Moving On

by

Jenny Piper

MOVING ON

Copyright © 2014 by Jenny Piper

ISBN # 978-1-907984-54-9

First published in Great Britain in 2014 by Sunpenny Publishing
www.sunpenny.com (Sunpenny Publishing Group)

MORE BOOKS FROM THE SUNPENNY PUBLISHING GROUP:

Blue Freedom, by Sandra Peut
Brandy Butter on Christmas Canal, by Shae O'Brien
Breaking the Circle, by Althea Barr
Bridge to Nowhere, by Stephanie Parker McKean
Dance of Eagles, by JS Holloway
Don't Pass Me By, by Julie McGowan
Embracing Change, by Debbie Roome
Far Out, by Corinna Weyreter
Going Astray, by Christine Moore
If Horses Were Wishes, by Elizabeth Sellers
Just One More Summer, by Julie McGowan
My Sea is Wide, by Rowland Evans
Someday, Maybe, by Jenny Piper
The Mountains Between, by Julie McGowan
Uncharted Waters, by Sara DuBose

To my R.

Chapter 1

D o you want to drive round the block?"
"What for?"
"I don't know. Have a last look?"
"No."
"Okay, then." Valerie stared out through her side window at the passing promenade wondering if he had said 'no' because he was as happy to be leaving the place as she was, or because it would hurt too much. "The sea looks almost blue today. Shall you miss it?"

Andy glanced across through her window and shrugged. "Does, doesn't it? Almost inviting."
"Still."
"Yep."

Hardly anybody in sight, just one young mum with a pushchair and an anoraked elderly couple with a straining black dog on a lead. The small, once-ornate shelters punctuating the grey tarmac every two hundred yards or so were all empty, most of them almost derelict, not inviting at all now. The ground around them was littered with bits of broken seats and shards of glass and discarded fast food wrappers; you could sense that they would smell of fish and chips and urine if you ventured under their canopies. Rummaging for the tube of soft mints in her handbag with a sigh, she gasped, alarmed. "I've still got a key!"

He frowned, annoyed. "Have you?"

She fished it out. "Here, look, it was at the bottom of my handbag. Must be the one I give Susie when she comes up without one."

"Well, I'm not going back. How many have you given

1

them?"

"Three for the front door, two for the back, one for the shed and two for the French windows. This is a front door."

"They won't need it, then." He set his jaw. "Anyway, as I said: I'm not going back."

"No." Still feeling faintly flushed with guilt, she fell back to staring out at the passing view. "The pier looks a right mess now that they've barricaded it off, such a shame. Remember going dancing in the Pavilion?"

He grinned. "I remember the bar."

The hotel on the headland was all boarded up, too: another one gone. You'd have thought somebody could have made a go of it with that wonderful view. Same story, though, all over town: all the lovely big Victorian buildings boarded up or turned into run-down bedsits or torn down and replaced with characterless blocks of flats for Housing Associations or old people's sheltered accommodation. Same story, too, with the shops: there had been such a lot of lovely shops once, really nice shops! Oh, one or two she hadn't cared for much, like the Home and Colonial, which always smelled strongly of faintly-off bacon, but that had been in the really old days; still, in the main, till the last few years, you were quite spoiled for choice – and look at them now.

She sighed again, watching the town slide past, shabby and characterless, mostly just charity shops and 'Everything For a Pound', those places that were still open. Fast food litter in the streets, graffiti everywhere. All the lovely trees that used to line the streets chopped down to save the council money. Used not to be like that. Such a pity. Still, not their problem now.

She squeezed herself in excited disbelief. Can't believe we're finally doing it at our age, Andy pushing seventy – well, sixty-nine, getting on that way – and me only a couple of years behind! Never thought he'd do it. All these years in the same town, not even once moved house, all very familiar and safe and then suddenly – oof! Into the unknown. Not like deciding to sail around the world or emigrating to Australia, of course, but still! Never thought we'd do such a thing.

Her toes curled up with excitement. "No. No, you're

right. We're not going back."

The soft mints were finished and they were on the motorway before they spoke again. He slowed the car a little, nodding at the passing sign for motorway services. "You okay if we keep going till we get past Birmingham?" "Do you need to stop?" "No, I don't need to stop." "You sure?" "I'm fine." "Go on to the next one, then." "All right."

Opening up the glove compartment, she checked unfruitfully for any partial bags of forgotten chocolate caramels or mints before taking out the glossy brochure, admiring the photograph of the long, low house on the cover before scanning through the description for the umpteenth time.

A charming 17th century house listed Grade II with eight acres of garden and paddocks, double garage, heated swimming pool, enjoying the most lovely views southwards... She hugged herself with pleasure. Fancy! Oh, it did look nice.

He noticed what she was doing. "Just wish they'd let us see it before they went ahead. Worries me like hell that Oliver hasn't had a full survey done. Beats me where all these people are who've got all this money for cash buys."

"Well, Ollie's one of them, isn't he? I suppose they're mostly like him, earning huge salaries and bonuses in the city, or else they've inherited houses." She read on. *Six bedrooms. The first floor master bedroom, which enjoys views over the garden and countryside beyond...*

He groaned. "Wish I had my house down there. Think what I could have got for it!"

Valerie sighed. Not again. "I know, but it's not, and you couldn't, so it's no use thinking about it."

"When I think what I've got for it, beautiful house like that... Half a million down there. You know we'll never be able to buy anything else if this doesn't work out, don't you? Not down there."

They'd discussed all this till the cows came home and though, not too deep down, the thought worried her too, she shrugged philosophically, returning to the details. "Well, we'd have to come back, I suppose."

The first floor master bedroom, having delightful views over the garden and surrounding countryside has been fitted with a range of hanging cupboards and benefits from an adjoining part-tiled bathroom with a further range of fitted cupboards and separate shower cubicle...
An en-suite. No trip down a cold, draughty landing in the middle of the night. What a joy.

"Bloody hell, look at this lot." He slowed to a crawl behind a long line of traffic. "I hate the M6." He shook his head, his face darkening. "Wouldn't have my lovely house back again, though, would I? I've laboured over that house."

She humoured him. "I know you have. You might."

"Yes, but whoever's living there will have wrecked it by that time, let it all go, turned it into flats or something." He was winding himself up. "Mind you, that's probably all we'd be able to afford, a flat. That's my greatest fear, you know; that we've handed over our future. We're in Oliver's hands now."

He was quite right and she felt sorry for him suddenly. It was hard for a man. She glanced at him, worried. "But you don't regret it?"

"Just hope the day doesn't come. Jumping into the blue; we don't even know where we're going."

"Yes, we do: Lynton Stacey." She loved the name. It was very pretty.

"Yes, but we don't know the area. We haven't seen the house." He cast her a wary glance. "Hope we're not going to become glorified babysitters? That's not what I agreed to move for."

She shook her head firmly. "Oh, of course not. Don't be silly."

"That's what they want us for, though."

"Don't be so mean! Of course they don't."

"Why do they want us, then? I can't get my head around it."

"Susie grew up with her grandparents living with us, just as I did with mine. It's always been the way in my family, taking in the parents as they get older. My mother and father played a big part in her childhood; she just thinks it's the natural thing to happen now we're getting on."

Mother and Daddy gave my Nana and Grandpa the best room when they moved in with them; history does repeat itself. Susie might expect to do the same for us, with a bit of luck.

He was still suspicious. "And what does Oliver think about it?"

"He's very fond of us, you know he is. He's enjoyed being part of a family, not having any parents of his own – happy to keep up the tradition. He's just trying to be nice. He wouldn't have offered if he didn't like the idea."

"I suppose not." He nodded at another sign. "There's another services coming up. Do you want to stop?"

She arched herself. She was a bit stiff. "Might as well, stretch our legs, have a cup of coffee."

He steered the car carefully into the approach road. "What kind of rolls did you bring?"

"Egg and onion salad."

"Good. Any Kit Kats, anything like that?"

She smiled indulgently. "Yes, I've got Kit Kats."

She could almost hear his tummy rumbling. "Good."

Before they got out of the car, he squeezed her hand and kissed her on the cheek. "Happy New Life, pet."

She kissed him back, beaming. He hadn't shaved this morning; his face was all stubbly. "Happy New Life, sweetheart."

The countryside as they neared Lynton Stacey was very beautiful. In the open areas, lush hedgerows and rolling fields of green and gold and beige and rust and ivory rolled out gently on either side and occasional farm buildings and clusters of little cottages, some of them thatched, crouched comfortably and picturesquely together by the sides of the lane. From time to time where the roads narrowed the branches of the trees on either side arched and linked overhead so that it was like driving through dappled tunnels. It was very different from the North Wales scenery, softer somehow, less harsh and threatening and it delighted Valerie. "Oh, it's glorious, Andy!"

"Hm, yes. Very nice." He sounded drained. She glanced at him; he was looking tired. It had been a long drive. She read out the approaching sign with excitement:

5

PLEASE DRIVE SAFELY THROUGH OUR VILLAGE

"We're here, Andy! *Our* village! Lynton Stacey!"

The directions were easy to follow. *The Bury* was almost the first house in the village. Wanting to study it, they deliberately drove very slowly past. It was big, as Susie and Oliver had said, and it looked very much as it did in the photograph, wood framed, long and low, with a central porch. The only difference was that it was unexpectedly close to a row of smaller, newer houses opposite and looked just a bit uncared-for.

"There isn't a lot of garden at the front," she said, admitting a little disappointment.

A flint wall separated it from the road. Andy nodded at it. "That wall's crumbing." He craned his neck. "And look at that bloody roof. That bloody roof is going to cost a fortune."

"A pretty colour though, those tiles. Aren't they, Andy? Very pretty. Sort of greeny-grey."

"That's moss." He curled his lip. "Look at those walls! They're in a hell of a state. It'll all need re-rendering. Bloody hell!"

The village seemed to consist of two rows of houses, a mixture of old and comparatively new, facing each other across the narrow road, though there were a couple of side roads, one a cul-de-sac. They passed a tiny village shop, a freshly-painted village hall on a green with a duck pond, swings and a few wooden seats, then a pretty little graveyard with huge yew trees and a flint-built church, and at the far end of the rows of houses, a pleasing looking pub, *The Black Jug*, with colourful window boxes and tubs and an old wooden bench outside. Valerie could just imagine three old codgers – Andy and two of his soon-to-be-made new mates, perhaps – sitting there with their pints watching the sleepy world going by. A sandwich board by the door advertised meals and bar snacks. Valerie nodded at it happily. "They do food! Oh, Andy, that looks nice!"

He nodded grudging approval. "Might take you there for a pint later." Reversing into its car park, he turned the car round and headed back again, cruising past *The Bury* once more at a snail's pace. Val peered up past the side.

"There's a car up the drive."

He was engrossed in taking an inventory of the building. "Look at that guttering! Half of it's coming down."

She shook his sleeve. "Andy, there's somebody waiting. It's probably the estate agent with the key."

"Eh?"

"I saw him standing in the drive."

"What time did you say we'd be here?"

"Probably between two and three. It's half-past, now."

"Right." Executing a rather splendid three-point turn, he turned back and manoeuvred the car gingerly through the gateless pillars between dense, overgrown shrubbery at the side of the house. "That's a bit tight!"

"Might be better approaching from the other side."

"Too late now. Won't get the furniture vans up here, that's for sure."

"They'll have to park in front."

"They'll block up the road."

"Well, we can't do anything about that."

It was a shock to the senses to come up into the open space behind the house. Fields and woods and low golden and lavender hills stretched far away into the misty blue distance. Valerie gasped. "Oh, Andrew – just look at that view!"

The tall man in a dark suit whom she had seen was standing with his back to them talking into a mobile telephone. Becoming aware of the car, he turned, raising his eyebrows in greeting, then finished his conversation quickly, slid the mobile into his pocket and strode down towards them, smiling, as they climbed out.

"Mr and Mrs Bryce? Malcolm Rathbone – Brookner and Partridge. How was your journey?" He had greying hair and a rather nice face for an estate agent, Val thought. He spoke very well, too, very plummy.

Andy stepped forward to meet him, throwing out his chest and strutting a little, and shook his proffered hand. "Andrew Bryce, my wife Valerie. Oh, not too bad; bit of trouble with roadworks on the M54 and, then of course, the M6." Mr Rathbone assumed a sympathetic expression. "Took what?" Andy glanced at his watch. "Five hours? About five and a half? Mind you, we did stop, twenty minutes, maybe; Valerie'd made some sandwiches."

"You're probably anxious to get inside. I'll give you a quick tour. Mr and Mrs Dowling have left the electricity on, I believe, so you will be able to have a cup of tea." Mr Rathbone led them down some worn stone steps towards the back door and sorted through a bunch of keys. "I believe you're going to be on your own for a while. Mr Drewitt – your son-in-law, is that right?"

Valerie nodded, smiling. "That's right."

"He told us that he and his family won't be joining you for a few weeks yet."

"They're coming as soon as their little girl finishes school for the holidays. She's almost seven. She'll be starting down here, then, in the autumn"

He tried unsuccessfully to turn the large rather rusty key he had selected. "Hang on." He examined the bunch of keys, then reinserted the same one in the lock, frowning. "Yes, that's the right one, sure it is. Try again!" He twisted and then pushed hard. "Nope, won't budge. What's the matter with it?" A second key yielded no more success. "Tell you what, we'll go round to the front door."

They followed him back up the steps and though a splintery door set in an arched wall. Having managed to open it with some difficulty, he couldn't close it properly again. "The hinges must have dropped." He was beginning to look a little embarrassed.

"How much did you say they'd paid for this?" Andy muttered to Val out of the side of his mouth as they walked along the front to where a stable door was set in a deep, ivy-covered porch. Mr Rathbone batted his hands about, frowning in distaste and brushing down his sleeve before inserting the key. "Sorry, a few cobwebs. Don't think they used this door much. Here we go..."

The door opened outwards, which meant that they all had to back out of the porch again before he could reach inside the lower half of the door to slide open the bolt. It seemed rather reluctant to shift. "Possibly a bit rusty. As I said, the Dowlings didn't use this door."

"Not surprised." Andy was fingering the wooden jamb around the door. "This lot all needs replacing. Woodwork's rotten."

Mr Rathbone looked as if he was pretending not to hear him. He stepped outside the porch again, brushed back his hair and opened the lower door with a grand gesture, leaving room for them to pass. "Here we are, then, Mr and Mrs Bryce – welcome to your new home!" Brushing a cobweb aside, and trying not to catch Andy's eye, Valerie stepped inside. She was in a medium sized, dark room, which smelt very musty. A steep wooden staircase rose opposite the entrance and to her left was a dark oak door. Ahead of her and slightly to the right was another, and set into right-hand wall, a large Art Deco style mantelpiece with tiles of brown and fawn. It was very ugly. Mr Rathbone moved past her and opened the door to her left. He seemed to be in a hurry. "Through here is the snug, if you'd care to...?"

Trooping after him obediently, they found themselves in a smaller, dark-beamed room, lined all round with shelves. The main feature of the room was a huge open fireplace surmounted by a high, dark oak beam. A small and dusty log basket sat looking lost on the wide hearth amongst a scattering of ashes. Mr Rathbone gestured to the fireplace proudly. "One of the main features of the house. Very cosy in here on a winter's day."

"I'm sure it is. Yes, indeed." Valerie was trying not to notice that Andy was tapping suspiciously at the plaster on a wall. Smiling, she nodded obligingly for Mr Rathbone. "Lovely!"

Frowning, Andy stamped warily on the worn carpet. "Solid floor, is it?"

Mr Rathbone consulted his notes. "Yes, that's right, solid floors throughout on ground level."

Andy grimaced. "I imagined that they'd all be oak. You know, nice wide floorboards. Gleaming."

Valerie felt a bit cross. "You saw the brochure, Andy."

Mr Rathbone looked crestfallen. Valerie smiled comfortingly at him. "This is better for us, really. We like carpet."

He seemed surprised: probably wasn't the 'in thing'. He stared at her, fingering his chin, ruminating: "Yes, yes, of course," then shrugged, moving on quickly to the next door. "Well now, next we have the family room." This room was bigger again, running from front to back of the house with windows at either end.

Valerie beamed. "Very pleasant room! Room in here for Susie's piano."

"Wood burner." Mr Rathbone nodded proudly at another large fireplace in which was set a heavy dull black stove, before moving on swiftly to the room next door. "Dining room."

"Uh-huh!" Val nodded appreciatively, though she didn't care quite as much for this room. Wood panelled, it seemed very dark and gloomy with just the one small window opening into it at the front and a huge white marble fireplace appeared out of place and seemed to dominate the space.

Mr Rathbone led them through another door at the back of the room and into a narrow, windowless passage with a staircase leading up. "Scullery, utility, handy lavatory. Um, storerooms. That way to the side door. And in here we have the kitchen." He stood back to let them enter. "Lovely floor in here. The original brick."

Uneven and mellowed terracotta bricks were arranged in a herringbone pattern in a fair sized room, with a window at each end, but despite the pleasing flooring, Valerie's heart sank. What a disappointment! The kitchen had looked really nice in the brochure. 'Fitted kitchen with all appliances' had brought to mind something very stylish, but these wall cabinets and worktops were ancient, Formica-topped and scarred and very shabby.

"Electric cooker, washing machine – oh." Mr Rathbone paused, puzzled, peering under the worktop by the discoloured sink. "Mrs Dowling appears to have taken her dishwashing machine." He straightened, looking anxious, "I do hope that's not going to be a nuisance?"

"Oh, no, no!" she said immediately, wanting to please, but Andy looked more dubious.

"Depends if it was included in the details, doesn't it? My son-in-law might have a problem with that."

Mr Rathbone nodded, and then glanced at his watch. "I'm so sorry to rush you round," he told them moving swiftly to another door, "but I do have another appointment shortly. Very rude, but could I just run you round the rest of the ground floor and then hand over the keys?"

On the kitchen table in their old house, Valerie and Andy had left a carefully prepared list of suppliers, receipts for accounts paid in the last year and anything else they decided might be useful ready for the new owners and she looked around for one here. "Did Mr and Mrs Dowling leave a list?"

"A list?"

She nodded. "Yes, you know – who supplies the services, where they got their logs from, when the rubbish is collected, things like that."

Andy growled. "What the dickens we do about the swimming pool: are we supposed to put anything in it, servicing and things."

Valerie smiled ingratiatingly at Mr Rathbone. "You know."

"Oh!" The penny struck. "Oh! Yes, yes, of course. Now, have they? Have they?" They all looked around, but there didn't seem to be a note. "Oh dear me." Mr Rathbone shrugged. "Of course, all the information you need will probably be with the details."

Andy scowled. "Yes, but my son-in-law has them."

Mr Rathbone looked disconcerted. He clearly wasn't used to this sort of two-generational arrangement. "Yes, of course." Moving across the kitchen quickly, he threw open the final door. "The Drawing Room."

Valerie moved into it slowly. It was much larger than the other rooms and much lighter. "Oh, this is a nice room, Andy!" she breathed, delighted. "Nice and big."

He nodded grudgingly, staring round at the patchily painted pale green walls. "Hm, yes." He glanced at Mr Rathbone. "Extension, is it?"

"A fairly recent extension, yes. Most of the house is Jacobean, partially Georgianised in the eighteenth century, but with some fairly recent modifications. Log-burning stove in here, too."

"Hm." Andy moved around slowly, gazing up at the ceiling. "Bit of a damp patch there?"

Mr Rathbone joined him, staring up at the brown mark on the greyish white ceiling. "I believe the en-suite to the master bedroom is above. Must have had a leak at some point."

"Must have, yes. Hope it's been sorted."
Mr Rathbone nodded enthusiastically. "I'm sure it has.
I'm sure it has, oh, yes." He glanced at his watch again and
drew in a deep breath. "Mr and Mrs Bryce, I must crave
your indulgence, I really do have to fly. I'll let myself out
at the front door. If I give you the keys? Could you possibly...?"
Andy took the keys from him, frowning. "Nothing else
we need to know?"
"No, I don't think so, no. Keys are labelled, water is on,
apparently, and so is electricity. If you do have any prob-
lems or queries, of course, don't hesitate to ring the office."
Drawing his heels to attention, he proffered his hand. "Mr
Bryce, Mrs Bryce... May I wish you a very happy life in
your new home?"
Beaming, Valerie shook his hand. "You may, yes!"
He frowned. "Excuse me." Reaching out, he brushed
something gingerly from her hair. "Bit of a – bit of a..."
She touched her hair, puzzled. "What?"
He shook out his fingers delicately. "Tiny bit of a...
Sorry. Just a spider."

Chapter 2

When he had gone, Andy glanced at his watch. "Time is it? Bloody hell, a quarter past four; they'll be here in a minute; better get that back door opened. Don't know if they'll be able to get everything in through the front." He grimaced, looking uncomfortable. "Is there a downstairs loo?"

"I think there was one, yes. Have a look by the back door."

He set off hurriedly back through the kitchen. "Shall I get the kettle and stuff out of the car? They'll want a cuppa, I expect, before they start unloading."

"Better had." She followed him into the kitchen, still staring around her. The stove had seen better days; the rings were scratched and a bit rusty; something had been baked on hard round one of them. She opened the oven; a couple of rusty roasting trays festered inside. The whole thing was pretty disheartening. Somehow she'd imagined something really posh and up to the minute down here and in such an expensive house, like the ones she'd read about in glossy magazines, like a Smeg or a Neff, but it was just an old Belling.

There wasn't much depth to the shelves of the wall cupboards. There were lots of ring marks and a dusting of something like cocoa and sugar and a handful of Shreddies and a few pieces of dried spaghetti had been stranded at the back. She made a mental note to get out a dishcloth and some Cif before Andy could have a look inside. He'd have a fit.

Her stomach clenched a little. *Please let Andy like it down here. Please let him be happy.*

He'd feel better after that cup of tea. Crossing over to the sink she tested out the taps. They flowed smoothly. Good. Turning them off again, she peered up through the window at the blue sky and the trees and fringes of green lawn just visible above the steep rockery and caught her breath, feeling her anxiety dissipate in a sudden rush of joy. *And we are here. We're really here! We've moved at last!*

She wanted to pinch herself.

He was back, panting under the weight of a large cardboard box. She nodded. "You found one, then? You got it open, then, the back door?"

"Yep. Just stiff. Wood's a bit swollen. Must have had a lot of rain recently. Mind you, could do with a new lock." Setting the box on the work surface, he stripped off the sticky tape. "So what do you want out of here?"

"Kettle, tea, sugar, milk: hope it hasn't gone sour. Mugs. How many of them were there, do you remember?"

"Four, I think,"

"Four and us two, then: six." She gestured in the direction of the box before filling the kettle. "There's a packet of digestives in there somewhere too, and some teaspoons."

He set everything out beside the sink. "I'd better get out there and watch for them, warn them they're not going to be able to pull up the drive. I don't think they're going to like those steps. There's an awkward turn inside the door there, too before you come into the hall, difficult angle. Can't see them getting that big dresser of yours in."

"I'm sure they will. It comes in two parts, after all. They're very experienced."

"Hm, well, we'll see." He stood gazing silently out through the rather grimy window beside her for a few moments. "So what do you think, then?"

She could feel his disappointment – same as with her and the kitchen. He'd expected something more... more... She searched for the right word. He'd expected something a bit posher, something more *finished*, for the money.

She tried to distract him. "I want to see the garden properly. Have another look at that wonderful view, Andy."

He nodded thoughtfully. "Hm."

"T"hey're here!" he shouted up the stairs.
      "Coming!"
   Valerie took a last, quick look around the huge attic room with its boarded-over floor, pretty little windows and high, exposed rafters. It would make a really lovely playroom for the children. In the wall at the inner end there was a little door. Crouching awkwardly, she opened it and peered inside, making out a deep cavern of shadowy, silent raftered space, which presumably ran over the rest of the house. As far as she could see there was plenty of headroom, though heavy wooden waist-high beams ran crosswise at intervals. Room to extend into there, then, if they needed to, if the architect could figure out a way to do it, and if not – well, they'd have lots of storage space!
   She straightened cautiously, unkinking her back with care, and peered again through one of the small windows, shaking her head in wonder at the view. You could see over right the lawns to the swimming pool, and beyond the swimming pool to the fields and the distant hills. She chuckled again with delight, unable to resist the thrill of it all. A swimming pool, a *heated* swimming pool, whoever would have thought it!
   Andy called again. He was sounding harassed. "Valerie? Do you know where you want everything?"
   "Coming!" Tearing herself away, she clambered carefully down the narrow flight of splintery stairs leading down to the landing, making a mental note that they'd need safety rails.
   "This for the master bedroom, Madam?" Two of the removal men were poised on the first floor landing with the king-sized divan. The mattress and the awkward bendy headboard with its bedside cabinets attached were propped up ready at the angle on the lower flight of stairs.
   She dithered momentarily and then led them into the best bedroom, the one with the en-suite bathroom and windows at both front and back. Could always move out again when Susie and Ollie came, if necessary. "In here, please. If you could put it against that wall." She hovered, watching and worrying if she'd picked the right place for it as they assembled the divan and headboard underneath the window on the back wall, and heaved the mattress

onto the top.

Whilst they went back down for the dressing table, she nipped back in to explore the precious en-suite bathroom a little more closely. The white enamelled bath was quite an old one, boarded in with splintery tongue-and-groove panels, also painted white. It was stained quite badly beneath its tarnished gold taps, but it was a good, long, deep one, and it had a handy handle with which to pull yourself out. It had a rather grand, if slightly tarnished, gold shampoo spray and stand attached, very posh: much nicer than the spray attachment she'd brought with her, the one she'd bought from Boots. It was always a bit of a bother trying to keep those rubber thingies on the taps.

The gold edifice wobbled precariously when she lifted off the nozzle. Seeing water beginning to trickle quickly from the joint, she rested it back quickly. Perhaps Andy would be able to fix it.

The toilet bowl looked nice and clean. There was one of those what-you-may-call-its – a bidet – squatting beside it! She hadn't noticed that before. She stared down at it, puzzling as she always did when faced with one. Which way are you supposed to use a bidet? Facing forwards or back? It looked very low either way. For experimental purposes, she gingerly attempted to lower herself onto it, choosing forwards, but feeling an unpleasant twinge, gave up quickly before her back caved in. *Shan't be using that.*

The tap end of the bath was beneath the window. Through it, she could see a bit of the lawn above the patio through the gaps between huge yew trees. She tried to imagine lying in the bath. What would you be able to see then? Just the trees, probably; the trees, and a bit of the sky. Still, very nice. Very nice seeing the sky from your bathtub. She looked down at the bath longingly. Be rather nice to give it a go.

The bare splintery floorboards beside it, patchily painted a wishy-washy blue and with wide gaps between them, didn't please her. Dust traps. Cold, too. Hard on the feet. Wouldn't want to have to get your slippers on every time you needed to pop in during the night. Have to get a nice bit of bathroom carpet, something soft and fluffy for bare soles.

One wall was lined with long doors, also made of white-painted tongue-and-groove. Inside there were shelves and, beneath them, hanging rails. On the back of one of the doors was a long mirror. Lovely! It felt a bit damp at the back though, when she put her hand to it – just flaking plaster, not wood. Must be against the outside wall. The floorboards in the bedroom creaked loudly. The men were back up, then. She closed the doors again carefully. Still, a dressing room! Just fancy!

She hurried back to direct them. "Underneath the window, please."

The familiar mock reproduction Louis Quatorze dressing table, bought with pride in the early seventies from Thomas Green & Co in Station Road – long gone – and scratched now, with its gilt ormolu work missing in places and its cream paintwork whitish in patches where she'd tried to rub off marks. It looked very shabby – and rather lonely, too, without its matching wardrobes. Mrs Miller, who'd bought their house, had offered her £40 for them, which wasn't bad considering they were nearly thirty years old. They'd been very tall, perfect for the old Edwardian house with its high ceilings, but unlikely to fit in the kind of house they'd be buying, Susie'd said.

She'd wanted Valerie to let Mrs Miller have the bedhead and the dressing table as well, she had grown rather sniffy about their bedroom suite, had Susie, since she'd been in London, but Valerie had dug in her heels. "I'll need to see myself, won't I? And your Dad will. It'll take us a while to order anything new."

First time she'd looked at herself in a mirror since the motorway café. What a sight! Whatever must that nice Mr Rathbone have thought of her? Needed a good wash. Needed a bit of powder on her nose! She'd lost a button from her pretty Windsmoor floral blouse, she realised, *bother it* – pinged it off somewhere. She'd been so pleased with this blouse, discovered in Oxfam on Station Square, such a bargain. She'd already used the spare button as it had had one missing from the neck, and they were unusual little blue buttons, nothing like them in her button box. Drawing in a deep breath, she refastened the side button of her skirt again with difficulty: been too tight for comfort in the car. Might have to start thinking about a size sixteen. She frowned at her reflection crossly, fingering her greying curls with equal annoyance. She should have known better than to turn up for an appointment at *His 'n Hers* on 'Pensioners 10% Off' day. She might *be* a pensioner, but she should have spoken up when Tracey started bringing out her pink, yellow and blue rollers; nobody had roller sets nowadays except really old, old people, but she hadn't had the heart. Tracy was such a nice girl, always made her a second cup of tea.

Need to find decent hairdresser though, if I'm going to be a Hampshire Lady now.

Andy met her down below in the hallway, looking gloomy. "Told you the dresser wouldn't fit."

"What d'you mean, it won't fit? Couldn't they get it in?"

"Oh, they got it in," he said, leading her into the sitting room at the far end where the upper part of the dresser was propped against a wall while the lower part blocked off the bottom of the narrow staircase. "But the ceiling's too low, you'll have to have it in the hall. Mind you, if it you put it there, nobody'll be able to get past."

"Oh, surely it's not that deep, is it?" Darting into the sitting room, she measured the lower part of the dresser with her hands, then hurried out into the hall, holding them apart.

He clicked his tongue. "You can't do it like that. Here, move, I've got a tape measure." Having measured it, he stood back, disconcerted. "Hm."

"Told you."

It took the men a surprisingly short time to finish unloading the van. Valerie and Andy had got rid of so much of their furniture that what they had brought barely made any impression over the two main floors. It had been a tremendous wrench; it wasn't valuable stuff apart from the dresser and the sideboard, but much of it had been in the family house for generations. Not knowing how much they would need, though, and not having seen the cottage or heard Ollie and Susie's plans for it, and most particularly in the secret hope that they might be able to buy new for once if they were going to have a bit of spare cash, Valerie had been ruthless.

"Don't worry," she told Andy, finding him standing looking anxiously at the single armchair and the small coffee table they had set out in front of the log-burner in the Drawing Room, as Mr Rathbone had called it, the big extension room off the kitchen, where the only TV point they could find was sited. "I'll sit on a cushion. You'll have to heave me up again, mind! When Susie and Ollie arrive with all their things, we'll be looking for space."

He looked exhausted, she noticed, for once showing all of his almost seventy years. If she cared to admit it, she herself was very tired and rather stretched out. All that long 'shall we, shan't we?' business, then all the keeping things tidy, showing round and selling, then the excitement when Susie had told them about finding the right house, then all the packing up and preparations for going. Not knowing exactly where they *were* going. Saying goodbye to Louis and Norma and everybody. There'd been a lot of nervous tension in the build-up to the move.

Andy gestured dubiously to the log burner. "Ought I to try to light that thing?"

"Do you know how?"

"Can't be too difficult. Have they left us any logs?"

"If they have, they'll be somewhere outside. Maybe there's a woodshed." She glanced at the window. The sky to the west above the patio wall was developing a rosy glow. The view ought to be particularly splendid if there was a nice sunset. "Come on, the light's fading," she urged him, scuttling excitedly towards the door. "Let's go and have a look. It gets dark earlier, doesn't it, down here?"

He followed her reluctantly through the kitchen and out into the narrow back hall. "Have we got anything to eat?"

"I brought some bread and corned beef and stuff. I could make some sandwiches."

He looked disgruntled. "Need something more substantial to eat than that."

She stood back whilst he tugged open the back door. "Well, let's go and have a quick look for some logs, then go down the road to that pub, celebrate our first night."

His scowl deepened. "I don't know if I feel like going out."

"Well, what can I make for you? If I had some potatoes

and onions, I could make a corned beef hash."

"But you haven't."

"No."

"Forget it, then. I'll have a sandwich."

She hovered outside on the gravel at the top of the steps, waiting, but he had been distracted by the stain on the wall beneath the window to the tiny downstairs loo, and was bending to prod and scratch at the plaster disapprovingly. "Got a horrible feeling there's rising damp."

Ignoring his suspicions and closing her eyes, she breathed in deeply. The air felt different down here. It was softer, somehow, like the scenery, without the sharper ozone-smell you got living near the sea. This air smelled sweetly of new-mown grass with faint traces of something like honey. Rapeseed, perhaps; there were a lot of bright yellow fields about.

Unable to hold back, she set off exploring, discovering first near the kitchen door an area where a stained and torn tarpaulin had been left lying in a stiffened heap on a scattering of wood shavings. She called back. "They haven't left any logs for us, not up here, anyway."

"Might have guessed." She saw him following her up the steps as she picked her way eagerly across a lengthy stretch of tussocky grass towards the swimming pool, which lay humming gently to itself beneath a taut green cover behind a recently planted yew hedge. Someone had made an effort to plant out a corner bank as a flowerbed near it, but had given up. She could see blades of iris and what looked like clumps of cranesbill and twisted, shrubby rosemary, but the bed was neglected and very much overgrown.

Crouching awkwardly and stiffly, she slipped a hand beneath the cover, testing the temperature. Lovely and warm! Wait for us, she told it lovingly. We'll jump in you tomorrow, promise.

Running the length of the lawn and one side of the pool area was an established hedge made up of hawthorns, hazels and other native plants, quite high, so that it was impossible to see any further. When she stood on tiptoe, she could make out some sort of high flint wall on the other side with trees and then one or two chimneys beyond.

From here she couldn't see much of *The Bury* either, just its extensive greeny-grey uneven roof, the twisty chimneys and the little attic windows. To her left, the gravel drive swept round in a turning circle and on the other side of that was more grass and then a long beech hedge, marking the demarcation of the property from that of the next-door house. She craned on tiptoes, but couldn't see it properly and couldn't remember what it had looked like when they had driven past.

In front of her, beyond the swimming pool, the ground sloped shallowly, falling away some considerable distance through overgrown fence-rimmed paddocks to where a dark fringe of nettles and brambles rambled thickly along the line of a tangled and overgrown hedge, with elders and hawthorns tall as oak trees. Beyond that were more deeply sloping fields, the grass in them knee-high. She shook her head. Just imagine! Eight acres! How much of that, then, was theirs?

Andy was strolling across the grass towards her. From this distance, she couldn't see how tired he looked or how grey his hair was; he looked quite youthful, tall and lean. With his appetite! It wasn't fair.

"Look, there's a little summerhouse with roses growing over it!" she called to him, spotting it suddenly up behind him near the left side of the lawn. "Ah, look, Andy! Oh, isn't that sweet! And there's a big tiled outhouse there, on the other side of the house. Wonder if it's some kind of garage?"

He followed her gaze. "Not much use as a garage there, is it? It's nowhere near the drive. Still, useful for storage. Wonder if it's got electricity?" He stared around. "Where's this tennis court, then? I thought Oliver said there was a tennis court?"

"It was a croquet lawn he said, wasn't it, not a tennis court? That part on the other side of this little hedge is lawn – that must be it."

He wandered off head down over the grass, hands in his pockets, and she trotted happily after him. It looked as if earth had been scraped up at some time to make the big rectangular lawn and then left piled up in a long bank on the far side. A few neglected shrubs crouched amongst fading daffodils and narcissi in a jungle of couch grass, dock leaves, nettles and thistles. She called to Andy, nodding at the bank. "Not gardeners, then."

"Doesn't look like it." He tested the ground, stamping up and down a little. "Not very even. Take a lot of rolling to get this any good."

Straightening, he stared out to where the sun was setting over the far fields and the lavender hills to the west. The sky was a blaze of pink and gold and amethyst. He shook his head in admiration. "Must say, that's quite a view." He whistled softly. "Yep, that's quite a view."

There was a tiny clematis-covered shed, the source of the humming noise, presumably housing the motor for the heating and the filtering. She squeezed his arm, grinning. "Fancy a swim, then?"

He smiled. "Maybe tomorrow. See what the weather's like."

She sighed. "Our own pool."

He nodded thoughtfully. "Hm."

They were both bone-tired by nine and Andy couldn't get the television to work. "It must be a duff aerial."

She couldn't find the bread knife or the butter, so had to saw off thick crumbly doorsteps with an ordinary knife and make the corned beef sandwiches without. Andy stolidly munched his way through them, but she didn't: didn't fancy them somehow. At last he left her to rinse out the things they'd used for their sparse meal, together with the collection of mugs used earlier, while he went off upstairs to unpack the bedding. The water was stone cold.

"I thought you said you'd found out how to turn the hot water on?" She called up from the bottom of the stairs.

"I did."

"You didn't." She heard him mumbling, but couldn't catch what he said. "What?"

He growled louder this time. "I said, 'Well, I'm not having another go tonight; I'm too tired. We'll have to wash in cold water.'"

She turned wearily back to the kitchen again. "Okay."

They were in bed before they heard the church clock chiming ten. It felt very strange. "Why did you do that?"

"What?"

"Get in on my side?"

"Thought you must have wanted to change sides."

"No, I didn't."

"Why are you on my side, then?"

With Andy heaving a big sigh, they clambered out of bed again, exchanging places. "That's better. You know what?" Val said, snuggling back under the duvet, "It's because the bed's the wrong way round. We're facing in a different direction."

"Are we?"

She raised herself a little and peered over the bulk of Andy towards the window at the back. "That's west, isn't it, because that's where the sun set, so if that's west... North, yes, we're facing north now."

"Is that a bad thing?"

"Well we never used to face north."

He heaved himself over, reaching for the bedside lamp. "Well, I'm not going to move the bed now. I'm knackered."

"I wasn't asking you too, don't be silly."

"Yes, you were, I know you."

It was very dark after he put the light out. Of course, no street lights here, she realised. Couldn't even see where the windows are. Should have gone out to have a look at the stars.

The air on her face in the darkness felt very strange, perhaps because the room was much bigger than their old one. Andy had settled down the wrong way, with his back to her. He was probably just so tired, but it was unsettling; she loved the snuggling down together now that the passion of their younger days had given way to the pleasure of animal comfort. At first, the gradual dwindling of sex had been a difficult thing to come to terms with, especially for Andy. He'd had a lot of trouble getting used to the fact that his body wouldn't keep pace with his mind any more. They'd had several of *those* conversations:

"Shall I get some Viagra?"

"Some what?"

"You know – Viagra."

"Oh."

"Shall I get some?"

"You don't need it."

"I think I need some."

"Do you?"

"I do, don't I?"

"Now you're fishing. No."

"Do you want me to get some? I think maybe I should get some."

"If you want to, I don't mind."

"I'll get some then."

"Do you want some more cocoa?"

"Good idea. Yes."

For a long time she had felt that he was blaming her and indeed, she'd blamed herself, because, of course, she wasn't as attractive as maybe she had been, but if truth were told, she'd reached the point herself when sex would likely have lost out in a straight choice between that and a nice hot cup of tea. It had been the nightly cuddle that she'd missed the most. The mumbled 'night-night' followed by a rolling over away from her had left her very lonely in the bed. As time had passed, though, the arm had crept back around her waist and a soft and well-padded belly had pressed once more against her cushiony bottom and they had both sighed heavily in contentment and settled down to sleep. Longing for the comfort of it now, she tugged at him until he heaved himself sleepily back over towards her.

Even curled up in their old, familiar position with his arm heavy about her waist and one hand cupping her breast and his breath warm against the back of her neck, it was very difficult to drop off, though. Her mind was still wired up with excitement, even though her body ached with weariness.

Well, we've done it now, haven't we? Burnt our what-you-may-call-its... Bridges. Burnt our boats.

Chapter 3

I t was a very bad night. It was fair to say that Valerie
hadn't been a good sleeper since that day long ago
when Susie had passed her driving test and she'd lain
awake worrying and imagining and waiting to hear her
driving safely in; but it hadn't worn off – it had become
a sort of habit. Nevertheless, this was a particularly bad
night. At first it had seemed very quiet as well as very dark,
but gradually she had become aware of noises, strange
noises, little noises she wasn't used to, noises that made
her prick her ears up and freeze, wondering if she should
wake Andy, wondering if somebody was breaking in. Then
her brain kept going 'tick-tock tick-tock', of course, thinking about the new house and worrying about if everything
was going to work out, and Andy, being overtired, had
snored very badly, and it hadn't been helped by all of a
sudden at some point finding herself pinned to her pillow
in a brilliant white glare.

It had even woken Andy, who had lifted his head with
a jerk. "What the dickens is that?" Clambering groggily
and irritably out of bed, he had peered through the front
window. "It's the house opposite – they've got on a security
light. It'll go off in a minute." He had crawled back into bed
and they had waited.

It hadn't.

People got up early too in Lynton Stacey and whatever other villages the road through the village was going
to. From first light, when the security light opposite had
finally gone out, there had seemed to be an unending trail

of heavy vehicles grinding along the road. "Of course, this is farming territory, they'll be tractors and things," Valerie told Andy, giving up any hope of sleep and wearily slipping her legs out of bed. "We'll get used to it."

He turned over huffily, heaving himself automatically into the place she had vacated and pulling his pillow over onto her side. Funny how each of them did that, whichever one got up, she thought, pulling on her dressing gown. Made you feel safe and secure, somehow, snuggling into the place where the other person had been. Funny.

She opened the bedroom door quietly, or tried to. It was very creaky, like the floorboards. "Do you want a cup of tea?"

"Bit later."

"Okay."

Waiting for the kettle to boil for her own cup, she stood on tiptoe staring through the window. She could hear the birdsong even in the kitchen. How lovely! It was going to be a beautiful day. Thinking pleasurably of drinking her tea out in the early-morning garden in her dressing gown – because here, of course, nobody would be able to see her – she tried to open the back door, but no matter how she tugged at it, it wouldn't open. Disappointed, she went back to the kitchen and debated with herself, sipping the scalding hot tea. If she went out at the other door, at the front, she would have to go upstairs and get dressed because of the houses opposite, then she might waken Andy if he had dropped off again, and he probably needed his sleep. *Better to leave it for now.*

She felt full of energy, though, despite her sleepless night. Yes. What she would do in the meantime was to clean the kitchen.

She found the cleaning equipment in one of the cardboard boxes marked 'kitchen' and stockpiled in the corner ready for unpacking, and set to work, tying on an apron and pushing up her dressing gown sleeves. It took three bowls of dirty water down the sink before the cupboards were clean enough to pass muster for Andy.

Fancy leaving your house in such a state! She wrung out the cloths crossly. We worked like Trojans, making sure that everything it was possible to leave squeaky clean, was squeaky clean. Mrs Miller won't be doing this, not in our old house.

There was a heavy creaking overhead. He was up, then, and she hadn't taken him any tea. He looked very bleary-eyed and saggy when he walked into the kitchen, fastening up his dressing gown cord. "What a night!"

"We'll have to get a black-out blind," she told him, handing him a steaming mug.

He sipped it, disgruntled. "And ear mufflers. I thought the traffic at home was bad enough, but at least that didn't start going till a respectable hour!"

"Should we tell them, do you think? About the security light?"

He frowned warily and shrugged. "Dunno. Might have been a one-off. Let's wait and see. Don't want to get off on a bad start with the neighbours." He looked around. "Don't suppose there's anything for breakfast?"

She went to the box she was using as a bread bin. "I've got a crust of bread left. I could try to toast it."

He grimaced. "Must be a Tesco or a Sainsbury's or something down here that's got a café. We'll need to shop. I'll get something there." He turned to the door, carrying his mug. "I'll go and have a shave."

"There isn't any hot water."

He'd obviously forgotten. "Bloody hell. Have to take up the kettle."

Eager to find food, he was ready before she was, and she found him nibbling a digestive biscuit and stowing away the dry goods and utensils and kitchen crockery from the boxes when she came back down ready with her bag. *Good thing I'd cleaned the shelves out: very good thing.*

"Where d'you want these things?" he asked, waving a packet of Brillo pads.

"Under the sink, I suppose, lovey."

He opened the under sink door then paused aghast as a scummy wash ran out over the lip and onto his shoes. "It's soaking wet in here. Look!" He hopped back, shaking his feet. "Hell's bells! Must be a leak!" Muttering to himself, he crouched, and she bent down beside him, both of them peering inside. He fumbled under the sink, then straightened. "That's what it is."

She struggled to see what he was talking about. "What?"
"Would you credit it?"
"What?"
"Mean bugger!"
"What!!"
"See this gap next to the sink? That was where the dishwasher was, right?"
"Right." She was puzzled.
He pointed underneath. "Well, when he took it out, he should have put on a cap. It linked in here, see, to the pipes. Water's running straight through the sink and emptying into the cupboard."
She was shocked, thinking of all the bowls of dirty water she'd tipped down the plughole. "No!"
"Bloody hell!"

They spent the morning familiarising themselves with the area by getting lost at regular intervals on the way to the nearest Tesco and a plumbers' merchant, and had to stop and ask directions at least twice before they got back to *The Bury*, but having had a satisfying All Day Breakfast at the busy supermarket café, Andy was more cheerful and in the mood for more exploration when they got back.

He unlocked the door of the outbuilding first with a huge and rusty key. As Valerie admired the white Montana and the Mile-A-Minute growing so thickly together over the building that they almost formed a second roof, he eyed them with animosity. 'They'll have to come down."

"Don't listen to him; over my dead body," she muttered to a Montana flower as he stalked inside.

"See what I mean?" He pointed up at the cobweb-draped roof space and round the ill-fitting windows where invasive cords and tendrils had come poking and slithering through.

She followed his gaze. "Hm."

"Roof's corrugated at the back; thought it was all tiled."

She nodded, taking in the hanging hooks on one wall. Would get all the spades and hoes and things on those nicely. How convenient.

He was waiting. "Val?"

She nodded, smiling. "Hm."

He mooched around a bit, inspecting the cobweb-draped plaster walls and crouching here and there to inspect the cement floor. "Seems dry. It'll do well enough for storage. Bit of damp there round that window, but it has got a broken pane. Quite useful." He peered up again into the recesses of the roof space, shaking his head gloomily. "Mind you, we will have to replace that roof."

She slipped the hook and lifted the lid of a large rectangular splintered wooden chest that stood against the same wall, catching her breath as a big black spider scurried quickly out of sight. "Val? Have to replace that roof."

The chest would do nicely for things like bags of Bone Meal and Clematis food, perhaps even flowerpots. Dropping the lid with a thwack, she dusted sticky cobweb off her fingers, nodding happily. "Hm."

The little summerhouse was full of spiders' webs, too, but quite dry, with a sound wooden floor raised from the ground and wooden benching all round the inside walls below windows. She saw Andy balefully eyeing the little yellow rose rambling profusely over it and moved him on quickly, leading the way round the far side of the summerhouse and along past the end of the bank to find out what was behind the high flint wall.

What was hiding was a special treat. The wall didn't just run along behind the bank, but continued round four sides of a large rectangle. At the far end of the north-facing wall was an arched doorway, and when she pushed it open, she found – oh, joy of joys – a walled garden; a neglected one, certainly, but what a treasure! She clapped her hands in delight. "Look, Andy, look!"

It was knee high in weeds and uncut grass, but in the midst of it all she could make out gnarled fruit trees espaliered against the walls, raspberry canes and rhubarb, the outlines of raised beds, apple trees and plums, a pear, something that was possibly a quince, and in one corner a large glass house with many broken panes. She was beside herself with pleasure. "A greenhouse! Oh, look, Andy, I've got a greenhouse!"

It was full of old flowerpots and half-used bags of moulding compost and bone meal and nameless substances providing homes for earthworms, woodlice, snails and the ubiquitous spiders, and it smelt heavily of earth and something chemical and long-ago tomatoes. It was full of weeds, some of them so tall that they poked up through the broken roof glass. Crawling and twining over the walls and roof was an ancient jasmine with long tendrils poking through the glass wherever it had been able to find a hole.

"Have to keep the kids away till it's been cleared out and had the panes replaced." He cleared a space with his foot. "See here, it's all broken glass. Could be lethal." But he smiled and nodded, knowing how much it meant to her, so she knew he would be putting it on his list.

They wandered down to the bottom of the grassy paddocks, but weren't sure how far they could go. Andy was very law-abiding. "Have to check with Oliver which hedge marks the bottom of our property."

Valerie peered over the hedge at the land belonging to the people next door. "Oh, look, Andy, how pretty! They've let the grass grow high and somebody's mown paths through it – we should do that over here. It looks ever so nice."

There were no further buildings except the detritus of something that could once have been a stable or a night shelter buried in the long grass, and a fearsome stand of nettles at the bottom of the long meadow leading to the southern hedge. He stood looking back up towards the cottage. "We could do with a decent garage. Going to need a sit-on mower – can't do all this by hand."

"Let's have a look around the front."

The strip at the side of the road behind the low flint wall was only about six foot wide, but there was a narrow border running along the house wall, where borage, forget-me-nots, thistles, pinks and peonies, thirsty lace-cap hydrangeas and untended ramblers, which had layered themselves, all struggled for space. A small green gate opened from the road to a narrow path leading to the front door steps, and at the very far end, past the front of the cottage and a second arched doorway going through to the back, they found a well. It was covered with convolvulus and brambles, but it had a tiny roof, almost complete with tiles, and beneath it a stout wooden bar from which the bucket would have hung, and a rusty iron handle at the side. It had been filled in with rubble at some point and was full of brambles and other weeds, but it was the second treasure of the day, and Valerie was enchanted.

It was really very warm now for fairly early in the year. An image of the pool swam in her mind's eye. "How about it, then, Andy? Are we going for a swim?"

Andy grinned. "Oh, hell, why not? Where are my trunks?"

She felt excitement rising. "I did unpack them, just in case. Bottom drawer of the dressing table, on the left."

He rose with some alacrity. "Righto. It's almost teatime. You going to make some sandwiches for after and bring them out?"

She was eager to please. "I can do, yes."

"And a nice jug of iced lemonade?"

"If you like."

He came back downstairs fairly quickly wearing the ancient and faded swimming shorts bought long ago in Corfu, and his cricketing sunhat, and with a pile of towels neatly rolled under his arm. "Where are my flip-flops? Have we got suntan lotion? Have you seen my book? Where would I find my reading sunglasses?"

When she had finished equipping him, they set off across the lawn. She felt a bit daft parading down the garden in just her bathing costume – very conspicuous. Too dumpy now to look decent in a bathing costume, but at least it held her in quite nicely, though her thighs felt winter-white and very bare.

Andy spread a towel and a cushion on the solitary steamer chair for her. Nice of the Dowlings to leave it for them, though it needed some cushioning. It was a bit green and splintery and weather-worn.

The bath towel softened the hardness of it somewhat. Lying back with a sigh of pleasure, gazing out over the sprawling fields and low hills in all their shimmering shades she sighed with delight. "Oh, Andy, we could be in Tuscany or somewhere when you look out there, we really could."

"Hm..." Andy had seated himself on the grass at her side. He had a silly smile on his face, too. "Pass me a sand-

31

wich, please."

She did so. "What about this, then, eh? This is the life!"

"Yep. This is the life."

They munched their way through their picnic in companionable silence, staring out around them like a couple of contented cows in a field, and then Andy set down his plate on the ground. "D'you fancy a dip, then?"

She pushed her plate and glass under the steamer seat in case she trod on them. "Aren't you going to let the food go down a bit first?"

"Only sandwiches."

"Oh, okay." The water felt cold at first, though it wasn't really, and she soon got used to it. Andy splashed vigorously up and down doing lengths, and she bobbed around more decorously for a while, before they met for a brief canoodle in one corner. "Are we overlooked?" he asked, drawing her towards him.

She glanced around. "Don't think so."

"Somebody might have his field glasses out."

"Does it matter?"

She giggled, nuzzling into one of the warm, wet saltcellars at the base of his throat and enjoying the feeling of his still-sturdy thighs imprisoning hers between them. "I don't think so. No."

He stared out over her head and the rim of the swimming pool. "Have you seen the state of that back wall?"

"Shut up, Andy."

"Hm..." He sighed, holding her tightly against him with the blue water lapping gently about their necks. "Oh, yes. Oh, yes. You know what, Val? This is definitely the life."

They walked down to *The Black Jug* afterwards for a bite to eat at about eight o'clock, just to have a look at it and to celebrate their first whole day. There was a huge open fireplace in the small lounge bar, and lots of low beams, some of them wreathed in festoons of dried hops. Photographs of the village cricket team and faded sepia ones of the village as it used to be were dotted here and there on the whitewashed walls. Above the scratched and polished dark wood bar hung an array of tankards and all around there were lots of gleaming brasses. It smelled of hops and beer and old log fires. It was very cheerful.

There was a kind of a stir when they went into the bar, a few heads turning, that kind of thing, and the barmaid was welcoming, but nobody else said hello. They had a whole range of local beers that Andy didn't know, so he had a difficult time choosing one. He was very pleased with his final choice, though. "Here, Val – go on, taste that!"

"They're a bit stand-offish," he muttered as they eventually took a small table at the back of the room and picked up the bar menus.

"Give them a chance! They all know each other. It'll be fine once they've got to know you, too." Actually, she admitted to herself, she felt a weeny bit awkward and overdressed in dress, beads and court shoes. It relieved her that they were sitting at the back. All the women seemed to be in jeans and tee shirts or trousers and sweaters, hardly any make up, really casual. None of them had had their hair done in curlers.

Funny, she'd expected them to be very smart and dressed up in the South. And to think she'd even thought of buying a hat.

Andy shook his head, studying the menu. "Bloody hell, have you see these prices?"

She had, and they were alarming if they were going to be eating out very much. "There are more things on the blackboard," she pointed out. "'Today's specials: Loin of Pork with a Prune, Sage and Apple Stuffing; Roasted, Slashed Fillet of Sea Bass; Pan-seared Scallops served with Crispy Prosciutto, Roasted Tomatoes and Puy Lentils.' Oh, my goodness, Andy! Twelve pound sixty for sausages and chips!"

Eventually they settled on ham, egg and chips for Andy and scampi and chips for her. They were very nice.

The phone rang just as they entered the house afterwards. It was Oliver, sounding bright and breezy. "Ah, Nana, so you're in there, then! Sorry we couldn't ring last night but we didn't get back till all hours. Susie tried this morning, but you were out. Well then, so what do you think?"

She had no hesitation. "Ollie, it's lovely, dear!"

He was pleased. "You like it, then?"

"I think it's wonderful!"

Andy was hovering at the door. "Is that Oliver? Ask him if it's been rewired."

"Ollie? Andy wants to know when it was rewired." She listened. "He says he thinks about five years ago, but he's going to have it all checked."

Ollie was saying something about coming down that evening just for a quick look. She frowned anxiously, thinking about the lack of beds. "Of course, dear. Are you coming on your own? Will you want to stay?"

"No, no – I'll drive down and back again. Poppy's got Mini Tennis and then Karate, but we'll probably all be down at the weekend. Should be there about sevenish if I can get away. Actually, we've found a rather good designer, friend of our friends Marcia and Rupert, name is Camilla Fox-Bruton, hah-hah, bit of a mouthful, and I've arranged to meet her, let her have a look round. Hope that's all right?"

"A designer?"

"Yes, she's pretty good apparently, and she doesn't just do the interior design, she'll sort out an architect and get estimates and has got some good builders on tap, so she might be useful. Might put it all in her hands." She felt a concerned and disappointed pang for Andy, who was probably expecting to do any overseeing himself. "I've arranged for her to meet us there at about seven-thirty. I've given her directions, but perhaps you could keep an eye open?"

She nodded meekly. "Of course."

When he had rung off, she wandered hesitantly into the kitchen. A designer! "Andy?"

He wasn't going to like this, not at all.

S he was very thin and tanned with a delicately streaked blond hair, the cut and colour of which Valerie knew must have cost a bomb; your hair wouldn't look like that if you'd been to *His 'n Hers* in the High Street. She wore a tee shirt which wasn't the kind of thing you picked up in Asda when you were doing your weekly shop, either, and her plain pale blue tailored skirt with a narrow belt, tiny gold leather sandals and all the gold jewellery spoke of somebody who had a lot of money to burn. She drove a low-slung red sports car, and spoke rather preciously with a slightly defective 'r'. "Mrs Bwyce? Hope we're not going to put you out."

Valerie straightened the skirt of the brown sprigged summer dress she'd bought from Country Casuals, one of her 'New Home' collection, carefully garnered from the Spring Sales and donned in honour of their first visitor. "Not at all. Do come in. I expect Oliver will be here in a minute."

"Yes." Camilla Fox-Bruton gazed dreamily around the garden. "This is very lovely, yes? What a marvellous view."

"Yes, it is. It is, isn't it?" Valerie ushered her through the back door. "This way." She took her into the kitchen, where she had cleared the table and set out four chairs.

Camilla clasped her beringed hands. "Oh, how quaint! I just adore this place! It has such incwedible potential."

"Um... Yes." Valerie avoided Andy's eyes. "This is my husband, Andrew." She'd forgotten her surname. "This is Camilla er... Andy."

He shook Camilla's languidly extended white fingers heartily. "Did you have any trouble finding us?"

She waved her free hand airily. "No, no. May I go through while we're waiting? Have a little explore?" She disappeared into the snug without waiting for a reply.

Valerie waved her own hand. "Carry on."

Andy helped himself to one of the Cadbury's shortcake biscuits she was setting out on a plate. "How long do you think this is going to take?"

"I don't know. About an hour?" She was making him wait for his dinner. All their married life they'd eaten at half-past six, and his tummy was probably rumbling, but with Oliver coming it would have to be a much later meal. It was going to be vegetarian today, too: a low-fat vegetarian lasagne in honour of Ollie; Andy didn't know that yet. He wouldn't be too happy.

Ollie arrived about five minutes later. He looked very tired, but he couldn't stop grinning. "Great view, that, isn't it?" he said, as he entered the back door. He was still wearing his city suit, slightly crumpled, though he had loosened his tie.

She embraced him with warmth. "Fantastic! Your lady is wandering round somewhere. Do you want a cup of tea?"

"We'll all have one, shall we? While we're talking? Are we sitting in here? Andy!" He slapped Andy on the back. "What do you think, then, Andy? Are you pleased with your new home?"

Valerie wasn't going to have Andy spoiling Ollie's pride and pleasure by voicing any disappointment. Seeing him frown and clearly ready to launch into a catalogue of all the things wrong with it, she sat down quickly and kicked him under the table. He winced and caught her eye. "Eh? Oh." He nodded at Ollie. "Oh, yes. It's got a great view. Tell you what, though, Oliver, we've got our work cut out –"

"Yes, yes, we'll discuss it in a minute." Ollie disappeared through the inner door. "Camilla!"

"Oliver! Dahling!" Valerie and Andy heard them chattering and laughing somewhere in the far sitting room.

Valerie picked up the kettle then put it down again. They were probably going to have a look round the whole place before they sat down.

When they did eventually did so, Camilla seemed taken aback when, after setting out the teapot and tucking on Granny's handmade padded cosy, the one that looked like a little thatched cottage with roses round the door, Valerie took a place again next to Andy at the kitchen table. "Oh, you're joining us, are you?" she asked, raising a finely arched eyebrow.

Disconcerted, Valerie glanced at Ollie. "Well, yes, I thought so."

He nodded, beaming. "Well, yes! I may be paying the bills, hah-hah-hah... But Andy and Valerie have got to live here. I'm sure their input will be very valuable."

Camilla smiled thinly, showing tiny, pointed teeth and nodded graciously. "Of course. Do let us know what you think. Any points you want to make..."

Encouraged, Andy leant forward. "Well, the first point is, that roof. We need to think about –"

Camilla turned deliberately towards Ollie. "It's all quite, quite wonderful, dahling, what a clever man you were to find it. We're going to have such fun. Now, as to an architect, dahling, I've got the very man." Unzipping her leather briefcase with a flick of her wrist, she consulted her notes. "Anthony McKenzie of Downall and Wichardson. He's a specialist in the renovation of listed buildings and he has the ear of the planners, so he's a jolly useful man to have on your side; they can be such beggars!"

"Now, shall I tell you how I see it, dahling?" She began to scribble on a pad. "Obviously this kitchen is absolutely hopeless as it is, far too small, so my suggestion would be that we make the Drawing Room into the kitchen, knock a door through here –" Valerie strained to see, but Camilla's elbow was obscuring the pad. "This to be the dining room, with maybe a gorgeous big conservatory with some lovely blinds leading off from the new kitchen."

Ollie brushed back his fair hair. "That sounds good! What do you think, Nana?"

It sounded wonderful but like a very big alteration. Valerie raised her eyebrows. "Well..."

Andy leant forward with a furrowed brow, "It sounds all very well and good, but before you get round to that you need to think about –"

He was talking to himself. Camilla was sweeping towards the back door. "Now, through here, Oliver! Come and have a peep." Scraping back his chair, he followed her obligingly into the back hall.

Valerie angled her ear toward the door and listened hard. Eavesdropping was down to her; men weren't good eavesdroppers, and in any case Andy was too deaf now to pick up much. "Obviously these good people will want to be tucked away," Camilla was pronouncing authoritively, "so I suggest we make a dear little kitchenette for them where the small utility room is now, and build a wall across here." Valerie could imagine her gesturing expansively with a dramatic arm. "So that they're nice and cosy. That will give them their own sitting room and cooking facility with the existing back door as a separate entrance. After all, you won't want –"

Her voice dropped annoyingly to a low murmur ending in a brittle, disparaging-sounding tinkle of laughter, and Valerie frowned, frustrated. What was it she thought Ollie wouldn't want? Annoyingly, she couldn't hear him answer.

Camilla lifted her voice again. "Fortunately, there is already a staircase in the sitting room, so they can scoot up there when they want to go up to bed in the end room.

We can seal that off from the landing somewhere. Then, on your side, knock through the back wall here and extend into the patio area to make a new porch and decent sized utility room and loo –"

She heard the stairs creak. Camilla's voice grew muffled and then became inaudible as they moved upstairs. She caught Andy's eye. He cleared his throat meaningfully.

"Well?"

She nodded thoughtfully. "Hm."

Chapter 4

They had a blissful day on Saturday with the family. The little ones were just lovely, with Poppy galloping round and round the huge garden and leaping over the yew hedge being a horse, and little Thomas toddling after her, occasionally falling flat on his nose. Of course, the towels and armbands came out, and a lot of the time was spent around the pool. Susie and Oliver went off to do some shopping and came back with a picnic barbeque and briquettes, bags of rocket and what Andy called disdainfully 'frizzy' lettuce, as well as granary rolls, hummus, cartons of olives and parmesan shavings and lots of vegetarian sausages and Quornburgers. Valerie was able to find some ordinary Birds Eye beef ones for Andy in the deep freeze. Ollie also produced with some pride a shop-bought 'home produced' chocolate cake as a special treat. The one Valerie had made and filled with butter cream and topped with a chocolate ganache she hid quickly in a tin at the back of the cupboard.

Andy managed to contain all the bad news he was collating about the state of the cottage to a passing mention of the condition of the roof, which Ollie took with equanimity, so that wasn't as bad as she had feared.

When evening came and the children started to get tired and crabby, the men, of course, disappeared. Andy took himself off to a distant garden seat with a newspaper and Ollie pronounced a short run necessary before driving back up to London, and set off up the drive in lycra shorts and running boots. He was a very long time.

"So, are you definitely going to have Camilla overseeing everything?" Valerie asked as she helped a clearly resentful Susie to load all their belongings back into the Discovery. Susie shrugged. "Oh, yes, it'll save a lot of trouble. Of course, she's still got to get the plans from the architect, but we've agreed to most of her ideas and she's getting a contract ready for us over the weekend. She's got several builders in mind she's going to interview when the plans come through."

Valerie cast a glance down across the garden to where she could see Andy, bare head buried in his newspaper. "Dad would do it for you, you know. Oversee the building work. He'd love it. After all, he's been in the building trade most of his life. He's only waiting to be asked."

Susie didn't seem to hear her.

As Valerie tried to persuade Poppy that the 'My Little Pony" collection that she had bought for her to play with should stay here rather than going back to London, and Susie struggled to pin a shrieking Thomas down so that she could put on his training pants before the journey, Susie frowned. "Actually, Mum, we were thinking it might be better if we stayed in London whilst the building work is being done."

Valerie sat down at the table. "Were you?"

"Makes sense, doesn't it? We can extend our lease for another six months, a year if necessary."

She was taken aback. "A year?!"

Susie widened her eyes. "It's a very big job, Mum. It won't be much fun with everything going on. It'd be very bad for the children."

She nodded carefully. "For the children. Of course."

"Don't want them breathing in brick dust and stuff."

"No." The thought was worrying, especially with Andy's heart. Had thought it would be just a matter of titivation, minor repairs, a bit of decorating. Didn't expect there to be so much construction work going on. It wouldn't be easy. "No, of course not. No."

Susie reflected. "I suppose you and Dad could move out yourselves. Rent somewhere for a little while."

It was an idea. "How much do you think that would cost?"

"I don't know – twelve hundred? Fifteen hundred?" Valerie heard herself squeak. "Fifteen hundred pounds a month?"

Susie shrugged. "That'd be for a small house or a cottage. You might find a little flat for seven or eight hundred."

She was aghast. "Goodness gracious! Beryl Holmes next door only got £400 a month for the house in Llewellyn Road and it had had four bedrooms and one of them en-suite – four bedrooms and two reception and a nice little private garden at the back. It's a nice road, too – quiet and no DSS bedsits, not yet, at any rate."

"Well, that was there. It's different here."

"I'll say." Whilst Susie darted off again to the Discovery, Valerie sat down with Thomas on her knee and tried to scribble out a quick calculation.

Fixed income now, just the two small state pensions, plus maybe a bit from investing what we can out of the money we got for the house when this one is finished. Paint and wallpaper, curtains and carpets for our own rooms and some new furniture once all the renovations are complete. The garden, a sit-on mower and a hedge cutter, lots to spend out there not forgetting plants and compost and fertilizer and things. Hope we won't need a new car, but there's the MOT every year, bound to find some things going wrong. Road Tax. Insurance. Replacing appliances, dental charges, spectacle replacement for both from time to time, we're both getting wonky.

Don't know yet what our share of the electrics and so on will come to; that Aga is likely to be expensive, being oil. Council Tax. TV Licence. Telephone. Insurance. Hopefully, our pensions will cover those things and still leave enough for food and petrol but if they don't we'll have to draw out of savings every month. Have to hang on to some of it, too, for Christmases and birthdays, clothes, of course. A little holiday now and then, maybe. Bound to be other expenses.

Ooh.

She sat back in her chair, staring at her jotting pad and locking her hands tightly round Thomas's middle. No. Renting was definitely out. One hundred and eighteen thousand pounds had sounded like such a lot of money when they had sold the house, but some of it had gone already on removal expenses and solicitor's and estate agents' charges, of course, and if they had to start renting somewhere as well at those prices and have all the expense of moving in and out again and that kind of thing on top, it wasn't going to go anywhere.

Susie was back, glancing at her watch. "Poppy, leave those, hurry up, have you been to the loo? Mind you," she added thoughtfully, gathering up the remaining scattered items and tossing them into Thomas' changing bag. "It would be very valuable to have somebody on site, I suppose. You know what builders are! I don't imagine Camilla will be able to get here every day to keep an eye on them."

Valerie nodded silently. *Indeed, we must hope not.*

"I'll get this out to the car." Susie glanced at her watch again and her lips tightened. "We're going to be late, where's their father? Leaving it all to me. The kids are shattered; we need to get them home. Selfish bastard."

Valerie hitched Thomas onto her hip and followed her out. "I think we'd better stay put, you know, dear, ride it out," she told her thoughtfully. "The building work, I mean."

"Are you sure?" Susie glanced up the drive as Ollie, hot and perspiring, panted in from the road, and pulled a disdainful face. "Here he is back now. He'll insist on a shower now, I suppose. Can he use yours for now?"

"Yes, of course."

Exhausted but exhilarated, Ollie threw himself down at the top of the back steps. "Whew!" He glanced at his watch, clearly pleased with himself. "Eight miles. Not too bad for an eight mile run!"

Susie bustled past him, raising her voice sharply. "Oliver, we need to go; Sarah and Dane are coming for supper, remember. It's going to take us at least an hour and a half to get back and we need to do some shopping on the way. If you're going to have a shower, use Mum and Dad's, and do it quickly."

"Ah." He raised his eyebrows, grinning at Val. "Looks as if we're off, Nana."

She smiled feebly. "Hm."

"Oh, well, we'll be here permanently before long. No

more peace and quiet then, eh? Looking forward to it, are you?"

Catching sight of Susie's tightly frozen scowl, her smile wavered just a little. "Oh... Oh, mm."

Contentment in a wife, Valerie had found over long years of marriage, was very dependent on how happy one's husband was. They could be miserable little buggers when things weren't going their way.

Apart from his discovering more and more things that were wrong with the building, the first few weeks were fine. There were lots of good days. They both enjoyed the swimming pool when the weather was sunny. They both liked getting in the car and tootling off on what they called their 'little outings' – exploring the countryside or paying visits to nearby places like Winchester and Salisbury. They were very taken with their nearest little town, where colour-washed and elegantly brick-fronted houses crawled up and down the sides of a shallow hill. To their great pleasure, there was no Thomas Cook or Thompson's Travel, no Carphone Warehouse or Vodaphone, no McDonalds or Boots or Poundstretcher or WH Smiths or Waterstones, just three or four really nice looking pubs, a tiny library and a couple of banks, and a small collection of independently owned shops and cafes with carefully-arranged window displays and assistants who smiled and actually seemed pleased to see you.

They were a bit pricey, though. Valerie was enticed into popping into a clean and fashionable-looking hairdressers to see about getting herself a restyle, but came out again, white as a sheet, when she saw the prices. "Good heavens, I'll have to think about buying myself a nice wig!"

Andy, who had been hovering outside the salon, checking the stucco work, was feeling expansive. "You have it done, pet, if it pleases you."

He was used to paying £4 at the barbers in the Glyn. He'd have a fit. Still shocked, she shook her head. "I'll have a look at some other places first."

There was a lovely 'Help the Aged', too. She made a mental note to come back and investigate it properly when she hadn't got Andy hanging around outside, looking bored.

He was showing no serious signs of wishing that they hadn't come, but as time went on he was definitely getting a bit ragged round the edges. The whole thing about the house was worrying him to death, she knew – the state of it as well as the thought of what it was going to cost to do up. The architect had taken weeks to draw up and submit his plans and when he eventually did there had been many things to iron out, like the fact that he had obviously been instructed to include the 'apartheid system' after all.

Camilla battered her eyelashes, the picture of innocence, when Valerie and Andy challenged her. "I had no instruction about that from Oliver."

When Andy asked Susie about it on the phone, Susie said that it had been made clear by him when the architect and Camilla were walking round and that should have been good enough.

"But did he put it in writing, Oliver?" Andy asked, frowning.

Susie was amused. "Good lord, shouldn't think so; he hasn't got time for that. That's not Ollie's style. No, he'll just have to pay for the architect to draw up some different plans."

"They don't half waste money," Andy said to Valerie, shaking his head worriedly.

By the time the Planning Officer had agreed to the plans in principle, Valerie and Andy found that on top of the basic costs of the architect's fees and the other building work, which now also included under-floor heating in the conservatory and all sorts of other, to them, very extravagant things. Oliver was also going to have to pay for all new windows – twenty six in all – with small, individually handmade panes of glass in each one because the existing ones were deemed too modern, new cast iron guttering because the existing guttering was PVC, reclaimed tiles of the correct period for the huge roof and that of the old storage shed, solid oak staircases and seventeen solid oak doors, which each had to have five separate coats of fire-resistant varnish. Even the bolts and latches must be in period and had to be specially ordered. There was to be no double-glazing – not allowed. Only a special traditional plaster mix could be used for the exterior, and a new soak-away had to be dug.

"Tell you what, don't let me ever buy a bloody listed building!" Andy snorted, pouring himself a large medicinal whisky. "They own you, these bloody planning people. It isn't right!"

For a man who'd already had one heart attack, the amount of whisky he was comforting himself with these days worried Val rather more.

He was missing male company a bit too, she knew that. He was a man's man, Andy, and he needed a good chat with the lads over a pint from time to time, but he still hadn't taken kindly to the pub. He went occasionally on a Saturday to watch the village cricket team in action, but so far had dug his heels in about volunteering to umpire for them, even though they were obviously in need of somebody. "If they want me they'll ask me."

"Do they know how much cricket you've played, Andy?"

"Don't suppose so."

"You haven't told them?"

"They haven't asked."

"Why would they?" She sighed in exasperation. "Look Andy, nobody knows you down here and if you don't say, they never will know, will they? One the things about down here that I've noticed is that nobody asks any questions. It's not like it was at home –" She corrected herself quickly. "Not like it was before. Nobody wants to ask who you are or what you did for a living, they're waiting for you to tell them."

"You're right," he admitted gloomily with a shrug, helping himself to a KitKat from the fridge and unravelling it disconsolately from its wrapper. "Nobody in the pub seems to want to know."

She spread out the collar of a shirt and bent over it, wielding the iron with heavy precision. "Bet they're talking about you, though, I bet they are! Like I said, I think they're waiting for you to tell them what you want them to know. It's not that they're not interested, they're just trying not to be nosy."

He shrugged again. "Maybe."

Neither of them had got to know anyone very much yet.

The second week they were there, Elizabeth and Howard Blackwell, who lived next door in 'Mulberry Cottage' – which wasn't really a cottage at all but quite a big house – had invited them in for some drinks, which was very kind of them, but they hadn't seen much of them since. Valerie felt she should have invited them back, but Andy didn't feel they were up to offering hospitality just yet and he was probably right.

But matters on the social front did get better.

"That's it. I've had enough." Valerie woke, startled, one night as Andy threw back the duvet roughly and swung his legs out of the bed. Pushing back her 'Deep Sleep' eye mask and pulling out one earplug, she raised herself anxiously onto one elbow and switched on the bedside lamp.

"What's the matter?"

He shuffled into his slippers angrily and reached for his dressing gown. "That bloody security light. I'm going over."

Reaching over for the alarm clock, she peered at it closely. "Andy, it's ten past two."

"I don't care." He sounded almost tearful and appeared to be fighting a losing battle with his dressing gown.

"You're in the wrong armhole, pet." She lifted her eyes to the ceiling. "Oh, my goodness, listen to that rain!"

"I have been listening to it, for hours – and that bloody tarpaulin."

"You should put on the sleepmask I bought you from Boots like mine – and you never wear your ear plugs."

He strode over to the door. "They're no bloody good. I shouldn't have to."

Wearily she forced herself out of bed and reached for her own dressing gown. He glanced back. "No, you stay there; no point in us both getting up."

She fished out her slippers from under the bed. "I'm awake now. I'll have to have a cup of tea."

"Suit yourself then."

She followed him down the stairs, shivering in the blast of cold, wet draught allowed in by the tarpaulin which had been stretched over the bones of the roof and down over the breach in the back wall of the cottage. The draught and the continual flapping and snapping as it fought against the wind together made it sound and feel as if they were clambering down some rickety companionway on a ship at sea. She groaned. "Oh, my goodness! My! I see what you mean."

He stood by the removable flap that covered the void that had been the back door, already wearing his old trilby hat and pulling on his raincoat over his dressing gown. She reached for an umbrella. "At least take this with you. Do you want a torch?"

"Don't need one, do I, not with that light on? Go on back to bed." Unfastening the flap and ducking his head against the driving rain, he stepped out into what appeared to be an ink-black lake rather than a patio. She drew in a sharp breath. "Andy, you've still got your bedroom slippers on!" Too late. She could hear him swearing as he splashed over towards the back steps.

He seemed ages. With difficulty, stubbing her toe on a protruding half-brick and wincing, Valerie picked her way across the kitchen to the kettle. The kitchen had become a bombsite. The whole house had, really.

They'd had a fairly long period of calm. Finding a builder who could actually come in the next year or two had proved rather difficult, even for Camilla. At last, though, she had identified two of whom she approved and who might – only might, they each warned separately – might be able to start in the next few months, and this time Andy had made the advance decision to accompany them around so that he could suss them out.

It was plain that Carmilla had been rather taken with the first builder, a sleek young man wearing an expensive suit and carrying an important-looking briefcase who had an impressive-sounding building company, was quite good-looking, and who had flirted madly with her. Val had been so irritated by the two of them that she didn't even offer him a cup of tea.

Andy, though, had gone for the older man of the two, a Mr George Bailey, who was only a small family builder but who seemed to know what he was talking about. He also talked a lot more to Andy, Val had noticed, which had pleased him, and seemed to be listening with interest to what he had to say. He did get tea and a chocolate biscuit in gratitude; she had even offered him a second.

They had been both relieved and more than a little triumphant when Oliver had overruled Camilla and gone along with Andy's choice.

It had been late October before building work had actually started. Although Autumn had set in fair, the fine weather had only lasted long enough for the tiles to be taken off the roof, the old boiler to be removed and the back wall to be taken out, then the temperature had dropped, the wind had got up, the clouds had piled in from the Atlantic and the rain had started tippling down with a vengeance.

Mr Bailey and his men had done their best, rigging up huge tarpaulins over the roof struts and fixing them to a frame erected where the new back wall was to be, but the combination of the sound of the torrential rain drumming on the tarpaulin and the continual flapping and snapping as it fought against the wind, together with the nagging irritation of the light from across the road, which still penetrated the bedroom nightly round the edges of the blackout blind, had clearly brought Andy to breaking point.

Turning back from the kettle, Valerie stubbed her toe painfully yet again. "Ouch! Dammit!" It had been resolved that the kitchen would remain in use for the time being, so that they could actually eat. Camilla, though, had decided that she wanted the brick floor in the kitchen taking up and big stone floor tiles laying there instead.

"Oh, you must! You must! It'll look absolutely marvellous, dahling!" She had fluttered her eyelashes at Ollie and invited him and Susie to supper, so the beautiful old bricks had come up, creating huge amounts of dust and leaving craters underfoot. Whilst Camilla and Susie and Ollie spent a lot of time spent humming and hah-ing over which fantastically expensive flooring stones out of her glossy catalogues should take their place, Val and Andy's toes were accumulating a patchwork dressing of sticking plasters and their elderly ankles were feeling very fragile and strained. Quite apart from the discomfort, Valerie was disgruntled all over again every time she went into the kitchen. She had loved those mellow old bricks.

Trying not to think about it, she made and drank her

tea and ate a couple of ginger biscuits, peering out through the front window from time to time, but apart from the lashing rain revealed in the beam of the security light, it was impossible to see anything. She wandered through the gap that was to be a new doorway into the draughty, echoing room that was to be the new kitchen to see if she could see any better out of the front window there, but it was much too cold with the huge tarpaulin-hung hole in the wall that was going to lead to the new conservatory, so she turned back quickly and instead climbed back upstairs. Switching off the lights in the room and peering with cupped hands through the bedroom window, she thought she could make out a faint light somewhere across the road, but the security beam blinded her too much to be certain of it. Shivering, she went back downstairs again and warmed up a hot water bottle, which she tucked into the top of her dressing gown, tying the cord tightly so that it wouldn't slip down.

As the time ticked by – half an hour, three quarters – she began to panic. Andy might have tripped over the builders' materials lying on the drive. He might have hit his head and be drowning in the water rushing down the drive. He had been very angry; he might – terrible thought – have had another heart attack.

Peering out through the flap through which he had disappeared and straining to see through the rain she called questioningly, but there was no answer. In desperation, pulling on her wellies and throwing her mac on over her coat and dressing gown, she tied on a scarf and picked up the torch, then took a deep breath and stepped out into the waterfall of rain spilling over the rim of the overworked guttering.

She couldn't see anything beyond, even before the rain got in her eyes and blinded her. Dabbing them with the soggy end of her scarf and carefully avoiding the area at the side of the steps where the builders had been digging out earlier for the new soakaway, and dodging the piles of bricks and building rubble heaped along the sides of the drive, she made her way up to the road, casting around with the feeble light of the torch and projecting a hoarse whisper; "Andy? Andy?".

There was no answer.

It was bitterly cold and very scary. The wind howled and screamed amongst the swaying trees and the road was pitch dark except where the arc of the security light, neatly pinpointing their bedroom window, pierced the blackness. There were no lights at the windows of the house to which it was affixed, no other lights anywhere; she must have been mistaken when she thought she had spotted one.

Images sprang frighteningly into her mind. Andy knocking angrily at the door, complaining, and this huge burly tattooed yob coming out and beating him up; the people in the house with the searchlight all turning out to be druggies, a Columbian drug gang or something. He had caught them in the middle of doing some – what did you call it? – dealing, and had been shot or knifed by this out-of-his-skull druggie. Andy lying unconscious in the gloom beneath the hedges along the road...

Did she dare knock at the door? Should she go next door and ask for help? Mr and Mrs Blackwell were probably sound asleep. This was Lynton Stacey, not Brixham or Peckham or wherever. It was probably just a nice old lady who had the security light because she was afraid and hadn't realised it was faulty.

In which case, where was Andy? Should she call the police? Maybe she'd better.

Anxiously debating with herself, she made her way back to the house. Have another cup of tea first yourself, she advised herself once back inside. Don't want to cause an unnecessary fuss. Even your dressing gown's sopping, look, silly woman; get it off first and put on something dry.

When he did come back dripping wet, almost another hour later, after she had picked up and put back the telephone receiver at least three times, he came wearing high green waders, a glazed look in his eyes and a silly smile. The fumes of alcohol were barely dissipated by the draught.

She met him angrily. "Oh, there you are! I was going to call the police!"

"Sorry, were you worried? He's a nice fellow; plays cricket."

She sniffed, handing him a towel. "Must be a nice fellow,

then."

He leant insecurely against the only solid bit of wall. "Oopsie! Going to take me fishing. Got a permit somewhere. Nice fellow. Lent me these waders. You'll have to give me a hand."

It took several goes, but she managed it eventually. His stripy pyjama trousers were soaking. Grinning, he pinched her bottom as she positioned him at the bottom of the stairs. She smacked his hand. "Go on, get up there; you're drenched. He was in, then, I take it?" she asked him crossly as she climbed up behind him.

"He was, yes. He imports bananas, you know. Gave me a pineapple. Don't know what I did with it. He was in a kind of shed thing round the back. I heard some voices and I saw the light on so I went round there instead of knocking at the door."

"That was lucky."

"I'll say it was; he was having a tasting of his home brew with some mates."

"Beer?"

"And wine. Oh – and then he got out the whisky." Stumbling against the bedpost, he fell heavily into the bed. "Going to fix the security light. Good man. Nice crowd. Plays cricket. Going to take me fishing – did I say?"

Chapter 5

As time went on, Camilla began to arrive ever more frequently with arms full of heavy brochures and colourful designer swatches. Either Susie or Oliver, sometimes both, came down almost every weekend and he or she and Camilla had summit meetings at which they endlessly discussed the eventual décor, lighting fitments, appliances, floorings and soft furnishings. All these things would naturally have to be sourced from exclusive specialist suppliers and therefore needed to be ordered quite far in advance, to which end Susie did try to involve Valerie, but Camilla dismissed her suggestions with such patronising disdain that she blew up regularly in private.

"Honestly, Andy, she doesn't take the slightest bit of notice of anything I have to say. Do you know what she did today? She took Susie off into our bedroom – *our bedroom* – and shut the door so that I wouldn't hear what they were saying! Of course, I went straight in. They were discussing doorknobs. Do you know how much each one she wanted Susie to buy was? No, on second thoughts I'm not telling you. You'd have a blooming fit."

He shook his head with a knowing grimace. "10%"

"What?"

"She's getting 10% of anything they buy."

"She's not!"

"On top of her fee, of course."

"She's not!"

"She is."

Valerie was flabbergasted. "That's terrible!"

Since neither Susie nor Ollie seemed to be interested in whether or not they were being persuaded to spend too much money, and equally because they couldn't stand her, Valerie and Andy decided to keep out of any meetings where Camilla was involved. Valerie eavesdropped with glee, though, relaying their discussion *sotto voce* to Andy who inserted the deaf aid, which he normally disdained, especially for the purpose. It was useful sometimes not yet having a proper door.

"She's got some wonderful cabinet maker in mind who can make hand built units to fit for the kitchen and the children's bedrooms. He's going to do the doors and the staircases and the windows and the conservatory as well."

"Hard wood or soft wood?"

"Eh?"

"The conservatory!"

She listened again. "Susie doesn't know. She's going to ask Ollie. Ooh, we're going to have underfloor heating!"

"With an Aga? You'll roast, woman, never mind the Sunday joint."

She grimaced, listening. "Ooh, I don't like the sound of that."

"What?"

"They're talking about painting the kitchen units in that 'distressed' look. You know, where they put all the paint on and then wipe it all off again to make it look old?"

"If they want old, why didn't they leave us with the old stuff? Tell them I'll paint it for them, get a really nice shine."

She moved hurriedly away from the door. "Look out, staircases next, they're coming through to have a look at the hall!"

Over the next few weeks, plumbers, electricians and builders jostled for space. Brick dust filled the air and pieces of brick and other debris cluttered underfoot. Doorways were sealed up and knocked out, the joists up in the attic were secured, and the old sanitary fittings from the first floor bathroom were lifted down the stairs and out. The conservatory beams went up and a shiny, dark green Aga was brought in, a cause of great excitement.

Oliver's wetroom turned out to be a room with a viciously strong shower with nozzles at varying heights and the walls all tiled so that the whole place became a shower cubicle. Camilla had persuaded Ollie to have not only the tiles of heavy stone, but also to have the floor made out of a solid sheet of granite. It took six men to lift it, gave Mr Bailey sciatica and dropped on his son's toes so that he had to have them X-rayed, then it wouldn't go up past the turn in the stairs. They dropped it again, and it cracked. Camilla blamed Mr Bailey, and he argued that he had advised her against it. In the end, Ollie lashed out for another one. Camilla smiled, writing out the order form.

This time, when the new piece of granite arrived they took the lower staircase out first and hauled the thing up on ropes. Mr Bailey put up a ladder so that Valerie and Andy and anyone who needed to could get up to the first floor, but with a loo, a night time necessity, not being up there any more anyway, Andy and Valerie made themselves up a mattress bed in the snug. Hauling herself up from such a low level did Valerie's back in, and being on the floor and so close to the old carpet with books all around and brick and mortar dust filling the air as well as wood smoke, they both had to pay their first visits to the surgery and came back each clutching a nasal spray for chronic rhinitis. Andy had to have an inhaler as well; his chest got very bad.

The only other problem was the downstairs loo. They could get to it by going round through the little sitting room instead of clambering over the cratered kitchen floor, but being sheltered only by the tarpaulin, it was bitterly cold on their frequent nocturnal trips.

Otherwise, the arrangement was fairly cosy.

Over Christmas Mr Bailey and his men took the whole fortnight off, naturally, but they left the cooker standing, and the sink, and the wall cupboards where there still were any walls, so it could have been a whole lot worse. Susie and Ollie had invited Valerie and Andy up to London for the two days of Christmas, so they didn't need to worry about that.

They received an invitation to a pre-Christmas cocktail party at the Blackwells next door, which gave Valerie the opportunity to wear the black cocktail dress with the pleated gauze sleeves she'd invested in from The Clothes

Exchange in Chester for just such special occasions. She had her hair streaked and cut at last, too, and she was very pleased with it, though she was finding the blow-drying for herself rather difficult and she hadn't dared to tell Andy what it had cost. The whole experience, though, had been a real treat. They had given her a complementary head-and-neck massage with the essential rose oil she had chosen out of the proffered range of little bottles – and she had been offered, and had accepted, real coffee, which came in a proper pot with a cream jug and brown sugar on a tray spread with a crisp white tray cloth carried by an apprentice. Not a bit like *His 'n Hers;* Tracy's coffee, when she had remembered to offer any, had come in a mug and had tasted like weak ditchwater.

If Valerie had wanted to be critical, she could have complained that both the cups she drank turned out to be a bit cold, because she was only able to take quick sips between foils due to not wanting to hold up the colourist, but it was meant well and she appreciated it.

At the party, Marjorie Blackwell volunteered to drive Valerie down to a huge M&S at a place called Hedge End if she wanted to do some Christmas shopping, which was very kind. Excited, she took a long time getting ready, choosing her new lavender tweed suit, frilled floral blouse and her black courts for the occasion. She was somewhat disconcerted when Marjorie turned up in a long sleeved plain tee shirt under a sleeveless puffa jerkin, a dirndl skirt and no make-up. Valerie felt decidedly overdressed and made a mental note for future occasions that that was obviously the correct sort of outfit to wear if you were a Hampshire Lady going shopping.

The big M&S was amazing; she managed to find almost everything she wanted: a soft, cosy dressing gown for Susie, a plain turtle-necked light blue sweater for Ollie (she kept the receipt, so that Susie could change it and buy something for the children if he didn't like it) – a second one in dark green with a V neck for Andy, pretty pink pyjamas and slippers with a furry trim for Poppy, and for Thomas an appealing black-and-white mechanical puppy to be addressed, according to the box, as 'Patch'. The way it yapped and flipped disconcertingly over when wound up was so charming that she couldn't resist going back and buying another for Poppy, this time 'Goldie', a little golden retriever kind of thing, which meant, of course, that she had to buy Thomas pyjamas and slippers as well.

She managed to buy most of the little presents she needed for other people, and came away too with a selection of Christmas cards, six rolls of wrapping paper and a basketful of silver, gold and glass baubles and other decorations. Well, they were a bargain, being Three For The Price Of One, and they needed them because they had got rid of the ones that they'd had for years when they had left the old house.

It wasn't till she had paid for them that she remembered that they would be going to London for Christmas, and that anyway, with all the building works there would be no point at all in trying to make the place look Christmassy.

Christmas in Susie and Ollie's loft-style Dockside apartment was interesting. It was definitely impressive, though not exactly what you would call homely, with its double-height ceilings, exposed pipe work and other apparently much sought-after factory features. Thomas' and Poppy's toys and paraphernalia really looked quite out of place scattered everywhere, and though it was lovely and light with huge curtainless windows, there were no doors to any of the areas except the loos and bathrooms. However did they ever get the children to sleep in the evening, Valerie wondered?

The answer, as she found out when she and Andy eventually went to bed a little before eleven in the little angle known as 'Poppy's room', leaving Poppy and Thomas still wide awake and bouncing, was 'with great difficulty'. Valerie and Andy didn't get much sleep either. They could hear the giant flat screened television wherever they were in the flat and whilst Susie was rustling about wrapping up the stocking presents, Ollie was watching some very noisy 'Bang-Bang-You're-Dead' film involving lots of sirens and screeching car chases till half past two in the morning.

They kept on smiling; it was Christmas Eve, after all, and at least Susie and Ollie hadn't offered them their own giant queen-sized bed, for which they were extremely thankful, since it was very exposed, parked out like an island in the middle of the floor.

Christmas Day was lovely, spoiled a little only by a distinct tendency between Susie and Ollie to contradict anything the other one said and to pick arguments with one another over nothing at all. Watching the children's faces as they opened their presents was delightful. Andy wasn't exactly thrilled with stuffed red peppers followed by nut roast instead of turkey and chipolatas for his Christmas dinner, but he put a good face on it. At least there were roast parsnips and a Christmas pudding; low fat and vegetarian, naturally – with *crème fraiche*, not rum sauce – and no brandy butter.

They got a bit more sleep on Christmas night. The children were worn out and Ollie went to bed at half past nine, which, as he was effectively in the middle of what was also part of the sitting room, made them feel rather awkward. They retreated to Poppy's 'room' shortly afterwards.

Nice as it had been, they were both quite glad, though, when they were on their way back to Hampshire, uncomfortable as it was with the building works. Valerie was especially pleased when Andy had referred to the journey as 'going home'. It meant they were settling down.

Things carried on in the New Year much as they had before Christmas. When the panes of double-glazed reinforced glass for the conservatory finally arrived after months of waiting, they turned out to be the wrong size. The tarpaulins went back over the huge wooden frame and slipped and blew off regularly over the passing weeks whilst new ones were being cut. It was very draughty in the kitchen, though once it was installed the Aga kept it reasonably cosy up at the far end. The cost of oil when the first bill came in frightened Andy half to death.

Some of the cottage windows had been measured up incorrectly too, and had to be remade. Camilla took it quite calmly. Andy shrugged sardonically. "Is she bovvered? 10%!"

Her cabinet-maker's men set about fitting in the new kitchen units next, though the process was a very leisurely one. They seemed to have very short working days, 'popping back to the workshop' frequently, sometimes vanishing for days on end, and then stopping coming entirely. Camilla announced with relish that it was because Valerie and Andy had been 'howible to them.'

This surprised Valerie and Andy, who, as far as they were concerned, had done nothing more horrible than pass the time of day and offer frequent cups of tea. Susie told Camilla on the phone that she really doubted that her Mum and Dad had said anything and by the way, did she realise that the men hadn't been in at all again last week? Camilla said that wasn't true. Susie said, yes it was, and they'd only been in two days the week before as well, Mum and Dad had told her so. Camilla said, "Sebastian assures me that they were here all week, your pawents are lying to you!"

Susie blew her top. "How DARE you!" She even burst into tears. Valerie was very touched.

"Kick her into touch, Susie," urged Andy, rather hoping that his hour had come. "Now's your opportunity. I'll keep an eye on things. She's just costing you a fortune. You don't need her."

To his disappointment though, Susie demurred, sniffing. Another dinner party at Camilla's house, she explained awkwardly – friend of a friend; it was very tricky. Andy stomped off, harrumphing, to sort out the tools in the shed.

George Bailey's men came in to level the kitchen floor and lay and seal the new and wickedly expensive cream stone tiles and the house was filled with noxious fumes from the sealant, which made Valerie and Andy feel quite ill. "Bloody dangerous, that," said Andy, who went round flinging open any windows or doors which were not letting in a howling gale already due to glasslessness or framelessness. Valerie took to wearing a pom-pom hat and her thick woolly dressing gown on top of all her clothes.

As it transpired, Sebastian's men had refused to come back because they had been getting snide comments from one or two of George Bailey's men with whom a not insubstantial degree of rivalry had built up. Camilla had a loud and furious row out on the patio with George about it. Valerie and Andy listened through the tarpaulin, hugging each other and jumping up and down with glee when he eventually got so irate that he called her a stupid bloody rude woman who knew nothing about the building industry and couldn't oversee a paddling pool, and that she knew where she could put her job. It took lots of conciliatory beers at the pub from Andy and a lot of tea and sympathy and slices of home-made cake from Valerie to calm him down again but eventually, for their sakes, he agreed to carry on. So, unfortunately, did Camilla.

Then the Planning Officer had an objection to the roof tiles George had sourced and he had to take them all off and start all over again. Camilla gloated.

Neither the Whirlpool washing machine nor the enormous dryer would go through either of the back doors and the new door that had just been put in had to be taken out of its frame and the doorway widened. The ordering of another solid oak door the appropriate size was, of course, necessary. Andy nodded knowingly. "10%"

Valerie slipped on the ladder and twisted her ankle, which left her in a lot of pain. Andy confronted Camilla on her next inspection visit instead of vanishing quickly as usual for a walk. "When are they actually going to finish the stairs?"

She waved an airy hand. "Sebastian will finish when he's weady. He's a craftsman."

Andy went quite red. "Don't tell me about craftsmen, I appreciate a craftsman as much as any man, I've been one all my life, but this is getting ridiculous! We're getting on. We're pensioners! We're sleeping downstairs on a mattress! My wife's hurt her ankle now. I can't have her forever clambering up and down a ladder!"

Camilla smiled patronisingly, rolled her eyes and shrugged. "Maybe, Mr Bwyce, you would have done better not to have wejected moving out." She swept on, leaving Andy floundering.

They both knew she was right.

Despite all the problems and the discomfort, matters were slowly beginning to take shape. Huge double doors were constructed between the kitchen and the conservatory and, to everyone's relief, the correct panes were delivered at last and fitted into the giant frame of the conservatory, and the last tarpaulins came down. The weather brightened immediately. The kitchen units were suitably 'distressed,' to Andy's matching dismay. Valerie secretly decided they looked rather nice. A double butler's sink with double drainers was set in place beneath the side window, as was an enormous dishwasher. The sink had a waste disposal unit which terrified Valerie into thinking of chopped up fingers, and a special high-spray gadget on the tap for cleaning off your carrots, which fascinated her, though she didn't think she would ever use it.

A gloriously complicated Smeg electric hob and fan oven was installed in the granite-topped island unit and a highly sophisticated and far-too-complex-for-Andy-and-Valerie-to-use microwave oven was fitted into a space beneath a wall-unit. The splashbacks in the kitchen were tiled in rustic-style creamy white. Loopy ivy-green writing across consecutive tiles dotted here and there hinted at tempting delicacies to come. George was so pleased with the result that nobody liked to mention that, for example, *Omelette aux Fines* would have made a little more sense had the isolated word *Herbes* been attached, instead of on the other side of the kitchen next to *Patisserie*. Even Camilla, whose relationship with George was now all but non-existent, held her tongue and merely rolled her eyes and fluttered her lashes sardonically.

Wandering around the immaculately-fitted kitchen and opening the doors to see the light automatically turn on in the big walk-in larder cupboard, Valerie had a brief flashback of her very first such, the one she had been given by her mum when they had got married. Small, cream-painted, with rather splintery wood and wallpaper on the shelves and never sufficient space on them, but she could remember clearly the pride she had felt as she had placed her purchases on its shelves with care.

She closed the door again with something like disbelief. They had built up a very nice home over the years, had she and Andy, comfortable and shipshape – everything in its place and a place for everything – but nothing like this. This house was something special. Who would ever have guessed!

The wonky units still remaining in the previous kitchen were removed and big smooth flagstones were laid over the rubble that had been the beautiful old bricks. Big French windows leading from it onto the patio were set in place and a new wood-burning stove was installed in one corner. George Bailey took out the ugly old fireplace in their sitting room and replaced it with a dark oak beam for a mantle. To Andy's great delight, as there was no cellar, he also built a huge wine rack to fill the gap beneath the stairs.

As a special favour George, who was becoming quite a friend, sent in one of his men one weekend to sort out the broken staging and panes in the greenhouse and all through the months, whenever it wasn't too cold, Valerie laboured in the garden. But even with the staunch assistance of Andy – which was in any case a mixed blessing since he was an enthusiastic hacker-back and digger but didn't know a dandelion from a delphinium – knocking it into shape was too much, really.

She was staring at it all through the kitchen window over the pastry board and feeling quite despondent when her surprise birthday present from Andy arrived, in the late afternoon.

The man on the steps was tall, tousle-haired and forty-ish with a sweetly abstracted and faintly worried-looking smile. He was wearing muddy gumboots and an ancient jerkin over a checked shirt and faded jeans. "S-sorry I'm late." He had a slight stammer. It made him sound very shy.

She was puzzled. Was she supposed to be expecting him? "Are you?"

"G-got a bit held up."

"Ah." Valerie rubbed the end of her nose in case there was flour sitting on it. "Did you want my husband?"

"S-sorry, you are Mrs Bryce?"

"I am."

"May-maybe the best thing would be to wander round?"

"Yes. Yes, of course. Um – would it?"

"You can t-tell me what ideas you have as we go. What you might have in m- mind. Then I'll go away and think."

She was totally mystified.

"Sorry, sorry, I'm M-Matthew Crossley."

That didn't help much.

"C.G.C. Crossley Garden Construction. Mr Bryce asked me to design and sort out the garden for you. I'm here to give you a quote."

She hugged Andy to within an inch of his life when she found him. He went all pink-faced with pleasure. "Well, I'm fed up with bloody digging. Bloody gardens... Happy Birthday. Don't go too mad, mind!"

She was in seventh heaven. Trotting along beside Matthew, practically drooling, she listened avidly as he proposed lots of lovely things like delphiniums, shrub roses, agapanthus, marguerites, tulips, veronica, penstemmons and hellebores, echinaceas and salvias to go in a long border all down the side of the croquet lawn. Two of his men prepared and planted the border up, scarified, fertilised and rolled the lawn, cleared the little well and sorted out the front garden. They built an archway for climbing roses over the gate, installed a heating system in the greenhouse, prepared the raised beds, sorted out the wheat from the chaff in the walled garden, and dug out and planted new borders round the swimming pool. Susie gave her *carte blanche* and contributed too. It cost a fortune, though despite his warning Andy didn't complain, and it was quite enthralling.

She was so carried away with it that when she spotted a poster on the notice board of the village hall inviting villagers to enter their gardens for an Open Gardens Day, to raise funds for the village hall later on in the summer, she put her name down immediately, then got very worried about it afterwards. "It won't look at its best, of course, not for a year or two. Am I being too hasty? It'll be a dickens of a job keeping it looking tidy. What have I let myself in for?"

"Hm?"

"Is it just showing off, Andy?"

"Is what showing off?"

"What I've been telling you."

"What was that? I didn't hear you."

"About the Open Gardens. Why don't you ever listen to a thing I say?"

Chapter 6

The staircase was installed eventually towards the end of April, and to be fair it was beautifully made, but whilst they all were clustered round in the hall admiring it – even, grudgingly, George Bailey – someone raised the question of how they were to get Susie and Ollie's furniture upstairs around the bends. The spindles, newel posts and banister rails had to come out again. George Bailey guffawed and gloated. Nevertheless, the treads and risers did provide a way upstairs

The bathrooms were tiled, the children's in white with individual tiles bearing motifs of sea shells and goldfish and green water-weed dotted here and there, and Susie and Ollie's en-suite in pale beige and very expensive stone. The guest en-suites, the downstairs loo and big utility room, and the kitchen and the walk-in larder, followed. New lavatory bowls and basins and baths, very swish, free-standing on iron claw feet – smooth and deep and white for the en-suite and guest rooms and bright sunshine yellow for the children's floor – were carried in. Valerie and Andy had decided to keep the big bath with its tarnished taps and wonky shower stand; nothing much in the posh catalogues Susie showed them provided much temptation, it was easy to get in and out of and they had grown to love lolling in it gazing out at the treetops, listening to the radio or, in Andy's case, luxuriously sipping a glass of wine. It didn't seem worth the bother. Andy asked George's plumber to take out the bidet instead. They filled a spare corner with a white painted wicker Ali Baba basket that

Valerie had fallen for in John Lewis.

Cupboards, walk-in wardrobes and other storage units were constructed, and then the final choices as to colours had to be made before the decorating could start. The cards and wallpaper books Camilla worked from were all designer labelled, expensive and trendy, with no regard paid, as Andy saw it, to coverage or durability. To ruffle his feathers even further, she and Susie settled on what were for him alarmingly bright colours like Sundance Yellow, Cornflower Blue, Peppermint Green, Paris Pink, Burnt Orange and Argyle Green. Andy's taste tended towards off-whites, pale yellows, beiges and browns and unobtrusive grey-greens, and to good old Dulux paint.

It led to a few arguments, but a compromise was reached eventually: Andy was to decorate the little sitting room, the hall by their front door, their bedroom and the en-suite to his taste and Valerie's without interference, and the rest of the house was up to Susie and Ollie and Camilla. Even then, the two of them still had a bit of an argy-bargy as to what colour carpets they should choose; for the sitting room Andy wanted a sort of mushroom colour which Valerie deemed dull and boring, and favoured a sort of greeny-grey for the bedroom, for which Valerie fancied a nice off-white. She won. The greeny-grey carpet was to go into the sitting room where it would go very nicely with the rose-coloured curtains. For the bedroom and the en-suite walls she chose a soft, pretty shade of primrose yellow, and when she had hung the pretty muslin curtains sprigged with tiny white flowers, and the blinds in a darker shade of primrose yellow that she'd found on Special Offer in Homebase, she felt satisfied that it was all going to look very nice.

It wasn't long after Andy had started on the decorating of the en-suite that Camilla sent peremptory instruction via Susie that Andy and Valerie should arrange for their furniture to be moved and stored whilst they vacated for three days the following week so that the new carpets could be laid.

"Oh, and by the way," Susie added as an afterthought, "the armchairs and the sofas we've bought and had recovered for the snug and the dining room are going to be arriving on Thursday – can you make sure somebody's in, please?"

Valerie knew her breathing was getting jagged. "One minute you're telling us to put our things in storage, then you're telling us more stuff is arriving! Where on earth are we supposed to put those?"

Andy asked the same question. "Where are we supposed to put those?"

Valerie shrugged. "In storage with ours, I suppose."

"They can't come and lay carpets yet, can they?" Andy snarled. "There's a hell of a lot still to do; the dining room floor's not done, the windows aren't all in and hardly any of the decorating's been done. They'll bloody well have to wait."

Valerie steeled herself to confront Camilla. "Why can't the carpet fitters move the furniture?"

Camilla rolled her eyes. "Oh, for goodness' sake..."

"It's ridiculous! It'll cost a fortune, getting them in to take all the furniture out and then in again to put it all back. When I got the ones from Prestige Carpets on the High Street back home, they moved everything for us on the day, even the big heavy dresser and sideboard and the television. What about the decorating? How do they do the skirting boards? Going to get paint all over everything."

Camilla fluttered a disinterested hand. "Oh, goodness, it won't be a pwoblem. The decowating won't take any time at all."

Valerie puffed out her cheeks. "Don't tell Andy that. The decorating means a lot to him. He's got his standards. Why on earth can't they hang on to the carpets till we're ready?"

Camilla sighed. "They don't expect to hang on to them once they're weady. They need the space."

"In our experience they do. They hang on to them in the warehouse."

Camilla rolled her eyes again. "This is a *specialist* firm. The carpets were specially woven. They don't have the huge trade warehouses full of all that fwightful mass pwoduced stuff."

Valerie was very unhappy.

To cheer her up, Andy agreed that they would indeed take themselves for a bit of R&R and be blowed to Camilla and to the carpets – and to her 'window tweetments' as she called the curtains, which made them giggle, and which she had announced further would shortly be coming in. They'd even take a look across the Channel, since they weren't far away, he added grandly, if Valerie cared for the idea? "I'm not driving, mind. I don't much fancy driving on the other side of the road."

It was very exciting. "Couldn't have done that the same from North Wales, could we? Take a good bit longer from up there!"

"Cherbourg, then, or Caen, or St Malo?" Valerie offered, having made the necessary enquiries. "St Malo sounds ever so nice. It's a walled city. There's a ferry goes from Portsmouth or from Weymouth. Which would you prefer?"

St Malo, it was. Valerie was very excited. Andy's new friend Nick, across the road, told them of a farm not far away which had storage facilities and offered to come in with some of the lads from the Cricket Club and shift everything and then bring it back after; if Andy would like to hire a couple of U-Drive vans, it would save them quite a bit of money.

Going over on the ferry was a doddle, with the parking very easy, to Andy's great relief. Valerie would have preferred it if they'd not been on the high-speed one. She had been looking forward very much to standing up on deck, but when she ventured out cradling a plastic beaker full of coffee, she was glued to the spot by the wind and the coffee blew right out of her cup and landed all over her face and her front. She put her raincoat on after that, even though she stayed inside. Embarrassing, otherwise, with all those coffee stains.

They really liked St Malo. Their hotel had seen better days, but was quite acceptable. Andy didn't mind the continental breakfast, because he was a bit under the weather all the time, which was rather a shame. Valerie did worry a bit about him. The rhinitis and the shortness of breath triggered by the dust in the house seemed to have left him a little lacking in energy.

Even so, after a peaceful couple of days exploring and eating *galettes* and things, they returned relatively revived, promising each other that they would do it again sometime. It was amazing, really, knowing that they could actually be on the Continent while still being so close to home.

The carpets did look smashing. Nick and the boys brought back the furniture next day and the gathering afterwards at the pub and later in the shed behind his house was memorable.

The Open Gardens Day was supposed to have been in June but was delayed until the last week of July because some people couldn't make their minds up whether they wanted to take part or not, which was just as well because it was the end of June before the new back door and final window frames were in place and the decorating finished, and mid-July before George had finished the soakaway and other bits and pieces. But then Sebastian, George, their men and – heaven be praised – Camilla, all moved on and it was just the bills that kept on coming.

When Valerie and Andy totalled up what they'd spent on their little holiday and Christmas and everything else on the house, they had spent over forty-four thousand pounds.

"That leaves seventy-six thousand four hundred and fifty," Valerie said, staring anxiously at her little account book. "It isn't half going down fast!"

Obviously worried, Andy was heavy-browed and silent for the rest of the day, and Valerie tiptoed round him, eyeing him warily. He perked up again though, to her relief, when his old friend Leon from Glynogol telephoned early that evening. Reaching for the wine bottle standing by the bread bin, he sank into a chair at the table with a delighted grin, gesturing widely for Valerie to pass him a wine glass and then the bottle opener. "How are you doing, my son?"

When she came back in from the garden a while later, he was still on the phone and there was an almost empty bottle at his elbow. "Oh, she's here, hang on, I'll ask her now. Val! Val, no reason, is there, that Leon and Norma can't come down the first week in August?"

She was delighted. "No, that'll be lovely."

He returned to the phone, his face beaming. "No, that's fine, Leon! Look forward to it, be great to see you both." He listened, grinning, then threw back his head with a guffaw. "That's a good one, my son, a good one! I'll have to try to remember that!"

Once the receiver was down he took out another bottle, still beaming. She watched him open it resignedly. He rubbed his hands gleefully. "Good idea, eh, anyway? Be nice to see them, show them round!" He sniffed appreciatively at the casserole she was heaving out of the oven. "Smells good. What are you going to give them when they come down?"

She clicked her tongue. "For goodness' sake, it's ages yet, I've no idea!"

He was so excited, bless him. The four of them had been very good friends and always supportive of each other in times of trouble, ever since they had first got together when the kiddies were still at Junior school, but they were none of them saints; they did like to have a bit of a show-off from time to time. It was accepted with tolerance and amusement; it was understood. He'd take Leon for a pint or two of the local beer, no doubt, show him how well he'd settled in. She could hear the lads at the bar now, Nick and the others, when he and Leon walked in. "Andy! What are you having, mate? Your usual? No, no, this is on me!" He'd be ever so proud.

For her, apart from showing off with garden and all the mod cons and gadgets, the high spot was going to be the swimming pool. She couldn't wait to say, 'Whew, it's hot! Do you fancy a little swim, Norma? So refreshing. The water is lovely and cool."

It had blooming well better not rain!

As she'd feared, after the chicken casserole and the bread-and-butter pudding that she'd made him for after, came a whisky, and after that, he thought he might wander down to the pub. "Just a couple of pints. I won't be long. You don't mind, do you?"

She clicked her tongue. "Oh, Andy, you don't need beer as well."

He was already changing his slippers for his shoes. "Then I'll stick to whisky."

"Oh, for goodness' sake!"

"You don't really mind, do you?"

She sighed again. "No, I suppose I don't mind."

She wished she had said she minded next morning, when she found him curled up in agony on the landing, his face contorted, and with one hand clutching his chest. "Val..." he muttered feebly. "I think you'd better ring the doctor. I've got this terrible pain..."

For a few moments she thought he was joking, and then she saw the fear and real pain in his pillow-creased and unshaven face. "What is it, love?"

"Chest. Terrible pain in my chest."

"Oh, oh, pet!" She could feel a little pulse beating at the base of her throat and her head felt strangely swimmy. Should she ring for an ambulance? She decided to ring the surgery first.

The voice at the other end of the telephone was calm. "Where is he?"

Her hands were trembling a bit as she clutched the telephone. "Well, he's sort of curled up on the floor on the landing. He's just got out of bed."

"Is he talking to you? Is he able to speak?"

"Tell them I feel like a tube of toothpaste," Andy mumbled.

She glanced at him, bewildered. "Pardon?"

He gestured ineffectually. "It's tight round here, round my chest, and it's sort of squeezing."

"Is it?" She relayed the information anxiously, trying not to squeak. The receptionist put her through to a doctor straight away.

"How old is he?" the disembodied voice asked briskly.

"Um, he's seventy."

Andy groaned, his face contorted with pain.

"Any history of heart trouble?"

She bit her lip. "Well, yes, he did have a heart attack – a mild one, mind, but that was, oh, over twenty-five years ago, and he's been as right as rain ever since. Should I ring for an ambulance, do you think?" she asked, trying to keep her voice from quivering.

"Don't want to take any risks in that case. I'll see to it. They shouldn't be very long."

Having checked his vital signs, the paramedics seemed relatively unworried. "Did you have very much to drink last night, sir?"

Valerie sniffed. The air on the landing around him did smell very strongly of stale alcohol.

He groaned, looking rather sheepish. "I did have a bit, just a bit...."

The paramedic chewed his bottom lip reflectively. "Mm. Right. Well, we'll take you along, sir, let them have a good look at you."

Valerie stood back as they wrapped him up tightly in a warm green blanket and carried him carefully downstairs. She felt reassured by their lack of panic. Andy couldn't be having a heart attack; it wasn't possible, the silly boy.

He peered up at her over the edge of the blanket as they manoeuvred the stretcher through the door, with big, sad eyes like a puppy, and murmured feebly, "Don't worry, love..."

The paramedic winked at her. "I shouldn't think she is, sir. Don't *you* worry."

Andy looked crestfallen. "Oh."

She grasped the paramedic's sleeve. "It's all right if I come?"

He grinned. "You might want to get a coat or something, love?"

She was still wearing only her pink cotton nightie, she realised with horror. Mortified, she reached for the nearest thing to hand, Andy's beige raincoat, which was hanging on a peg by the door. She buttoned it right up to the neck with fingers that seemed remarkably stiff, and stumbled a bit as she clambered into the ambulance.

The air inside the A&E Department smelled of antiseptic and something not very nice. She tried to stay calm and breathe deeply, but it wasn't easy. There was a lot of noise and clattering. People kept hurrying past her, and bells and bleepers seemed to be ringing constantly. A little nurse with tired eyes bustled out of the cubicle and wanted to take down a few details.

Valerie's mind was a blank. "His birthday – yes, his birthday, it's the 8th of March – no, or is it February?" Perspiration started breaking out on her forehead. She stared at her feet, trying to concentrate. They were still clad in her fluffy pink bedroom slippers, she noticed with embarrassment. "This is so silly, I know perfectly well. I ought to! Hang on now, let me have a think..."

The nurse frowned. "Are you all right, dear?"

Valerie nodded. "Oh, yes, I'm fine, thank you! I'm fine."

The nurse studied her face intently. "No, you're not, look at you – you're shaking."

Valerie looked at her hands. The nurse was right, they were shaking; in fact, now her attention had been drawn to it, she could feel that her whole body was locked into a kind of rigid St Vitus's dance.

The nurse tucked her clipboard under one arm and put the other about her. "Come on, I'll get you a chair somewhere and you can sit down and have a nice cup of tea."

Valerie dug in her heels. "No, no, thank you; I had a cup before I left." She bit her tongue. That sounded silly, as if she and the ambulance man had settled down over the pot for a leisurely chinwag before setting off.

A white-coated man trotted up the corridor pushing some sort of small trolley and slipped into the cubicle too. With a call over her shoulder of "Be back in a minute," the nurse darted after him, pulling the curtain closed again. Feeling panic rising, Valerie waited. As the nurse re-emerged after a moment, she tried to peep inside.

"Was that a doctor? Is that another doctor? Why does Andy need two doctors? He is going to be all right?"

He was. The hospital wanted to keep him in for twenty-four hours, though, and she had to make her way back home on the bus wearing Andy's raincoat and her slippers and using the three pounds in loose change she'd found in his pocket, but the relief to Valerie was enormous. Of course, she had forgotten her key, but fortunately she had forgotten to lock the door too, so that was all right.

It was a strange and difficult day, and unsettling trying to sleep that night without Andy beside her. It was a quite different feeling from the kind she had when she knew he would be back at some point. She felt empty and lonely, and she didn't really drop off properly till almost half past three.

He was home again by twelve o'clock the next morning, though, baggy-eyed and sheepish. "Yes, okay, I had too much to drink. I know I did. Bloody chest still hurts, though. Not sure how I did it, but they said it's only muscular."

Her tongue was sharpened by relief. "Really, Andy, you ought to have more sense! You can't do it any more; it's very bad for you. It's got to stop. What have they said, anyway?"

"Oh, you know the form; they're all preaching it these days, just want you to be miserable: lose a bit of weight, cut down on salt, red meat, dairy products... Take plenty of exercise, avoid stress."

"And booze?"

He frowned. "Hm. Maybe. "He looked round the kitchen hungrily. "They only gave me a drop of cereal and a cold piece of toast for breakfast at the crack of dawn. I'm bloody hungry. What can I have now?"

She put her hands on her hips. "Well, not bacon and sausage and fried bread, I can tell you! You scared me, you know, Andy. You can have some shredded wheat and grapefruit, or a poached egg. I haven't got any muesli."

He grimaced. "Well, don't get any. I'm not going to eat muesli – horrible stuff. It gets right under my denture plate."

He settled, wincing, onto one of the new cane chairs in the conservatory with a thick cushion behind him as she bustled about boiling up a small saucepan of water and making some toast. "What was all that about feeling like a tube of toothpaste?" she called.

He looked blank for a moment. "Toothpaste? Oh, oh, yes – I read that somewhere. Apparently it's one of the signs."

"Of a heart attack?"

"Mm."

She made a mental note. "And it felt like that, did it, as if it was squeezing? That's what you said."

"Well..." He was looking sheepish again. "Well, I suppose I was exaggerating a bit. Just tight and very painful." He winced again. "Got a nasty great bruise and a cut on my shin, too. Lord knows what the hell I did."

Breaking an egg into a saucer, she slipped it carefully into the pan of simmering water, carefully omitting any salt. The white drifted off into long strands. She contained it as best as possible with her spoon. "So what were you up to that evening, anyway? I saw Nick getting out of his car last evening and he had a big raw graze all down the side of his face."

He perked up a bit at the news. "Did he?"

"Whatever were you up to, the pair of you?

"It beats me."

"Were you at his house? Did you go back to his shed?"

He wrinkled his brow. "No, I don't think so." His expression cleared. "No, no, that's right, I remember: Pete Parkinson asked us back to his place for a nightcap. Great place he's got, Val, used to be the old vicarage. You'd like it, love. He's got a Snooker room."

She rolled her eyes sardonically. "Oh, I would like it then. Oh, yes, I'd be bound to like it immensely."

He chuckled, then winced and clutched his chest. "Oh, come on, don't make me laugh. You know what I mean."

The reason for his painful muscles and the cut and bruise became apparent later that day when Nick called while they were having their tea. Faced with a salmon salad and with the thought of no cake for after, Andy was being decidedly grumpy and they both welcomed the interruption. Andy pushed his plate aside eagerly. "Come in, Nick! Fancy a glass of wine?"

Valerie smiled weakly at Nick, hoping he wasn't going to say 'yes'. She had set out a jug of plain water on the table, and so far not of drop of anything else had crossed Andy's lips. He shook his head, though, reluctantly. "No, thanks." His usually bright-skinned round face face looked somewhat grey and drawn and he had a sticking plaster on his balding crown.

Andy looked at him, surprised. "You on the wagon too?"

"Bit fragile still, me old mate."

"You and me both." Andy nodded at the graze on Nick's cheek, which looked very sore and painful. "How the hell did you do that?"

"Don't you remember?"

"I don't remember a bloody thing, other than the fact that we went back to Parky's."

Valerie shook her head. "You must both have been in a terrible state. Andy ended up in hospital."

Nick was astounded. "He didn't!"

Andy rolled his eyes. "I bloody well did! What the hell were we doing?"

Nick frowned. "We fell down."

"We didn't!"

"We did. Don't you remember?"

Andy shook his head. "Told you, I remember going back to Parky's, I think we played a bit of snooker, that's about it. What time did we leave?"

Nick shrugged. "Lord knows. I know I was in the doghouse. Anyway, we thought we'd take a shortcut home across the churchyard." He paused. "You don't remember at all? You don't remember Bob Thom and Little Stevie?"

"Were they with us?"

"With us at Parky's, yes. They'd left before us, though, and had cut into the churchyard ahead of us, apparently, because they wanted to have a pee – and it was bloody pitch dark, wasn't it, and when they came out in front of us from behind that big angel monument thing in the middle, it knocked us for bloody six. You yelled, we turned to run like hell, crashed into each other and tripped over one of those old headstones. And you don't remember that?" He fingered his cheek ruefully. "I had a big interview yesterday, too. Looking forward to getting out of bananas. Shouldn't think I got the job."

Valerie was torn between amusement, delight that Andy had settled in so nicely, and exasperation. "Oh, Andy, really! Really, the pair of you! You're just like little boys!"

Chapter 7

U p early because of excitement and nervousness on the Open Gardens Day, she took her morning mug of tea on an early walk through the garden and the paddocks and it all looked beautiful. The sunshine spilling over her face and body was already faintly and deliciously warm. The birdsong, though not as symphonic as it had been in the early spring was still magical. Bees were already buzzing lazily amongst the roses and lavenders in the long border and the honeysuckle twined about the swimming pool gate and the scent, mingled with the sweet smell of the dew-drenched grass and the incense-like scent of a balsamic poplar or something in the Blackwells' garden, almost made her weep with pleasure.

The increasingly golden and silver and beige fields lying quiet beneath a clear blue sky tempted her down through the paddocks. Like the Blackwells, Andy had carefully cut pathways with the motor mower through the long grass leading down to the bottom, and oxeye daisies, cornflowers, field scabious and meadow buttercup, ragged robin and musk mallow and many others that she hadn't yet identified were flowering in the remaining stands of pale, silvery, whispery grass. At the space in the bottom hedge where you could really see the view, he had made a seat out of a fallen trunk and she sat on it, quietly sipping her tea. From here, she couldn't hear the road. She was aware of the drone of a distant tractor, but no other sounds of habitation. So peaceful here, it was. So beautiful.

Andy's voice shattered her reverie. "I hope nobody's

going to fall into that swimming pool. Should I tie up the gates, d'you think?"

Startled, she glanced round and then moved along the fallen log a little, making room for him to sit. "Didn't expect you to be up yet."

He sat heavily beside her and stretched out his legs, sighing luxuriously. He hadn't shaved yet, she noticed. Still, it was early for him. "No, well... It's a beautiful day for you."

"Yep. Have you had a cup of tea?"

"Yep."

They sat silently for a while, then Andy stirred. "D'you know what?"

"Hm?"

"I don't ever want to leave this place."

A sunburst of relief and happiness broke inside her chest. "You don't?"

"Nope."

"Hm." She inched closer, slipping her hand into his and nodding. "Hm. That's good."

"No. Don't want to leave here till they carry me out in my coffin."

"Don't."

"Sorry."

Hands comfortingly entwined, they sat staring out at the view until Andy stirred again and straightened suddenly, squeezing her fingers abruptly. "Now, then, what about this swimming pool? Should I put up a danger sign?"

A surprising number of people came to wander. The space outside the village hall had been designated as the official car park, but even so, several people left their vehicles at the sides of the narrow road, causing a number of hold-ups and one very nasty altercation with an irate tractor driver, so Andy nominated himself as parking warden, and stood in the road shepherding them to the correct place. It meant that he had to remove himself from swimming pool duty, leaving the gate unguarded. To be on the safe side, in case people missed the sign printed in large letters saying 'NO ENTRY', he tied the gates together with a length of cable. "That should do it."

Valerie hadn't anticipated a visitation from the family, but finding the effort of taking tickets at the entrance to the driveway, selling them to those who hadn't already bought them, accompanying where necessary and trying to answer questions very tiring, and heavy-going on her poor feet, she was relieved at first to see the Discovery pulling up the drive. Reinforcements! Poppy was leaning out of the window, looking very excited. "Hello, Nana! Come and see what we've got!"

She made her way, beaming, across the lawn. " Hello, sweetheart! This is a nice surprise!"

"Look, look, Nana!" Poppy opened the passenger door and then disappeared with a cry of mingled hysteria and rage. "Henry!" Valerie took a step backwards in shock as a very large furry animal clambered over Poppy and leapt from the Discovery like a great black and caramel woolly bear emerging from its den, launching himself upon her, panting like a steam engine and grinning happily.

"Oh, my goodness!" She struggled to hold him at bay and to stay upright. "Oh, my goodness! Where have you come from, eh?"

Poppy jumped out after him. "He's a Bernese Mountain dog. His name is Henry. Henry! Henry, get down!" She dragged ineffectually at his tail.

Ollie leant over from the driving seat, grinning. 'Hello, Nana! Thought I'd bring the latest member of the family to meet you!"

Valerie tried to keep her face away from the huge animal's lolling tongue whilst simultaneously struggling to hold his heavy, furry bulk still enough to allow her to grasp his collar. His enormous head twisted, nudging brutally into her stomach. "Oof!"

"Henry! Sit down!" Ollie shouted sternly, climbing out of the driving seat and slamming the door. "Henry!" To Val's relief, the dog turned and galloped back eagerly to Ollie, clambering over him with his paws on his shoulders and licking at his ears. He glanced smugly at Valerie. "His Master's Voice, eh? Ha ha..."

Valerie closed her eyes. Her poor garden!

"Lovely, isn't he?" Ollie ruffled Henry's fur. "Yes, who's a good dog, eh? A colleague of mine from work, transferring to the New York office: I said we'd take him. Plenty of room for him here."

Rising to his feet, he reached into the Discovery and pulled out a red rubber ring, hurling it over the yew hedge onto the lawn, and slapping the animal on the rump. "Go on, then. Go and have a nice run!" With a bark as deep as a roar, Henry charged excitedly after it.

She heard a shriek from the lawn and remembered. "Oh, wait, Ollie, wait – there are people!" Ignoring decorum and her weary legs, she hobbled after the creature. Suppose someone was afraid of dogs? Suppose he knocked somebody over? "Here! Here!" What was it his name was? "Here! Dog! Dog!"

The damage wasn't too bad. One child flattened, a lady with torn tights and an old gentleman with palpitations, and several copious quantities of wee spilled out over the carefully renovated lawn, but it could have been worse. Indeed, the most severe damage was done to her precious borders once Henry had got bored with charging around like a steam train and knocking people for six, and had turned his attention to exploring and hole-digging. Tulip bulbs and irises flying, salvias and peonies trampled. Ollie and Poppy thought it very amusing.

To make things worse, Ollie decided to untie Andy's cable and invited people in to look at the swimming pool, at which Valerie's blood pressure rose still higher. Henry, of course, plunged in immediately.

Ollie roared with laughter. Everyone else scattered, squealing, as Henry heaved himself out of the pool and galloped round and round the pool shaking off his wet fur vigorously before leaping back onto the lawn.

Then, to Valerie's equal distress – having had to concentrate on the garden she had had no time to do a proper clean-up inside – Ollie, determined to play the munificent host, unloaded a crate of champagne from the back of the Discovery and ransacked the cupboards for all Valerie's wine glasses, including the ones that had been cracked in the removal and which she had boxed ready to discard at the tip. Andy, scenting a party, relinquished his traffic duty and, having greeted Ollie and Poppy and blanched at the sight of Henry, settled down happily to shepherding people into the conservatory. Once they had each been given suitable refreshment Ollie, patently very proud of his expensively extended and renovated new house and accompanied by a dripping wet Henry, eagerly conducted guided tours.

Valerie, watching the visitors troop in, was mortified. She couldn't remember if she had even made the bed.

D espite all this, she had to account the day a success rather than a failure when she took stock of it that night. Quite apart from having raised a fair bit of money for the village hall, which was very nice and a small contribution from the two of them to village life, it looked as if the event might have brought both her and Andy new acquaintances and lots of new things to do. Everyone had been very complementary about the garden.

She'd plucked up the courage to invite the Blackwells in at last for an evening meal. She had been invited to join the Horticultural society. She'd met a very nice woman called Martha who lived on the little estate and who came from Lancashire and knew North Wales very well, having spent a lot of holidays there in her childhood. Though quite a bit younger than Valerie – she had two sons still more-or-less based at home – she even vaguely remembered the trams and the Tinkerbell Railway at the funfair in Colwyn Bay, and the boat trips to Liverpool and the Isle of Man, all memories of the past that Valerie treasured. In the convivial glow of joint recollection, Valerie even found herself telling her all about Susie and Ollie being the owners of the house and about how she and Andy were just pensioners who didn't have any extra income except a little bit every month from a dwindling investment, and how they were just crossing their fingers that it was going to last them both out. She wished she hadn't as soon as she'd said it, but "Thank God not everybody in this village except me is bloody rich," was all that Martha had to say.

Andy got himself roped into Bell Ringing for the Church and Petanque at the Black Horse. Valerie had no idea what that was and didn't think Andy had either; as far as she could make out both activities were designed basically to provide an excuse for a night out in the pub, but there!

He had chatted cricket for ages with Nick and with Jim Haughton, the Captain of the village team, and his tongue had been sufficiently loosened by the flowing champagne provided by Ollie for him to let drop enough clues as to his impressive past form to feel that an offer to umpire would be appreciated. Nick and his mates had arranged to take him fishing at last. Martha and she were going to have a get-together the next evening to reminisce more and chat. She had been quite exhausted by it, of course, but was also very happy. It was a lovely life.

Her elation didn't last long once she had found Susie in the kitchen. Susie had been in a tight-lipped mood all day; she had been snappy with Poppy and hadn't seemed to be talking to Ollie at all. She was slumped on one of the kitchen stools now at the island unit, studying Andy's newspaper and looking tired and strained.

"Dad's still drinking a lot, I see," she murmured as Valerie walked in. Her tone was flat and dull.

"Oh, he has been trying, but you know what he's like, he doesn't take much encouragement. Anyway, he's fine. D'you want a piece of flapjack?" she added, reaching for the cake tin.

"No thanks."

"Different recipe this time." She helped herself, feeling a bit guilty. She hadn't told Andy that she had made any; he'd had some sliced peaches and plain yoghurt for desert. "Must say, it's very nice. Nice and chewy." Susie smiled briefly without looking up and turned over the page. "The Aga cooks things like this very well. I do love having an Aga."

Silence. She helped herself to another piece of flapjack. "I think that all went very well, don't you?" Silence. "The garden looked nice." She could hear the clock on the wall ticking. "It's really nice that they do things like this down here, brings the village together. I was saying to Martha today – I met this woman called Martha and she seemed ever so nice – I was saying to Martha it's so nice too, being in a place where they don't have rubbish at the sides of the roads and old supermarket trolleys in the stream and horrible language in the streets, and where practically everybody you meet seems very happy."

She was beginning to feel a bit fraught. "It's money, I suppose. They're much more affluent; well, most of them, not all. The charity shops down here, have you seen them? Everything neatly pressed, no smell of perspiration and old clothes, just nice floral air spray and a touch of dry-cleaning fluid – and people down here throw out such wonderful stuff. Designer labels! You can get real bargains. I saw a beautiful coat from – from whatsit, MaxMara, the other day, only it was too small, and they had a lovely blouse from that place you like – Whistles? D'you want me to get it for you? A lovely blouse, it was, your size, sort of pale silvery blue, you'd pay a fortune for it in London."

Merely a mute shrug. Reopening the tin, Valerie took out a third piece of flapjack in desperation. "Oh, and the stars at night!" she mumbled enthusiastically through a mouthful. "I'm going to get Dad a book, or some kind of a map, you know, *The Stars At Night* or something, so he can work out what's what. He's always been interested in stars." She shook her head with a contented sigh. "Oh, yes, we're ever so happy here. Oh, yes."

"I'm thinking of taking a lover."

Panic-stricken, Valerie dropped the remnants of her flapjack "Oh, lovey! Why? Whatever do you mean?"

There was a long silence and then Susie shrugged, crumpled up the paper and pushed it away abruptly. "Oh, it's all right, don't worry, I'm only joking. I'm just fed up with bloody Ollie, that's all."

Andy'd be looking for that, he did enjoy his paper and he'd not had time to read it properly today. Reaching for the newspaper pages, Valerie straightened them up and folded them as best she could. "What's that matter, then, pet?"

Susie shrugged. "Oh, you know. Just the usual." Glancing at her watch with a heavy frown, she slipped off the stool. "I can't believe how late it is! We've got to go. Where's Oliver? She hurried onto the patio, raising her voice stridently. "Ollie! *Ollie!* What time did you say they were coming?"

Valerie followed her. "Why are you in such a rush?"

"Oh, he's invited somebody from work and his girlfriend for supper. I told him we were coming down here, but of course he didn't listen." Susie clambered up the steps onto the lawn, shading her eyes from the golden glare of the setting sun, then pattered back down onto the patio, looking furious. "He's not gone off running again, has he? I've no idea what we're going to give them to eat. We'll have to stop and get something on the way back." She disappeared inside again, raising her voice angrily. "Ollie! *Ollie*, where are you, come on, it's half past eight, we've got to go shopping, it's over an hour to London and you invited Piers and Pauline for nine. You'd better get on the phone and tell them we'll be late. Come *on!*"

Stretched out in the late afternoon sunshine on the spare sun bed with his glass in his hand, Andy gazed out contentedly over the distant hills and heaved a long sigh of satisfaction. "Ah, yes, yes, yes, yes, yes..." Valerie studied him with amused affection. He'd been strutting like a peacock all day.

"Mm?"

"This is the life, eh, Leon? This is the life, isn't it, old son?"

Leon stirred lazily in the wicker bath chair. "It is, it is. I'm very envious."

"Have you got a drink?"

"I have, mate, thanks."

"What about you, Norma?"

"I have, too, thank you, darling." Norma raised a glass from where she was lying, plumply overflowing in a tight and brightly flowered bathing costume on the steamer chair, now fully furnished with a comfy green cushion from B&Q. "This is delicious."

Worse than I am. She really has put on just a little bit more weight.

Andy quaffed the remains of his chilled Chablis with gusto. "Mm, not bad, is it? Waitrose, special offer. You don't have Waitrose up there, do you? Worth popping in, maybe, see if they've still got the offer running before you go back." He beamed smugly at Valerie. "What about you, Val? Want another drop of wine?"

"I'm all right at the moment, pet."

"Go on, have another glass of wine." He half rose eagerly.

"I'll get you another glass of wine."

"No, Andy, I'm all right," she told him firmly, pushing herself out of her deckchair. "I think I'd better go back and start getting on with the dinner. I'll set the table in the conservatory. It'll be lovely in there with the doors open."

"That sounds very nice." Norma raised her head again. "Can I give you a hand, Val?"

Valerie waved a hand. "No, no need – you stay there. I can manage."

She checked everything carefully before calling them. Norma was rather a whiz at cooking; everything needed to be right up to scratch: a delicious-smelling leg of lamb from the Farmers' Market resting nicely, mint and redcurrant gravy ready, roast potatoes crisped up very well, new potatoes dancing in their pan on the oven top, asparagus and the peas and baby carrots from the garden ready to simmer gently in their pans. There was a Gooseberry Fool and a Chocolate Raspberry Pavlova in the fridge ready for after, the double cream to accompany them already beaten and waiting in a cut glass jug. Too rich for Andy now, really, but it was a special treat. Cheese, butter and biscuits ready, freshly ground coffee beans waiting in the cafetiere. Pudding bowls and coffee cups ready. Milk and cream jugs. Brown sugar lumps in the bowl. Yes, everything ready. Everything looking fine.

Andy was still glowing as he led Leon proudly into the conservatory. "Anywhere? Anywhere, is it?" He rubbed his hands. "My goodness, that looks good!"

"Yes, do sit anywhere." Valerie was so pleased to see him so happy. Do him good to show off a little bit. Why not! She was, too. Who would have thought that one day they'd be living the high life in a beautiful house such as this?

And it was lovely to see Leon and Norma too. Funny, after only, what, fifteen months, she'd almost forgotten that any other kind of life existed. They might have been merely figments of her imagination, people she had only read about. It had been quite a jolt, seeing them clamber out of their car: quite a surprise to find she hadn't sort of, well, made them up in a way. But there they'd been, large as life and looking just the same: Leon with his soft, collar-length white hair, short and dapper and elegant as always otherwise in dark blue blazer and sharply-creased grey flannels, and Norma, comfy and messy in contrast in her old pale blue track suit – handy for travelling, had it for years – chubby and smiling and so familiar with her smudgy pink lipstick and untidy fly-away greying hair .

She dished up the asparagus carefully, then, smiling, ran her eye over the table once again as she set down the plates. It did look nice, like something from *Homes & Gardens* with its vase of white roses and its pale green linen tablecloth, and Granny's silver cutlery and cruet, and the best glasses and the new Lilies placemats she'd bought from the china shop in town. Scented candles, too.

"Light the candles, Andy, will you, pet?"

She sniffed, testing the air, when he had done so, but the scent of the roses on the table and of the jasmine wafting in from the open doors overwhelmed the candles rather. They were supposed to smell of Gardenia. She'd tried to get Lily but they hadn't got any. Still, the Gardenia were very nice.

Leon took a seat at the table. "You've amazed me, you know, Andy."

Andy looked puzzled. "Have I?"

"I was really worried about you. I really didn't think you'd ever leave."

Norma shook her head. "He didn't, did you, Leon? You kept saying, didn't you, 'Brycey'll never move'?"

"'He won't leave Glynogol; he won't leave that house of his,' I said. 'Not in a million years'." Leon chuckled. "And here you are. Amazing. And this house is fantastic."

Andy nodded, frowning. "It's funny, you know, if you'd asked me a few years ago if I'd ever move I'd have said, 'No, never.' Now, though, I wish we'd done it years ago."

"Do you really!"

Valerie glowed and Andy preened, his face shining. "And wait till you see my pub!"

I t was only a short visit, but after they had gone both Andy and Valerie went around for days with quiet, complacent smiles of pride and satisfaction. No doubt they'd be telling everybody up in the Glyn how nicely they were doing. "Oh, yes, he's got it made down there!" Andy could just hear

Leon say. Norma would be nodding, red curls bobbing. "Oh, and you should see Valerie's new kitchen – and the swimming pool!"

Their self-indulgent enjoyment of luxurious tranquillity lasted too short a time, though. Having the family moving in proved a bit traumatic.

They brought far too much furniture, and most of it was really much too big for a house with low beams. The huge bed wouldn't go up the attic stairs. Even when it was taken all apart and Camilla had summoned Sebastian to come round with one of his men and, grumbling heartily, dismantle his banisters once again, it still wouldn't go up. Valerie and Susie had to offer to swap beds, which didn't please either Ollie or Andy, both of whom went off in a sulk.

The removal firm turned out to be a very posh one; they all wore dark green overalls and white cotton gloves. To Valerie's dismay, because it would have been so much easier to sort things out later on their own, the men insisted on unpacking all the glassware and china and spreading it out on all available surfaces, even cracked pieces – of which there were, embarrassingly, quite a few. Thomas broke onto hard tiles of the kitchen floor every one of a couple of dozen fresh farm eggs that Valerie had just bought from the farm shop and had moved temporarily onto a conservatory chair.

The children were over-excited and the dog, equally affected, drove everybody mad. Charging about, he managed to brush all Susie and Ollie's best wine glasses off a coffee table with his enormous tail, knocked Thomas over several times and set him howling, discovered and gulped down the packets of digestive and bourbon biscuits that Valerie had bought for the removal men, smashed a huge vase, wee'd on a big, brightly coloured Cath Kidson rug intended for the family room, chewed up one of a pair of hand-embroidered fringed cushions, tore Poppy's skirt and, when thrown out into the garden, ended up burying Andy's best slippers in the middle of Valerie's dahlias and making an enormous great crater in the lawn. He then took off excitedly, disappearing down the road.

Ollie seized on the opportunity, changed eagerly into

his running gear and set off after him. "Bastard," Susie snarled. "That's the last we'll see of him, then, for the rest of the day."

Her mood didn't improve when Ollie accounted himself very tired and in need of a long hot soak in the bath when he eventually got back two hours later with a wet and muddy Henry, panting and straining, attached to his lead. "Only seven miles. Not up to my standard, but not bad considering I had to look for the dog."

Valerie stared in horror at the muddy creature. *What about the new carpets?* "Wherever has he been, Ollie?"

He shrugged. "In the village duck pond, I think, ha ha! God knows, Nana. I came round a corner on my way back and found him lying plonk in the middle of the lane, just up by the church, enjoying the shade of the yew tree; wasn't there before. There was an irate chap in a 4x4 there, trying to get him to shift, but he wasn't interested, obstinate brute!"

Swelling a little with pride, he ran his fingers casually through fair hair made lank by perspiration. "No problem, though. His Master's Voice, hah-hah! I managed to heave him out of the way and get his lead on." Snapping his fingers with authority, he energetically led Henry towards the kitchen. "Come on Henry, let's get you some water. You'll have to make sure he has plenty of water, Nana; he dehydrates very easily."

She trailed after him, feeling a bit rattled. *I'll have to, will I? I'll have to?* "Right-ho. Yes. I see."

Chapter 8

Next morning very early she heard Ollie's alarm clock ring, and the water running and the tank overhead refilling noisily as he took a power shower. One thing they hadn't reckoned with was the fact that the cistern and the main water pipes seemed to be running directly overhead and, of course, being so old, the floors and walls were very thin. Susie was up, too; she could hear her clattering downstairs in the kitchen. She seemed to have high heels on. After a few minutes, her voice rose in a shrill stage whisper from the hall. "Ollie? You're going to be late. You're going to miss the train."

Valerie heard him call back something, but couldn't make out his words and neither, it seemed, could Susie. Her whisper was even more penetrating this time. "What? What did you say?" Mumbling, Andy turned over heavily and pulled the duvet up over his ears.

Ollie's roar this time was panicky and full-throated. "I said I can't find my wallet! Where are my clean socks? And where is my other black shoe?" From his small bedroom next to Valerie and Andy, Thomas started to wail.

Susie's footsteps clattered angrily up the stairs. "Now look, you've woken Thomas up!" There was a knock on the bedroom door, and she entered, tiptoeing unnecessarily across to the bedside. "Mum?" she whispered. "Mum, I've brought you some tea."

"Oh!" Valerie struggled sleepily up on one her elbow. "Oh, that's very kind, dear, thank you."

Susie set the mug beside her. "I'll put it down here.

Have to go, we're late. I'll take Thomas, he's yelling his head off."

Valerie glanced at the thin wall between the two bedrooms. "I know he is, dear."

The bedroom door slammed behind Susie. "Ollie? Ollie, come on, for God's sake! You've no idea how late we are! You're going to miss it!"

Ollie's footsteps thundered down the stairs.

Valerie peered drowsy-eyed at the clock. Five thirty seven. Sighing, she reached for the mug and then put it down again quickly, wrinkling her nose, having tasted it. Oh, dear, dear, what a disappointment. Very cold Earl Grey.

The back door opened and slammed. A few moments later it reopened and Ollie's footsteps thundered back up the stairs. Susie clattered back in after him from the patio, calling angrily from below. "Now what are you looking for?"

"Where have you put my bloody season ticket?"

Andy groaned. Closing her eyes, Valerie sank back down upon the pillow. She sincerely hoped it wasn't going to be like this every morning.

It was. Still, she told a grumpy Andy confidently over a breakfast at which they were both too half asleep to know where they really were, these were minor matters, teething troubles. They would all soon adjust and everybody would settle down.

They did, to a large extent. Having the family around fulltime proved to be, like Andy's attempts at helping in the garden, a mixed blessing: lovely, but extremely tiring. The times when the house and garden rang with laughter were wonderful; the frequent angry words and spats between Susie and Ollie were worrisome and unsettling.

Weekends proved to be another problem. To Susie and Ollie, the main point of having a house in the country seemed to be in order to invite town friends down for long and boisterous weekends. To Andy and Valerie, weekends had meant for years a nice quiet time, more often than not spending the days pottering around and the evenings peacefully reading or watching telly. Bedtime was the same as always, round about half past ten, Saturday was for fiddling around in the garden and Sunday was reading the papers, usually followed for Valerie by ironing, writing letters or perhaps making a cake whilst Andy popped to the pub, and then a nice roast dinner. Resting, recuperating, rebuilding one's resources, that was what weekends were for; weekdays were for gadding about and being sociable. Once upon a time they might have coped with it, but no longer.

"What's the matter with them?" Andy muttered as they sheltered from the mob for a while in the early evening, having long succumbed to eating the previously disdained microwaved meals on trays propped on their knees in the little sitting room. "Don't they want any time on their own?" Grimacing, he set his stodgy macaroni cheese down in the floor. "This stuff is horrible. What happened to my Sunday roast?"

"I'll sneak in and get us some crackers and a nice bit of cheese in a minute," she promised. "I just couldn't face that kitchen, love, not with them all in there. I'll have to start cooking more than we need and freezing some of it. I'm sorry, but you know what it's like: people everywhere, the sink will be full of washing up and so will the dishwasher. I'd never get near the Aga, and I'd probably end up peeling dozens of extra potatoes and things and spinning the joint out for everybody again once they'd seen what I was about. Not that it would have been big enough, I only got us a small bit of topside."

"You'd think he'd want a rest with all that commuting!" Andy muttered.

Valerie was distracted. It had just occurred to her that having visitors kept Susie and Ollie from shouting at each other for a little while, so maybe there was some benefit to be had from it. The relationship between them was getting very worrying. She nodded slowly. "Hm."

It was quite hard work, too, all living in the one house. Sometimes Valerie found herself hankering for a nice long stretch of peace and quiet, on their own, just her and Andy. Late in the second spring, she was halfway up the bottom stairs carrying an armful of discarded toys and clothing which she had previously gathered and put on the bottom step ready to be taken up, and which, naturally, had been ignored by everybody, when a glowering and heavily-laden Susie burst into the hall accompanied by a sullen-faced and pink-eyed Poppy who marched straight over to the family room door. Valerie was sure the words she muttered vehemently before slamming it vigorously behind her were, *Bloody pig!*

She was shocked. Such language!

"Little cow." Dumping half a dozen Waitrose carrier bags onto the floor, Susie darted outside again.

More squabbles. If it wasn't one pair, it was another. She was still deliberating between continuing up the stairs with her burden and descending to see if she could soothe the storm clouds, and to carry the carrier bags into the kitchen before someone fell over them, when Susie reappeared with more carrier bags and two dry-cleaning bags containing suits of Ollie's.

"Will you take these up if you're going upstairs? Just dump them anywhere or sling them on the bed."

Valerie waited patiently whilst Susie draped the dry-cleaning bags over her arm before hurrying back down the stairs. "Oh – and Mum?" she added with a bright and wheedling smile, turning from making her way back to the door. "Do you think you could baby-sit tonight? Ollie's promised to come home early so we can go out and have a drink and a nice chat."

"Of course we will." Reluctantly she said goodbye to *Coronation Street.* They hardly ever went out together. It'd do them good.

"Thank you! I'll just get Thomas. Put the kettle on Mum, will you? I'm simply dying of thirst."

That child is getting out of hand."

"It's no wonder the little lass uses that kind of language, all that rowing." Andy shook his head disapprovingly. "She hears it all the time from Susie."

"And from you."

"I don't swear!" Talk about innocence betrayed. "I *don't!*"

"Don't you?" She let it go. "We're babysitting tonight, by the way. You haven't got anything on, have you?"

"Are we? Why?"

"Ollie's promised to come home early so they can go out and have a bit of time together." She was surprised how pleased she felt; might have been her own special arrangements she was making. "I could manage on my own."

He shrugged. "No, no, all in a good cause." He returned to his newspaper. "Anyway, wouldn't leave you on your own."

Whilst Valerie and Andy and the children were having their dinner, Susie went off upstairs happily to get changed. Valerie heard her singing happily above in the power shower and smiled. "Nice to hear her so happy for a change!"

"Eh?"

"Susie. She sounds happy." She listened head cocked. "Aah, isn't that really nice."

Andy took the children out onto the garden after dinner. She was relishing the comparative quiet of the kitchen and smiling as she listened to the children's distant shrieks and Andy's shouts as they chased about in some rowdy game on the lawn, was washing up steadily when Susie zoomed in excitedly, fastening on an earring and looking gorgeous in a short pale blue linen dress and high sandals and with her long blonde hair shining, "Have you seen the car keys?"

"I haven't seen them, love." She nodded approvingly. "You look very nice."

Susie smiled fleetingly. "Bugger it, what have I done with them?" She whirled around the kitchen like a noisy dervish, clattering dishes as she searched.

"Not in your handbag? Sure?" Valerie dried her hands patiently. "Shall I double-check?"

"Well, you can do, but they're not here." She upended her handbag herself onto the worktop, sorting frantically through the contents.

"Isn't the taxi picking Ollie up?"

"I've cancelled it, bit of a surprise, I'm going to pick him up. I thought we'd have a drink and then I've booked a table at the new Italian in town." She rummaged frantically in the fruit bowl. "*Where* are my bloody keys? Don't stand any nonsense from Thomas; put him in with Poppy, if you like. *Where* have I put them? They're not bloody here. Did

I leave them in the ignition?"

She darted out through the patio door, calling stridently, "Poppy! Thomas! Mummy's off now, I'm going out with Daddy, be good for Nana and Grampie, now. Thomas, have you had my car keys?" She was back before Valerie had dried her hands. "In the ignition. Right then, I'm off. I've got my mobile. Will you be all right?"

"You look lovely. Yes, yes, of course we will. You have a lovely time."

"If you have a moment, any chance you could run a quick iron over a shirt for Ollie for tomorrow? I meant to do it, but I haven't had a chance. Must look for an ironing service – and we really need a cleaner. Maybe you could scribble out a couple of cards for the shop?"

"Okay."

Susie hadn't finished. "Oh, and Mum, if Poppy's going to have a pony, we're going to need some decent post-and-rail fencing around one of the paddocks at least. Could you have a look through the local paper for a fencer? The one nearest the house where we can keep an eye on it would probably be best – or perhaps we should fence round two so that we can move the pony over from time to time, give him some fresh grass. Then of course we'll need a stable, or at least some kind of shelter, but there's no immediate hurry with that. You can leave that to me."

"Thank you," Val murmured dryly.

"Oh, and Ollie fancied us keeping chickens, what do you think? It would be lovely to go out in the morning with the children, wouldn't it, hunting for freshly laid eggs? Or ducks, though I don't know if we'd like duck eggs. And what about a goat? Goat's milk might be good for the children."

Valerie grimaced. "Oh, I don't want a goat, they eat everything! They'd eat all my flowers."

"Well, maybe not a goat, then. Where could we put a run and a chicken coop? What about in the walled garden?"

"But it's lovely now; I've just had it all laid out!"

"Well, give it some thought. Got to go. I'll be late." She glanced at the kitchen clock. "Oh, God, is that the time? I must fly." She darted hastily for the conservatory doors.

The kitchen seemed very quiet and empty after she had

gone.

The game of football didn't last as long as Valerie would have liked, though probably long enough for Andy, who was red-faced and out of breath when he followed the children in. She eyed him anxiously. "By the heck, he's got some energy, that lad!" he panted. "Mind you, that Poppy's not bad, either – got a good eye for a ball."

Poppy darted towards the family room. "Now can we watch a DVD?"

Valerie reached into the games drawer. "I thought we'd have a nice quiet game of something. How about Snakes and Ladders? Or Snap? You'll keep an eye on Thomas, won't you, Andy?"

He looked justifiably aggrieved. "Here, I've done my stint!"

Well, I did it!" Valerie finally tottered into the sitting room and sank gratefully into her armchair. "Not as early as I'd have liked, but better than usual!" There was some sort of very noisy high-speed police chase going on the screen. Reaching for the remote control, she tried to turn down the volume surreptitiously. Andy caught her.

"What are you doing?"

"Need to be able to hear if they call."

He grimaced tetchily. "Well, might as well switch it off, then. I can't hear it at all now."

She turned it back up a notch. "Don't be so silly." She watched it for a minute. "What is this?"

He shrugged. "I don't know. I was half asleep. I'm worn out."

"You and me both." She watched the screen for a few moments, but was a bit too rattled to make any sense of the story. "They've noticed, you know, the children. All the rowing."

His eyes were fixed to the screen. "Ah. Hm."

"I feel sorry for them. They shouldn't have to listen to it. It's them I feel sorry for, poor kiddies."

He heard her this time and nodded, frowning. "They want to get their act together, Susie and Oliver; it's a bloody shame."

"See, you do swear."

"No, I don't."

"You just did. You said 'bloody'."

"They're not here, though, are they?"

"You don't know when you're doing it. You've got into the habit."

"Hm..."

"Still, things might get better now when they've had a nice night out and a bit of a chat."

"Maybe." He yawned.

She struggled stiffly to her feet. "Shall I make us a cuppa? What d'you want? Hot chocolate?"

"That'd be nice." He glanced at the clock. "We're not stopping up, are we? We're not waiting up for them?"

"It's only just gone nine."

He grimaced shamefacedly.

"All right, then. You go on up and get the bed warm; I'll bring up the hot chocolate."

He switched off the television eagerly. "Lovely."

"He's messed up the bed a bit," she warned him, remembering.

He straightened, shocked. "What? He hasn't...?"

"Eh? Oh!" She chuckled. "No, no, He's been bouncing; you'll need to straighten it up again, that's all."

She must have missed hearing the car engine. Susie was in the kitchen, sitting slumped on a kitchen stool. She stopped short in her tracks. "Hello, what are you doing back here, pet? I didn't hear you come in."

"I came in by the conservatory; the doors were still open."

"Where's Ollie?" Susie shook her head disconsolately. "Ah, what's happened, then, pet?"

"Oh, the usual sort of thing." Susie shrugged stiffly. "He wasn't on the train, so I tried to ring him, but his mobile was turned off. I waited for the next train: still no Ollie; still no answer on the mobile. Still no bloody sign. He rang as I was driving away from the station. He'd had to go to a meeting."

"Oh no!" Valerie felt as disappointed as Susie looked. "Did he have to go?"

Susie shrugged. "Said so. He was still there."

"What a shame." Valerie bit her lip. What a pity. "Oh,

well. Another time then."

"Yes." Susie shrugged again. "Another time. Oh, and thanks, Mum, anyway."

The truth of it came out the next day. Susie's face was like a fiddle when Valerie went through to help with the tidying up. "Never mind, love," Valerie said sympathetically. "I know you were disappointed."

"Disappointed?" Susie, who had been in the bath with Thomas, attempted to drag a wide-toothed baby comb through her long, tangled wet fair hair and, defeated, threw the comb into the wastepaper basket. "He promised me! He said he'd come home early last night so we could go out together and talk. He knew you and Dad were all ready to baby-sit." Her face was crimson with rage. "He knew! I'm furious with him!" Gathering up a handful of jigsaw pieces, she threw them all into the wrong box.

Valerie attempted to sound soothing. "We'll do it another day, pet. It doesn't matter to us. What about today? Or tomorrow?" She glanced round the room. "Where is he, anyway?"

"Taking Henry for a walk."

"Oh, you could have gone with him!"

Susie's face turned thunderous again. "I don't want to go anywhere with him; he makes me sick. Anyway, he's gone running. He had his stupid running kit on. Henry was just the excuse."

"I thought it wasn't his fault last night?"

Susie nodded furiously, her eyes narrowed. "Yes, that's what he told me. Now I find out, don't I? D'you know what time the bloody 'meeting' was? Five thirty. D'you know where it was? In the pub. In the bloody pub! How do you conduct a business meeting in a smoky, boozy, noisy city pub? And how long did it go on for anyway? An hour? Twenty past one when he got home, smashed as a rat. Absolutely out of his tree. Couldn't even get his key properly in the lock. And I find out he's got himself talked into another investment policy. Again. "

Her hazel eyes were filled with tears and anger. "He can't keep on burning the candle at both ends like this, can he, Mum? It's ridiculous! I know everybody thinks he's lovely, and he can be, but when he gets overtired he can get really nasty and he's no time for Poppy or Thomas, never mind for me." She shrugged hopelessly. "Oh, what's the use? If I say anything, it's wrong. He only says I'm nagging."

Moodily she retrieved the comb, tossing it onto the sofa. "That's four times on the trot he was out last week only getting four or five hours sleep – if you can call it sleep; he's too tired and wound up to sleep properly when he gets to bed, he just tosses and turns, he's furious with me if Thomas gets up and climbs into our bed, then the alarm goes off and it's five thirty and time to get up and I'm tired, too, but I still get up and run him to the station, don't I, but if I dare to speak to him he only snarls. At weekends, we have to have people down or we'd just start shrieking at one another, but he's exhausted, I'm exhausted, the children get on his nerves. It's hopeless."

So she'd been right about the weekend visitors. Valerie nodded thoughtfully. "Has it made things worse between you, d'you think, love, having Dad and me here?"

Susie reached for a WetOne from the packet lying on the sofa, and blew her nose loudly. "No," she replied, sniffing. "As far as that's concerned, it's just a bit of a waste. Ollie and I could be going out together every evening."

Hm...

"No, no." Susie shook her head vehemently. "He likes having you here."

She was relieved. "Well, if you're sure about that."

Susie smiled. "Oh, don't be silly, Mum. If you weren't here to keep an eye on the children so that I can drive him, he'd have to get a taxi every morning to get him to the station as well as every evening back."

That night Valerie clambered into Susie and Ollie's big, high bed that took up so much space and always seemed cold and unoccupied until she had reached out a hand or a foot and found a reassuring patch of warm Andy, and wriggled herself along the mattress until she was pressed up to his hunched back.

He was still half awake. "Oh, there you are," he mumbled sleepily.

"Mm."

Turning, he put an arm about her, drawing her even

closer against him. "Hmmm..."

She squeezed him tightly. "Hmmm."

It felt safe and comfy, but she was still unsettled, and stared out into the darkness. The alarm clock ticked softly. An owl hooted. As if sensing her disquiet, he stirred.

"You all right?"

"Mm?" She squeezed his arm reassuringly. "Mm, yes. Yes, I'm fine. I'm fine."

But she wasn't.

She confided her worries, at last, to Norma when she probed. "There's something worrying you though. I know you, Val. I can tell."

Valerie sighed, twisting the cord round the receiver. "Oh, it's nothing, Norm, it's just, well – I'm sure it's nothing, really, just a bad patch, only temporary. It's Susie and Ollie, Norma. Their relationship is worrying me. It seems to have gone just a little bit to pot."

Afterwards she had wished that she hadn't said anything, because she would really have preferred to let Norma carry on believing that everything about their new life was perfect, but on the other hand it turned out, in some funny way, that saying something about it out loud seemed to have done the trick – a bit like the way weather had a habit of turning really cold and chilly as soon as you said you were going to put your winter coat away.

Over the following months, things started to get a lot better. The arguing went on, but at a somewhat lower level, became just bickering, really; the flow of weekend visitors slowed down to a trickle and though Ollie still came in very late most nights, he and Susie actually spent quite a bit of time chatting together, late into the night with the door closed, bobbing about in the swimming pool, or out somewhere on the darkened lawn. Susie even started going running with him, which Henry clearly thought was wonderful. All in all, Valerie did too. Now things were really settling down. This was the way it ought to be. She felt much happier.

Her happiness didn't last long, though. One Friday early in October, Susie packed a couple of bags and hurried off to sweep up the children after school. "Mum, we're going up to London for the weekend. We're going to stay with

Alistair and Charmain. Back late Sunday night."

They were backwards and forwards to London for a number of weekends, and then one day towards the middle of November, Susie accosted Val in the little sitting room. "We've come to a decision, Mum." She had a smile on her face, but the slight tremor in her voice made the words sound ominous. Valerie's heart plummeted, though she smiled back, attempting to sound unruffled.

"Oh, yes, dear? What's that?"

"Well..." Susie fiddled nervously with the ornaments on the oak mantel. "Oh, that's nice, isn't it?" she added, picking up a small gilt carriage clock. "Where did that come from?"

"It belonged to my grandmother. I don't know if it's any older than that; she always had it on her mantelpiece. Doesn't work."

"You should have it mended. Oh, look, is that me?" She picked up a small photograph frame closely decorated with tiny pale pink shells. "Ah, sweet! How old was I there? I don't look like either of the children. What is it I have in my hand?"

"Let me see?" Valerie screwed up her eyes. Really must see about getting some new reading glasses. "I think it was a chunk of bread. We'd just been to the shops. You can see the edge of my basket."

"Ah...!" Susie placed it back on the mantel and then took a deep breath. "Well, um, the thing is, Mum, the thing is, we've decided to go back to living in London."

Valerie nodded slowly. "Ah."

"The commuting is too much for Ollie; I think that's been a great deal of the problem: he's always so tired. If we're in London he won't have to get up nearly so early and he's promised that he'll come straight back home most nights. Besides, if we are there I can go and meet him after work sometimes, I can go to his gym at work with him at lunchtimes, we can go out together, it'll be a whole lot better."

Valerie found she had had an itch on her anklebone, a bite, maybe. She scratched it vigorously. "Mm, I see."

"Besides, there isn't much point in having a country house when you and Dad aren't comfortable with having people down for weekends. That's what we wanted one for, really."

"Mm, I see." Valerie repeated slowly, still scratching at her ankle. Dratted mosquitos!

"You know we've been going up to London a lot recently; well, we've been looking around. We've been to see a few properties, but there's a house has just come on to the market, in Primrose Hill. Well, between Primrose Hill and Camden, actually, which is actually better because you can walk into Hampstead and you don't have all the tacky side of Camden, but you can walk there easily as well. It's a lovely house, Georgian Terrace, incredible Wisteria growing all over the front, very pretty. Camilla Fox-Bruton mentioned it to us, actually."

Valerie sniffed. "Oh, her."

"It's one she had her eye on, only her husband doesn't want to move and won't let her put in an offer. She's feeling sick as a pig."

Oh, good.

"Well, we offered them the asking price and it's been accepted."

She'd never noticed before, the pale greeny-grey on the walls didn't really go with the shade of the carpet. It was the wrong tone. Next time they decorated, she'd get Andy to think about a pale pink. It would look warmer, too.

"Mum? It's been accepted; so I'm afraid we're going to have to ask you to move."

Chapter 9

Valerie drew herself together and rose stiffly. "I think your dad should be in on this, don't you? Hang on a minute, love." She felt her head singing as she went to fetch him from the conservatory. He looked so happy, so at home, ensconced comfortably in one of the oversized wicker chairs next to a huge potted palm with his feet in his old brown leather slippers crossed comfortably on the matching footstool, that it took her a moment to speak. "Looks as if we're moving on, pet."

"What?" He looked up from his newspaper. "What do you mean, 'moving on'?"

She beckoned with her head. "Need you in the other room." She gave him the gist of it as calmly as she could whilst they were moving through the house. He was taut with shock by the time they got to the small sitting room. "So, what's all this, then? What happens about us?" he asked Susie.

She shook her head emphatically. "Oh, you'll be all right, Dad – we're not going to leave you in the lurch. Has Mum explained?"

He sat down in his easy chair, though he didn't look comfortable at all. He was making a great effort to keep calm, Valerie saw. "Well, sort of, the gist of it, yes. It's a bit of a shock."

"Oh, don't worry, don't worry!" Susie spoke very brightly and earnestly, though Valerie could see that her hands were trembling just a little bit. "I don't want you worrying, Dad. We will have to sell this fairly quickly, I'm afraid; the new house is very expensive. Ollie can get a bridging loan and increase the mortgage without any problem, but we'll need the money from this, too, or at least some of it, so Ollie and I have agreed, you two can find somewhere that you like – whatever you like, so long as Ollie approves. Have a look round, have a look on the Internet, ring some agents. Whoever sells this might have somewhere you like on his books. It'll be fun!"

Andy looked panic-stricken. "Don't know about that. I could do without that sort of fun. We're not ones for moving much."

"I know that."

"We never have. We've always tended to stay put."

"We'll fix a budget, obviously, but whatever you decide on will be yours. Well, ours nominally, of course, unless we put joint names on it, but then there'd be a problem if you have to go into a nursing home one day and they make you sell it. You can do whatever you want with it, decorate it how you like, whatever, and it'll be your home, not ours." She smiled brightly. "How do you feel about that?"

Valerie studied her hands. *Numb, actually.* All she could think was, *Poor Andy,* and then, as anger built in her, *What a waste. What a waste. All the money that's been spent on this house; all that time spent choosing doorknobs and having things made to order. All that putting up with all those months and months of building work, getting rhinitis and asthma from the dust. All the money from the old house we've invested in this one. The new friends we've made. All the time, the money, the effort. My wonderful greenhouse. All my plants!*

Her hands were trembling. *Well, we can't stay here. Even if they didn't need the money, we couldn't afford it. Run a heated swimming pool, on a pension? Have all the hedges cut? An Aga running non-stop – all that oil?*

Look on the bright side. She drew in a calming breath. On the bright side, it is kind of them to make the offer. Very generous. Another adventure. It might be good for them, Susie could well be right about that.

It'd be nice for us, too, being able to treat a new place exactly as we want, with no Camilla hovering. Peace and quiet. It'd be a relief not have to have to fit in with anybody else's way of life or to live with all the quarrelling. As time goes on, I'm not going to be able to cope with all this garden, be sensible, it's bad enough trying to do it as my knees are now.

But – moving again? All that hassle?

Pride crept into it, too. *Having to tell everybody we're downsizing, just when Leon and Norma will have told them all how lucky we are...*

"Dad? Mum? Are you all right with that?"

No point in being angry. "Well, of course, we don't want to stand in your way."

They walked slowly together down through the gossamer-strewn paddocks later. Valerie slipped her cold hand into his and he pushed them both into his pocket. "There's a right nip in the air."

"There is." The air smelled as if someone somewhere had a bonfire. Most of the trees and the hedgerows tangled with thick garlands of wild rose hips, old man's beard and blackberries – fruitless now, the birds and Valerie had had them – were still in thick leaf, though the colours were changing. No mists about this evening. The sky was still a bright blue. It was certainly too cold to sit for very long on their seat.

Andy stood staring out while she perched on the edge for a minute. Rooks were cawing, preparing to make their evening racket high up in the trees. A flight of migrating birds circled and swooped gracefully, forming and reforming across the cloudless sky. Below them, a faint whisper of white smoke rose from the hollow beneath the bottom field, curling up very slowly into the almost still air. It was old Alf Lord who had the small cottage down there who was busy; Valerie could see his tiny figure and hear the faint clang of his spade. Nice old man. Been very helpful with her vegetable patch. She'd been about to ask Susie if she could offer him some regular work.

Most of the fields were brown and beige now that the hay and the corn and other crops had been harvested, but scattered about were still the soft greens and golds. As always, the view brought a lump to her throat. So beautiful, it was – so beautiful.

What had he said? '*I don't ever want to leave this place.*'
Poor Andy. He looked so woebegone. And it had been such
a big thing for him, the move. He'd done so well, settling.
She could have wept for him.

He kicked at a clod of soil. "Will we stay around here?"

"Oh, yes." She shrugged. "Well, I suppose it depends on
what we can find within our budget, whatever that turns
out to be. It's not the cheapest of areas. Susie suggested
Cornwall."

He rocked back on his heels. "Cornwall?!"

She chuckled, though it wasn't funny really. "She and
Ollie love Cornwall, apparently. Or Italy: she did mention
Italy, perhaps you'd fancy that."

"We'd be further away from them there than if we'd
stayed in North Wales." He hunched his shoulders sardonically. "Though maybe that's not a bad idea."

"Would you really want to?"

He stared out beside her. "No."

What's our budget, then?"
"Somewhere around four hundred thousand." The
figure sounded enormous.

"And how much is this one on the market for again?"

" Nine hundred thousand seven hundred and fifty."

"Bloody hell." She knew what was coming. "Just think
what I'd have got for my lovely old house!"

It sounded like an awful lot of money, four hundred
thousand pounds, but it frightened Valerie and Andy how
little they could buy with it when they started to look
around. There were houses to be had, of course, but even
if they themselves might have settled for a nice little post-
war semi, they were constrained by Ollie's and Susie's
taste; they held the purse strings and it was their investment. Something that would grow or at least hold its own
in value; nothing new build and not on an estate.

Somewhere with character. That meant somewhere old.

"Surely they don't want to buy another one that's falling
to bits and listed? You'd think they'd had enough after this
one" Andy was astounded. "What about a nice Victorian
house, or Edwardian?"

"Hm." Valerie nodded, pretending to consider it. "Something high-ceilinged and solidly built?"

He nodded approvingly. "That's it."

"Something that's been well-maintained over the years?"

"That's right."

She was smiling now. "Something just like our old one?"

"Mm."

Poor old thing.

"Pricewise, though, it would probably have to be a semi or a terrace."

"Well, nothing much wrong with that."

"No, no. So long as you've got a bit of a garden. And nice neighbours."

"Neighbours?"

"Quiet ones. A party wall? "

"Oh! Hm."

Victorian and Edwardian houses were vetoed, though. The only ones in the right price range seemed to be pretty ugly, in the middle of suburban nowhere, or on the cheaper fringes of town. Susie turned up her nose. "Ollie won't like that one, I'm afraid. Nor that."

They really wanted to stay in the village. Susie's eyes got a little shiny when she told her so. "Oh, Mum, I'd love you to, but you just can't."

"There is one for sale, look, in today's paper. No, no – two!" Valerie flattened the page. "Oh, this is a nice one, look! I know where that is, it's up by the pub. Oh –" Her eye had caught the price. "Oh. No."

Susie sighed. "That's what I mean. They're all going to be around that mark, if not dearer. It's a very desirable village, very sought-after. The only ones within the budget might be the modern ex-council ones up the cul-de-sac if there were any for sale."

Where Martha lives? Those ugly little semi-detached brick houses with their pocket-handkerchief back gardens and their wheelie-bins stuck outside their front doors? And no view? After The Bury?

Valerie shook her head. "Oh, no, Ollie wouldn't agree to that, I'm sure." She was immediately ashamed of herself.

I've turned into a right old snob.

Susie pulled the paper towards herself. "Where's the other one? *The Old Post Office.* Where's that?"

107

Valerie tried to picture it. "It's up near the green on the opposite side to the shop. Semi-detached. You know it; next door to the Bacons."

"The Bacons?"

"Yes, you know – she's got white hair. President of the WI. He's famous for his sweetpeas."

"Don't know them. Maybe worth looking at."

Valerie felt a prickle of excitement. "But it's too much."

"Four hundred and thirty five..." Susie cogitated deeply, frowning. "Mmm..."

Valerie was ever so disappointed with it and Andy – well, Andy was just plain shocked. "*What* are they asking for this?" he scowled.

The poor little dark-haired woman from the Estate Agents looked quite terrified. "Four hundred and thirty-five thousand."

Disbelieving, he ran his fingers through his hair. "*Four hundred and thirty-five thousand pounds?*"

"Um, that's right, yes."

"God save us. It hasn't even got an upstairs bathroom."

Valerie bit her lip. "It's got a nice little garden. Private." So private that it hardly got any light. "To whom do the Leylandii belong?"

The woman gazed helplessly through the window. "Um..."

"No upstairs bathroom. What are we supposed to do in the middle of the night? Come traipsing downstairs? Down that staircase?"

"It is a bit steep, the staircase, yes."

"And the treads are too shallow. Can't get your whole foot on a step. Death trap, I'd say, if you were half asleep."

They walked upstairs again, just to make certain. The woman left them alone to do it this time. "It's bloody horrible," Andy muttered.

Valerie grimaced. "It isn't very nice. I suppose we could have a bathroom put in."

"Where?"

"Well, would we really need three bedrooms?"

"It'd cost a fortune, all that plumbing. Besides – " He rapped at a wall with his knuckle. "Cardboard."

"What?"

"Probably just two bedrooms originally. This is a flimsy partition wall."

"When was it built?" she asked the woman when they got back downstairs into the hall-come-living room with the strange front window that must have belonged to the Post Office.

"About eighteen hundred, I believe. Eighteen something. The kitchen's a more recent add-on, obviously."

"Obviously."

"By the look of it, it was some kind of shed."

They walked dejectedly home afterwards. "She said we'd have no problem getting planning permission."

"To do what?"

"Oh, I don't know. "

He looked at her, surprised. "You didn't *like* it, did you?"

"Eh?" She shook her head. "Oh, no, no."

"You just want to stay in the village." He stared at her for a moment and then caught her hand and squeezed it. "It'll be all right, wherever we end up, you know that, so long as we've got each other. So long as I've got my Val."

She gulped. There was suddenly a lump in her throat and she had to blink hard to keep sight of the passing ground, which was suddenly hazy. Clutching his hand tightly, she squeezed it back hard. "I know that, pet. Yes. Mm."

S he made them a cup of tea when they got home and they sipped it together whilst browsing through various offerings on the Internet. Few of the properties currently for sale around about seemed to meet the requirements; the majority were too expensive, too much in need of 'modernisation', too ugly, or on some kind of housing estate. It was all very headache-making.

Andy nudged her. "Here, what about this one? That's not bad! Shedley. Where's that?"

She frowned. "I don't know."

He frowned intently. "Got to be something wrong with it. 'Period property, delightful cottage, three bedrooms, two reception, country-style kitchen, recently updated... Secluded garden.' Two hundred and eighty-five thousand."

Valerie felt excitement rising. Two hundred and eighty-five thousand? "Where? Let me see! Where?"

He clicked his tongue crossly, sagging back in his chair. "Thought there was a snag. Wrong section. It's in Northumberland."

With the aid of the Internet and the paper, they somehow managed to draw up a shortlist of three that might be worth looking at, and Andy went to telephone the agents whilst Valerie opened up a tin of soup: no appetite at the moment. She badly needed to talk to someone about the whole thing, but she still didn't want to ring Norma. It felt as if, as long as she didn't tell her, she might only have imagined it or Susie would tell them any minute that she and Ollie had changed their minds, or that it had been an April Fool, even if it was late October. Then it would be all right; she wouldn't have to tell Norma that they might have made a terrible mistake selling up and coming all the way down here, or that Andy'd been quite right when he'd worried about giving up control of their lives and being in Susie and Oliver's hands. But she did need to chat about it to somebody. Martha or Norma?

She chose Martha, and popped round to see her whilst Andy was having a bit of a snooze after lunch. She was shocked, but pragmatic.

"Well, I'm really sorry you're going, of course I am – what am I going to do without you – but if you think about it, what the hell are you worrying about, Val? You're still so lucky. You wanted to move, didn't you? From what you've said, you'd never have been able to afford this area without Susie and Ollie, and they're still promising you a house. How many daughters and sons-in-law would do that?"

Valerie felt quite ashamed. "You're quite right."

"Besides, won't it be better on your own? Go on, now, Val, be honest."

Valerie hesitated. No noise, no continual clutter, no hoards of exuberant visitors, no extra washing, no rows... "Well, in a way, I suppose so, yes."

"Go on with you, then!" Martha waved a dismissive hand. "We'll find you something. You can make another home, you know you can, you and Andy, you're real home-bodies – and think how much fun you'll have doing up another garden."

Valerie pictured her precious borders wretchedly. "I suppose I'm not allowed to take any of my plants?"

Martha chuckled. "Well, not officially, but you can take cuttings, or specify which ones are going with you."

Valerie was fretting. "It's the wrong time of the year."

"Well, what we'll do is dig a lot of them up and then you can say you're taking all plants that are in pots. Buy in some compost and plenty of big tubs." She shook her head. "I tell you what – I wish I was looking for a nice new house!"

The light was growing dim already as Valerie started walking home; no blue skies today. The clammy air smelled of a mixture of wood smoke and mould, partly sombre and partly thrilling. Damp autumn leaves that had been run over by passing vehicles clung to her shoes. A gust of cold wind whistled down between the hedgerows, making her turn up her coat collar. She turned, suddenly feeling very lonely, and waved back at them. Martha uncharacteristically blew her a kiss. "'Bye-bye."

Andy was waiting. "Looks cold out there. What's for dinner?" After the previous evening's offering, he'd clearly been thinking about his tummy now for quite some time.

She shrugged off her coat. "Oh, I don't know. I'll find us something."

"You've got a bit of lamb, haven't you? That lamb thing you do with lemons and green beans and potatoes and things would be nice. Does it take long to cook?" he asked hopefully, following her into the kitchen.

"Depends what time you want to eat. It's half past four already."

Mention of the time must have nudged his memory. "Oh, the agents are bringing some people round to have a look around at five, by the way."

She hadn't had the heart for a tidy-up. She looked at him aghast. "Five o'clock?"

He looked puzzled. "What's the matter with that? I said it was all right."

"Oh, Andy!"

It turned out, actually, as Susie had suggested, quite fun, looking at houses. It hadn't dawned on Valerie before; it was quite nice being nosy. She had found a brand new game. The various Estate Agencies had been told that the actual purchasers were Susie and Ollie, but word didn't seem to have filtered down to the people showing Andy and Valerie around and it was rather jolly, pretending to be affluent enough to be buying, and even more so to have a house worth nine hundred and fifty thousand pounds to sell – because of course the agents wanted to know if their own house had been sold yet but as soon as she told them blithely, waving a casual hand, "Oh, don't worry about that, we're effectively cash-buyers, there is no problem with a bridging loan!" and where the house was, they were quite obsequious. It made a nice change.

The search for anything close at hand proved impossible. The same was true when they extended the search to a twenty-mile radius. There were just a few that they listed as 'possibles', but they all turned out to be a waste of time.

"Should we be looking in a different area entirely?" Andy wondered morosely at last, surreptitiously removing a bit of cress that had got stuck between his teeth: they always treated these wanderings as 'outings' and had a spot of lunch. Egg-and-cress sandwich for Andy today at a little café they found on their travels between viewings; tuna mayonnaise for Valerie. "This seems hopeless."

Despite the disappointments, though, Valerie was quite enjoying herself. The fact that they were actually going to move seemed vaguely unreal. "Let's have a look at the next one before we think about that."

When they got home that evening, though, tired and even Valerie a little bit dispirited – Andy was getting crabbier and crabbier with each reject that they crossed off from their list – they had a bit of a shock. Susie was waiting in the kitchen with a big smile plastered all over her face. "Well, we've had an offer!"

Andy gaped. "Good Lord above! Already?"

"Ollie's just rung."

"How much?"

Susie's beam broke into a triumphant grin. "The full asking price."

Andy scratched his head. "Good Lord."
Valerie had to sit down. "Oh, my gracious me. Who, lovey? Which ones?"
Susie bustled about the kitchen. She seemed to be making a cake; there was flour and cocoa powder everywhere. "The Martingales? The ones who came round first? You remember – you said they had twin girls and a little boy."
"Yes, I remember." There had been a big fight over having a ride in the pedal car of Thomas's that they'd found. Very aggressive children. Valerie felt a bit of a headache growing. "So, are you going to accept?"
"It's tempting." Susie waved her wooden spoon excitedly, sending dollops of chocolate coloured batter spattering. "The people we're buying from are keen to close the deal. Ollie had him on the phone today, too, asking if we were anywhere near setting a date for exchange. He liked us, but he had another offer and he won't hold it forever. What do you think, Dad?"
Andy shrugged helplessly, frowning. "Oh, don't ask me. I've no idea, pet."
Susie resumed her beating energetically. "On the other hand, we've already had a lot of interest. It might be worth hanging on for a while. I don't know. I'll talk about it with Ollie later. I'm making him a chocolate cake to celebrate. He won't eat it, but he'll like the gesture. It'll make him feel loved. It's sort of symbolic, isn't it, cake?"
"Dad'll eat it for you." Surreptitiously Valerie dabbed away as many blobs of cake mixture as she could reach, particularly those on Andy's Roberts radio.
Susie chuckled. "I know he will." She glanced across, raising her eyebrows. "Have you had any luck today?"
Valerie felt suddenly drained. "No, nothing at all. Well, there was one that we quite liked, the last one we saw."
Andy snorted. "Service Charges! 'How much?' I said. 'That's bloody criminal!'"
Valerie shook her head. "No, you didn't."
He looked surprised. "I did."
"You didn't say 'bloody.'"
He sighed heavily.
Susie looked reflective. "If we accept the offer, you know

you may have to think about renting till the right thing comes on the market."

Valerie felt her heart pitter-pattering. All that money, more of their money, just sort of oozing out.

They made one last foray. *Very versatile accommodation with views to the west over adjoining countryside*, it had said in the blurb. It turned out to be a shabby, run-down box of a thing, isolated by barbed wire from surrounding muddy cattle pasture, besieged by flies and squatting forlornly all alone at the top of a long lane. The 'view to the west' was negligible. No one was living in it, and judging by the musty smell it had been empty for ages. It was 'carpeted throughout' as the details promised, but in shag-pile man-made fibre in a startling sort of electric mauve, faded and stained in places. Whoever had lived there had liked bright colours; all the walls, except for the small, dejected-looking kitchen which had been done out in imitation pine, had been decorated with woodchip and then painted. The sitting room had a ceiling and one wall in a deep shiny claret and the remainder in raspberry pink. Someone had replaced the original fireplace with a crude sort of construction of indeterminate stone, which had been painted white.

Andy had a field day with it; ill-made and creaking stairs, external window frames that hadn't been painted for God knows how many years; ill-fitting, draughty windows with cheap and nasty UPVC window frames, leaking drainpipes causing damp inside and out, broken guttering that needed replacing, and so on and so forth... Valerie tuned out eventually. "And they want *how* much for it?" He was practically foaming at the mouth.

There was one little cottage that was really rather sweet. "They've got some lovely furniture," whispered Valerie covetously into Andy's ear. "Look at this lovely old carved dresser – and this chest!"

He was more sensible. "Yes, but imagine it, love, with all this taken out and our stuff put in instead. It wouldn't look right." The thing she could imagine most clearly was their television. There would be no escape; the sound of it, at Andy's usual volume level, would echo round the house.

"You're right."

At each end of the single room there was a steep and narrow circular wooden staircase with a thick rope hand rail winding up to a low-ceilinged bedroom and small bathroom on each side. The doorways were ever so low; Andy and the young man both cracked their foreheads on the lintels as they made their way around. "Divided house," the young man explained, patting the doorless wall between the two halves upstairs. "Keep the kiddywinks at bay! Probably two houses once, each separated from the other by this."

What finished Andy was a sort of trapdoor in the floor. "It's a coffin hole," he informed them with some relish. "You wouldn't get one down the staircase, you see, so if anybody dies, you build it up here and sort of – well, lower them through."

"We're too old to want to hear about that."

There were several more viewings of *The Bury* that week, and two more offers came in within the next few days, one a little above and one just below the asking price. "It's about right, then, the Martingales' offer," Susie said. "And they're cash buyers. The people who've made the higher offer have still got a house to sell, though they're not expecting the sale to fall through."

"So what are you going to do?"

"Mm?" Susie, who was searching for her car keys again, was very abstracted. "Oh, we've done it. We're going with the Martingales. Ollie's accepted it."

Chapter 10

Valerie's game was over. It was quite hard keeping the situation to themselves, particularly hiding it from Norma and Leon. She couldn't help feeling like a fool. Norma's response, though, when she finally summoned up the nerve to do it, was very different to Martha's; she was so full of sympathy that she made Valerie cry. She was very angry with Susie. "After having you living all that time in a building site, Val? It's too bad! Having all that upheaval and just getting nice and settled? You can tell Susie her Aunty Norma says she's a naughty girl."

Dismissing the fact that she'd had much the same thoughts, Valerie found herself defensive. "But she's not, is she, Norm? They're not leaving us stranded; they've offered us another nice home. We can do what we like with it, they said."

Norma sounded doubtful. "Yes, well, that's good, that's generous, I suppose."

"And we'll never be able to buy one for ourselves again. We've spent a lot of our money on this house, you know – oh, not by Susie and Ollie's standards, but by ours."

"You wouldn't have done that, though, would you, if you hadn't thought you were going to stay?"

"No, no, we wouldn't."

"And you wouldn't have moved if you'd thought you were going to have to keep moving."

"No, no, we thought we were here for keeps."

"Well, then." Norma sighed heavily. "Oh, Val, lovey, it is a shame!"

With the day of exchange fast approaching, it was practical Martha who came to their aid. She had been keeping her nose to the ground. "I've been thinking," she murmured reflectively as she stirred her coffee cup one morning. "Don't want to get your hopes up too much, but I think I might just have the answer. There's this lovely old boy..."

"And his wife is in there as well, Andy," Valerie told him excitedly later.

He rustled the newspaper vaguely. "Oh yes?"

"He sounds ever such a sweet old man. Such a good husband, Martha says."

"Uhuh..."

"Are you listening to me?"

He lowered the paper a little. "Yes, yes, I am. Who is?"

"This old man. Listen, listen, do! In this nursing home. In this nursing home I've just been telling you about that Martha goes to visit her friend at, Andy, *Greenacres,* it's called, near Basingstoke."

"What about him?"

"Well, she's been in for a long time, his wife, got Alzheimer's, I think, poor thing, and he's been wonderful, Martha says. Visited her every day for years, he has, and stayed every day from nine in the morning till nine o'clock at night, bless him."

"I'd do that."

She was touched. "I know you would, pet."

He frowned. "Well, I don't know though, maybe not all day long."

"Oh. Well, anyway, listen, he's been staying there with her for the last few weeks to see how he'd like it if he moved in too so he wouldn't have to go backwards and forwards. They haven't got any children or anyone, apparently, and I mean, obviously, he's getting on, too"

"How old is he?"

"Oh, I don't know; somewhere in his eighties, it doesn't matter."

He raised an eyebrow. "Bet it does to him."

"The thing is, Andy, he's got a little cottage and he's going to sell it because he's decided he does like it there, I mean, in the nursing home. He hasn't put it on the market yet and Martha says she's going to have a word with him and see if he would mind us looking round and if we like it, if he'd be happy to do a private sale. That way, of course, he'd cut out estate agents' fees, so it'd be good for him too. Eh? So, lovey, what do you think?"

He looked very doubtful. "Oh, I don't know! What kind of cottage is it? What kind of condition is it in? Where is it? And how much?"

"It's in Hetherfield, it's supposed to be a nice village and not that far away."

"Hetherfield, you say? Don't know it." Putting down the paper he rose and took his car keys from their hook on the dresser. "I'll go and get my Road Atlas."

"And what's he wanting for it?" he asked, returning and putting on his glasses before settling with the Atlas at the table. The wonky arm must have fallen off again; he had it wound on with sticking plaster. Would he go, though? Get some new glasses? Would he, thump!

She peered over his shoulder. "Hetherington... Hetherfield! There it is!" She stabbed the open page excitedly with her finger. "Ooh, it's not far away at all!"

"Can't see it. Where? Move your finger..." He peered closely. "Oh, yes. Not far as the crow flies, anyway. And how much did you say?"

"I didn't." She grimaced bashfully. "I don't know any more, not till she comes back to me. She said she'd ring this afternoon or this evening as soon as she had had a word with him."

"Then you don't even know if it's in our price range?"

"No, but Martha said he told her probably about three hundred and twenty five."

He shook his head gloomily, drawing in a whistling breath. "I doubt that."

"How do you know? You haven't even seen it yet."

"Must need a lot of work doing on it then. Well, has he called in an agent? Had a valuation?"

She felt like wringing her hands. "Andy, I just don't know!"

Wiping her hands on a tea towel, she made her way eagerly to the telephone as soon as it rang after tea. It was Martha, and Valerie listened carefully, trying not to

let her disappointment show. "Oh, I see. Hm... Oh. I see! Oh. Right. Well, no, of course. Of course! Yes. Yes, okay."
He looked up when she walked back into the sitting room. "No good?"
"Oh, yes, yes, well, no. Yes and no. He's happy to sell direct to us –"
"But?"
"Apparently, the Estate Agent went round yesterday afternoon."
"And?"
"Four hundred and thirty five thousand."
He whistled. "Well, I'm not surprised. Old boy's probably out of touch. That's that, then."
She didn't want to let the possibility go by. "Well, it's not necessarily 'that', is it? I mean, Susie was happy about us looking at the other one that cost very much the same."
"Which one was that?"
"*The Old Post Office.*" She was feeling impatient with him. "You know!"
"The rip-off one, you mean?" He shrugged. "Oh, that."
"Shall we go and have a look at it at least? We might as well."
"Oh, I don't know."
"He says it's got a garage," she offered temptingly. "With electricity laid on. And a tool store."
"A garage, eh?" She could see he was thinking about it now. "Is it a double garage?"
She crossed her fingers. "Um... Possibly."
"Well..." He shrugged. I suppose it wouldn't hurt for us to take a little look."

Hetherfield seemed a nice enough village. It had a church and a decent looking pub, though no Post Office or village shop. The cottage was, as she had somehow known it was going to be, just perfect. Well, almost perfect: as Andy pointed out; it abutted directly onto a narrow lane, which could prove troublesome.
Washed a creamy, very pale apricot, it had a mossy thatch, small, low-set leaded windows and a rose-wreathed porch over the front door. Possibly 'the garland', she decided, examining its dense, twiggy growth, or maybe

'rambling rector', in view of its numerous small rosy hips. Lovely. The name was a pretty one, too, *Penny Cottage.*

"Why *Penny Cottage,* do you think?" she asked Andy, who was standing back weighing up the roof. He shrugged, abstracted.

"I don't know." He frowned deeply. "Don't know that we want to be doing with a thatch."

"Perhaps they once collected some kind of toll? Oh, look, Andy, there's a clematis in here as well..."

"Maybe not in too bad a shape. Wonder if that's all right?" Taking out the front door key, he inserted it in the lock. "Are we going in, then, or are you going to hang about all day examining the greenery?"

She withdrew her fingers from the entwined mass around the door. "I'm waiting for *you!*"

"Oh, are you? Thought you were thinking about going back to get your secateurs."

The front door opened directly into a good-sized sitting room on two levels divided by a shallow step. The place smelled of old ashes and ancient wood smoke and, faintly, of rotting flower water, and it was all very dusty. The ceiling beams and irregular struts dividing wattle-and-daub wall panels were of faded, almost bleached timber. The floor was carpeted in a faded apricoty pink, much deeper than the outside of the house and very threadbare, but it was right, somehow, she decided. It gave some warmth and colour to the whitewashed walls. Andy sniffed hard. "I don't detect any smell of damp."

A rocking chair stood beneath the deep-silled front window, and nearby a vase with crumbling, unidentifiable and forgotten flowers stood on a small table topped with lace-trimmed white cloth, which was stained with the brown ring-marks of cups and displayed an open photograph album. Crammed, white-painted bookshelves reached up to the low ceiling at the far end of the nearest part of the room, and more books were piled up on the floor around a pair of armchairs set with a low oak table between them. More books still, photographs and documents filled every other available surface An incongruously modern-looking light oak dining table layered with dust sat in the middle of the room, surrounded by hard-backed chairs. Two tall oak cupboards stood against the other wall.

"Proper dining hall, then."

"Be very draughty."

Below the step on the far side of the table the ceiling was a little lower, and in front of a faded floral cretonne-covered sofa and armchair, their seat cushions well used and sunken, a wood-burning stove crouched in a deep, brick-built inglenook with snug leather-covered brick benches built into either side. A dull brass hood rose into the wide chimney above it and a long-unpolished brass scuttle beside it held a shovel, a blackened poker, and some tongs. A pile of browning newspapers lay heaped up near the hearth beside a basket full of shavings, boxes of matches and one or two rough-hewn pieces of log. A small-screened, old-fashioned-looking television sat on a low table facing the armchair.

At one side of the fireplace sunlight spilled in through a low, arched doorway where wide steps led down. There didn't seem to be another door. She looked around, frowning. "How do you get upstairs?"

"Hm?" Andy was studying the open photograph album. "Suppose this is his wife? Must have been missing her, poor old chappie. Good looking fellow, by the looks of it, in his younger days."

"How do you –" Valerie tried again, but she had found the door. "I thought this was a cupboard! I thought this was a cupboard, look, Andy! That's clever!"

Andy glanced round. "Hm. Shall we finish the downstairs first?"

The steps beneath the arch led down from the sitting room into a medium-sized sunshine-filled kitchen with an iron grate at one end in a blue-and-white-tiled surround. The window at the back was a modern one, and rather ugly. He examined it carefully. "At least they haven't used UVPC."

Though the cupboards and units fitted around the walls were not to Valerie's taste, being a rather gaudy yellow, they did add to the glowing effect in the room. There was a small range, though a Rayburn, not an Aga, but she didn't mind that; presumably they would operate pretty much the same. The old man had left three pots of pelargoniums on the windowsill. They looked dead, but she half-filled up the kettle and watered them just in case it might bring them back to life.

Outside the door at the opposite side to the grate, a tiny cloakroom lead off from a shelf-lined storage and cluttered utility room where an ironing board stood at the ready, and a small washing machine and a refrigerator huddled beneath a laden worktop. This finally led to a porch where a pair of large, cobwebby Wellington boots and some walking sticks were standing in the corner.

They walked out into a small, cobbled courtyard, where an espaliered peach tree grew against one mellow, rosy-golden brick wall of what proved to be the promised workshop, complete with old-fashioned tools and a carpenter's bench, dusty and redolent of resinous wood chippings. An old and somewhat dilapidated lean-to greenhouse with an earthen floor stood at one side of a splintery potting shed. The overgrown lawn stretched out between gnarled fruit trees towards a containing fringe of small trees and shrubbery.

Andy scratched his head. "So where's this garage, then?"

She pointed to a flint-built green-roofed building at the side. "I imagine that's it."

He looked puzzled. "How do you get to it, then?"

She had wandered off. "Apple. Pear – and, oh, look, he's got a weeping cherry, and I think this is a medlar! A medlar, Andy! How amazing!" She tootled round slowly happily mentally listing the visible contents of the garden whilst he headed off to look at the garage.

Another apple tree. Raspberries. Gooseberry bushes. Plum. Her heart was racing a little bit. Oh, yes. Oh, yes, I like this very much.

He came back smiling. "Only a single garage, but it seems watertight."

"How do you get to it, then?"

"There's a gate at the side; must be a drive or a lane running up. We must have missed it. I'll go and have a look from that side."

"I'm going upstairs," she called after him.

A narrow, twisting stair led up from the hidden doorway to a small landing where more shelving laden with books had been built between the wooden architectural struts. The same faded apricot carpet ran throughout. There were two little bedrooms at the front, each with a small leaded window and a hand basin, then a bathroom and a separate lavatory, basic and a bit shabby but white, which should please Susie, and at the back a much larger room, low ceilinged but sunny. It had no en-suite though.

It looked as if the old man had used one of the smaller rooms. The bed in the main room was neatly made, whereas the left hand room at the front had a single bed in it, more roughly thrown over. A torch, an empty medicine bottle, a small radio and a couple of books stood on the bedside table, and a chequered woollen dressing gown hung on the back of the door. All the bedrooms had wooden wardrobes built in; he'd probably made them himself, in his workshop. Poor lonely old man; she felt so sorry for him.

Imagine, if I had no Andy.

On impulse she threw open the back bedroom window and called to him. "Andy?"

Oh, I would miss him so.

Would the Master and Mistress approve of it, then?" Martha had a sardonic twinkle in her eye.

Valerie nodded enthusiastically. "Ooh, I think so, yes; it's got a lot of character."

"Out of the question, I suppose, is it?"

She sighed. "Oh, yes. Well, no – Well, I don't know. It's a lot more than Susie and Ollie said we could spend and it's quite likely to go for even more if someone comes along with money to do it up."

"Look, I promised Margie I'd pop over to see her today." Martha glanced at her watch. "I'll be going in an hour or so, they have tea about four. What's Andy doing? Come with me and see Mr Cotton, Val."

"Ooh, I don't know."

"He'd like some new visitors, I'm sure. He's very devoted, but his wife sleeps a lot now; he probably gets very bored. He used to be a Spitfire pilot with the RAF; he loves to chat about that. Andy might find him interesting."

"Hm..." Valerie considered the prospect as she picked up her handbag. "I'll see what Andy says; we might well do that. Yes."

They hovered in the entrance hall. Andy was clearly feeling a bit awkward. "We're not going to stay long, are we? Are you sure he'll want to see us?"

"Well, I don't know, but Martha said so." She nudged him as a weary-looking bottle-blonde woman emerged from a room from which came the blare of a television and the clatter of crockery. She was wearing big hoop earrings and a pale blue hand-knitted jumper patterned by what was possibly a circle of prancing reindeer, though they could have been puppies. Valerie smiled hopefully at her. "Mr and Mrs Bryce, Andrew and Valerie? We've come to see Mr Cotton. Martha – Mrs Porter – said it would be all right to come. "

"Our Sam!" The woman smiled toothily. "Ah, yes, he's just gone into the communal room. Teatime, you see. Yes, come on; come on through." They followed her back into the room that she had just vacated. Valerie found herself fascinated by the pattern on her jumper. From the back, the prancing figures appeared to be dolphins.

Most of the occupants were distributed in groups of between two and four about small Formica-covered tables which had been set up in the centre of the room, though a few dozed or stared at a large television screen from an ill-matched assortment of armchairs pushed back against the walls. The blonde woman twinkled. "They do like their tea and bickies! Though we have a special treat today, cook's made some ginger cake." She glanced over her shoulder flirtatiously at Andy. "Who knows, we may even be able to rustle you up a little slice!"

Valerie sniffed. The room smelled of cabbage, over-boiled potatoes and disinfectant rather than of freshly baked ginger cake. It was very depressing.

Mr Cotton proved to be one of those sharing a table. His companions were another elderly man who was solemnly masticating a rather dry-looking slice of cake, and a thin, upright, very wrinkled old lady, who seemed to have given up. Her plate and the table around it were all covered in crumbs. Valerie, who was nearest to her, couldn't help noticing that she smelled very strongly of wee. She gave the lady her best smile when she glanced up, to make up for noticing.

Mr Cotton put down his teacup unevenly on the saucer and stood up at once when they reached him. He was a short, neat man with wispy grey hair and a moustache that might once have been sandy, and pale blue watery eyes. "How very kind of you to come." He had an extremely nice voice, like the Blackwells: very educated. "Martha told me you might be good enough to call. Will you have some tea?"

It was when he went across to the tea urn that his age became more apparent. Wearing down-at-heel carpet slippers, he shuffled rather than walked. He had a slight stoop and his hands, when he came back carrying the cups and saucers, trembled noticeably. He insisted on making another trip to fetch them some of the famous cake, too, which made Valerie feel very guilty. After all his efforts, it was beholden upon them to look as if they were enjoying it, but the cake was indeed very dry and clearly mass-produced, the kind of thing Valerie occasionally used for trifles, and it had been standing on the shelf for far too long, surely far past its sell-by date. Even Andy struggled with it, and he did like cake.

"And how are you getting on here, Mr Cotton? Are you finding it comfortable?" Valerie asked, trying to do her best with it. The tea was stewed, too. He chuckled.

"Oh, it's not too bad, you know, saves me driving back and forth – not too good with the old eyesight these days, unfortunately! I have got my own room, of course, next door to Mary's, so that is rather nice. Would you like to see it? Yes. Yes, come and say hello to her, she'd like that. Yes, do." He rose with some alacrity, so they left their cups and followed him compliantly out of the dining room and into a small lift.

Mary Cotton was plainly asleep when he knocked softly and opened a door on the second floor. "Ah." He closed it again gently with a finger to his lips. "Ah. We won't disturb her, if you don't mind. An ex-colleague of hers called to see her this morning and it has quite tired her out. She used to be a University Lecturer, you know, yes, in Political Studies. She likes to see an old face from the past."

Political Studies? Valerie was very impressed. And look at the poor thing now. What's she come to? We really ought to count our blessings. Life is a funny thing.

He led them into the adjoining room. Just as at *Penny Cottage*, books, photographs and bits and pieces covered every available surface and were piled up next to the bed, but here a big reproduction oil painting of a World War II aeroplane took pride of place above a high chest of drawer. Andy, who had been primed by Valerie, gratefully picked up the cue. He pointed at the oil painting. "Is that *The Darlington Spitfire,* sir?"

Mr Cotton's face lit up. "You recognise it, Mr Bryce?"

Andy nodded fervently. "I do, I do! I believe you were a Spitfire Pilot, sir. My father was a pilot too; he used to talk a lot about Sergeant Kingaby, was it? Was it 92 Squadron he was in?"

"Kingaby! Lord, yes, Sergeant Kingaby! 92 Squadron, was it?" Mr Cotton frowned. "92? Now let me see..." He lowered himself stiffly into one of the only two armchairs and Andy settled comfortably in the other. Valerie perched herself awkwardly on the side of the bed as Mr Cotton stared up at the oil painting, tilted his head contemplatively and drew in a long, whistling breath "Well, now – !"

A ndy, we never mentioned *Penny Cottage!*" She clicked her tongue, suddenly realising, as they drove home.

"Why, is that what we went there for?"

"We should have mentioned it; it was good of him to let us go and look round."

"Enjoyed that, actually. What a very interesting man. Fascinating. Might call again. Like to have a chat with him again some time. Might go again next week."

"You seemed to be getting on like a house on fire." She stared reflectively through the side window. "I wouldn't like to be in a Home, Andy. You won't put me in a Home one day, will you?"

"I will if you don't behave yourself."

"That woman said they were going to have a little sing-song later, and a nice game of bingo. Can't think of anything worse."

Chapter 11

Andy paid a few short visits to Sam Cotton, but it was Martha who conveyed the news. "Hi, Val, it's me. Don't know if it'll make any difference, but –"

Valerie found Andy up in the storage part of the attic rummaging through the stored bags and boxes. "I'm looking for my father's service record and his discharge papers," he told her, "And I've got a log book of his somewhere. Thought I'd take it along to show Sam Cotton."

She leaned over a dusty crossbeam, excited. "Andy, I've just had Martha on the phone."

"Can't see them. Have we got another box we keep them in?"

She pointed at an old, battered Gladstone bag in the far comer. "Well, there's that."

Clambering over, he opened it. "Ah, yes, think this is the one!"

"I've just been talking to Martha."

"Hm?" He withdrew a battered and faded photograph. "Well, I'll be blowed, me and old Duffy Roberts outside Montgomery Barracks in Kladow when we were doing our National Service! Didn't know I'd got that." Shaking his head nostalgically, he rummaged in the bag again.

"Apparently, Mr Cotton told her that he'd liked us very much, and he said –" She sighed. He clearly wasn't listening. "He said he'd give us a million pounds."

He nodded vaguely. "Hm. That's good."

She clicked her tongue crossly. "Andy! This is important. Listen!"

He looked up, frowning. "I *am* listening; go on."

"Well, you seem to have made a hit with him! If it's us, he's willing to take an offer lower than what the Estate Agent said. Four hundred and ten, Andy!"

"Ah, no, no, it wouldn't be fair to do that!" He bent back over the bag.

Goodness only knew when those bags and boxes had been opened last. "You're going to get dust right up your nose, you know," she told him fretfully. "You'll have your rhinitis back if you're not careful." After a moment, realising that she had lost his attention again, she withdrew regretfully.

Susie didn't rule the possibility out of hand when Valerie went back downstairs and found her. "That's a good price. At least, I assume it is, from what you've told me."

Valerie felt her hopes stirring. "Oh, I think you'd like it; it's a dear little cottage – and it's available as soon as we like. Might you and Ollie like to have a look at it, do you think?"

Susie shrugged. "Maybe. I'll see."

It was a week before Ollie managed to find the time to look.

"And you like it, do you, Nana?" He asked as he sat down afterwards and pulled on his cycling boots. Henry rose at once and crossed over to him, his huge tail wagging. He pushed his huge nose away. "No, Henry, I'm not taking you!"

She switched on the food disposal unit and waited while it growled and gobbled up the remains of his supper, couscous and salad and a nice little fillet of Sea Bass. "I thought it was very nice." She wiped nervously round the sink. "I mean, what did you think?"

He ruminated. "Not bad, not bad at all. 'Course, we'd have to have a survey. But you'd be happy, there, you think, you and Andy?"

She squeezed the dishcloth, trying not to get too excited. "Oh, yes, I'm sure we would."

He stood up, stretched, shook his feet and made towards the door, nudging aside Henry. "Stay, Henry, Stay! Back in an hour or so, Nana, maybe an hour and a half. Susie should be back about ten. You'll be all right with the children, will you, till then?"

She waved the dishcloth. "Yes, yes, we'll be fine. Take care, now, on these lanes, won't you? They get very dark at night."

"Hah-hah." He didn't like that, she could tell. Must smack of nannying. He vanished quickly into the hall, calling back as he strode through. "I'll give the surveyor a bell in the morning, get him to go ahead."

Valerie nervously studied Susie's expression, watching her carefully for clues. "Uh-huh... No. NO! Oh, but, Ollie – Mm. No." Catching her eye, Susie put her hand over the receiver. "I have tied the gate up, but would you mind just popping out, Mum, and checking that Thomas and Henry are still in the garden? Can't hear him shouting. I dared him to go anywhere near the swimming pool."

Valerie sighed, eavesdropping frustrated. Damn. "Okay."

They were fine, chasing each other round one of the paddocks. She repeated the warning about the swimming pool, then, panting, made her way back and into the kitchen, where Susie was on the perennial hunt for car keys. "Keys, keys, keys..."

Impatient to know the outcome, Valerie took the bull by the horns. "So? Well? What did the survey say?"

Susie frowned. "Um..."

Valerie's hopes floundered. "Oh."

Susie upended the fruit bowl. "Damn. Where the hell have I put them?"

"I don't know. Where did you see them last?"

"I'm supposed to be picking Poppy up from riding in ten minutes." She darted to the hall door. "Might have left them upstairs."

By the time she had found the keys on top of the laundry basket in Thomas' bedroom, there was no time left to talk. By the time she came back, almost two and a half hours later, Valerie had mended a scratch on Thomas' knee with one of his special coloured dinosaur plasters, soothed his tears, prepared and fed the three of them with steak-and-kidney pie and apple crumble for their supper, filled the dishwasher, fed Henry, got Thomas into bed, put another load in the washing machine, cleared up the mess of toys in the family room, sorted out a pile of ironing for the morning – hers and Andy's, an Ironing Lady came in now to do all the rest – and Oliver was back. She heard his taxi turning in the drive just before the Discovery.

Susie bustled in first laden with carrier bags and breathless. "Sorry, sorry! I had to wait after all and then one of Poppy's friend's mothers had rung the stable to say she couldn't get there to pick her up so I drove her home, and it was miles away in Eastham and then I remembered I'd forgotten the dog food and the soya milk this morning and I needed some other things, too, so I thought I might as well nip into Waitrose and –"

"Darling?" Ollie called impatiently from the back door, interrupting the flow. "Are you coming?" Hearing his voice, Henry lurched to his feet and darted excitedly towards the door. Ollie sounded full of beans. "Yes, Henry, yes, Go on then, fetch your lead!"

"I'm just going for a short walk with him, Mum." Susie pulled on a jacket. "You don't mind getting Poppy into bed and checking that she doesn't carry on reading in bed for too long, do you? Maybe just pop up again in half an hour or so if we're not back."

Valerie called after her, "Susie? What did the survey say?" – but she had gone.

She and Ollie were at the conservatory table with an open bottle of wine between them when Valerie came back wearily downstairs an hour later after turning off Poppy's light for the second time. "My goodness, she does love her reading, doesn't she? There's hardly room in her bed for books."

Ollie looked across with a slightly strained smile. "Well, it's good news, Nana."

Her heart leapt up again. "Is it?"

"Yes. The survey was – " He hesitated. "Well, there were a few things that'll need attention, but on the whole, it's in, um, well, quite good shape. Listed, of course. Did you know it was built about 1660?"

"As old as that? Oh, my goodness me!"

Susie jumped up animatedly. "Anyway, we can go ahead now. Isn't that exciting!"

Valerie was elated. "It is, it is, we were getting worried! We were beginning to think we'd have to rent after all or move a lot further afield." She made excitedly for the door. "I'll just go and tell your Dad. He'll be ever so relieved."

He was, at first, before he started worrying. He came back with her and had a glass of Ollie's wine to celebrate. Ollie raised a toast: "Well, here's to your new home! Cheers!" and they all clinked glasses happily. It was all very jolly. "And to our new home, of course, too, hah-hah!"

"I'd get on with booking your furniture removers straight away, Mum," Susie said, once the excitement had died down. "Ours are coming down from London. I don't know how busy removal companies are down here."

Ollie nodded. "I'd get three estimates, Nana."

Andy looked doubtful. "If we can find three – don't know, at this time of the year."

"Of course, you might still have to rent for a while." Susie shrugged nonchalantly, reaching for the wine bottle.

Valerie frowned, puzzled. "Oh? Why?"

"Well, think about it. The completion date on this is the twenty-fourth of next month. That's only four weeks away now."

Ollie nodded. "I'll hurry them up, of course, as best I can, with the legal side of things and see if they'll cooperate on the date, but it doesn't allow a great deal of time. As Susie says, you might want to think about finding a short-term lease, or maybe even a hotel for a week or two or three. Have a bit of a holiday, perhaps? Where do you fancy, Andy? Nice bit of sunshine. Bermuda? Mauritius? A cruise? Why don't you pop over to Oz?"

"'Pop over to Oz'!" Andy growled later, when they had retired to the little sitting room. "Ridiculous! This move alone is going to cost a bloody fortune. What does he think we are? Made of money?"

She shook her head. "Oh, he was just being expansive, love, he doesn't realise. He assumes that as he's providing us with a house, we're free to spend the money from our old one; he's no idea what it's like living on a small pension."

The creases about Andy's nose and mouth were getting deeper; his shoulders were getting hunched. She sighed.

She knew the signs: he was going into a real grump. He opened the wood burner with an exaggerated shiver and reached for some logs. "Bloody cold in here! And these are still wet. Bloody hell." Slamming the glass fire door shut, he sank grouchily back in his chair. "Money going out like water. And what happens if it all goes wrong, eh? Tell me that."

She tried to make light of it, hoping to cheer him. "Then we'll live in a caravan or something. Who knows, it might be fun!"

Her efforts didn't work. He looked like a little black cloud, hardly spoke again that evening, snored badly that night and passed wind loudly when he was in the bathroom, always signs that he was in a bad mood.

He slouched out into the garden after a silent breakfast. She couldn't find him at first when she went out to look. After a long search, though, she caught sight of him, a distant, forlorn-looking figure, at the bottom of the lower paddock. She made her way down towards him. He was on their special seat, silently staring out over the fields and hills.

She sat down quietly beside him. After a long time, he took her hand. It was always nice when he came back to normal. She leant against him, resting her head on his shoulder. "Hm."

"I like this house." He sounded like a little boy.

"I know you do."

"Don't want to leave it."

"No. Nor do I."

They shared the view and the cooing of pigeons and the cawing of rooks in the trees for a while and then she lifted up her head. "It'll be nice to have a house that's just ours, though, just the two of us again, won't it?"

He sounded a little ratty again. "It won't *be* ours, will it?"

"No, but you know what I mean."

After a while, he frowned again. "It worries me a bit, though, you know, Val. It's all been a bit of a rush. At least with this one I know I shouldn't have to worry about things going wrong or needing replacing. Everything's been done, top notch, too. The boiler at the new place looked a bit ancient. Wish I'd had a better look round for damp."

"Oh, the surveyor would have picked it up if it was anything major, and there's bound to be some damp in such an old place. 1660! Think about it, Andy." She loved the thought herself. Imagine all the people who've been living there! Over three hundred years old! What kind of lives did they lead? What did they wear? What were they all like?

He shook his head gloomily. "Going to need a hell of a lot of maintenance. There's re-thatching alone."

"When it comes to it."

"It'll cost us a fortune over time, you know."

She held onto his warm hand tightly. It was very comforting. "Hm."

"Hm..." He squinted into the middle distance. "And the oil tank looked extremely rusty, too."

It was all a bit of a headache, though, of course. They did manage to find three removal companies who were prepared to come round and give a quote, but Valerie had a terrible shock when the estimates came in and Andy nearly blew a gasket. "Good God! Good God! Good God!" was all that he could say. Needless to say, they chose the cheapest one. She spent a long time in the kitchen with her little account book after Andy had gone to bed.

The next urgent matter was finding somewhere to live temporarily. Renting a flat or a house by the week or just for one month was out of the question. Ordinary rentals were bad enough, but they'd be looking at holiday lets, which were hugely expensive. The date set for completion on *Penny Cottage* was for a month after they were going to have to vacate, which meant that the furniture would have to be put into storage, then brought out again and delivered when the time came. "Four weeks at... Plus the actual removal... " Valerie's headache became a permanent thing and her account book got to look quite dog-eared.

Martha tried very hard to help; Val was extremely grateful. "Martha's so good, you know, Andy. She had such a good idea: we could rent *Penny Cottage* just till everything's gone through. She put it to Mr Cotton."

Andy looked up hopefully. "And?"

Val sighed. "He said no."

"Ah." Disappointed, he returned glumly to his perusal of the local paper.

"He was ever so apologetic, Martha said, but he wanted to feel he could pop in and out and take his time about clearing things out, deciding what to keep. Old things, you know. His wife's things. Important things. Memories."

"Ah. Mm. Of course." He shrugged. "Shame."

Tears swam into Val's eyes. Poor Mr Cotton. "It's understandable. We can't push him."

"No, no."

"He's been very good."

"He has."

Martha also offered to have them to stay for as long as they needed and so did Nick, which was very kind of them.

"Do you want to do that?" Andy asked doubtfully.

She sighed. "Oh, I don't know. A month's an awful long time, even two weeks if we did it half-and-half. You know what they say about visitors; they're like fish. After three days they start to, you know, stink."

He was looking very anxious and careworn. "What do you want to do, then?"

"It'd be different if we were staying with Norma and Leon, they're like family." She hesitated. "D'you fancy going up to Wales?"

Glynogol felt like somewhere they were just exploring on an outing. It held no real draw any more for them at all.

"It hasn't changed much."

"Did you expect it to have?"

"I did, somehow."

"What, did you expect them to have had a what-you-call-it, a Debenhams or something, moving in?"

They cruised slowly through the town towards Leon and Norma's, scanning the passing shops. Closed. Boarded up. Oxfam. Computer repairs. New Look. The British Cat Society. A fluorescent sign: 'Grab-Yourself-A-Bargain'. She pointed. "That's new." Closed. Threshers. "No, nothing new." She sighed. "Well, you never know, they might have done."

"Haven't spotted anyone we know, have you?"

"No."

"Feel a bit like a stranger."

She chuckled. "Yes, me, too."

It was lovely spending time with Norma and Leon again. Norma had planned an extra special meal for their first evening and the wine flowed from the moment they entered the front door. They sat in the kitchen for ages, but then Norma shoed them out to sit at the dining table whilst she finished off this and that. It was good to get things off their chests. Naturally, they had told them everything.

"Maybe we should have kept the house up here, rented it out instead of selling it," Andy said at last, morosely.

Val rolled here eyes. "I suggested that, Andy."

"No, you didn't."

She was stung. "I did! Would you like to rent it out instead? I said."

He shrugged. "I don't remember that."

"Well, I did! No, you said. Too many worries about maintenance, things going wrong – having to come up here every time."

"Susie might have liked it one day."

Leon frowned. "Would she want to live in the Glyn?"

"I wouldn't think so."

"Well, then."

"Point taken."

"What point?"

"Well..." Leon hesitated, frowning. "What was I trying to say?"

"Um... You were saying... What were you saying?" Andy shook his head. "What was he saying, Val?"

"I've lost me fread. Come on, you're younger than me, help me, Val. What was I saying?"

She had no idea.

"My brain doesn't work any more." Leon shook his head dolefully. "D'you know, I can't stand the pace any more either. Boozing like this – I can't do it any more. Do you remember when we used to be able to stay up all night nattering? Get up and do a day's work afterwards?"

Andy shook his head sorrowfully. "Can't drink like I used to, not any more."

Valerie narrowed her eyes. *You give it a pretty good try.*
"So how old are you now, Leon?" Andy asked, reaching
clumsily across the table for the almost-empty bottle of
wine.
"Seventy-one. What are you?"
"How old am I, Val? Um – seventy-three. I'm seventy-
three, aren't I? No, tell a lie, I'm two years older than Val so
I'm seventy-two. Seventy-three next February."
"God, are you really? You're really old, aren't you? How
did you get so old?" Leon reached for a new bottle of wine
from the sideboard behind him. "Alright with Rioja this
time?"
Andy smacked his lips. "Lovely, my son!"
"What happened to our youth?" Leon sank back into
his chair with a theatrically mournful moan. "I want to
be young again! I want to be young like you, Norma!" he
added plaintively, catching Norma's eye as she bustled
in from the kitchen carrying a tureen of soup. "She's the
baby; she's only sixty five, you know."
"Sixty five? Do you mind? I'm only sixty four. Well, then,
are we ready to eat?" Norma scanned the table carefully.
"Leon, you haven't put out the salt and pepper! Will you
fetch them, please? And bring in some fresh wine glasses.
Honestly, call yourself a butler!"
He looked bemused. "I don't!"
"Don't what?"
"Call myself a butler!"
She rolled her eyes. "That's your role, Leon, that's your
role! I've cooked the meal, you see to the table and the
wine. Hurry up; the soup will be going cold. Salt, pepper,
glasses, some more wine." She glanced at Valerie. "Do you
want red or white, love?"
"Ooh, it doesn't matter." She was already feeling woozy
and was conscious that, tongue loosened by the flowing
wine, she had already said more than she really wanted to
about the move and about Susie and Ollie and everything.
No point in getting Andy all upset worrying that she was
worrying. Better to put on a brave face. Fortunately, he
was still smiling fuzzily; the more wine he had, the deafer
he seemed to get.
"White, please." She waved a hand, undecided. "Ooh,

I don't mind!" and then startled herself by giving a loud hiccup.

Leon returned bearing the cruet and a bottle of Cabernet Sauvignon. "Three for two at Asda," he told Andy with a twinkle in his eye. "Like the Rioja. You might want to take some back with you, my son!"

"Leon, you still haven't brought fresh wine glasses!" Norma returned bearing a tureen as he sat down. "What is he like, I ask you?"

Valerie chuckled. She had missed their bickering. At least with Norma and Leon, you knew they were only joking, only teasing each other. Not like Susie and Ollie. She hiccupped once again, this time more loudly. "Oh dear."

Leon eyed her thoughtfully. "Did I ever tell you about the time that Norma threw the dinner all over me?" he asked, picking up his soup spoon. "I mean, she was in a terrible mood, I mean, really terrible, and I only asked if she'd got a touch of PMT, that's all!"

"'What do you mean?' she asked, and her little eyes were like, like –" He demonstrated, waving his spoon and narrowing his eyes dangerously; "you know – like two beams of concentrated fury. 'I was only asking,' I said.

"'No, Leon,' she said, 'I am not premenstrual. As you well know, that kind of thing has not affected me for a long time now. What nasty little female hormones I have left are perfectly under control, thank you for asking.' And she stormed out, thump, thump, thump!" He thumped with his feet on the floor. "Thump, thump! And she slammed the door, really slammed it. The whole house shuddered. Well! I thought I'd better do something. I washed up: immaculate! Emptied the bin and washed the kitchen floor, then I went to find her. 'Hello,' I said – you know, all nice, all sweetness and light..."

He leant towards Norma, his voice taking on a childlike, obsequious note. "'Hello, are you feeling better? I've been a very good boy; I've even washed the kitchen floor for you."

"Well, she turned round and her eyes were like, you know..." He narrowed his own wrathfully once again. "And she said, all silky, 'For *me*? You've washed the kitchen floor for *me*?' Then she picked up the casserole and threw it at me."

Norma was laughing so much she was crying. She wiped her eyes. "It was Beef Carbonara."

"You can still see the bruise." Leon offered his cheek woefully to Andy. "Look, just here at the side."

Turning to Val as the laughter subsided, he patted her hand. "Don't worry about it, love. Susie and Ollie, they'll get over it."

They took the scenic route home rather than going down the motorways. Much as they had enjoyed it, they had both been ready to go back when the time came. Exhausted, actually. Ready for a few nice silent evenings in front of the telly and early bed with a cup of cocoa. Leon was right; they none of them could stand the pace.

After wandering round Glynogol again, even the thought of having to move again had taken on a bit of a glimmer.

"So you wouldn't want to go back?"

"To the Glyn, you mean? No, never." Andy nodded at the glove compartment. "I'll have another treacle toffee, though, please."

Valerie unwrapped one and held it out for him carefully so he needn't take his eye off the road.

"I was thinking, you know, I might start walking."

"Walking?"

"Yes, walking every morning. Get a bit fit."

"Hm, good idea." She unwrapped another one for herself. They were very more-ish. Very tasty.

He narrowed his eyes, chewing juicily. "Maybe we should both have a go with the start of our new New Life. You know, cut down on oil and butter, eat more salad. Use that stuff, whatsit – Flora, instead of butter."

Catching her sceptical glance, he shrugged, grinning. "Well, anyway, you know what I mean."

It had snowed a little in some parts. She gazed at the patchily white fields in amazement. "Early, isn't it? Very early for snow."

"Much warmer down south."

She felt smugly pleased. "Mm, yes, it is. Much warmer."

Should be lovely and warm and snug under a thatch. Dear little cottage. She shook her head. "D'you know, I always dreamed I would live someday in a cottage with a thatched roof and roses round the door."

"Did you?"

"Yes, when I was a little girl. I used to imagine it would have lovely flowers at the front and herbs and a pretty white cow in the back garden with a bell round its neck, and some white hens. A white cat, too."

"Everything white."

"Except my dress: that was always a sort of pale blue-grey and floaty. I had long, blonde hair, and big blue eyes." She sighed. "I was very beautiful."

"Well, you are. You are beautiful." He squeezed her knee, grinning, before turning back to the road and changing his tone mischievously. "So give me another toffee. Now! A fellow could bloody well starve."

Having stowed the paper bag away again in the glove compartment, and sucking contentedly, Valerie turned back to staring at the passing fields. "Strange how the snow is lying on some fields and not on others."

He was lost in his own thoughts now, not listening. "Mm?"

"I said it's strange how the snow lies on some fields more than others."

"I don't know."

"Wasn't asking. Just wondering."

"Wondering what?"

She had forgotten. "I don't know. What were you asking?"

Chapter 12

They arrived in Hetherfield before the removers' lorry and parked at the side of the cottage. Andy got out, stretching. "Well, here we are, then! Not a bad run. Expected a few hold-ups on the A34. Have we got anything to eat?"

Valerie gathered together her handbag and her mac. "Only another treacle toffee. I told you we should have stopped somewhere for lunch!"

"Didn't want them to get here before us."

"Have you got the keys?"

She jangled them triumphantly. "Of course!"

They stood together at the front door. "Ready?" she said teasingly, holding the key poised.

He sighed. "Come on, open it up. I want to have a good look round before they bring the furniture in."

In retrospect, it might have been better if the removers had beaten them to it; at least, it would have been if, of course, they had had a key. With everything brought in before he got there, Andy might not have noticed the state of the plastering straight away. As it was, his shoulders got more hunched and the lines around his mouth grew deeper with every step that he trod. "Bloody hell." She could hear him swearing to himself as he stalked heavily above her head exploring the bedrooms. At last he shouted to her. "Val? Come here, Val. Come here and look at this."

"Coming!" She tore herself away from poking gingerly at the big patch of black something-or-other that she could see stretching up behind the book shelving now that the books had all been taken away. As far as she could see for the layer of grey dust, the wooden skirting board at the bottom was crumbling. It certainly smelled of mould.

He's going to say it's rising damp, I know he is.

He met her on the stairs coming down as she was going up, and snarled. "Go and have a look. Main bedroom. Bloody hell. Talk about cowboys."

"Where are you going?"

"Need something – a stick or something – to knock."

The bedroom looked all right to her – a bit shabby, maybe, needed a lick of paint, and the plaster of the sloping ceiling did look a bit wonky in one corner, but she didn't study it in any detail; she was drawn instead to the view out to the back. The window opened easily enough and she leant out, resting her arms on the sill. It was cold, the air, but that didn't matter. Do it good, to air the room a little bit. Great deal of work to do, but lots of potential. A border, maybe two, leading up to the back? Fancy, having a medlar! You had to leave them on the tree till they were frosted and rotten or something; she'd have to look it up.

"Val?"

She looked around hastily. "Um, what?"

"Here, in the corner, look. The aerial lead." She crossed to where he was pointing. "Must have had a chest or something there that the television sat on, and now it's been taken away. Wish I'd seen that before. See that?" "That' was a gaping seven-or-eight inch hole through which the aerial lead protruded. Crumbling plaster lay scattered beneath it on the floor. "Whoever did that wants shooting." He began to prod at the ceiling with the tip of the cane. Flakes of plaster started falling. Valerie squeaked, alarmed. "Oh, Andy, don't do that!"

"We'll have to get a plasterer in before that ceiling falls down," he muttered over his shoulder as she followed him downstairs. "It'll be beyond me. Need a specialist, somebody who knows lime plaster."

"Lime plaster?"

"Wattle and daub, it's special plaster. We may need permission from the Planning Department, too, dunno. Listed building again, isn't it?"

She almost said it herself this time. *Oh, bloody hell.*

She stood in the hallway admiring the old oak beams and struts as he went through to the sitting room. Better to leave him alone. "It's all very pretty, though, isn't it?" she said cheerily when he came back through, hoping that he hadn't looked behind the bookshelves.

He had. "That is hardly the point."

She felt strangely stretched out, rattled. "Well, I like it. It's a dear little cottage."

He was tight -lipped. "Well, jolly good for you."

They'd both feel better once they'd eaten something. "I wonder where Jarman & Sons have got to. Shall we give them a ring?"

"Have they put the phone line back on?"

"They said they would. Did you give them this number or our mobile?"

"Can't remember."

"Where's their number?"

"I don't know; you had it."

"No, I didn't, you did!"

They were saved from further argument by the heavy grinding of tyres and a male voice shouting. Valerie glanced out of the front window. "They're here!"

Andy craned over her shoulder. "Where have they pulled up? Oh, not in the road!"

"Well, where did you expect them to park?"

"Not blocking the road." He opened the door, but he was too late; they were already downloading. The first two men were making their way through the gate bearing packing cases.

"Afternoon. These are marked 'kitchen', mate."

They'd be wanting tea! She'd forgotten about that. She tugged at Andy's jacket sleeve. "Andy, I'll have to go and see if I can borrow some teabags and stuff from some-body," she hissed.

"Can't you go to the village shop?"

"There isn't one. Pretend you can't find the kettle. Take your time looking for the mugs and things, please."

She trotted as quickly as she could to the next cottage, but there was nobody at home, or at the one on the other side, where a dog yapped frantically when she rang the bell. "Sh, sh! Oh, dear!"

The other houses were right up by the Church, except for two white cottages set back much further up the side drive. She made her way up towards them as fast as she was able, but she was getting breathless and her legs ached badly. No one, anywhere, was at home.

Andy and the removal men were sitting round the newly-installed dining table in the hall and leisurely drinking tea when she breathlessly staggered in. "Oh."

Andy raised his mug. "They brought their own, love." He was looking a lot more cheerful now; always did enjoy a spot of male bonding.

"We brought our own, love." The foreman nodded, holding up a large mug with 'HIS' emblazoned on it. "Emergency rations."

"Oh."

Andy sipped appreciatively from a red and white mug bearing the emblem of Liverpool Football club. "Thought you'd gone to India for it."

Feeling suddenly exhausted, she looked round for a chair. "Nobody in anywhere." They'd put an armchair that she'd marked down for the front sitting room in this room instead. She sank into it gratefully. Never mind.

"Lovely cottage, Madam," the foreman said, blowing onto his tea. "Very atmospheric."

She felt proprietarily pleased. "It was built in 1660, you know."

He shook his head in amazement. "Was it really?"

"Don't think anybody's done much to maintain it over the years. Needs a lot doing to it," Andy muttered disparagingly.

The foreman shook his head gloomily. "You'd be surprised what I've seen. Some people don't."

Valerie felt huffily defensive of Mr Cotton. "The previous owner was a very old man. His wife was an invalid."

The foreman nodded. "Seen a bit of history, though, eh?"

Andy pushed back his chair. "Do you want some tea, love? Have we got any more mugs? No, don't worry." He drained his mug. "Don't worry, you can use mine."

She felt better once she'd had a drop of tea.

The foreman grinned sympathetically as he got up and

stretched. "Well, better get on. The tallboy, love? Which room is it going in?"

"The front right hand bedroom, please. I'll be with you in a minute." She gulped the rest of her tea rapidly. "Why have they put this chair in here, Andy? We decided we wanted it by the fire in the other room."

"Dunno. I tell you what, though – our bed's going to be impossible to get up those narrow stairs. This room's going to get bloody cold in winter, too, I can tell you that, without a door. And have you see those radiators? Bloody ancient."

He stood up, and instead of being stiff and hunched, his shoulders drooped. He looked very tired. "What the hell was that surveyor playing at, Val?" he asked her quietly. "We've bought a pig in a poke. Well, Oliver has."

She hesitated. "It'll be all right, love."

He grimaced doubtfully. "Will it?"

It had to be. "I promise you it will."

He was silent for a moment, then he shrugged. "Okay."

Once the removers had left, it all looked, as Andy described it rattily, 'Like a right tip!' The main sitting room was heaped with boxes still to be unpacked and pieces of furniture that so far had no home, so that though it grew cold as the evening wore on and this time there were logs to be found in the garden, they couldn't get at the fireplace, so they had to do without. The downstairs rooms felt clammily chill. According to Andy, the cottage had been constructed directly onto the ground and they could feel the cold rising. He managed to get the boiler going, so that was all right, though the ancient radiators didn't throw out much heat. Valerie made hasty plans for some nice, heavy door curtains.

They were very hungry by the end of the day, especially Andy. "Don't feel like a pub."

"No, nor do I. I can't be bothered to change."

"We'd better go and shop." He eyed her hopefully. "But you don't want to be having to cook..."

She shook her head firmly. "No, I don't."

"Oh." He shrugged, disappointed. "So what do you want to do, then? Get a take-away?"

"I don't *mind*, lovey." She instantly regretted the sharpness of her tone. "Where from?"

"Must be a shop somewhere where we can get some butter and a loaf." He pulled on his coat and reached for the car keys. "Or better make that Flora."

"You won't like it."

"I'll give it a try. Oh!" He stepped back, startled, at the sight of an elderly woman on the doorstep with one fist raised. She dropped her arm, looking equally taken aback.

"Oh, I'm sorry! I was just about to knock."

Valerie peered round Andy's shoulder. The woman's wiry white hair was drawn up into a thin bun, and she had an intelligent, thin face and very pretty faded blue eyes. The rather stiff-looking red and blue waistcoat she was wearing over a checked blouse and dark blue woollen skirt looked hand-woven, or else it was a very stout piece of Welsh tweed. "I'm a neighbour, Lorna Sheldon," she explained in a brusque, manly voice. "Appledown Cottage: second white one, on the right."

"Hello!" Valerie stepped forward, smiling and wishing she'd run a comb through her hair. "Very nice to meet you. I'm Valerie, and this is Andy. We've just moved in."

"I know you have, that's why I'm here; I thought a few bits and bobs might come in handy. If you're anything like me, the last thing you'll want to do is to have to go off shopping after such a heavy day." She held out a wicker basket.

"Just a few bits and bobs. There's a small loaf in here and some farm butter and half-a-dozen fresh eggs from my hens – watch those, they're wrapped in newspaper, run out of egg boxes, I'm afraid. There's a homemade date-and-walnut loaf; I'm WI, you know; I keep a few ready in the freezer for the weekly sales. Perhaps you'd like to join us, Mrs Bryce, when you've settled down, we're a nice friendly little group."

She rummaged in the basket. "Oh, and a little casserole: it has been defrosted. Venison and pickled walnuts – hope you like venison. Damn: potatoes. Seem to have forgotten them."

"Oh, don't worry about them." Andy took the basket from her with alacrity. "Venison, eh?" Val smiled to herself; he was practically dribbling. "Just the job, eh, Val?"

Valerie nodded, beaming enthusiastically. "Yes, yes, indeed! That sounds very good! How very, very kind."

Andy nodded, still staring greedily into the basket. "You're quite right, we were just off hoping to find somewhere open, but we really don't feel up to it, do we, Val?"

"No, we don't! Thank you! Thank you so much!"

"I've put my phone number in there on a scrap of paper. Give me a call if you need to know anything. Sam and I are old friends." She set off briskly towards the gate and then turned back briefly. "Oh, by the way, will you want Tom to call?"

"Tom?"

"Tom is our milkman."

Valerie found the thought of having a real live milkman calling again really quite exciting. "Ooh, do we have a milkman? With proper glass bottles?"

"Most of us like to support the local Farmers' Cooperative. He sells logs and very nice honey too, and he also cleans windows in his spare time. Very handy."

Valerie sighed. This was even better than being in Lynton Stacey. Just like an Enid Blyton storybook! It was going to be a real rural idyll. "Oh, well, then, yes, please!"

Andy nodded heartily. "That's very thoughtful of you."

"Yes, indeed, yes – we're very grateful!"

Lorna Sheldon raised a hand stiffly in acknowledgement. "Neighbours are neighbours. What else are they for?"

It was just what they needed. Valerie heated the casserole up in the microwave whilst Andy cut some bread and butter and then they fell on it. As Andy had forecast, a distinct draught sneaked in under the front door and seemed to gain a further two or three degrees in iciness as it curled its way towards the dining table. They draped their knees with coats and Valerie made a mental note to fish out the picnic rug in the morning and to put some nice warm throws of some kind on their Christmas list.

"Very nice, too. We ought to get some venison, you know, Val," Andy said, pushing his plate away at last. "Did she say there was a date-and-walnut cake?"

"A date-and-walnut loaf."

"What's the difference?"

"You're supposed to eat it in slices with butter." She rose to fetch it from the kitchen. "But we'll have it without the butter, then."

"Why?"

"We've already had a lot of butter on our bread. I'll bring the Flora."

He shook his head, frowning. "No, let's have the butter."

"You were the one wanting me to get Flora."

"Yes, but you can't beat butter. Butter's very nice."

The bed frame, headboard and their mattress had all gone up the narrow staircase despite Andy's doubts. It was just as well Sebastian had been called back in to remove the bannister rails again temporarily, as they'd been able to swap beds back with Susie and Ollie; the huge one would never have made it. Mr Cotton had left the curtains up: as he had said, no point in his taking them where he was going. Valerie didn't care for the ones in the main bedroom much; they were a plain dark blue and a bit drab. It was their good fortune that the windows of Susie and Ollie's new house were much too big for the curtains from *The Bury*; they were all theirs to choose from. She fancied hanging the pretty pale blue *toile-de-joule* ones with matching linen that had been in the first guest bedroom, or maybe the lovely cream damask ones from Susie and Ollie's bedroom, if they'd fit, which was a bit doubtful without a lot of fiddling, but the dark blue ones were more than adequate for the time being.

They had had the forethought this time to make up a box of their bedding ready, so the bed was easily made. Andy brought up a bedside lamp and the small portable telly, and attached the aerial, muttering bitterly again about the hole. The telly worked, though, that was the main thing; in fact, the picture on it was very good.

With the thatch sitting over it like a tea cosy, the bedroom felt relatively snug, but it was cold in the bathroom, with no radiator and only a heated towel rail. They draped the towels over the side of the bath and hung their underwear on the rail instead, so that it would be nice and warm for the morning.

With the curtains drawn and with the glow cast by the

pale gold lampshade spilling onto the crisp white pillows, the bed looked very inviting to their weary limbs. They clambered in hastily and drew the duvet up under their chins.

"Ah, that's better!"

"Aah..."

"Hm.

"Hmmm."

"At last."

Andy, being Andy, was asleep within minutes. Valerie, though, found it impossible to settle. She'd got used to the oversised bed, and in this one she felt cramped now; Andy seemed to be taking too much room. They were facing a different way round again, which, like before, even in the dark made her feel disoriented and funny. The walls felt much closer, and the blur of moonlight delineating the rectangle of the window was on the wrong side. She had already forgotten the brick dust and the gale lashing in through the edges of the tarpaulin and had got used to the clean, fresh smell of new paint. Here, even with the window open, the air felt thicker somehow. It smelled of dust and old books and generations of wood smoke. It made her nose prickle and she began to worry if Andy had brought up his inhaler.

There were lots of strange noises, too. There had been owls to be heard at night at *The Bury* and occasionally, the barking of a fox or the high pitched squealing of a rabbit that had just become something's dinner – and, on one memorable occasion, a terrible howling and yowling which had tuned out to be the mating of two hedgehogs – so she didn't mind any more about those sorts of noises, or little settlement noises either, but here the creakings and groanings in the radiators and woodwork and strange little rustling and tapping noises from time to time seemed to combine to form a continual and disturbing symphony. She spent a long, long time lying on her back, holding her breath and staring wide-eyed into the darkness, listening and imagining things. Her brain wasn't helping, either, chattering on twenty to the dozen, and not just about potential burglars: about moving furniture, mostly.

Do we really need a dining room? The table and chairs

could go in the kitchen. Move the dresser onto the other wall – it'll look nice in the fire bit of the sitting room with the big Christening cups and Granny's plates on it. Is the ceiling high enough? How tall did we say the dresser was? She wielded an imaginary tape measure. Six foot?

At ten past three, when she saw that it had only been twenty minutes since she last looked at the clock, something skittered noisily overhead and she turned onto her back again and froze, eyes wide open, staring out once more. Whatever-it-was skittered back the other way, then round as if running in a circle with tiny clogs on. Mice in the thatch, perhaps? A bird? Not rats! This is an old house, suppose...

Forcing herself to close her eyes once more, she edged closer to Andy. She still didn't doze off properly, though. Apart from anything else, being overtired, he snored.

He was in action mode next morning, up early and dressed in his oldest trousers, with both a thin and a thick jumper over his lumberjack shirt. "Right. The first thing we'd better do today is to light the Rayburn, and then we must get that sitting room sorted and get hold of a chimney sweep."

Lighting the Rayburn wasn't too problematic; finding somewhere to put everything waiting in the cluttered sitting room was trickier. "Where are you going to put them? We need to be able to get at them."

Andy ran his fingers through his hair. "Dunno. The dining room? Not much use for anything else; too cold. Right!" He reached reluctantly for the nearest packing case. "Bloody hell, what have you put in here, Val?"

"Me?" She snapped at him, ruffled, ratty after her bad night. "Don't blame me, you packed that one. Oh, be careful!" she added as, mustering all his resources, he managed to heave the packing case off the floor. "Let me take an end!"

"I'm all right, I've got it. Right..." Moving slowly with it towards the doorway in which she was hovering, he jerked his head peremptorily. "Out of the way, Val. Get out of the blooming way!"

The day was quite satisfactory, though, in a way. They

managed between them to shift a lot of the stuff around so that the sitting room was a bit user-friendlier. Valerie rang Lorna Sheldon to ask her who her chimney sweep was, but she was out, so Andy went through the yellow pages. "This one looks all right, he's fairly local. Same code, anyway." He caught the man on his mobile and made an appointment for him to come and do it in a couple of weeks' time. "We'll have to do without a fire till then."

"Couldn't we risk it?" Valerie murmured hopefully. She had really fancied an evening by an open fire.

He drew in a whistling breath through pursed lips. "No, no, I don't trust it. You can't be too careful with a thatch. Don't know when it was last swept; Sam was a bit vague on that. He couldn't even remember the fellow's name who'd done it."

"It's funny, isn't it, really? You'd have thought he'd have been very organised and left us a detailed list, he seemed the type."

"Getting on, though, Val. Place is in such a state, I think he was just glad to get rid."

It was almost four o'clock before they decided they'd better leave the rest of the unpacking till the next day and went off to do a shop. Having had nothing since breakfast, Andy bought himself a Ginsters pasty to eat on the way home to stave off the hunger pangs. She felt she ought to remind him: "You shouldn't be eating pasties, Andy, not on your new regime."

Forgetting the regime herself, she added quite a large dollop of cream into the pork chops with cider and apples for supper, telling herself, when she remembered – well, it wouldn't be the same without.

Susie rang as she was washing the last pan: no posh dishwasher here; Valerie was surprised how much she missed it.

She sounded a bit flat. "Hi, Mum, it's me. Did the move go all right? How are you? How's it going?"

Valerie couldn't wait to tell her all about it. "Hello, darling! Oh, fine, fine! Hang on; let me dry my hands."

When she returned to the telephone, Susie was speaking sharply to someone. "You're not going out?"

"Why not?" Valerie recognised Ollie's voice, a bit further

away.

"But dinner's nearly ready! I've been slaving half the afternoon."

"I didn't know that, did I?" Brusque tone; the opening and slamming of some cupboard door.

"But you rang! You said you'd be coming home. I thought..."

Valerie couldn't pick up the next bit, just, sarcastically, "I *have* been working." Very terse indeed, the latter. Closing her eyes, she winced.

"And I've done nothing, I suppose?" Sharper, bitterer now and a bit tearful.

Something Val couldn't catch, then a door slammed. Silence. "Bastard."

Oh, no, they were off again. Twisting the coiled telephone cable nervously between her fingers, she murmured tentatively, "Hello?"

Chapter 13

Something clattered noisily by the phone and then Susie snarled again. "Bollocks."

"Pardon?" Valerie's stomach tightened further.

"Sorry, Mum. Oh, nothing. Just Ollie. Little bugger."

"Why, lovey, why? What has he done?"

"Oh, nothing, nothing. Par for the course; he's just gone out again. He was late back yesterday, and the day before it was past midnight. I know he's out tomorrow with clients, and then he's got to go to New York for the weekend. This isn't what was supposed to happen. I'm fed up with being on my own."

The ensuing prickle of anxiety really spoiled the rest of the evening.

She slept a little better that night, but not much; this time, of course, it was thoughts about Susie and Ollie that were playing on her mind. Andy seemed a bit restless, too. He was very snuffly and wheezy and his snoring reached new heights in terms of scale and range of notes. She realised eventually that some of the strange noises that were startling her were coming from his direction; if she hadn't been so tired, it might have been amusing. She wondered whether the extra wheeziness and clogginess was caused by the old carpet or perhaps – and she hoped very much it wasn't, but perhaps – something to do with the lovely thatch?

It was very cold when she got up early the next morning in search of a cup of tea. The heating wasn't due to come on for another half-hour or so, but the cool feel of the air when she opened the kitchen door took her by surprise. The Rayburn was on, all right; it felt quite warm when she laid her hand on it. She bent down stiffly and opened the works door and turned up the dial to maximum. Perhaps they'd set it a bit low.

She took her tea back up to bed in the hope that the cottage might have warmed up a bit more by the time she came back down, so Andy, rising about half an hour later, was the next one in the kitchen. He called up to her sharply from the bottom of the stairs. "Val? Can you come down here?"

She didn't want to get up again yet; she'd moved into the bit of the bed where he'd been, and it was lovely and cosy. "What? What?"

"Can you smell oil?" he asked brusquely as she shuffled half-heartedly into the kitchen.

The thick, cloying stench of the stuff filled her nostrils and she felt panic starting. "Yes indeed, I can!"

He gingerly opened the door covering the burner, then sprawled back on his heels in alarm. "Hell's Bells! Stand back, Val!" Even from where she was she could see that flickering flames were surrounding the outside of the burner.

"Oh, goodness!" Her heart jumped as he pulled himself back and reached tentatively for the control dial. "Andy, be careful!"

"I am, I am!"

"Be careful, be careful!"

"Okay, it's okay, it's off, now."

She rolled her eyes in relief. "Oh, goodness. Goodness me!"

"Now the oil's cut off, those flames should go out by themselves. Hope so, anyway; the last thing we want is a fire." He was watching them carefully, though. "Pass me that extinguisher in case."

He eyed her accusingly as she did so. "Did you turn it up? It was set right up."

She hugged her dressing gown about her guiltily. "I thought it was set too low."

The thing did die out and cool down all right eventually, but the burner was left covered in thick black carbon.

That, of course, meant a visit by the Rayburn service man who tinkered with it knowingly when he eventually came, several days later, by which time they'd found that the pub, *The Three Tuns*, didn't do a great choice of Bar Food, but very nice sandwiches.

Apparently the high fire flow rate was wrong. It also, unfortunately, had a leaking boiler. "See, if it's been standing unused for a while, the water can corrode the boiler," the Rayburn man explained. "It might be possible to get it welded, but..."

It wasn't just that boiler that needed replacing, the central heating one, too, turned out to be on its last legs. Mark Oates, the plumber whom Lorna Sheldon recommended, was very nice, small, bald and chatty, and suggested that they should replace the old Rayburn with another, perhaps second-hand if it came from a good source, of the kind which would provide all the hot water for the heating as well.

After a bit of discussions and much scribbling by Valerie in her account book, they agreed to that – it made economic sense – so it was off to a camping equipment shop to buy some sort of portable gas rings, and back to the Rayburn suppliers, who promised to see what they could do. Mark also advised that the oil pipes were a bit dodgy and that the rusty oil tank in the garden ought to go. He shook his head a lot, whistling, when he looked at it. "You'll get a huge fine, thousands, if it ever leaks into the water system." The tank installation company that he recommended promised to come soon and replace it with a modern double-skinned version and some new oil pipes.

The sweep arrived at last, but having spread dustsheets around very carefully, unpacked his gear methodically and stuck his head up the chimney, he backed away fast. "Sorry, I can't touch that, not safe. To be honest, anyone who lit a fire in that chimney would need his head examining."

"But Sam – the previous owner – said they'd had some lovely fires in here!" Valerie told him, distressed. "Roaring fires, he said!"

"I believe you, you can see they did." He beckoned with his head and pointed up the opening. "All charred that is, that wooden lintel. See? Can you see all that? Yes, they've definitely had some fires in here, and not the cosy kind, either! Look you can see where smoke has blacked all the ceiling." Val and Andy peered up with horror.

"Oh, my goodness me, yes!"

"How did I miss that?"

The chimney had to be lined and a wood-burning stove installed.

Valerie couldn't bear to open her account book: another thirty-two thousand pounds gone.

"What kind of a survey did you have done, pet?" she asked Susie on the phone late one evening. "He seems to have missed an awful lot of things. Mind you, your Dad did, too, not like him, his age, I suppose. He says you ought to sue."

"Oh, no, we can't do that." Susie was very quick off the mark.

"Why not?"

"Well, just because."

"Because what? Was it a bad survey, Susie? Did the surveyor advise against buying it?"

She was very cagey. "Well, sort of."

"So why did you let us go ahead with it, lovey?"

Susie gave a heavy sigh. "Well, we were making you move and you didn't want to rent and something had to be decided and there wasn't anything else on the horizon. And besides, well, because we knew you liked it."

"Oh, Susie . . !"

"Don't you like it, now, then?" She sounded very disappointed. Valerie hastened to reassure her.

"Oh, yes, we do, we do." She hesitated. "Well, I do, anyway. It's just the cost of it, such a lot to do..." She caught sight of Andy, mooching round, prodding at the windowsills and glowering. "Dad'll come round to it, given time."

Susie seemed relieved. "By the way, Mum did I tell you? We're going to go skiing with some friends for Christmas, hope you don't mind. What are you going to do? Have you got any plans?"

No children opening stockings this year?

"Christmas?" Valerie tried to inject a note of nonchalance into her voice. "Oh, no, no plans, but we'll be fine, don't you worry." At least it sounded as if things weren't too bad between them if they were going on holiday. "That'll be nice. Where? Who are you going with?"

"Meribel. Oh, just with some friends, you don't know them. And Camilla and her husband."

"Camilla?" She felt resentful. "So you're still seeing her, then?"

Susie sounded a little embarrassed. "It's her chalet we'll be going to, actually."

"I see."

She sniffed when she told Andy. "Feel a bit hurt. Can't blame them, of course."

"Thought they needed all the money they could get from *The Bury* for the new one?"

"Probably had a big bonus."

"Hm."

The chimney sweep wasn't going to be able to get the chimney done in time for Christmas. They would have to order the stove, anyway, before he could come, which was going to take four or five weeks.

"What are we going to do, then? Can't even cook a turkey." Andy had really been looking forward to his Christmas dinner and Valerie had been planning to take a turkey and all the trimmings including the cooking equipment with them to Susie's so that he wouldn't have to settle for nut roast. "Can't even have a nice fire."

"I hate this bloody place," he said, lying in bed that night, and uttering the words she had been dreading. "I wish we'd never moved. Why ever did I sell my lovely house?"

She didn't tell Norma that, of course, when next she rang. Norma invited them up as soon as she heard that they were going to be on their own, but she had her own family coming as well so really, all the beds would be taken, and besides, they didn't really fancy trailing all the way back to Wales so soon.

In the event, they stayed up really late and went to the midnight service at the little church, which was very atmospheric, and far warmer than the cottage, and gave

Valerie an opportunity to see what the villagers she hadn't met looked like, and then they had scrambled eggs made in the microwave and mixed with smoked salmon pieces for Christmas Day breakfast, and took them back up to bed on a tray, where they ate them whilst listening to Christmas carols on the radio. Valerie gave Andy a CD of Bryn Terfyl, a pair of brown leather gloves and a new book on English Cricket by Stephen Chalke; he gave her a pair of black boots that she'd chosen for herself and a lovely book on English Country Gardens.

In the afternoon, they went over to see Sam Cotton in the Home, and to take some little presents: gloves and a nice warm scarf in a nice shade of grey for Sam, which Valerie had bought at the WI Christmas Fayre in the village hall, from which she had also come away laden with jars of chutneys, marmalades and jams and a collection of lavender bags and handmade Christmas cards and gift tags, and having made a promise that she would go along to the first meeting in the New Year.

She took some Bronnley's Lavender talc for Sam's wife, a box of Sainsburys' 'Taste the Difference' mince pies and a tin of M&S Belgian chocolate biscuits.

There was a stronger and slightly spicier smell than usual of overcooked food pervading the hall today. They could hear the clatter of cutlery behind the euphonious clamour of carols from the television in the dining room. An arrangement of holly and red plastic flowers, draped with a piece of silver tinsel, stood on the reception desk and a meagre Christmas tree, desultorily decked with crackers, four or five strands of tinsel, a plastic Barbie-type doll 'angel' and a dozen or so red and gold baubles, stood drunkenly in a red crêpe paper-wrapped bucket in the corner. Andy nodded at a scanty bunch of mistletoe tied with a big red bow and hanging hopefully from the central light fitting. "Bit of wishful thinking there."

"You never know; you hear of late romance blossoming."

"It's probably for the staff."

"Some of us are a little late with our lunch today, I'm afraid," the bottle blonde proprietor told them toothily when she bustled out of the dining room to greet them. She had a piece of tinsel round her neck and the big central blob on the front of her red jumper today might well have been a reindeer – Rudolph, probably. At least, it seemed to have a red bouclé nose. "We had the Musical Players in to give us a little concert, *Music from the Shows,* and they overran a little. Do pop in and get yourselves a mince pie!" She hurried up the stairs.

Hesitating, Valerie peeped in and caught Sam's eye. He started to get to his feet, but she could see that he had a half-finished bowl in front of him, and so gestured to him to sit down. An attempt had been made to make the dining room looked festive, too. Each small table had been covered with a red or green paper cloth and set with an arrangement of a twig or two of holly in what looked like, on the nearest table at least, a little fish paste jar. An enormous blow-up Father Christmas with a stupid plastic grin was propped up in the bay of the window, backed by a much smaller blow-up Rudolph, both of them drooping over an obviously half-empty sack. Someone had scrawled 'MERRY CHRISTMAS' in white artificial snow and glitter across the central windowpane behind him and 'HAPPY NEW YEAR' and 'SEASONS GREETINGS' across each of the others.

Valerie glanced sideways at Andy. "You want a mince pie?"

"Do you?"

"Probably Cash-and-Carry. I've got another packet of 'Taste the Difference' at home."

"I'll wait then."

"Yes, I would."

Sam was very pleased to see them, and delighted with the presents. He insisted on taking them up to see Mary, who was as usual comatose. They came out from their visit feeling really depressed.

"I hate that place."

"Nice old fellow, but I wish he wouldn't keep telling me the same stories over."

"You'll be like that one day."

"I probably am now. I wouldn't know."

They called in at Martha's afterwards for a chat and a drink "You must stay for dinner!" she told them, pressing glasses of wine into their hands. Catching sight over her shoulder of the bird sitting in its roasting tin, Valerie saw that it was only a fairly small chicken. With Martha's boys both tall and hefty specimens, and an aunt and one of their girlfriends coming, it certainly wouldn't stretch to two more, so she caught Andy's eager eye and signalled to him, 'no'.

"That's very kind of you, Martha, love, very kind indeed, and we'd have loved to, but we've a nice little turkey waiting."

No need to say it was only a ready-stuffed, ready-cooked breast and waiting for the microwave.

It rained steadily till the end of December, and then it rained some more – all through most of January, in fact, and into February, and a great deal of it was torrential. With the rain pouring down off the thatch, looking out through the cottage windows was like looking out from under a waterfall. In February, arriving back from a trip to Tesco's, Valerie stared up at the roof through yet more driving rain.

"Um... Why have we got a green roof, Andy?"

He stared up at the green-covered thatch, scratching his head. "That's moss."

"I know it is. Is it all right like that? We could keep a cow up there."

"Supposed to be good for another ten or fifteen years apart from the ridge. Bloody hell, hope we don't have to have that thing done as well."

"Hope not." She pictured her little account book anxiously. The thatch *had* to be all right; they couldn't stand any more expense.

They had meant well, though, Susie and Ollie, and it was a dear little cottage.

They had meant well.

As the rain cleared, bit by bit the work gradually got done and by the time spring arrived, the moss had begun to dry up on the roof and there remained – and they both crossed their fingers superstitiously as they talked about it – just the decorating to do. Andy had brought with him five lots of paint left over from *The Bury* in colours of which he approved: the pale sage green from the kitchen, the yellow from their bedroom, cream, white, and apricot white. He painted the kitchen in the pretty sage green and white, the cloakroom in the yellow and the ceilings and panels in the hall, the sitting room in apricot white, cleaned up all the oak framing and beams, and was clearly feeling a lot cheerier.

"Thinking of doing our bedroom next. What colour do you want?"

She considered the matter carefully and decided on the *toile-de-joue* curtains. "Blue?"

He shook his head firmly. "Blue's a cold colour. It's a very cold colour, blue."

"Pink, then. Sort of pretty rose pink."

"Pink is too girlie."

"I am a girlie."

"I'm not."

"Oh." She knew what colour he wanted. "Okay, cream, then. But you'll have to make it into a kind of oyster cream." It would have to be the damask curtains.

Whilst he was busy with that, she got started on the garden. Sam had had a lot of daffs, which she dug up and buried in a trench over by the garage so that their leaves could die away before she replanted them or tossed them out. There were tulips – all of those would stay – and hundreds of blue and white and pink scillas: a lot of them would have to go. So far she'd seen delphiniums on the way and too many clumps of cranesbill, and some campanulas and lupins and peonies that could stay. It took quite a bit of sorting. Andy and Martha carted over the pots and tubs and cuttings from *The Bury* that Mr and Mrs Blackwell and Martha had kindly been keeping for her, and she got out as many as she could as the weeks went by; the rest stood around in their pots. It meant a lot of watering. It was testing work these days, gardening; she could only manage it in quite short bursts before having to sit down, and her back and knees and hands were paying for it. She used up two full tubes of Atrixo Special Treatment hand cream and had to take some Iboprufen most nights.

Andy, on the other hand, seemed re-energised by the

decorating, and remembered about walking. He began to set off every morning after breakfast to stride manfully along the lanes or across the fields – unless, of course, it was raining or *had* been raining; he was fussy about muddy paths – and came back fresh-faced, panting, and bringing with him a rich waft of country air.

He started to read items on exercise and weight loss in the Sunday supplements instead of ignoring them. "Val, what's my BMI?"

She was in the middle of making a fresh batch of Maids-of-Honour for the Tuesday WI stall and didn't really want to be interrupted. The last ones she'd made hadn't quite turned out to standard and she wasn't sure where she had gone wrong. She nibbled her lip, frowning as she popped the tray in the oven. "Your what? What did you say? Your BM what?"

"How tall am I? About six foot? Six foot one?"

"Well, more or less; you used to be, you might have shrunk a bit."

He looked shocked. "What do you mean, Val? Why might I have shrunk?"

"Well, we do, don't we, apparently, when we're getting on? I have, I'm sure."

"Don't think I've shrunk."

He was hurt. She shrugged indulgently. "Okay."

"I need my exact height in centimetres. Where's the tape measure? Oh, and have we got scales?"

"Yes, here." She pushed the kitchen scales towards him.

"No, no, to weigh *me* on."

"Oh."

"I need my exact weight in kilograms."

"You know we haven't."

"Oh."

She was pleased, though, that he was making an effort, and pointed out helpfully that eating his way through three of the first batch of Maids of Honour that were supposed to be cooling on their wire tray, whilst at the same time as reading up on diet and exercise, didn't just mean she would be a bit short for the WI, but might also not be the best way to proceed.

She tried to be helpful, reading out useful snippets occasionally from the paper or her magazine. "It says here that washing and waxing car, or washing windows or floors for forty-five minutes to an hour, is very good exercise. That's good! Ooh, and dancing. They do line dancing and country dancing at the village hall; I wouldn't mind going to that." She glanced at him hopefully out of the corner of her eye, but he was cocking a deaf 'un. She raised her voice. "Oh, and so is heavy gardening – you know, doing the digging..."

H is new regime went on and on, and although she knew it was sensible, it got her down a bit. She was glad to have a moan about it to Norma when, the following spring, she and Leon popped down for a couple of days to inspect their new abode and she and Norma were having a bit of a chin-wag in the kitchen.

"He's driving me batty, with it, Norma. He weighs himself at least three times a day. He's bought these scales."

"Yes, I saw them in your bathroom. I tried them but they were miles out. They said I was fifteen stone two and then, the next time, six stone eleven."

Valerie nodded, unsurprised. "Oh, they will be up there; the floorboards are too uneven. No, he brings them down here and puts them on the tiles. He used to leave them here but I kept falling over them, so I make him take them back up. 'Nother cup of tea?"

"Yes, please. I expect it'll wear off soon: Andy does like his food." Norma nodded through the kitchen window. "Nice garden, though, Val. Nice and private. Less work than the other one, eh?"

Valerie smiled, pleased, as she refilled the teapot. "Yes, it's looking quite good. It's big enough: all I can manage really, now. The other one was ridiculous, much too big."

"It was lovely, though."

She pictured it wistfully as she pushed Norma's cup towards her. "Oh, yes, lovely! Here you are, Norm, sugar's in."

"You've had a tossing time, lovey, one way and another, but you seem settled now. Has it been worth it?"

She sighed contentedly. "Oh, yes, yes, Norm – I love it here."

"And Andy? He seems happy, too."

Valerie hesitated. She wasn't entirely certain. All the walking and stuff might be just a diversion for him. She knew he was still worried about the cottage. He told her so often enough. "Oh, yes, he is, he is, though it needs a lot more doing than we'd bargained on."

"I haven't had a proper chat with him yet. What are they doing out there? Shall I tell them tea's ready?" Norma heaved herself up from her chair and opened the back door. "Come on, you two, tea's up!" She returned to the table, frowning. "Andy's not losing too much weight, though, is he, Val? He's looking a little bit – you know, well, skinny."

She made sure he had two apricot muffins with his tea, just in case he was.

It was lovely, having Norm and Leon there again, at long last. You couldn't beat old friends. They seemed to like the cottage; it cheered Andy up no end. The fact that they hadn't been able to get down to inspect before meant that the garden was going well and all of the urgent stuff and the decorating had been done. It did look nice.

In bed that night he reached for her hand and held it tight by his side as he lay smiling happily up at the ceiling and hiccoughing occasionally. He'd had an awful lot of wine. "You know what, Val? I've grown to really love this place."

She sighed heavily. "Honestly, Andy, you do my head in, you really do. I've been frazzled to death for the past few months, worrying."

He turned his head on the pillow, puzzled. "Why?"

"You know very well why. So you don't want to tell Susie and Ollie to sell up?"

"What, another move? Not likely."

"And you don't want to go back to Wales?"

"Did I ever say I did?"

"Not exactly, but –"

"Couldn't afford it now even if we wanted to."

She wouldn't let it go. "No, no, but would you? Do you? If something happened to me, would you?"

He gave a loud hiccough. "Shut up, you silly woman and put the light out. Now you're winding *me* up."

Chapter 14

With all the catching up to do, Valerie and Norma were up next morning well before the boys. With her face puffy from a too-heavy sleep and grey hair tousled and uncombed, Norma sat comfortably at the kitchen table in her dressing gown whilst Valerie, equally unkempt, busied herself at the Rayburn.

"So Andy doesn't want to move back, then?"

"He's said not, like I say, though I think he might, you know, Norm, if anything happened to me." Valerie prodded the tray of bacon and sausages and pushed it back into the oven. They were doing nicely. "Will Leon have one egg or two?"

"Two, probably, lovey."

"And the same for you?"

"Go on, then; I'll be a devil. Why's that, then, Val? I thought he liked it here?"

Valerie waved the fish slice around, frowning. "Oh, yes, he does, he does. It's just that, well, I think he'll be a bit lonely. Be better for him to have you. And whatever he says, I know he only moved for me, really."

Norma shook her head firmly. "He wouldn't have done it if he hadn't wanted to; he wouldn't, Val."

Valerie thought about that. "No, no, that's true."

"And what about you? I mean, what would you do if, heaven forbid, but *if* anything happened to Andy?"

She didn't hesitate. "Oh, I'd stay here."

"You would?"

Valerie reopened the oven door. Perfect! Just like the

cottage. "Give them another shout, Norm, will you, love? Don't want these going over."

Mortality seemed to be the topic of the day. "Did I tell you little Billy Watkins died?" Leon asked, digging enthusiastically into the jar of whisky marmalade. "You make this marmalade, Val? It's delicious."

With anyone else, she might have pretended. "No, no, it's WI."

Andy shook his head. "Good God, Billy Watkins! How?"

"Cancer, of course. Bowel cancer." He looked around hopefully. "Any chance of another slice or two of toast?"

Valerie sighed as she slipped another couple of slices into the wire toaster. "Another one gone! Dear me, we went to dozens of funerals the last few years before we left the Glyn, didn't we, Andy?"

He nodded morosely. "We did, dozens: Bob Roberts, David Carter. And, of course, there was Derek Mason!"

"Poor old Derek." Valerie nodded. "Though he was old, of course; well into his nineties. Then there was Noreen Studley..."

"Most of them younger than us, though. Martin Graves, he was only, what, 64, 65?"

She tried to remember. "65, I think. Mary Houndsworthy, she was 66; Sandy Pritchard, she was only 52. Poor Sandy. Don't know how old Carol Wheelan was, but she wasn't much older than me."

"D'you know," Norma frowned. "These days if somebody's lost weight, I don't think, 'Ooh, you've been on a diet, you look nice and trim'; I find myself thinking, 'Have you got cancer?'"

Valerie eyed Andy anxiously. Was that what Norma had been thinking? No, he looked fit enough.

"And Bryn, don't forget Bryn!" Leon added, helping himself to a slice of the fresh toast. "Thanks, Val. That was a huge funeral. That church was absolutely packed out; very popular, was Bryn, belonged to everything – Bowls Club, British Legion, Toc H, RAF club, choir."

"Won't be anybody left to come to ours." Andy tried to sound lugubrious, but they all chuckled.

"Save on the sandwiches, anyway."

"I'll come, my son – I'll come!"

Valerie pushed back her chair again, feeling a glow of contentment,. "More tea, anyone? Some coffee?"

"Coffee, please, Val."

"I'm going to go like an Eskimo granny," she told them as she spooned out the coffee granules. They wouldn't expect her to bother with fresh. "That's what I've decided."

"You mean, get left out on an ice flow?"

"Yes, if I get old and decrepit and lonely, I think that'd be for the best."

Norma chuckled. "You are funny, Val."

"I tell you what I'm not doing; I'm not going into a home," she told them firmly. "We might not set our old folk adrift on ice flows to die, but we do things worse to them – drugging them to keep them quiet and things, the way we do."

Andy grinned at her. "You just don't like Bingo."

"It's a myth, you know." Leon pronounced, waving the marmalade spoon.

"What is?"

"Putting your granny on an ice flow just 'cause you got – you know – fed up with them. They didn't do that at all. They only did it if the person asked them to."

"Like an assisted suicide?"

"Exactly. And if they did ask you to do it, you had a sort of moral obligation to go through with it, whether you wanted to or not."

Norma shuddered. "Hope nobody asks me."

Andy folded his napkin, one of Valerie's mother's starched white linen ones, horrible to iron and only used when they had visitors. "Apparently the best way of dying is to fall asleep in a snowdrift."

"Who says?"

"Well, I dunno; somebody must have almost died, I suppose and told them."

Leon was fascinated. "Or are they just going by – you know – physical things that they know will happen?"

"Dunno."

"Like, I've heard that though you hear people screaming as they're falling off a high building, the people who were falling said they didn't know they were screaming at all; it was actually quite pleasant."

"Pleasant?"

"Well – you know – interesting." He mimicked a grace-ful, slow motion fluttering plunge. "I suppose, look, wow, I'm falling... Falling! Whoo-ooo-ooo...!"

"What are we like?" Valerie chuckled. "We are morbid creatures, aren't we, discussing dying over breakfast."

Andy pushed back his chair. "You're right; change the subject. What shall we do now, then? It's a beautiful day. Want to go out? We could drive down to the New Forest. Fancy that?"

They had a lovely day out. It was nice showing Norma and Leon around; they hadn't stopped long enough to see very much the last time. They drove down through the New Forest counting ponies, only getting stuck at Lyndhurst in a traffic jam for about fifteen minutes, paused for a little while at Beaulieu (which Norma fell in love with), decided not to go the Motor Museum (to Leon's disappointment and Valerie's relief), but went on to Buckler's Hard instead, where they walked by the side of the river and had a drink at the pub, and then nipped over to Lymington where they had sandwiches.

On the way back they stopped briefly at Romsey to pop into the Abbey. Leon was very taken with it. "It's got a lovely feel, this place, hasn't it, Val? Very – um – what shall I say? Very peaceful; very healing. The sort of place you want to go to if you've got a troubled heart."

Later, Valerie rather wished the Abbey had been a bit closer. There was a message from Susie on the answer phone. She didn't say much, just "Hello? Hello? Mum? You there?" but Valerie knew her voice well. She bit her lip as she put the receiver down. "Oh, dear."

Andy frowned. "What's the matter?"

"She sounded as if she was crying."

"Going to ring her back?"

She picked up the receiver. "Of course." She dialled Susie's number carefully, and her mobile, but there was no reply.

Sighing heavily, Norma shook her head. "It doesn't get any easier, does it, Val, when they grow up? You never stop worrying about them, do you?"

"Wish they'd sort themselves out." Andy hovered by the tray of drinks that he had ready assembled on the table in

the window. "Glass of sherry, Norm? Or a glass of wine?"
She waved a chubby hand. "Wine, please."

Andy shrugged. "Oh well, she'll have to sort it out,
whatever it is." He rubbed his hands together. "Right, if
you ladies have got a drink, I fancy a pint. Fancy a pint,
Leon? I'll take you up to *The Three Tuns*."

Valerie and Norma exchanged glances. "Oh, Andy –
didn't you have enough last night?"

"Chauffeured you all round the countryside, think I
deserve one."

Leon put his arms round Norma and Valerie. "Oh, come
on, girls! You don't mind, do you, really? Just a pint or
two, we won't be long. What time are we eating?"

"Seven o'clock." It was only ham salad, but best not to
mention that, or they'd never see them. Andy seemed to
have forgotten about his diet now he was happy with Leon.

*Not going to say 'I don't mind', either: look what happened
last time.*

She nodded grudgingly. "Don't be late."

I t didn't take long to prepare supper: only the table to lay
and the eggs to hard-boil and the potato salad to make
and the lettuce to dress and the cold meats to lay out on
a plate. Pudding was already in the fridge, waiting – a nice
raspberry trifle with sherry and fresh cream. They were
soon able to settle down to wait. Nice to have a little chin-
wag on their own. They talked about their children and
grandchildren, mostly. Norma's son and daughter-in-law
were doing a fair bit of quarrelling at the moment as well,
apparently.

Norma chuckled. "We're a bit like dinosaurs, you know,
you and Andy and me and Leon. There aren't many couples
left who've stuck together for so long."

Valerie rolled her eyes. "Oh, I know, I know! It's all
'what *I* want.' They've got a sort of me-me-me mentality,
that's the trouble; not prepared to work at it like us." They
exchanged smug headshakes.

"You have to work hard at it."

"You do. 'You've made your bed, now you must lie in
it', that's what my mother used to say. I said it to myself
sometimes, when I didn't like Andy." She frowned. "You

don't sometimes, do you?"

"I know exactly what you mean; sometimes Leon really gets on my nerves and I ask myself, 'whatever am I doing with this man?'"

"I'm sure Andy's exactly the same way about me, but no matter what, neither of us can imagine life any other way."

"They give up far too easily these days."

"They do."

They shook their heads again gravely in concert. "If you think what he needs and what's best for him, and he does the same for you, you can't lose."

They were brimming with self-satisfaction. "Exactly."

Norma waved her hand in dismissal. "But they're all right, really, aren't they? Susie and Ollie, I mean. I mean, they wouldn't ever split up? That'd leave you in a very difficult position."

Valerie chuckled. "Oh, no, of course they wouldn't. Oh, no."

That was when Susie rang again, and said she was leaving Ollie.

She didn't hold on long enough to explain. "I'm at the gym, Mum. I'm just getting changed, and then I've got to pick up Poppy and Thomas. I'll ring you later."

Valerie's fingers were knotting themselves tightly round the telephone cord. "But, Susie –"

"Got to go. Is everything all right?"

"Er – yes, yes, we're all right here..."

"I'll ring you later, then. Bye-bye."

Valerie felt anger rising as she put the phone slowly down. Why ring and tell me that now, then? Now I'll be on tenterhooks for the rest of the evening.

Norma was staring at her, all agog. "What's up, Val?"

Valerie cleared her throat. "She says she's leaving Ollie."

"She's never!"

Valerie heard the gate creak. Andy and Leon were back, walking, grinning and jabbering, up the path. "I'm not going to tell, him, Norm. Not yet. Not till I know that she's serious and I've found out what's going on."

Norma wouldn't leave it alone, though. "So where does that leave you, Val? If she is?"

"Here, I suppose." She shrugged, trying to look nonchalant. "It's probably the best thing. It'll do them good to have a break, then they'll get back together."

"And if they don't?"

She made a supreme effort to sound confident. "Oh, don't you worry, Norma, no. They will."

O h, but lovey, why?"

It had been tricky, trying to find somewhere she could talk to Susie without big ears – especially Andy's – listening in. In desperation, she had taken the cordless phone from the bedroom out to the greenhouse in the dark, pretending the need to water. She had knocked over a few pots of carefully autumn-sown foxglove seedlings with her elbow as she'd been feeling her way in and could feel the soil from them crunching under her fluffy slippers. Damn.

Susie sighed. "Oh, I don't know, I just can't do it any more. We seem to row all the time now, Mum."

"Going back to London hasn't helped?"

"I think it's actually made it worse. I get so furious when I sit here on my own when he could be at home. I feel so helpless, hopeless, boring – and I know that the guys at work send him up about me; I can hear them laughing about me when I ring him. I'm a bit of a joke, the little leech who sits around at home all day spending his money and nagging all the time. None of them are married. They're all playing the field or they've got glamorous and successful girlfriends."

"Not all of them, surely!"

"He'd respect me more if I were career-oriented like Camilla, he's said as much. He's used to being a success. He can't believe I couldn't just walk into some high-powered position if I wanted to. But I can't; I'm not qualified for anything halfway interesting and I'm too out of touch. I can't even pick up a telephone these days. I'm terrified of going to interviews; I know my mind would go completely blank. I'm bloody useless. My brain doesn't seem to work properly. I think he's right; I am going round the bend."

Valerie felt a stab of indignation. "That doesn't sound like Ollie. Did he say that?"

"You only get the nicer side of him. Oh, yes, he said

it – you name it: selfish, useless, irrational, stupid, petty, self-indulgent, neurotic..."

"And have you talked about it properly, lovey, told him how you feel?"

"Of course I have, he doesn't seem to hear it. He's so bad-tempered these days. I even wrote it all down in a letter to him once or twice because he wouldn't listen." Her voice caught. "Oh, I don't know, Mum, sometimes we do try to talk, we cuddle, and we apologise – one night, we even both cried. I think: thank goodness, now we're on the mend... but then each time we seem to end up standing on a smaller island than the one we were on before, because nothing ever seems to be resolved, nothing ever changes. I hate him."

Valerie's heart twisted further. "Sweetheart..."

Susie sighed. "No, I don't, I do still love him, but I don't love him like a husband, do you know what I mean? More like one of the children. I don't *like* him. I don't want to live with him any more. So I'm moving out."

"I see."

When Susie had rung off, Valerie stayed in the greenhouse for a little while collecting her thoughts. She didn't want to witness Andy's happiness again just yet and imagine how his face was going to fall when she told him. Instead, crouching in the dark, she felt for the fallen flowerpots and took a long time trying to push clumps of the tiny seedlings and the compost back inside by touch. Poor little things. "I'm so sorry, pets," she told them abstractedly. "Clumsy me."

Susie'd go back to him before long, of course she would. They'd be a nice little family again. But, sitting eventually at the candle-lit dining table surrounded by jollity and laughter, she felt – well, she felt quite sick.

She waited until Norma and Leon had gone back home but, even so, it took her a little while to work up to telling Andy. He seemed, not surprisingly, somewhat hung over the day they left, too, so she waited till the one after and then made them both a cup of coffee and sat down with him when he came back from his walk.

He was flabbergasted. "What about the kids?"

"She's taking them with her, though she says she's

going to let Ollie have them as much as he wants."

"And it's a flat, you say, she's going to? The one we stayed in?"

"An apartment, yes. Don't think it's the same one, but it belongs to his company like that one did. They've got a few that they rent to people coming in on short term contracts or on loan from other offices, New York, Switzerland, that sort of thing."

"Well, I don't know." Andy's shoulders had hunched. His brow was furrowed; the creases running from nose to chin had grown much deeper. He was really upset. Norma was right, too – he *was* getting too thin; you could see how bony and skinny his legs were through his trousers. She shrugged helplessly.

"No, I don't, either."

"Hm."

Until now, every time that Valerie had arrived home at the cottage she had felt a lovely warm glow. It wasn't so much that when she had opened the front door she had imagined herself to be surrounded by invisible, benevolent beings from over the centuries drifting amiably around and welcoming her, but the sense that the cottage itself seemed to be happy to see her.

Now, though, a sinking feeling was what she felt as she opened the front door. Walking straight to the telephone, she picked it up right away, closing her eyes tight in case it was going 'be-buh, be-buh, be-buh," meaning that there was a message. It was always a relief when there was not; things might have got worse. Of course, it was never long before she had to pick up the receiver again and ring Susie anyway to find out how things were. At the very least, they weren't getting any better.

"I can't do anything with Poppy, mum. She's an absolute nightmare. Won't get up in the morning, won't do a thing that I say. I have to drag her out of bed and drag her to school. Mind you, that's nothing new. She won't do any homework..."

Valerie bit her lip. "Oh, she is upset, isn't she, poor little thing? What about Thomas?"

"Thomas? Oh, Thomas is okay, don't worry about him,

he's fine; he's a very well balanced little boy."

"They must both miss their Daddy."

"What's there to miss?" Now Susie sounded sulky and defensive. "He was never there until long after they'd gone to bed and gone before they got up, and at weekends he was either out running or cycling or down at the gym, and then too tired to do anything except read the papers. It's not as if we ever did anything as a family any more. Besides, they do see him; more in fact than they did when we were at the house. I make him take them as often as I can; I even get up at the crack of dawn and go over before he goes to work so that he can have them for the night sometimes. I don't want to deprive them of their Daddy."

Andy was very quiet about the whole thing, though, "Any news from Susie?" he asked occasionally. "Or Ollie?"

When Valerie shook her head, "Oh, not much; no real news," he just nodded and pottered on his way. Once or twice she caught him gazing at her with an odd, thoughtful look on his face and challenged him. 'What?'

"Nothing, nothing. Just wondered..."

"Are you all right?"

"Yes, I'm all right. Are you?"

"Who? Me? Oh – fine, fine."

"That's good."

Though Susie didn't have a lot to say, the phone seemed red hot these days. Norma was keeping careful tabs. "You don't think he's having an affair, do you? They do say that when the wife is having an affair she's extra nice to her husband, but when men have one, they're horrible to their wives."

Valerie gave her short shrift on that one. "Oh, I don't think so, Norma, not Ollie. Oh, I don't think so. No."

"You know what, Val? I think you're right. I blame that Camilla. That's who's put Susie up to this."

Valerie sank into her chair. "Oh, I told her, I told her, Norm! 'Don't listen to that woman,' I said, 'She's probably an unhappy woman and just wants you to be unhappy too.' I wouldn't put it past her."

"Nor would I. Horrible cow; she wants shooting." Norma was chewing something; Valerie could hear her jaws munching. "I meant to ask," she added, gulping eagerly, "have you spoken to Ollie recently?"

Valerie nodded into the phone. "I have, I have, I gave him a ring. I didn't know whether to or not, but, I mean, we feel as if he's our son, you know, Norm."

Norma was soothingly full of sympathy. "Of course you do, love! And how was he? What did you say?"

She reflected. "He sounded okay, quite upbeat, really, but then, whenever we speak to him, he always does. 'Well, I said, take your bit of space, the pair of you, but what you've got to do is to remember what brought the two of you together in the first place; it won't have vanished entirely. That's what you should concentrate on, what makes you good together not what puts you apart.'

"I mean, you fall in love *because*, you love *in spite of*, isn't that what they say, Norm? Like we said when you were here – what you've got to do is not be blind to some of the things you fell for in the other person, despite the fact that a lot of what they do now may just drive you batty."

"What did he say?"

"Eh? Oh, he just gave that funny laugh of his, you know – 'Hah-hah'."

"Eh, dear, poor lad. Poor Susie." Norma clicked her tongue sympathetically. "Oh, don't worry, Valerie, lovey, they'll be fine. Just give them a bit of time."

Martha was more pragmatic and impatient. "Honestly, those two! Are they sorry they moved? Don't they like the new house?"

"Oh, no, it's not that! No, I think the problem is that Ollie's not spending as much time at home as she'd imagined he would."

"That's a pity. Why not?"

Valerie shrugged. "Oh, I don't know... The rest of his colleagues all socialise in the evenings. He doesn't want to seem henpecked; doesn't want to be the only one out on a limb."

She sighed, unthinkingly tearing some petals off her best scarlet geranium. "He's been on at her to get a job, too, so she said. Resents the fact that he's the only breadwinner. She would like to do something for her own sake, but she hasn't worked for such a long time now. The best she could hope for is probably something fairly low-powered, at least to start with, maybe even just a job in a nice shop. She quite fancied retraining as a midwife, you know, but the hours turned out to be difficult, weekend and night shifts, you know, and Ollie wouldn't have that."

"Wanted to have his cake and eat it."

"Maybe."

Martha's tone took a scornful edge. "Anyway, she doesn't need to work, for heaven's sake! They've got enough money. How's she going to manage that with the kiddies?"

"She does have an *au pair*."

"Oh."

"And a cleaning lady."

"Ah."

"And she uses an ironing service."

"Uh-huh..."

"And they have a gardener."

"Mmmm..." Martha chuckled once again. "Here's an idea, Val. Why doesn't she get a job?"

Chapter 15

It was surprising how tired she felt these days. She woke up with a bit of a headache and it didn't seem to clear all day and for some reason, if she ever sat down in the armchair, within minutes she would be fast asleep. Andy caught her several times with her head lolling and her jaw sagging open, 'catching flies'. He said it wasn't a very pretty sight. She was sleeping quite badly, of course. "Hibernating," she told him, 'I'm just hibernating. I'll be all right in the spring."

He wasn't too good himself. His breathing seemed to be getting worse and worse again. Sometimes, especially in the morning and last thing at night, it was very laboured. He was convinced it was the spores from the moss on the thatch; Valerie thought it was anxiety. The doctor gave him a different inhaler, which helped a bit, but he was looking decidedly pale and peaky by the time the spring had finally warmed the soil.

Her little garden was really beginning to take shape when the spring came at last; the scent of lilacs and lilies-of-the-valley drenched the air and the tulips, scillas and forget-me-nots were beginning to struggle for space with the burgeoning aquilegias, achilleas and delphiniums. They spent a lot of time out there enjoying the early summer sunshine, she pottering about whilst Andy hid behind his newspaper at the garden table trying not to let her see that he felt guilty.

She tried to encourage him to join in; gardening was such a joy. Besides, she could really do with the help. It was all a bit of an effort at the moment.

"Do you want to tie in those sweet pea canes, for me, Andy?"

He rattled the newspaper disconsolately. "Eh? Oh, I suppose so... What with?"

She sighed to herself. *For goodness' sake!* "Try string?"

"Where is it?"

"What?"

"The string."

"Where it always is; in the greenhouse."

"Oh, all right, then." He got up grudgingly, frowning. "Right."

When she came back from the greenhouse, he was still securing the long tendrils to their wigwam with green twine. "Bloody gardening. I hate it."

"No, you don't."

"Yes, I do."

She stood still for a moment, watching him. He was very meticulous, much more so than she. He became aware of her stare. "This all right for you?"

"Of course." She caught her breath, loving him very much. "Do you know, we've been down here five years now?"

"Five years? Never."

"We have, altogether; five years this month."

He stepped back carefully onto the lawn. "We've never."

"We have. Three years at Lynton Stacey, and two here."

"The longest years of my life."

"What?"

He grinned wickedly. "Only joking."

She chuckled, relieved. "Oh, you! Do you know what else it is this month?"

He was looking blank. Pulling back the wrist of her gardening glove she squinted at her watch. "Ten past three: we'd probably be on our way by now."

"On our way where?"

"To Pwllglas."

"Pwllglas?"

Goodness, he could be obtuse at times. "Come on, when did we go to Pwllglas?"

He got it suddenly. "Is it our anniversary this month?"

"It is. It's our golden wedding anniversary on the twenty-ninth of June."

It didn't seem appropriate to have a proper party. Most of the people they would like to have invited would have had to travel down from the north and stay for the night, and Leon and Norma couldn't come – they were off to Turkey on a gullet cruise.

Susie and the children came down though, and they all went to a very nice meal at *The Bird in Hand,* which had had an excellent write-up in the local paper. They really pushed the boat out, too, food wise – no looking for the cheapest thing on the menu this time! The children behaved very well, though Poppy seemed particularly sulky and only ate the odd scrap here and there. They all missed Ollie, except Susie, who pulled a sour face every time they mentioned his name.

The best bit came at the very end of the meal. Susie called Thomas over to her and whispered into his ear and he squirmed and blushed bright pink and then, when she pushed him gently in her direction, slowly came to Valerie's knee and plopped a large red envelope decorated with a rainbow arc of glitter, colourful bits of ribbon and stuck-on hearts, onto her lap. "Happy Anniversary," he mumbled, grinning, gazing at the floor.

"For me? Oh my, what's this?" she asked, wide-eyed, holding it up in the air.

"What have we here?" Andy added, beaming from ear to ear.

"A little present for your anniversary." Susie looked flushed with pride. "From Dad and from me, and the children of course. And Ollie. I hope you like it."

"From Ollie, too?" Valerie stared around at the circle of happy faces as she carefully tore open the envelope. "Oh, but you shouldn't have, you sillies! There was no need."

Andy couldn't seem to stop grinning. "Susie booked them over the internet. Don't go and lose them, now!"

Susie leant forward and pointed to the small sheaf of documents as Valerie drew them out. "The first one's for the flight tickets, and the others –"

The others were the confirmation, booking vouchers

and itinerary for two persons, for a cruise.

Valerie drew in her breath sharply as she scanned them quickly then looked up with brimming eyes. "Venice! Oh my! We're going to Venice, Andy! I've always wanted to go to Venice."

"I know you have." He looked like the Cheshire Cat. "I know we are. That's why I chose this cruise. It's only a week, you know and I'm sorry it's not till September, but it was the only one with room available that went to Venice. Don't know how much we'll see of it, mind; we get underway later the same day."

"Still! Just imagine! Venice!"

"We go from there to Mykonos."

"Fancy!" She was jiggling as Thomas sometimes did with excitement. "Mykonos! That's Greece?"

"And from there to Athens."

"Ooh! Athens!"

"Then somewhere in Croatia."

"Dubrovnic? Norma and Leon went to Dubrovnik."

He frowned momentarily. "Um, no. Split."

"Split! Split! Well! Well, I never!"

He tapped the itinerary sheet. "And back to Venice. Hopefully we'll get a better look at it that day." He looked at her hopefully. "Will that do you all right?"

"I should say so! Oh, Andy! Oh, Susie!" Grabbing Thomas, she hugged him tight, pressing a big kiss to his cheek. "Thank you, Thomas, thank you for our present." Even Poppy was grinning now. As Thomas wriggled away from her embrace, Valerie reached for her, kissing her warmly too. "And you, darling. Thank you. Thank you all so much! Oh, Susie, Ollie too; it was so nice of him to contribute. I'll ring him of course, but still – tell him, won't you? Tell him I'm delighted. Tell him I'm ever so pleased."

It seemed a long time to wait till September, but when it came down to it, Valerie found herself quite pleased that it had been a bit of a way off. It had given Andy's breathing a bit of time to improve with the nice warm weather and not quite so much moss growing on the thatch. He needed to be feeling at his best on a special holiday like this. As Norma had forecast, he had forgotten all about his diet and was putting on a bit of weight again, now, and she was relieved – not least because what Norma had also said about cancer and his looking too skinny had played a lot on her mind. She watched him very carefully each time he came back from his walk, though, in case he had been overdoing it and was setting himself back. She knew now, too, that he had booked the cruise partially at least because he had been watching and worrying about her, as well.

Naturally, over the summer they both read up about cruising quite a bit and on the places they were going to. Every time one of them heard anything on the radio or the television about cruising, they relayed it to the other.

"Apparently you don't have to attend the formal dinners if you don't want to; you can have a buffet meal instead. That might be better for us. We can eat any time we want."

"And you can go back for more if you want to."

"Hm."

"Apparently there's a wave machine and a climbing wall and a miniature golf course on this one, Val. I'd like to see you shimmying up a wall!"

"Ooh, Andy, we're expected to tip the cabin steward and the waiters and everybody so much for every day! That's going to add up."

"After fifty years? Hang the bloody expense."

"Did you see *South Today,* Val? Apparently a lady went overboard on a cruise liner coming in to Southampton."

"They say you only last three minutes if you fall into the Atlantic in winter."

"This wasn't the Atlantic, this was the Solent."

As the date of departure approached, Valerie laid things out on the spare bed, changing her mind on at least half a dozen occasions. Dressing up for dinner always seemed to be a big part of the deal when you heard about cruising, and she hadn't got any suitable dinner dresses, except the black one she'd worn to the Blackwells the first Christmas and which had been at the back of her wardrobe ever since. She had, though, over the summer, taken to haunting the little charity shop she was so fond of and had acquired several little things with which she was very pleased. Why had people had got rid of them? she asked herself every time she looked at them; they were ever so nice.

"Difficult to know, isn't it?" she murmured for the umpteenth time, worrying at her lip. "I'll take two evening skirts and three tops and my black dress. Or these two dresses and one skirt? What do you think, Andy?"

"We're only going for a week."

"Yes, but they won't wear the same thing for evening every day. I hope we're going to have room! Shoes for evening. Sandals."

"Don't forget my navy shorts."

"Do we need cardigans and jumpers, do you think? What about our macs?"

"The temperature in Athens was 41 degrees yesterday."

"Yes, but they might have a thunderstorm."

"Hm. They might."

She made a 'his' pile and a 'hers', and Andy took to wandering in and out, putting things onto his pile and then taking them out again the next time round, which was very irritating. He hadn't got a dinner jacket and what's more, he had refused point blank even to hire one on the ship. "I'll take my grey suit and a decent shirt and tie and that'll have to do."

"Well if they won't let you in, we'll have to go to the buffet bar, I suppose."

"Of course they'll let me in. Don't be so silly." He began to riffle through his pile. "Have you seen my other blue tee shirt? I don't want these shorts, they don't fit me."

She clicked her tongue. "Well, you put them in!"

"No, I didn't."

She was getting exasperated. "Andy, you did! And stop messing up my piles!"

He had a faint glint in his eye. "I'm a nuisance to you, aren't I, Val?"

"Yes, you jolly well are!"

He sighed lugubriously. "Don't worry, I'll be going soon, anyway."

She tossed her head. "Thank goodness for that." She had more than her tongue in her cheek when she said it, though; she had her whole self. He meant he was getting old; he meant that one day soon he was going to die. If she dared to think about it, if she could bear to think about it even momentarily, the idea of a world without Andy in it turned her entire being inside out.

He had been right; they didn't get into Venice sightseeing. Getting everyone onboard and settled took up most of the day and then they were off, holding hands and smiling at each other from time to time as, accompanied by an enchanting salutation of church bells, the big ship glided majestically past St Mark's Square and the Campanile and all the little bridges that she'd seen in pictures and on telly. It was wonderful.

They had booked themselves down for the early sitting for dinners, but everybody dined in the buffet that evening, so they didn't have to put Andy's grey suit and her little black dress to the dress code test. The food didn't meet their expectations; it was nothing out of the ordinary, only average.

"What d'you think, then?" Andy asked putting down his spoon at last having finished off a slice of some sort of apple cake, a chantilly cream and a rather solid little block of lemon mousse. "What's yours like?"

"Mine?" she prodded at the bottom of her trifle bowl, trying to fish out a little chunk of peach. "Bit too much jelly and the cream's synthetic. It's that stuff you squirt out of a can."

"Hm." He turned round, eyeing the cluster of diners round the dessert section.

She shook her head in amazement. "You're not thinking of going round again!"

"Might have made the wrong choice."

After dinner they set off to explore the ship again from bow to stern and from deck to deck, starting at the bottom. It was amazing what they had managed to pack in there, really – a huge casino, several bars, three dance floors, a coffee bar and an internet café, a library, a huge theatre, three restaurants and the buffet bar, a solarium, a health spa, a kids' club and a crèche, and a whole row of shops, not to mention all the things that were up on deck. When they emerged outside at the top, Valerie shivered. She was glad she'd brought her cardigan. "Whew, bit draughty."

"Mm. Come here." He slipped an arm round her, drawing

her closer.

"This is lovely, isn't it, Andy? See all the stars." She could feel the forward movement of the ship, though when she peered over the rail and down over the cliff face of the side there was nothing to be seen but an oily, slowly rolling blackness with, close by, a streak of luminous greyness fringed with the white froth of spray from the bow wave.

"Do you remember that poor woman?"

"What poor woman?"

"The one who fell off that ship? On *South Today*. Do you think she meant to do it?"

He shrugged. "Oh, I don't know. Maybe."

"Was she an older lady?"

"I don't know, why?"

"Can't see how you'd fall by accident unless you were a young person fooling about on the rails." She reared up on tiptoes, peering over. "Could you do it?"

"What, jump?"

"Mm."

"Why on earth would I want to jump?"

"Well, I don't know, I mean, just imagine: when we were young, you used to say to me we'd be together forever. 'When we go, we're going to go together,' that's what you used to say."

He grinned. "Did I?"

"Yes, you did. Well, just suppose for a minute that there was something wrong with one of us – badly wrong, I mean, like terminal, and we wanted to keep that promise and I said, 'Okay, how shall we do it?' and you said 'Let's jump from the side of a ship.' Could you do it?"

"Can't see you getting up on that rail for a start."

She surveyed it, frowning. It did look awkward. "I suppose I could, just about, if you helped me. But I'd be a bit worried about when I'd got up there, before we – you know – jumped. I'd want to hold your hand." She raised herself on tiptoes once again. "It's a long way down."

He nodded. "Though that's good, though, isn't it? If it's far enough it'd be like hitting concrete. We'd be dead before we got our feet wet."

"That's if we dived. I couldn't dive, Andy. No, I'd have to jump. Would there be sharks, do you think?"

"Could be. Bit cold, though."

She shuddered. "Jellyfish?"

He chuckled. "Come on, now, Val, you're not going to be worrying about jellyfish, not if you're trying to do yourself in."

Their cabin was very comfy, with a picture window instead of a porthole, much to her surprise. It was amazingly quiet. There were twin beds, narrow, but very soft and snug, just close enough for them to reach out and touch hands – or, as she noted with satisfaction, for her to be able to reach over with only a little difficulty and shake Andy if he started to snore.

There was plenty to choose from for breakfast, though the bacon was American style, which Andy didn't care for, too thin and crispy, and Valerie didn't think much of the yoghurts, which were on the watery side. They were due to arrive in Mykonos in the early afternoon, so they spent the morning alternating wandering around, and reading, stretched out on sun beds. The pools were a bit too busy and noisy, but the quiet solarium, all marble pillars and pools and Jacuzzis under a huge glass roof, had very much more appeal. They promised themselves a little dip when they got back on board after Mykonos.

"Not many whitecaps out there," she murmured, linking her arm through his as they moved out for a second time onto the promenade deck to lean on the rail, staring out across the empty, gently rolling sea. "Looks black, doesn't it? Not blue or green. Looks very deep."

"Well, it is."

"It is, yes. Hm." Strange to think that there were things down there under the surface, live things, moving and hunting. What did they do when a pale, slowly sinking body fell into their midst? Scatter? The little ones would, probably, the great shoals of things, dancing and shimmering, but the bigger ones... She didn't like the thought of those at all. Did you struggle as you sank down, or did the icy blow of the surface knock you out? What happened if you changed your mind?

"When would we do it?" she asked him. "If we jumped. I mean. What would be the best time?"

He shrugged. "Night time, I suppose."

"Some people probably stay up very late, though, those who like dancing and things. Three or four o'clock, perhaps? They should have gone to bed by then."

"Darkest before dawn, anyway."

"What time is dawn?"

"Seemed quite light when I got up to spend a penny last night."

"What time was it?"

"Don't know; I didn't look."

It all went ever so quickly. My goodness, it was hot on Mykonos, and Athens was even worse! Interesting, though. Valerie was very taken with the windmills and the Acropolis. Andy was interested and disappointed to find he didn't much like Greek beer.

By the end of the sixth day at sea they felt like really old hands, as they dressed carefully for a formal dinner in the dining room.

Andy straightened his tie. "Right, are you ready?"

"Yes, I'm coming now. Do I look all right?"

He was hovering impatiently by the door. "You look lovely. Come on, want a drink at the bar first; I've got a terrible thirst."

She checked her appearance for the last time in the dressing table mirror. After much deliberation she had decided on a royal blue silk jersey top and long, matching flowered silk skirt that she'd bought in the charity shop, adding some dark blue beads. The black dress she'd worn the last time had felt decidedly dated and elderly; plenty of wear in it, but it would have to go. Her court shoes hurt like Billy-o: not used to wearing heels these days. All in a good cause, though! Never mind.

He held open the door and she swept ahead of him along the narrow, carpeted corridor towards the dining room, trying to look glamorous and regal. He sounded rather anxious when he called her back. "Val! Val! Come here..." Frowning, he pressed his mouth close to her ear when she reached him. "You've got a tag thing dangling on your skirt: *Help The Aged. £3.99.*"

They sat up on deck with their coffee and a brandy after dinner. "Don't they have a lookout?" she wondered, peering around and up.

Andy chuckled. "Well, he won't be in a crow's nest in the rigging – you're a bit out of date, there, Val! I imagine whoever's on duty would be up there on the top deck." He pointed. "That's the works, see? That's where the captain will be. By the Observatory Bar?"

She nodded. "If we were behind it, then, in that little sunbathing area where they have the nudists, they wouldn't see us."

He resumed the game with her, whistling and drawing in a breath. "Could be nasty. Might be a bit close to the ship's screws."

A thought struck her. "Andy, what about the other people?"

"What about them?"

"Well, look at them. They've paid a lot of money for this cruise and they're having such a nice time." There was dancing to a steel band at the poolside this evening; it was very popular and noisy. "They'd have to stop, wouldn't they?"

"Who would?"

"Well, I mean, the ship. The ship's crew. When they found us missing. It'd have to turn round. It'd hold up the whole holiday; they might have to miss somewhere out. Might not be able to stop at the next port. Wouldn't really be fair."

"Hm. You have got a point."

She thought for a minute. "How would they know we'd gone, actually, if we kept ourselves to ourselves? You know, didn't pal up with anybody. Would the cabin steward know?"

"How would he know?"

"I suppose sooner or later he'd notice if nothing ever seemed to be moved, you know, if our nightclothes were still on the pillow where he'd put them, with that nice little chocolate on top."

"Well, we'd mess up the beds, wouldn't we, surely? I mean before we –"

"Oh, yes. If we weren't going to – you know – till three or four in the morning, we'd need something to do, something to pass the time."

"We could watch telly. We'd probably have a snooze anyway, just for a few hours. We'd set the alarm."

"I suppose he wouldn't really find out till the next evening."

"Or the morning after that, really."

"The next morning, again, yes. He'd know you'd gone somewhere, mind you, as soon as he saw that you hadn't eaten your chocolate."

He pretended outrage. "Are you saying I'm a greedy pig?"

They had till mid-afternoon on the last day before disembarking and setting off for the airport. Leaving both bags just outside the cabin door, as instructed in the daily bulletin, they set off down the corridor.

"How long have we got in Venice?"

"Got to be back here by half past four."

Andy sighed happily. "Right then – do you fancy a nice ice-cream?"

They took a water taxi into Venice, because the main trip was going off to Verona instead. There was time enough to do as the guidebook suggested and start by taking the No. 1 vaporetto along the Grand Canal as far as St Mark's Square. It was so romantic, going everywhere by boat. They debated long and hard about whether or not they should have a ride in a gondola, too, but it was very expensive so they let that one go in favour of wandering through the warren of little shops selling glassware and beautiful masks, and then over small bridges and through little squares away from the main area. It was all that Valerie had hoped for.

"Sorry about the gondola ride," Andy said, slipping an arm about her as they rode back towards the dock. "I'll come up and sing to you next time you're having a bath instead."

She chuckled happily, nudging him "Oh, you!"

Chapter 16

They drove home from the airport in a little bubble of contentment. They had both got themselves a nice bit of sun tan; they'd seen a lot of interesting things; they were both well rested. It had proved to be a very lovely holiday for older people – no lugging luggage about and living out of a suitcase; medical facilities on board just in case. The car started first time, despite Andy's forecast of a likely problem.

"Do you know, I'm ashamed of myself, I've hardly given a thought to Susie and Ollie or the children whilst we've been away," Valerie told him as they turned down onto the A31.

He patted her knee. "Good! Do you good. I'm glad."

She gazed happily out through the side window at the familiar Hampshire countryside. "I've got a good feeling about them, you know, Andy. We're going to get back and find everything's back to normal."

He nodded, beaming. "You know Susie. They'll have made it up and she'll have gone back to the house with him, I'll bet you. All forgotten. You know how she changes her mind."

Penny Cottage had missed her. It reached out its arms to welcome Valerie; she felt it. She got on the phone to Susie the minute they walked in. "Hello, darling! We're back!"

"Did you have a good time?"

Lost in narrating an excited description of their adventures, she didn't notice at first that Susie sounded a bit strained. At last she hesitated. "Are you all right, pet?"

"Me? Yes, yes, I'm fine."

"Are you sure? You sound a little bit tense."

"No, no." Susie sighed heavily. "Oh, bother it; I was going to come down to break the news, but I might as well tell you now. Ollie and I, we – well, we're getting a divorce."

Divorce. So it had come to it, then. The very idea made Valerie's knees quiver, her toes curl and her tummy turn over: indeed, made her feel entirely unwell. She broke the news to Andy eventually, though not till he'd had a good night's sleep. It was as well that she had waited; when she told him what Susie and Ollie had decided, his face went quite grey. "This is exactly the sort of thing I was worried about when we decided to move. I told you, didn't I? I told you. We're entirely in their hands now." He was right, of course, and it made her feel sick, but he kept coming back to it. "The thing is, Val – the thing is, what I'm worrying about is, where does this leave us?"

"Oh, I don't think we need worry about it at the moment." She had a terrible headache. "Susie said, 'Oh, it's not going to affect you and Dad, don't worry.'"

(*Well, I don't think so. Well, not yet.* That's what Susie had actually said.)

"At the moment, eh? That means it will affect us. Well, of course it will, it stands to reason: they'll be dividing things up. How are they going to go about it? Are they going to court?" He was getting himself wound up; she hoped that this wasn't going to affect his heart.

"No, no, they want to come to some kind of amicable financial agreement between themselves. She won't make him sell the house."

"She won't?"

"She says she's leaving him, he didn't ask her to go so she won't take it away from him. He loves it too much."

He nodded grudgingly. "Fair enough; fair play."

She tried to smile. "We can always hope they'll change their minds; you know what they're like."

He got more and more worked up as the day wore on, though. "I knew it was the wrong move. Biggest mistake we've ever made." At last, at half past twelve, after a silent and only half-eaten lunch, he opened the front door and, glowering, dragged on his anorak, zipping it up with an ill-tempered flourish "Got to get out of here for a bit; I'm going for a walk." He paused. "We needed our heads reading selling the old house. We needed our heads examining, do you know that, Val?"

There wasn't an awful lot that she could say.

It's the kiddies I'm worried about more than anything, though," she admitted to Norma, summoning up the backbone to overcome her embarrassment that things were going even more awry. "Poor little things. Oh, it really breaks my heart."

Norma did her best to soothe her. "It might be better for them though, mightn't it, love, not having their Mum and Dad quarrelling and squabbling all the time?"

"Maybe." She could feel hot tears welling up. "But why ever can't they stick with things these days, Norma? It's not as if he was cruel or anything. Susie's not a battered wife or anything. I can't help feeling that they're missing out, you know. All that 'being in love' and stuff is lovely and exciting, but it's only when you've been through the rough and smooth and stuck it out together, held in there, and have come out at the other end knowing – just knowing – that you love somebody and somebody loves you, that you understand what love really means. Don't you think so, Norm?"

"You're right, you're right, I know, I know..."

"I really hope that Susie knows what she's doing. With no job, how's she going to make ends meet?"

"It's both of them though, isn't it, presumably, that have come to this decision?"

"Oh, yes, I think so, but I do wonder if he understands why. It's usually the man who doesn't see it coming, isn't it, who says he thought everything was all right? And Andy's ever so upset about losing Ollie, too, you know, Norm."

"I'm sure he is, love. Like you've said: he's been like a son."

"No parents of his own. Never had a real family before. He did seem to enjoy it." She felt so very sad. "Not likely to keep in touch, is he, if they're getting divorced?"

"Maybe not, maybe not. No."

"Poor Andy. Oh, I'm sorry to burden you, Norma." She blew her nose hard, stuffing the sodden tissue unthinkingly back up her sleeve to join the couple already there.

"No, no, I understand, no, no..." And then, of course, Norma *had to* ask, because Valerie had been wondering about it too: "Has she got somebody else, do you think, Val?"

She tried to sound as firm about it as she could. "Oh, no, Norm. Oh, I don't think so. No."

When the phone call was over, she went out and watered and pottered a bit in the garden and the greenhouse to try to distract herself. By the time she came in again to start getting a shepherd's pie ready for supper, the clock was saying it was almost a quarter to four. She stared at it, faintly puzzled. Andy was taking a long time over his walk; he was rarely gone more than an hour or so.

An hour later, with the pie ready for browning and a rice pudding in the simmering oven, she began to get more than a bit worried. If it had been even later, she'd have decided that he must have popped into the pub, but they didn't open till six. Of course, he could have gone there after a short walk and got involved in a lock-in; it did happen. She really rather hoped that he had not, and not just because it would mean he would have got himself sozzled; he might have started telling everybody everything once the alcohol had loosened his tongue. Keep family things to yourself as far as possible: that was her motto.

Besides, nobody in the village knew that they didn't own the house.

When it got to almost five she tried a few phone calls, starting with the pub. Nobody answered for ages and when the publican's wife, Gilly, eventually did, she had clearly been dozing: she sounded half asleep. There hadn't been a lock in, then. Gilly hadn't seen Andy, and nobody else had seen him either; Valerie really was beginning to fret as she finally put down the phone, having made the rounds. Half past five now! Wherever could he have got to?

There was nothing for it. Changing into outdoor shoes and pulling on her anorak, she opened the front door and started down the path, then hurried back, fumbling with her door key. Be wise to take her walking stick, perhaps;

could be a long walk. Getting dark a lot earlier now, too – better take a torch. Discovering a crumpled bag with a few humbugs in it in the torch drawer, she stowed it in her pocket. Might keep her going for a bit.

Once in the empty lane she paused, undecided about which way to go. It didn't look as if there had been any rain recently to turn the lanes and fields into mud – Andy didn't like having muddy boots – so there were a number of ways he could have chosen. He might have gone through the yard of Cribbs Farm and up through the fields, come down by the churchyard that way; or he could have gone up Pooks Lane, through the woods and down the lane by Fiddlers Cottage and come out by the bridge. He could have gone up White's Hill, over the top and down towards the river. He could have crossed the water meadows and gone along by the river that way, come out near Batts Farm and turned right for the village. With any of these, he should have been home long gone.

Her heart was thumping, and she felt almost worn out before she started, her feet already dragging through the first drifts of fallen leaves. By good luck, or else through some sort of intuition, she plumped for the right path.

It was something about the long, slowly winding crawl of White's Hill that drew her in that direction. Though she rarely went out on the walks with Andy, not being up to the sort of trek he did these days, she did occasionally set off with him at least, to show willing, and it was White's Hill she dreaded most. It had a slow, inexorable incline that took all her energy and was the very devil on her hip. With high hedges on either side, there was little to look at and little to hear apart from occasional bit of birdsong, the stomp, stomp, stomp of their own feet, and the rhythmic plonk, plonk, plonk of her walking stick When he chose that way, she just kept her eyes fixed firmly ahead and plodded. It was very boring, hypnotic, almost; would have been a good walk to do if you were upset, worried or angry – she'd thought that about it every time.

Once at the top, he said – she'd never been all the way to the top, she usually turned back by Pipers Cottage – you had a choice: you could either come back the same way, or follow a signed footpath off to the right and go along the top of the fields and down through the woods to the river and from there across the bridge and back up to the village along the main road. She hoped she was going to meet him coming back, otherwise wasn't sure that she was up to it: one heck of a long way.

It was indeed a long, long, long, long drag all the way up White's Hill; it was all she could do to keep her aching legs moving, In fact, the only way she managed to reach the top at all was by making herself do a sort of head-down Scouts' Pace, only with the number of paces gradually coming down to five with a stand-still in the middle. Slow, short steps, not getting very far and very slow: one, two, three, four, five. A bit more effort, longer strides, covering a bit more ground: one, two, three, four, five. A pause, looking up, chest heaving, heart sinking; still no sight of the top. Still no sign of Andy coming down.

When she finally reached the brow of the hill, to her dismay there were three signs, not the one that Andy had described, and all of them said 'Footpath'. One indicated a narrow track at the top of a field to the left, so that clearly wasn't the one he had been talking about, but at the side of a splintery stile on the right, two fingerposts were marked 'Footpath', one heading slightly up, one down. The lane itself began to run down between high hedges, heading towards the west and a faintly lighter glow in the gradually darkening clouds that meant a setting sun. Goodness only knew where it led to; she wasn't intending to find out.

Nowhere much to do it, but she had to sit down; her left hip was giving her gyp, not to mention her knees. Perching precariously on the least spiky bit of the steep bank that she could find, and wedging herself awkwardly against a protruding bit of rock in order not to slip down, she stared, shivering, at the fingerposts, reflectively sucking a humbug. Which way? Should she turn back? Blasted Andy. It was probably just another false alarm, like the last time; he was probably somewhere nice and warm and cosy having too many drinks. But he might not be, he might not be...

She chose the downward-pointing track when she finally forced herself to her feet. It must be downwards, surely, to the river?

The path led down along the side of the hedge and then cut across again, leading off to the left, over another stile. Popping another humbug into her mouth for the energy, she heaved herself onto the track, straining to see where it led next. It seemed to run off into the distance alongside another hedge. The mist was mainly below her in the valley, but there was very little light left in the sky, too little to see much at all. Keep on ploughing on, she told herself, lifting her body painfully over to the other side and trying to avoid a cowpat. *Just put your torch on, keep ploughing on, keep sucking the humbugs! Come on now, you can do it.*

It was a long stretch of the path, this one; must have been a big field. At least the beam of the torch kept her on it, though by the time it had led her through a thick hedge of whispering tall dark trees and into another field, it was almost pitch dark and the small circle of light it cast seemed to be growing weaker. Sloping, this time, the field, steeply sloping. She played the fading beam around, looking for another signpost, but couldn't see one. *You'd think they'd have put another signpost!* Down again, presumably; she had to keep going down. She tried a few shouts before setting off, though. An owl hooted, but nobody answered her call.

It was difficult to make out where the path was supposed to be. There being nothing very obvious, she stuck fairly close to the overgrown hedge, hearing her breath sawing and rasping as she picked her way down over what seemed to be very uneven ground. She could smell the strong odour of manure. The wavering light of the torch seemed to be revealing the edge of a deeply ploughed field vanishing on her left side into blackness. She tried to speed up a bit, stumbling heavily now, her shoes sticking in gluey mud within the ruts, her breath sawing and whooping in her ears. The ruts got deeper; some of them she practically had to climb over. In one of them, she left her shoe behind. *Oh, stupid... Stupid!*

Reversing her stick, she felt around and hooked it out to where she could reach the shoe. The battle to try to get it on again without sitting down in the mud almost had her in tears.

She was hanging onto a thorny outspur of the hedge,

resting from the struggle for a moment, when a shiver ran down her spine. Something was moving in the darkness; something huge and dark and breathing heavily, a moving, thicker patch against the darkness of the field. As she watched, it loomed even closer. Startled out of her wits, and ignoring the pain in her knees, she began to lurch downhill again, half shod and calling hoarsely at the top of her voice, "Andy! Andy!"

It was down by the fringe of the water meadows that she found him, or rather, that he found her. Staggering, wearing only one shoe, her foot sopping wet and with mud encrusting her shaking legs, she had finally found herself at a point where she could see the river, or rather the faint lights of Mill Cottage, which was pretty much the same thing. She couldn't get to it, though, or even somehow attempt to make her way across the soggy water meadows in the dark without falling into the rivulets. What appeared to be an endless barbed wire fence was solidly barring her way. She just had time to realise the extent of it before her torch finally gave out. When nobody heard her calling, she just sat down.

That was where he found her sitting – lying down, really – with her head slumped forward and her back against a bit of a fallen tree. An owl swooped silently over the riverbank, and she heard another one calling far away as he cradled her in his arms.

"What are you doing here, you silly old sausage?"

She was glad to be lying down, though the grass was very damp; couldn't have gone another step. She tried to smile, though her lips seemed very numb. "Couldn't go any further."

"Silly old sausage."

She closed her eyes. Nice being here with Andy. "I knew you'd come."

So instead of Andy, it was she who ended up in a hospital bed. Exhaustion and a touch of hypothermia, they said: good thing it hadn't been December. "Where had you been? Where had you got to?" she asked him when she was feeling a bit more herself. "And how the dickens did you find me?"

He shrugged. "Just walking. Needed to think. Must have gone miles; I did the whole round trip. Carried on when I got to the top of White's Hill –"

"So you did go that way. I thought you would."

"Sat for a while. There's a good place to see the view a bit further down, you can see for miles, right down to the Isle of Wight. Must show you some time."

"Not on your blooming life."

He grinned. "Then I carried on and came out by the crossroads at the bottom. Walked back to the village along the fields next to the road. I called in briefly at the pub."

"I thought you'd do that, too."

"Gilly told me you'd been looking for me so I only had one pint, and then went back home. Paul came with me. We had quite a search party out looking for you. All the lads from the pub..." He frowned. "Why didn't you take the mobile?"

It would have been such an obvious thing to do. "Should have done, yes. Didn't think about it. Not used to having it. Why didn't you?"

He dodged the question "We've got to start taking it with us from now on. Bit more up to date than a paper trail."

"Paper trail?"

"Hare-and-Hounds. You know. Humbugs."

"Humbugs?"

"You must have been chewing humbugs."

She was ashamed of herself. "Did I drop the wrappers? Surely not."

He grinned sardonically. "One or two." He shrugged, frowning. "Mind you, it was lucky I took the bottom footpath. Nearly didn't."

"Must have read my mind." She reached for his hand. "Glad you found me."

He held her fingers tightly. "Hm. Yes. I am. I am, too."

They kept her in, just for twenty-four hours, which quite surprised her; you heard so much about hospitals not having enough beds. She was glad of the rest, though: never felt so tired in her life.

Andy made a fuss of her when she got home, and cooked for her as well, though in the course of it he swore an awful lot at the Aga. The anti-inflammatory tablets the hospital had given her weren't working terribly well; she was glad to doze on and off at odd times during the day.

By the end of January, they had got over the shock of it all and Susie and Ollie had finally come to an agreement. "I'm going to have *Penny Cottage* and an allowance," she told Valerie, who wasn't sure about the feeling that news gave her.

"You want to live here?"

Got used to being on our own again now. Imagine all that extra work! The noise! The chaos everywhere! Besides, with all their stuff, it'll be dreadfully cramped. Will they have to bring that dog with them? She tried to imagine it.

Susie gave a hoot of laughter. "Oh, for goodness sake – I'm a London girl. No! I'm going to buy a flat."

Valerie knew now what Susie was going to say. She felt sick.

"I really want to be somewhere fairly close to Ollie so he can spend time regularly with the children and you know what it's like round here – and of course I can't get a mortgage until I've got a job. And even then because I'm probably going to have to start from scratch, so to speak, it probably won't pay enough..."

She interrupted her quite sharply. "You want to sell *Penny Cottage*."

"I really didn't want it to come to this, Mum."

"No. No, I'm sure you didn't."

"I don't want to do this to you, I really, really don't." Susie sounded truly remorseful. "But I'll help you, of course. I'm sure we can find somewhere nice."

Valerie could feel both panic and anger born of self-preservation rising. "But what are we going to move with, Susie? We haven't got enough money to buy anything again, even if we went back to Glynogol. What were you thinking? That we would find something to rent? How long will our money last if we're going to have to rent?"

Would it see them out?

"Do you *want* to move back to Glynogol?" Susie's voice brightened. She sounded as if she thought that might not be a bad idea.

Valerie shook her head firmly. "No, I do not!"

"Because with prices up there being so much cheaper – I suppose they still are still cheaper – if you *were* thinking about that, I'd probably be able to help you buy somewhere. I should have something left over. I'd be able to put some money towards it if you did."

Valerie brushed her fingers against her forehead. She had a nasty, dull ache again spreading in her head. "But surely you're going to need all your money, aren't you, Susie? I mean, you'll need something behind you, at least until you get a decent job."

"I'd manage…"

She needed to think. "I'll have to talk about this with your father." He won't want to go back to the Glyn, will he? It would look like failure. Not unless his beloved house happens to be on sale, but it won't be. That would be too fortuitous. Where else is cheap?

Susie sounded hugely relieved now to have got it off her chest. "Well, look, I'll come down; we'll talk about it. Don't worry about it till then. I should be able to come down on Sunday morning; Ollie's having the kids."

Valerie phrased and rephrased how she would break the news to Andy, but by Sunday she still hadn't quite steeled herself up to it. His worst fears realised! She couldn't bear it. By the time she caught sight of Susie's car drawing up at the gate, she had been in to him three times that morning as he sat comfortably reading his Sunday paper in front of a roaring log fire, then finding herself asking him instead if he would like some more coffee. He had got quite cross eventually.

"For goodness' sake, woman! I've had three cups this morning already – I'm swimming in it! You keep making me lose my place."

Wiping her hands on her pinny, she hurried, panicking, to the gate. "You're early, pet. I haven't told him yet," she panted hastily and shivering without her coat as Susie wound down the window.

Susie beamed. "Don't worry too much, Mum – I've got good news!" She glanced behind her up the lane. "I can't stay long. Am I all right parking here or shall I move it round the back by the garage?"

Valerie thought quickly. "Move it round the back, love – we can have a chat in the kitchen before we talk to Dad."

She hurried back to the kitchen, trying to structure all her thoughts. Perhaps we shouldn't go. Perhaps I should just tell Susie we aren't moving. She has some responsibility towards us, after all, having persuaded us to come down in the first place; she should have thought about the repercussions before she decided to leave Ollie. I'll do that. I won't say anything to Andy and I'll just say that to Susie.

But what then? What's she to do then?

And then again, we didn't have to move. We should have thought it through more carefully, too. Susie and Ollie have been generous with us in the extreme. She's got her own life to lead; it wouldn't be fair to stand in her way now.

Susie seemed to be glowing that morning. She burst in through the back door in a scarlet duffle coat, blonde hair and thick white woolly scarf flying, and her rosy cheeks looked polished and her eyes were sparkling as ice crystals. "Good news, Mum! Solved the problem! Ollie has obviously been thinking about things and what I was going to tell you was that he's started doing some 'buy-to-let' with some colleagues at the moment, and he had said that, if you like, as I'm letting him keep the house, he'd set aside one for you. "

Relief washed over her. "That's so kind, Susie. I mean, very kind of him when he doesn't have to." She sank down at the table, knees feeling a little weak.

Still had to break the news to Andy, of course, but at least it wasn't going to be the open road just yet, then, just her with an old perambulator and Andy with a haversack and a red-spotted hankie on a stick. They were still going to have to suffer the wrench of leaving *Penny Cottage* and the daunting practicalities of the whole thing – sorting out and packing up and everything – and get used to somewhere yet again, but still...

"Can I make a cup of coffee?" Susie clattered at the cupboards. "Oh, well, we moved you, after all; you used your money on our house." She shook her head firmly, taking down the coffee jar. "Ollie accepts that he has responsibility towards you, Mum; the house he's offering would have been part of his investment portfolio, that's all, just with the profit a bit delayed."

Valerie shook her head. "Well, well, what can I say?" It was all so sad; he was a lovely lad. "Where are these buy-to-let places then, Susie?"

"Bulgaria, I think he said."

Valerie could feel her eyes popping. "Bulgaria?"

"Bulgaria, and – was it Bratislava?? Can't remember; I remember thinking that they all began with B..." She nodded happily, spooning coffee granules into a mug. "That's right, Bratislava, and a whole block of apartments somewhere; I think he said Berlin."

Valerie swallowed hard. "I don't think your Dad would like living in Bulgaria, Susie."

"What? Oh!" Susie rolled her eyes and chuckled. "Oh, no, Mum – like I said, that's what Ollie *had* intended, but things have changed; no, no, he's had a small bequest."

She was surprised. "I thought he hadn't got any family?"

"Oh, it's some great-aunt or – I don't know, great-second-cousin of his, or something, apparently: some relative of his father's anyway he didn't know he had. It's not much, but she's left him a small house, too, I mean, really small, even smaller than *Penny Cottage*, and he says you can have it. He suddenly thought of it this morning. Well, I say, have it, I mean use it, until –" Her sentence trailed off. Valerie finished it for her.

"Until we don't need it any more. Well! Well, that's really ever so kind. He's a very generous man, your Ollie."

Susie's tone was sharp. "He's not my Ollie."

"No. Sorry."

"But he is generous, though; I won't fault him on that score." Susie hesitated. "The thing is, Mum, how would you and Dad feel about moving, well, just a bit further north?"

"Like, what, like Basingstoke, you mean?"

"Well, not exactly..." Setting down her mug hurriedly, she darted to the back door. "Hang on – I stopped and brought us down some carrot cake. Left it in the car. I'll just nip and get it. I'm starving!"

Somewhere near Newbury, perhaps... Valerie ran over the page of Andy's A.A. Road Atlas in her mind's eye as she waited for Susie to come back. Pity it wasn't Basingstoke:

there were some nice little villages round there. Wouldn't even mind going as far north as Berkshire, Henley, perhaps, or Sonning. Or Windsor! Windsor would be even better; she might get to see the queen.

"So where is this house, lovey?" She asked, almost excitedly, as soon as Susie returned,

"Sorry, got to eat something." She unwrapped the greaseproof paper greedily.

"Where is it, then, love?"

"Where's what? Oh, the house? Oh. Colbury."

She furrowed her brow. "Colbury? Where's that, love?"

"Where did he say? Um..." Susie screwed up her eyes. "Oh, yes. Somewhere near Bolton."

Valerie blinked. She must have heard wrong. "Bolton, Lancashire?"

Susie shrugged. "Is it in Lancashire? Yes, I suppose it is."

"Bolton, Lancashire." Valerie blinked hard. "Oh. I see."

Chapter 17

Bolton? Bloody Bolton?" He had calmed down now; at first she'd been afraid he'd really have another heart attack. He had got very aerated at first and had launched into a distraught tirade along the lines of 'It's not just you and Ollie concerned in this, you know' and 'knew this sort of thing would happen – should never have moved – in their hands – I told you this sort of thing would happen, Val!' For which she had been waiting, but which still made her cry a little when it came. She had got a bit defensive of Susie, which had made him worse, and then defensive of Andy, which had got Susie in a tizzy and which had made her cry, too, but eventually it had all subsided and Susie had gone off eventually with a bit of a smile back on her face. Since then, though, Andy had been brooding. "Bolton. Bloody Bolton!"

They both felt helpless. "I don't know what else we can do!" Valerie said at last. "Ollie could sell the house, perhaps, but it wouldn't raise enough for anything very much down here, maybe just a small flat." If only it would!

He shrugged. "Of course not. No, I appreciate what he's doing; it's very good of him. But it's north again. I thought you didn't want to go back north." He scratched his head, bemused. "Bloody Bolton!"

"I don't know it at all, do you?"

"No, I don't."

She was trying desperately to look on the bright side. "We haven't seen it yet; it might be very nice."

"What's the house like, then?"

"Small, Susie said, very small, I gather. We'll have to go and look at it."

"Have to get the car looked at before we do a long journey. Need a couple of new tyres, don't like the noise it's making when I start it up. I don't want it conking out on us half way up a motorway. M6. M62, I suppose." He grimaced. "Bloody M6 again!"

He was silent for a long while and then he shrugged. "So what do we do now, then? Put this place on the market?"

It broke her heart to say so. "I suppose so. Yes."

Ollie was quite friendly on the phone when they rang to thank him. "Moving on again, then, Nana, hah- hah! Hope you'll find it's all right."

"I'm sure we will."

Andy was morose all evening. "We won't see him again, then."

"It doesn't look very likely, no."

Martha was flabbergasted when Valerie told her. "So you're on the move again? Oh, and you liked it there!" She was very practical, as always. "You ought to have a bit of security, you know, I mean, like a document saying you have the right to live there, that it's in Trust. I'm surprised you haven't had one before."

Valerie was quite shocked. "Oh, no, we couldn't ask Ollie for that, not after all he's doing for us, not now he's not going to be our son-in-law. It wouldn't seem right."

"We can't, can we, Susie?" she asked her later. "I wouldn't like to ask him. He wouldn't kick us out anyway, would he? Not Ollie."

Susie was doubtful. "I can try, but now's not the best time."

The demand for period cottages, particularly within a commutable area, was enormous and even though there were plenty of things left to do, like the thatch, by March they had had three firm offers, one of which had been accepted. It made Valerie feel ever so sad. She stared miserably through the kitchen window the afternoon that they heard it had gone. "Another garden, then. Andy, too: all that work, and I'm leaving another garden."

"Look on the bright side; you wouldn't be able to garden

much anyway any more, not with your hip."

"No, there is that, I suppose." She frowned, moving to put the kettle on. "We ought to go up to London again, you know, before we go off to Bolton, now you're better; we haven't been there very much. We should pop up for the day and see Susie and the kiddies. We could go up on the train, if you don't want to drive."

He nodded dubiously. "Uh-hum."

They went up the following Sunday, so that the children would be off school. Valerie quite enjoyed the train journey, though it was a bit cramped and incredibly expensive. "The ticket office man said we should have booked ahead."

Andy was very disgruntled. "How are you supposed to know when you want to go anywhere? It's ridiculous."

"We should have got those Pensioners' whatsits, card things, that would have cut it down a bit."

"It wouldn't. If we'd bought cards, we'd have had to pay out even more. What's the point in paying even more for pensioners' cards when we hardly ever go on a train? No, forget public transport – next time we're sticking to the car."

Waterloo Station seemed to have got busier and noisier and shinier since they had last been there, several years before. There were ever so many coffee places and bars and places offering baked potatoes and croissants, sandwiches and crepes. If they hadn't been so expensive, too, she'd have had some difficulty getting Andy to the underground.

Susie's flat was in a modern brick building in a quite nice area. It had a neat, narrow strip of well-tended grass around it and a large, gated car park. Valerie was saddened by the absence of a garden. "Nowhere much for the children to play."

On the front steps they stood staring at the battery of numbers on a shiny plate outside the door. "What do we press? It says 'enter code.' What's the code?"

"I have no idea."

"Well, have you got the what-you-may-callit – the mobile?"

"It's in my handbag."

He nodded. "Go on, then – give her a ring."

"She's not answering."

"Where's she got to, then?"

"I think I've got her mobile number on here somewhere too." Just as she found it, the front door clicked and opened and a tall thin man clad in a city suit and a cycling helmet emerged.

"Going in?" he asked politely, holding the door open.

"Oh, yes, yes, thank you very much!" They stepped inside quickly. "We must look trustworthy," she whispered as soon as he was out of earshot. "Sure he's not supposed to let just anyone in, really. Bit worrying, actually."

"Don't think we look like dodgy characters."

"No, but we could be anyone."

"We are."

It was a little bit claustrophobic inside but quite pleasant really, clean and tidy, with a nicely carpeted floor and polished wooden fire doors. She noticed Andy checking the light green wallpaper for seams as they waited for the lift to the fifth floor. Catching her eye, he nodded grudgingly. "Hm! Not bad."

The doors on the fifth floor looked liked that PVC or whatever Andy called it, she thought to herself as they waited outside number 19; they were a very shiny cream. Clean-looking though.

After a second try on the bell, she frowned. "I don't think she's in, Andy."

"I told you we should have rung."

She was disappointed. "Wonder where she's got to?"

"Could be anywhere. You wouldn't have it; 'Let's surprise her', you said." He was beginning to look pinched and crabby. Hungry, probably; she should have let him have a salad sandwich or something after all when they got off the train. "What shall we do now, then? I don't want to trail round shops."

"I don't know." She was already very tired. "Do you fancy Madame Tussauds?"

"I'm not standing in that bloody queue and neither are you. Same goes for a museum; too much standing around."

"Covent Garden?"

"We always go to Covent Garden." He shrugged unhappily. "Oh, well, I suppose so, if you like."

"Let's go there anyway, first, and find somewhere to eat." About to turn away, she paused. "I thought I heard something." She listened for a moment intently, her ear close to the door. "Yes, hang on, I'm sure somebody's in there. I'm going to ring again."

This time, when she did so, a voice called back. "Hang on, with you in a tick…"

She frowned. "That was a man's voice, Andy."

"Was it?"

"Couldn't you hear it?"

"No."

"Well, it was. Have we got the right flat?" She checked the number plate at the side of the door. "19, it says. That's what she said."

The man standing at the door when it opened was fair, tanned, crop-haired, tall, wet and wrapped in a white bath towel. Valerie was flustered. "Um – Susie?"

He looked faintly amused. "No, I'm Joe."

"Is Susie in?"

"No, sorry, she's out."

Valerie felt very awkward. "Oh, I see. Will she be long, do you think? We're her Mum and Dad."

He grinned. "Oh, hi there! No, she's gone to the gym, I'm afraid. I'm not sure when she'll be back. Sorry about the…" he added, gesturing at the towel. "I was just having a shower. Did she know you were coming?" He opened the door a little wider. "Would you like to come in?"

They backed away together, shaking their heads.

"– No, no, we won't stay. We were just going to surprise her."

"– No, no, we don't want to disturb you. Just called on the off chance."

"Flying visit."

The damp man nodded, clearly relieved. "Oh. Okay. Well, that's a shame… I'll tell her you called, then?"

"– Yes."

"– No." Andy and Valerie looked at one another.

"Or of course you could come back?"

"Oh, it doesn't matter." Valerie wanted to ask where the children were, but she didn't like to, so she just smiled. Andy was already halfway back to the lift. "Thank you. Sorry to trouble you. Bye-bye."

"Who was that?" Andy hissed out of the corner of his

mouth as she caught up with him.

"I don't know."

"From Down Under, wasn't he?"

"Think so"

They travelled to the ground floor in silence. "Well, well, well," Andy murmured as they set off along the street.

"Mm."

"So she's got a bloke..."

"He could be just a friend."

"Seemed pretty much at home."

"Could be a lodger."

"Did she say she had a lodger?"

"No. I wonder where the children were if she was at the gym? I suppose they must be with Ollie. Should we go and see them?"

"What if *he*'s got someone there? Could be very awkward."

"Do you think he has?"

"Has what?"

"Got somebody."

"Do you think he knows?"

"Knows what?"

"That she's got a fella."

"*We* don't know that, do we?"

He looked at his watch. "A quarter past twelve. What shall we do now, then? Covent Garden?"

She could do with a sit-down. "I suppose so." She set off towards the tube station. "Come on, then, but you're not having chips."

He didn't argue; he was still wondering as they rode down on the escalator. "Well, well, well... well, well, well."

Covent Garden was packed, so after a snack in Frank's Cafe, Andy's favourite, where he looked longingly at the egg, ham and chips but settled for a substantial Ploughman's, they wandered round the bookshops on Tottenham Court Road, briefly popped into the National Portrait Gallery, nipped into St Martin's–In–The–Field for a sit-down, and then made their way back to Waterloo. Valerie was exhausted by the time they got there; far too much walking: it hadn't been wise. On their way onto the swarming concourse she thought she saw Ollie, and got quite excited for a moment. "Ollie! It's Ollie, Andy!"

He looked around, startled. "Where?"

"Over there! He's just going through the barrier onto the platform. Is it him?" She stood on tiptoe, craning, trying to follow the fair head and the broad shoulders moving through the crowd. "He's talking to someone. Don't know if it is him. Look, with that blonde woman, there!" Disappointed, she sank back on her heels, frowning. "No. Too late. He's gone."

Allowing Andy to shepherd her onto their train, she settled gratefully into a window seat. "Oh, I don't know, London's too much for me these days." Her hip ached like billy-o and her feet were red hot and glowing. Andy said his hurt, too.

Susie sent them a text message on their mobile when they were halfway home. They'd been sharing a KitKat and chatting about marriage and long-term relationships.

"People used to die in their forties if not before; you can't expect couples to stay together for so long now we're not dying till we're so much older. If they find someone else and they're married, they don't have an affair and get it out of their systems, perhaps not as often as in the old days, any way. They move out of the marriage; move on."

"If you think about it, though, people get married much later now. If you don't get married till you're thirty-eight and you live till you're seventy-eight that's the same as somebody marrying at twenty-three and living till they're sixty-three."

She was thinking through the maths when the sudden buzz of the mobile made her jump. "Ooer!" She opened the message, feeling quite proud of herself; she was getting quite adept at this. "It's Susie. She says 'Sorry 2 mss u r u ok'.

"Ask her who the bloke was."

She typed the question in carefully, question mark and all. "It's much better now that you've stopped the automatic spelling thingy, Andy; it does what I tell it now." The answer came back quickly. "She's just saying, 'Joe.'"

He was frustrated. "We know that! Ask her who he is."

She waited, but Susie wasn't being very helpful. "She just says 'Friend.'"

They were both bursting with curiosity when Susie and the children came down next, both about their prospective new abode and about the man they had come to call The Lodger. She was full of some photography course she wanted to take. "It's expensive but it's something I'd really like to do."

Valerie nodded, interested. "And then what? What would you do with it after? Set up a studio? Do wedding photographs and stuff?"

She gave a short, dismissive laugh. "Oh, good heavens, no!"

"Children, perhaps? You'd be very good at photographing children. You've taken some very nice snaps."

Susie didn't know a great deal about the house, and as far as The Lodger went, she wasn't giving very much away. He was somebody she knew, had needed somewhere to stay whilst he was in London and as the flat he was moving into wasn't ready, was staying a short while whilst the children were with Ollie. He wasn't married, though Valerie got the impression he might once have been. He was a New Zealander, not an Australian. He seemed the travelling type; he had just come back from South Africa. She had met him at the gym. He was very nice.

Valerie nodded. "I'm sure he is, lovey. And what does he do?"

Susie hesitated, then smiled brightly. "He's a sports photographer."

Valerie and Andy glanced at one another.

"Hm."

"Hm." Valerie nodded. "A photographer? I see."

Poppy cornered Valerie in the kitchen after Susie had taken Thomas out for a walk. "Can I come and live with you and Gramps, Nana?"

"With us, dear? Why would you want to do that?"

Poppy poked a nail sulkily into the loaf of bread, hooking out a large crumb. "I can't stand it. It's not fair. It was bad enough that they were quarrelling all the time, but now they're trying to make us choose." There were tears in her eyes, Valerie realised. Her face crumpled and a big splash landed on the crumb. "I hate them! I hate them, Nana!"

"No, you don't, lovey."

"What am I supposed to say, though? I don't want to hurt either of them. We shouldn't have to choose!"

Valerie's heart turned over. *No more you should, pet: not in an ideal world.* She put her arms about the stressed little girl. "They both love you and want you to be happy, that's all, lovey. They just want to do the right thing."

"Well, they're not." Poppy drew away sniffing and began abstractedly to attack the loaf again, digging practically her whole fist into it this time.

"You'd be bored with us, Poppy, though, wouldn't you? I mean, you're a teenager now – well, just. You're going to want a bit of fun. Not that we wouldn't want you, of course, we'd love to have you with us, and it would be an adventure, 'cos we're moving."

She looked startled. "You're moving again? Are you?"

"And I understand it's a very small house and it is a very long way away. And then there's Thomas; Thomas needs you, pet, he really does. He shouldn't have to have anybody else now moving away." The loaf was now in crumbs and chunks all over the breadboard. She watched Poppy pushing them about with her finger, shifting them into patterns. "Did you mean to leave me any bread?"

Poppy reddened. "Oops! Sorry!"

Valerie chuckled. "Doesn't matter."

As Poppy began to gather them together Valerie waited with the dustpan, considering her dispirited little figure. Not so little, either: she was fast growing up. "Have you decided which one to choose? Which way you're going to go?"

Poppy shrugged. "With Mum, I suppose. I had been thinking perhaps Dad, but he..." Her voice trailed off.

Valerie nodded. "But you'd be able to see a lot of Daddy, stay with him a lot."

There was an oddly guarded expression on Poppy's face. "Yes, but –"

"But what?"

"Nothing."

"Come on, pet, you can tell me."

"All right, but don't tell Mum."

"Don't tell Mum what?"

"Daddy's got a girlfriend."

Valerie's heart gave painful lurch. "Really!"

Poppy grimaced. "I don't like her."

Before Valerie could ask, "Who is she?" Susie burst in at the back door, bringing with her a waft of fresh air and energy. "Poppy, we've got to go, we're late, I can't tell you how late we are. Have you got your things? Come on!"

They had disappeared back to London within ten minutes.

It was most frustrating.

They chose Chocolate Limes and a Toblerone for the inspection journey up to Bolton, a white chocolate one just in case it melted. With the M6 ahead of Andy, and all the money they'd had to spend to get the car through its MOT, and with a poor night for sleeping behind them after the anxiety-provoking sit-down financial assessment they had gone through the night before, they were both in ratty moods and were still dwelling on the money question as they set off in the car.

"The insurance is due next month, too, and the Road Fund Licence the month after. I reckon we'll have to risk just having Third Party; can't afford to keep laying out all we do each month. And the oil's gone up yet again. Hope this new house hasn't got a bloody Aga."

"I doubt it."

"Eh? Did you say it has?"

She raised her voice. "I don't know, do I? I shouldn't think so." He had the radio on so loud it was hurting her ears and she reached, wincing, for the volume control.

He didn't like it. "What are you doing?"

"Turning it down a bit; it's really distorted. Are you sure it's tuned in?"

"Leave it, leave it." He turned it back up again. "I need it for road bulletins."

She felt unusually resentful. "Andrew, for goodness' sake, why can't you wear your hearing aid? It isn't fair! Do you want me to get deaf, too?"

They travelled most of the way up to Birmingham in faintly aggrieved silence, lost in their own thoughts. Valerie spent a lot of the time wondering about where they were going to. "It's a funny address," she murmured, as they passed the signs for the NEC.

He glanced at her. "Eh?"

She repeated it louder. "I said it's a funny address: '3 The Ginnel'. It's a bit ugly, isn't it? Does it mean something? What's a ginnel?

"Sort of an alleyway, isn't it, I think, through sort of back-to-backs?"

"Sally... Sally, pride of our alley..." The song popped into her head.

He grimaced. "Do you have to?"

She chuckled. Hadn't realised she had been singing it aloud. "Got to drown out that racket you're listening to somehow."

He grinned. Reaching for the volume control he turned it down a little at last. "That better?"

The journey was pretty uneventful – only a couple of hold-ups on the M6, and the M62 was busy, but not too bad. They stopped for a nip into the toilets and a browse around the shop at a Grenada Services, and then ate their cheese and tomato sandwiches and drank their coffee in the car park outside. It was quite mild. She was surprised. "I thought it'd be getting colder."

There was a twinkle in his eye. "Being further north, you mean?"

"Mm."

"I dare say they have nice weather up here too. We used to have."

"In Wales?"

"Yes, of course. We had that Easter, don't you remember, when Susie came home and brought Ollie for the first time, and we were sunbathing all day."

She didn't want to think about that. "I don't remember."

He pressed the lid onto the plastic picnic box. "You ready?"

"Don't you want a Penguin?"

"Yes, give me one; I'll eat it on the way."

Things got ratty again as they approached Bolton. Valerie had the road map spread open on her knee and was looking out for road signs, marking their journey so far with her finger. The roads were much busier now, and Andy was getting very tense. He scowled, forehead furrowed, as he stared out at the congested road. "Left, here?"

She checked with the map. "Mm, right." Feeling the bearing of the car, she glanced up, surprised. "Where are you going?"

"You said right."

"I meant, right, it's left. You said left. I said left, right. Left, that's right."

There were a lot of road junctions and roundabouts. It was very confusing. "Which way now? Left?"

"Right." He was going the wrong way again. Goodness knows where they were going now. She reared up in her seat, pointing. "No, not left – right!"

"You said it was left!"

"No, I didn't!"

"You did! I said 'left'? And you said 'right.' Left, that's right."

"No, I meant: right, go right!"

Steam was practically coming out of his ears. "Oh, bloody hell!"

Colbury, when they finally found it, seemed insignificant and very dreary, with rows and rows of houses in varying degrees of size and preservation stretching out on either side of the road. At what appeared to be the middle of it was a small garage with, next to it, a lacklustre pub advertising karaoke and 'Two-For-One' bar meals, and on the other side of the road, a small supermarket and a short parade of shops. Valerie spotted a launderette, a unisex hairdresser, some sort of an electrical supplier, a Chinese takeaway and a chip shop.

"Where's this Fosse Road, then?" Andy asked, peering through the windscreen. "Have you found it on the map?"

She peered around. "It's on the left, somewhere. Should be about around here... Yes, Fosse Road, there it is, that's right." She did her best to make it very clear this time. "Turn left, Andy. *Left.* Here it is: to your *left.*"

The semi-detached houses on Fosse Road varied in size from small to middling and seemed generally well maintained, which came as a relief. Cars were parked on either side of what was a long, long, long, long road and a very,

very steep one. Valerie frowned. "I hope The Ginnel isn't near the top, Andy."

"You won't manage this climb, not with your hip."

"I won't. I hope it isn't."

It was, of course. It was the last small entry on the right and they missed it the first time, driving on past and finding themselves heading out into open, hilly countryside. She shook her head. "This can't be right. Go back."

"Nowhere to turn." Spotting the entrance to a field, he slowed, glancing in his mirror, but then grimaced. "Damn it, someone on my tail. Always somebody behind me when I need to stop..." The road was very narrow and they had to drive on for two or three miles before he finally managed a turn, but at last they were poised once again at the top of Fosse Road. "Keep your eyes peeled this time."

"I was, before." She spotted the sign suddenly, tucked away at the side of the grey stone wall as soon as they started down the hill. "There, Andy! Here, *here*, look!"

Chapter 18

The Ginnel was indeed an alleyway, only a few feet wide. Andy was worried about the car. "Have to park on the road, I suppose. Hope it'll be all right."

They climbed out stiffly. Valerie shivered. "It *is* colder here. The air feels different."

"We're at the top of a hill."

"But it's different from the south; I told you it was."

He was already stalking into the alley. "What number?" She trotted hastily after him. "Number 3." On her right, a long wooden fence protected the backs of the terraced houses in the row below. On her left, the short grey-stoned terrace of houses sitting above the narrow passageway presented its front aspect, "They're not back-to-back, then Andy!"

Each house, with a single window beside a porch and another one above, had a small gate leading into a narrow garden. The numbers ran consecutively. Number 1, on the corner, appeared to have been extended to the road side with a small conservatory and it seemed to have spread into Number 2 as well; there was a fence enclosing the two gardens, making just one. She could see that the garden was quite a pretty one, and well tended. A wooden seat hung beneath a blue-painted trellised arch, and there was a pretty paved sitting area with lots of tubs and flower pots nicely placed about.

In contrast, the garden of Number 3 looked as if someone might have grown things in it some time, but not for a very long while. It had no garden gate, just a couple of stumps with rusty sockets where a gate might once have hung. Number 4 looked empty. Its windows were blank and its small garden was a wilderness, with grass and weeds grown several feet high.

Oh dear.

Andy was already poking miserably at the flaking paint-work on the bottom floor windowsill of Number 3 when she reached the top of the path. "I tell you, it's in a right old mess."

"Uhuh..." Not wanting to look at him, she fumbled in her handbag. "Now where did I put the envelope with the key?"

Cobwebs draped the upper corners of the interior of the tiled porch. "There's some nice stained glass round the top," she pointed out. The front door needed painting badly, too. Her hand shook a little as she turned the key. "Here we go, then!"

It opened directly into a small, square room, empty save for a faded blue carpet, worn away in patches, and a coal bucket sitting by a green-and-red tiled hearth with a high wooden mantle above. As she stepped inside, she wrinkled her nose. Andy, following close behind, must have done likewise. "Pooh! What's that nasty smell?"

"Smells like cats."

"Did she have a cat, then?"

"I don't know, do I? Must have."

"Let's get some air in the room." He forced open the high sash window with a grating jerk, and then they both turned to survey the room. "Hm."

"Hm." She struggled to find something good to say about it. "Still the old fireplace: like the tiles."

He scuffed with his shoe. "Pretty mouldy old carpet."

"Mm. Wonder what's in here?" The door which she opened, at the back of the room and beyond a steep and narrow staircase leading up behind the sitting room wall, led into a small dining area, just big enough to hold the folding Formica-covered table and two small upright chairs which had been set back tightly against the party wall, and partitioned from a tiny, square kitchen by a set of empty, head-high, green-painted wooden shelves. Someone had scrubbed around recently; it smelled very strongly of Vim.

Dispirited, she moved into the kitchen area. The stove was an old electric upright. A split and faded orange plastic washing-up bowl sat in a small, cracked, butler's sink, and a rusty pan scrubber and a dishcloth, dried out into a solid grey lump, had been left inside a sink tidy. There were open shelves up on the other party wall, still lined with stained strips of floral wallpaper, and below them a narrow width of pale blue Formica-covered worktop, with open shelving below both it and the sink.

Andy moved in behind her. "Bloody hell, it's small!"

She looked around, frowning. "Where have they put the back door?"

"Doesn't seem to be one."

"That's odd." She hesitated for a while, puzzling about it, and then shrugged. "Shall we look upstairs?"

At the top of the stairs a miniscule landing led up towards the back of the house to a small bathroom and to bedroom big enough perhaps for a cot and a little chest of drawers. In the other direction, it led to a somewhat bigger bedroom overlooking the front.

They walked back downstairs in silence. Valerie was beginning to feel very anxious, very frayed. "What are we going to do with all our stuff?"

He shrugged, equally at a loss. "Dunno."

It's really not on, pet," she told Susie when they had settled back at *Penny Cottage* the next day. "It's ever so kind of Ollie and it's not a bad little house, quite sturdy, and there's some nice countryside at the back, but I don't think we can do it; it's too small and the hill is too steep."

Susie sounded a bit abstracted. "That's a great pity. What are you going to do now?"

"I rather hoped you might have some bright ideas, pet. I mean, we're a bit stuck. Do you have a definite date yet for completion?"

"The twenty-first of June. Don't know if we could put them off..." She hesitated. "What you could do, Mum, is to put your things in storage, the things you don't need, and just try it for size. And you and Dad always do everything together, don't you? "

"Well, more or less."

"So you won't really need to walk."

"Perhaps not."

Susie sounded relived now that she had thought of the idea. "Well, that's what I'd do: see what you really need, pack the rest away and give it a bit of time. You might like it, and if you do, you can get rid of the things you don't want then."

It'd cost quite a bit, long-term storage. "And if we don't? If we can't settle?"

Susie sighed. "Well, then, I suppose you'd have to ask Ollie how he feels about selling and buying something else instead. At least, by all accounts this one has a bit of character and should hold what value it's got; don't know what you'd be able to find for the same money instead."

"No, nor do I. It's only a small terraced."

"Wouldn't get very much for it, then."

Valerie suddenly felt very, very old and very, very tired. "No."

Tom the postman agreed to drive a large Self-hire van as they weren't taking that much stuff, and to bring his son Barry, who worked in Safeways, as long as it was on his day off, to give a hand with the shifting. Everything they hadn't thrown out or thought they could manage without was stored safely in a secure locked storage unit that he had recommended. They did an awful lot of squabbling about what to take and what to store. The monthly rental cost an awful lot.

Saying goodbye to *Penny Cottage* was a terrible wrench. Valerie felt like weeping as they drove away. Poor little thing, it was going to miss her. She kept her eye on its rose-covered porch and its thatched roof until it had vanished out of sight. "That's that, then."

Andy shrugged. "Say goodbye to the spiders."

She sniffed and attempted a chuckle. "And the mice."

"The damp in the walls."

"The rats in the thatch."

"The moss *on* the thatch."

"The oil charges."

"The cess pit."

"The medlar tree."

"The pub."

There were tears in her eyes. "Oh, I am going to miss it!"
"Don't, love." He squeezed her fingers. "Yes, I know."

Susie rang on the mobile as they were turning onto the
M62. She sounded enraged and tearful. "You're going
to love this, Mum."
"What's that, love?"
"You'll never guess who he's been seeing."
"Seeing?"
She was impatient. "Seeing, seeing; having an affair
with."
"Who? Ollie?"
"Bastard. Only bloody Camilla."
Valerie's eyes flew wide open. "You're joking!"
"I am not."
"Camilla! No! Hang on a minute, love..." She turned
breathlessly to Andy. "Ollie's been having an affair with
whatsit. Thingy. Camilla Fox Doodah."
"He hasn't!"
"He has."
He looked as shocked as she was. "Bloody hell! Well,
I'm blowed!"
Camilla was 'Daddy's girlfriend'! No wonder Poppy had
said she didn't like her. She turned back to the mobile,
shaking her head in disbelief. "Camilla!"
"Bitch."
"I thought you said you were both still seeing her before."
"Seeing her, yes, seeing her, not *seeing* her! I knew she
was popping to the house from time to time to see him, but
she told me she was just keeping an eye on him and I was
pleased about that. She'd tell me things he was up to, how
he was getting on. I do still care. I thought she was just
being a friend."
"But she wasn't."
"I can see it now: no wonder she kept encouraging me to
leave him, telling me I ought to get a divorce."
"Hasn't she got a husband of her own?"
"She did have, but he left her. They've had a divorce"
"And I don't blame him!" She turned to Andy again.
"Her husband left her."
"Whose?"

"Camilla's, of course!"

"Who'd want a woman like her? She's a bitch."

"Well, Ollie, presumably."

He sniffed. "Very surprised. Thought he had more taste."

The mobile squawked angrily. "I don't believe it! Little bitch!"

Valerie returned to Susie quickly. "So where are you now? I mean, what's happening?"

"I don't know, I don't know, I've only just found out. The cleaner told me and Poppy says that it's true. I've just been on the phone to him. He isn't denying it." She spoke through gritted teeth. "I'll tell you one thing, Mum, she's not having my kids!"

"Would she want them? She didn't strike me as very child-friendly."

"I'm not letting her have anything to do with them. If Ollie wants her, he can do without them, too." Her tone was cold as ice now. "If he sticks with Camilla, he can bank on it: I'll be taking them away."

"Well, well, well, well, well!" Andy shook his head as Valerie switched off the mobile at last. "Sauce for the gander, I suppose, sauce for the goose."

"We don't know that Susie's going out with that man, not for certain. I don't think Susie minds so much that Ollie's having an affair, but that it's with somebody she thought was a friend. Camilla was the one pushing Susie into leaving Ollie! I think she feels betrayed. Horrible woman!" She looked down at the half eaten bag of sherbet lemons on her knee; she seemed to have lost her appetite. "Do you want another one?"

He glanced with similar aversion at the bag. "No, not for me. No."

As they neared Colbury, Andy glanced in his driving mirror. "Is Tom still following behind?"

She craned around. "Can't see him."

"Must have got stuck at the last lights."

"He might miss The Ginnel like we did. I'd better hang about on Fosse Road."

Andy unloaded the car and went ahead to Number 3 whilst Valerie waited half in and half out of The Ginnel, poised to flag Tom down. She hoped he wasn't going to be very long; there was a chill wind blowing.

A middle-aged woman was in the garden at Number 1-and-2, hanging out her washing, and she smiled at Valerie. "Hello!" Friendly, then. Good. Strange to hear a northern accent for a change.

"Hello!" Valerie gave an exaggerated shiver. "Good day for drying but it's a little bit cold; warmer where we've come from."

"Where's that, then?"

She was very proud of it, somehow. "Hampshire."

The woman seemed suitably impressed. "Hampshire! You've had a long drive."

"We have." Valerie nodded down at the road. "Just waiting for the furniture van in case he misses The Ginnel."

"Yes, people do. Number 3 or number 4?"

"Pardon?"

"Which house are you moving into?"

"Oh!" Valerie waved a hand. "Number 3."

"Ah. Wondered who had taken Sally's house."

The woman approached her back gate and opened it, balancing her washing basket on her hip. She looked very nice. Her neat dark hair was smartly cut, and she was wearing lipstick, even if she was only doing the washing. "Miserable affair, moving day. Let me know if you need anything. I'm Shona, by the way, Shona Birkhead."

Valerie beamed. "Oh, how do you do, I'm Valerie Bryce. Hang on!" Bobbing out into Fosse Road again, she peered down the hill before returning. "I'm watching for the furniture van. Your garden looks very nice," she added, peering nosily past Mrs Birkhead. "I love the trellised patio area you've made. You've got both numbers, have you – 1 and 2? Made them into one? And you've found room for a conservatory. You're lucky, being at the end."

Mrs Birkhead nodded. "You're more restricted at Number 3, aren't you? You can't go sideways like we have, there's no room at all at the back and you would have to stay within the building line. We wondered if someone would buy 3 and 4, with both being empty. In the old days, families would have piled about fourteen children into one of these, but nowadays, people expect a bit more, don't they?"

Valerie shook her head. "They do, they do indeed."
Including us.

As she popped out into Fosse Road yet again, Tom's big van was just turning slowly and noisily round the corner at the bottom. She hurried out into the road, waving a hand vigorously and he flashed his headlights in acknowledgement. Relieved, she returned, puffing, to Mrs Birkhead. "They're here!"

Mrs Birkhead stepped back from the gate. "I'll get out of your hair, then. Pop round if you need a – you know – a cup of sugar!"

Maybe this won't be so bad. People were really nice, weren't they? You can always find nice people, wherever you go.

Valerie was already panting towards Number 3 to alert Andy. "I will! I will! That's very kind."

The moving in of a comparatively small number of items of furniture shouldn't have taken all that long, though it did. The table and chairs they'd brought wouldn't fit into the dining space if they were going to have room to walk through, so they had to put the Formica table and the two small chairs back where they had been against the wall, which left the dining set over. By the time Tom, Andy and Barry had managed to get that, the three armchairs they'd brought, the dresser and the sideboards, the television and the coffee table into the sitting room, there wasn't room for anybody to manoeuvre, and they still had all the boxes. The only good side was that it hid much of the old, moth-eaten carpet, though she could still smell cats.

Andy stood there, hunched and glowering. "We've still got far too much stuff. They'll have to take back that dresser and the dining table and chairs."

She was affronted. "I want the dresser!" She felt oddly tearful. "It's the only really good piece of furniture we've got – that and the sideboard."

"It looks daft. It was all right in the cottage."

"I don't care. We left enough of the old stuff when we left North Wales."

"Takes up far too much room, and collects dust, anyway, with all those ruddy plates you put on it. We never use those plates."

"We might do, one day. Christmas."

"Never have yet."

"We might."

He looked exasperated. "What about the sideboard, then? We definitely don't need that."

"It goes with the dresser! And where would I put the spare crockery? The nice tea set and stuff? All the decent cutlery? Tablecloths and napkins? The tablemats? Where would you put your bottles and your best glasses?"

"The other sideboard, the smaller one."

"We didn't bring it."

"Oh."

She shook her head. "The kitchen shelves are spoken for; there aren't enough of them really, I've still got stuff all over the kitchen. There isn't going to be an inch of room."

He sighed heavily. "Oh, blast it. Why don't you make us all a cup of tea?"

She was prepared this time; tea, sugar, milk and biscuits, teaspoons and a set of mugs. She had also put a tin of red salmon and some butter and bread and tomatoes and the breadboard and knife into the Handy Bag to make some sandwiches for everybody before Tom and Barry set off back again. She'd have to balance the breadboard, if she could find it, on top of the stove to make them. No room anywhere else.

Whilst they were waiting for Tom and Barry to get ready for the off, she gave Andy the gist of her brief conversation with their new neighbour. "It could be very handy for us, you know, pet," she told Andy as they eventually waved goodbye to the van in the dusk. "I mean, if we don't like it here, if it is too small and things. If Number 4 is for sale and if there are people looking to buy two together, Ollie might get a good price. It might be enough to buy something else, something on the level, perhaps a bungalow or a small semi. We'll have to get a local paper, have a look around and see."

He was too tired to consider the subject. "Let's just settle in first."

She nodded. She was too tired as well, really; in fact, she felt exhausted, though her brain was a bit wired up. One day at a time: that way would be the best.

They did a bit more sorting out, made their bed and found their wash and night things, and then Andy nipped down to the chip shop on the main road for two fish-and-chips and mushy peas for supper. They were an improvement on Hampshire's, but they ate them without chatting and then went straight to bed without even clearing the salt and vinegar away.

It wasn't a good night's rest. When Valerie did drop off, briefly, just before morning, she found herself having a terrible row with Camilla. She hit her over the head with a big, black folded city gentleman's umbrella and woke up again just as she was poking her in the supercilious blue eye.

In the cold light of day Number 3 looked even more miserable, sending Andy into a deep depression. He couldn't seem to get going. Whilst Valerie struggled to fit their kitchen equipment away on the shelves, he sat slouched despondently in an armchair squashed into the corner of the room between the sideboard and the dresser scanning some old copies of the local paper that had been left some time in the porch. When she went in to ask if he wanted a cup of coffee, he shook his head morosely. "Don't think I can be doing with this, Val."

She couldn't bear to look at his face. A most uncomfortable hot spot had developed somewhere underneath her waistband. She rubbed it, frowning. "Shall we go out for a bit, lovey? Forget all this putting away and have a breath of fresh air?"

He shrugged disinterestedly. "If you want." She left him to it.

The prices he saw in the paper seemed to cheer him up a little bit, though, as the morning wore on. He followed her into the kitchen, carrying a newspaper and looking brighter. "It is possible we could find something, you know, Val."

She was relieved. "Oh, that's good! Shall we go out, then? Have a look round?"

"We might as well. Do us good. See where exactly we're at."

They drove up Fosse Road first and out along the narrow

road they'd followed for a short while the day before. It was really quite pleasant, hilly, farming country with farms having strange, oddly romantic names like Top O' th' Hill, or Tutt's Bottom. After about half an hour, driving down a single-track lane they found themselves at the small car park for a walking place, amongst a fringe of trees around a large, tranquil, silvery-grey lake nestling in a wide basin, where rugged hills reached downwards towards a band of forestry around the water's edge. They could see the sun glinting on the windows of a car parked on the far side of the lake, but nobody else seemed to be about and it was silent apart from birdsong, very peaceful. Valerie nodded. "They've even got picnic tables, look. Shall we have a stroll?"

He shrugged dispiritedly. "If you want to. I don't mind. Why not?"

The air felt very fresh and smelled of wild garlic and pine. It was good to be out and about. The path was quite rough and pebbly, and quite up and down in places, and it didn't take very long before her hip began to ache, so they cut their walk fairly short. "Be a good place for you to go though, Andy," she told him as they got back into the car, "when you start doing your walks."

He looked unconvinced. "Hm. Hm."

"Shall we go down and have a look at Bolton?"

They parked in the town centre, where Valerie wandered round the shopping mall while Andy went off to have a quick look at the square and the Town Hall then they met up again for a cup of tea and a bite.

"What do you think, then, eh?" she asked, eying him over a crumbly Chorley cake. He still looked very tired. Seventy-five, he was now; too old for this lark.

"Not bad. Very, um – cosmopolitan."

"Oh." She mused, looking about her. "Cosmopolitan. Yes, very."

"Be interesting."

"It will."

They called into the small supermarket at the bottom of Fosse Road on the way home to stock up their supplies. There wasn't a great deal there. Andy scanned the bakery shelf hopefully. "Have they got any of those whatsits?"

"What whatsits?"

"Those Chorley cake things. They were very nice."

She couldn't see any. "They've got Eccles."

"They'll do." She slipped an up-to-date copy of the local paper into the shopping trolley. "We'll have a look through this tonight, just to see."

That evening, after a supper of salad, new potatoes and slices of boiled ham, followed by the Eccles cakes, they browsed through the Estate agents' advertisements in the paper. "There's one here, Merryweather Road, a bungalow, three bedrooms, a hundred and twenty one thousand. Doesn't look too bad."

"Where is it?"

"Bolton, I think. "

"No, I mean, in the paper."

"Oh. Here."

She studied the smudgy photograph carefully. It didn't call to her at all. "Hm. Hm."

"And another one, a semi. Blackthorn Road, wherever that is. One hundred and ten. There's no shortage" He frowned. "Would you want to stay round here?"

She shrugged. "Don't think we have much choice."

"We can't afford to go back, that's for sure."

"No, we certainly can't." She stabbed at the paper with her finger. "Look at this one, bungalow, three bedrooms again, two reception, garage, forty foot garden. Modern and on an estate, but that'd cost at least four hundred and something where we were."

"And the rest! And how much is it here?"

"One hundred and twenty eight." She shook her head. "Even the Glyn has gone up an awful lot, Norma was saying." She hesitated, eyeing him warily. Could he bear to hear it? "I wasn't going to tell you this, but our old house has just gone for –"

He held up a hand. "Don't tell me."

She was relieved. "Okay, I won't."

Andy returned to his newspaper. "Ollie's not going to get that much for this one, anyway. There's a similar sort of property here to this: two up, two down, terraced, with a countryside view, which this one hasn't got, eighty-five thousand."

She shook her head. "Oh dear. Hm."

He got up and wound his way to the window, biting his bottom lip as he peered through the yellowing net. "I wonder if he'd go for it, anyway? He doesn't like modern, does he?"

"No, he doesn't; he said 'no modern', when we were looking before – though he can't really lose out on property whatever it is, can he?" She pushed back her chair wearily and made for the kitchen. "Perhaps we should have a look at one or two – get some general idea? See if we think we'd like it better anyway?"

He peered over the top of his reading glasses. "You're not going now, are you?"

"Eh? Of course not, not *now,* silly. It's nine o'clock at night. I was going to get our cocoa."

His eyes were twinkling. "Right."

Chapter 19

They set off first thing on Monday morning to browse round estate agents' windows, and then made appointments to see a couple of test cases, a small bungalow and a slightly larger semi.

29 Daisy Court, which Valerie had chosen largely because of the name, proved to be a miniscule, unadorned, pebble-dashed, rectangular bungalow crammed cheek-by-jowl into a tight nest of identical bungalows amidst what seemed to be an otherwise mostly grim industrial and trading park. She took against it immediately. "Ooh, no, I don't like it round here, Andy. No views, nothing nice to look at. Very ugly."

"At least you'd be on the level. There aren't any hills."

"Yes, there is that."

"If you have an op on your hip eventually..."

"Mm, it would be handy then. Still... "

"Still..."

"Shall we move on?"

18 Sycamore Road was a three-bedroomed semi on a sprawling estate which had no sign of a tree. There were a couple of rather battered cars and an abandoned shopping trolley at the sides of the road instead, and quite a bit of rubbish lying about. The small front gardens had mostly been concreted over for parking and bins.

"UPVC windows again, though. Got a few loose tiles."

The house was empty, and the young man said he had a few calls to make on his mobile, so he let them wander round by themselves. She tried to look on the bright side.

"It's not bad, is it, Andy? Very light. Makes a change from the last."

"You could say that, yes."

He trailed reluctantly in her wake as she made her way into the kitchen. "No better than the other one. Still couldn't swing a bloody cat."

"Stop swearing." She had hoped for something a little bigger.

"Laminated units: plastic coated. That floor is badly scratched."

She stared at the small upright cooker. "Gas'd be quite nice for a change, you know, Andy. Very manageable, you know, gas. You can simmer properly." Her tummy was beginning to hurt again; it kept doing it. That Irritable Bowel thingy; she was definitely getting it.

Outside at the back there was a garden about twelve or fourteen foot square, consisting mostly of dusty beige earth and patchy grass. A collapsed red plastic paddling pool lay crumpled up against a small, corrugated green plastic tool storage shed in one corner. Not a sign of plants, except for an unrecognisably shrivelled dead something in a small plastic flower pot with a Homebase price sticker still on it: Two for £2.99.

She squinted, searching for the sun. "Which way is south, do you think?"

"Dunno." He stared up at the grey sky then waved a hand. "Behind the house, I think. Dunno."

Slipping a hand inside her coat as they made their way back inside, she undid her skirt button, sighing as she felt a little release. Felt a little better, though the hurty spot still ached.

There was only a comparatively short flight of stairs, fairly shallow. "Just look at this." He shook the newel post. The staircase rattled.

She nodded thoughtfully. "Hm."

"It's rough, you know, Val. Look at the way those ceilings are cracking already. Have to put some Anaglypta on those."

Somebody had left a small mock crystal chandelier dangling in the hall. Whoever had live here had liked Homebase; she'd seen the same one there.

Two people passed them whilst they were saying goodbye to the estate agent, an old man and a harassed-looking young Asian woman in a long coat and a headscarf, pushing a pram. They both stared, but neither returned Valerie's smile. As they got in their car, a sporty red one with flames painted luridly on the sides came racing round the corner with a boom-boom, headache-inducing bass rhythm blaring, and screeched to a halt outside the next-door house. It seemed full of young men.

They were both very quiet on the way back to The Ginnel.

"What d'you think then?" she asked Andy when they'd had their tea – pilchards and salad this time, they hadn't done any more shopping. He was looking very depressed again: combination of the pilchards and the house. "The semi. Did you like it?"

He hesitated. "Well..."

"I didn't." She shrugged. "Of course, it's not the only one – there are plenty more we could see. I tell you what: I'm going to ring Susie in a minute anyway. I'll ask her – put it to her, just as a general principle – just ask her how Ollie might react. What do you think of that?"

He shrugged. "I suppose so. Might as well."

Susie seemed distracted, but much jollier. "Sorry, Mum I was just on my way out."

"Going anywhere nice?"

"Manna."

"A manor? You mean, out in the country?"

"No, Mum. It's a veggie restaurant in Primrose Hill."

Valerie chuckled. "Oh, I see! Who are you going with? Anybody nice?"

"Oh, just Joe."

"Seems to have cheered up a lot. She's off out with that Joe," she told Andy, when he came downstairs in his dressing gown after his bath and joined her in the sitting room.

"Is she indeed!"

"She is."

"Kiddies all right?"

"Yes, yes, they're both fine. I had a word with both of them. Thomas is in the school rugby team; he's very proud. Poppy doesn't say a lot these days; bit unforthcoming. I expect it's being a teenager as much as anything; they get like that."

Andy got up again and went out to the kitchen where she heard him rummaging in the biscuit tin. He came back nibbling a chocolate digestive and with the packet in his hand. "Well, we didn't have any pudding," he told her defensively, when he saw her looking. "So what did Susie say?"

"She's a bit doubtful."

He sank into his chair. "Thought she might be."

"She said we'll have to ask him ourselves, she isn't speaking to him. She said the house is between us and Ollie, nothing to do with her and she said this might not be the best timing." In just a couple of weeks or so! She'd thought a divorce would take much longer. It had been a shock. "The paper work's all been completed, apparently, and it's gone up to the judge, so the *decree absolute* should be through very shortly. "She doesn't know whether it would be a good thing to bring up the thing about the house just at the moment."

"No, probably wouldn't. It was just a thought."

"Not as if we've seen anywhere we like. Shall we sit on it for a while; see how we get on where we are? It's very early days. At least we've got a bit of a view up here."

"From the bedroom window."

"From the bedroom window at least. And it's a sturdy little house."

"It is. Thick walls. And Mrs Birkhead seems nice"

"Whole place needs decorating, of course."

She sighed. "Give it a few months, maybe, eh? Let the divorce settle down."

"Can't keep on paying storage charges for ever, though."

He called after her hopefully as she was making her way through to get their cocoa: "At least he'll have to keep in touch with us to some extent, eh, Ollie? Because of the house, I mean, even if they're divorced?"

"I suppose he will, lovey, yes."

"That's one good thing."

Ah, bless him. Poor Andy. "Yes, it is!"

He went off to bed before her, and when she got up there the light was out, the little portable television was on and he was propped up on the pillows with his eyes closed. Left his glasses on again, she noticed: dropped off. He'd break them if he went to sleep like that. He opened his eyes and spoke sharply as she reached quietly to take them off. "What are you doing?"

He made her jump, "Oh, you're awake!"

"Yes, I'm awake. I was just listening."

"I was going to take your glasses off."

"Thought you were about to strangle me!"

It made her chuckle. "Well, I do feel like strangling you sometimes."

He grinned. "Trying to strangle me!"

Lying side by side in the flickering light of the screen, they tried to concentrate on Jeremy Paxman, but giggles kept shaking them.

"Shut up."

"I can't." Her tummy hurt, this time from chuckling.

"It wasn't that funny."

That started her off again. "Yes, it was."

Turning onto her side when he had put off the television, she snuggled down contentedly into the nest created by his arm, his warm tum and his bony knees. She could feel his body shaking with laughter still from time to time, and she sighed softly.

This is nice.

It was almost three months before Susie was able to come up to visit and when she did, it was plain that she was a bit taken aback by the size of the house. "You haven't even got a back door."

"We know we haven't."

"Couldn't you have one knocked through?"

"Well, we could, but it'd only lead straight out onto the road above."

Thomas was staggered. "Haven't you got a back garden, Nana?"

"We haven't, Thomas. You could play with your ball in the Ginnel, though mind it doesn't go out in the road. A bit later on, we'll take you to the park."

Andy nodded. "I'll have a knock-about with you then, lad."

Thomas didn't look all that enthusiastic. "Okay."

Poppy slouched up the stairs. "Where am I sleeping?"

Valerie followed her with Susie trailing in her wake. "Well, I thought you and Mummy could sleep in our bed, and Thomas could go on the floor in his sleeping bag. He did bring a sleeping bag?"

Susie was puzzled. "Where are you sleeping, then, Mum?"

"Oh, there's a nice little bedroom at the back." She opened the door. "See? We'll be all right in here." She had done her best with it. It smelled very fresh now that Andy had painted it, and the patchwork-patterned duvet and pillow set in shades of rose pink, green and white with toning pink curtains from the spare room at Penny Cottage looked very pretty. Andy had painted a chest of drawers white for under the window, and she'd bought a white-framed mirror from T.K. Maxx to go on the top. She'd hung up some white muslin curtains as well, as the little room was overlooked by the road, and had put on the pale green walls a set of small flower prints in dark red mounts that they'd had at *Penny Cottage*. The colours went quite well. A nice little rug was on the shopping list for next to the bed, but they hadn't got round to buying it yet. It would be the finishing touch.

Susie shook her head firmly, though. "Oh, that's no good, Mum, it's ridiculous. You and Dad can't sleep there: it's only a single bed."

Valerie was flustered. "We can't fit you and the children in here, and I wouldn't like to leave them downstairs."

Susie was dismissive. "Oh, they'll be fine, Mum. They're not babies any more."

How time flew. "No, I suppose they're not."

Susie disappeared and Valerie followed to see her peering through the bathroom door. She didn't like it much, she could see that right away. "We'd have liked to replace the bath and things."

"Well, at least they're white."

"We should have bought a Put-U-Up, you know," she told Andy as they were getting into bed later that night. "I said we should."

"And where would we have put it?"

"Got rid of one of the armchairs?"

"Not getting rid of mine."

"No, well, mine, then. What if we have an intruder?"

"We won't have. For goodness sake, stop worrying! Susie isn't."

"No, but still..."

They didn't have an intruder, but the car got stolen; Valerie heard a car alarm going off at half past one. At first, she didn't bother to waken Andy, because they hadn't got an alarm on their car after all, but then she suddenly remembered that Susie's was parked on Fosse Road too and it was nearly new and bound to have an alarm. She and Andy both met her on the tiny landing as she pulled on her dressing gown. "I'm sure that's my alarm." They followed as she hurried down the stairs and through the sitting room, rummaging frantically through her handbag. "Keys, keys, keys..."

Thomas stuck a sleepy head up from his quilted cocoon between the coffee table and the sideboard. "What? Mum? Where are you going?"

"It's all right, just checking the car's all right. We can hear an alarm."

"Wow! Cool! Pops! Pops, hey, wake up! Yeah, baby! Cool! The car's been stolen!"

It was a very dark night but Susie had a small torchlight on her key ring and Andy had snatched one up from the porch. Susie's BMW was parked in Andy's usual spot a little way up Fosse Road, and it was indeed her alarm that had been blaring.

Thomas emerged excitedly in his pyjamas and unlaced trainers from the Ginnel as Susie turned it off. "It's all right, it's all right," Valerie told him. "The car's still here. It was a false alarm."

He was patently disappointed. "Aw..."

He trailed behind them as they made their way back along the alley. "Wonder why it went off?"

"Hasn't done that before."

"Hang on." Andy, who was leading the way, pulled up suddenly, bringing them all to a halt. He walked off back into Fosse Road and they all followed, puzzled. "I'm sure I parked..." He strode out into the middle of the road. "I did!"

He crossed back over to a space a little further up from Susie's car, just above Mr Birkhead's red Toyota. "I parked it here. I know I did. I moved it out of my usual place so that Susie could be nearer to the Ginnel."

Valerie stared at the vacant space in horror. "Oh, Andy, where's our car?"

The police found it at eight o'clock the next morning, burned out at the side of a road running over the moors. Joy riders, they said: very frequent, these days. They were a menace.

"Third Party. Bloody Third Party. And I did it without theft." Andy had his head in his hands as she brought him a hot cup of tea. "I need a whisky, Valerie. I don't want that."

"You can't have whisky at this time of the morning."

"Yes, I can. I've had a shock. Put a drop in that mug then; that'll do for now."

Susie was disbelieving when she followed Valerie into the kitchen. "You didn't do it Third Party. Not without fire and theft."

"I'm afraid we did."

"But why?"

"It's not worth much, pet. And we couldn't afford it."

"Don't be so bloody silly."

Valerie let drop a smidgeon of whisky in her own tea, just a splash. It was that or a tear. "Well, we didn't, and it's gone."

"Bloody hell. What will you do now, then?"

Valerie pictured the long, steep incline up Fosse Road. "Don't know, Susie. Have to use the bus."

The generally black cloud that hung over Number 3 for the rest of the day was due in part to shock and in part to tiredness. Valerie tried to get them all out for a while, but it was difficult. Susie just shrugged with one eye on her mobile and said "Don't mind," to everything that Valerie suggested. Andy shrugged and said "I'm not in the mood. You go. I'm all right here." Poppy seemed content to send and read endless text messages while shut up in the bedroom or curled up in an armchair with the television on. Thomas had his Gameboy and seemed happy enough with that, though he proclaimed himself disappointed –

nay, outraged – that Andy hadn't fixed up the computer.

"We haven't got room, lad. There's nothing to put it on."

"Why don't you just get a laptop?"

"You may well ask why."

They did go out eventually, even Andy, and had a walk around their favourite lake, though nobody seemed to appreciate it much. Poppy, sour faced, trailed about half a mile behind the main party with Valerie, whose hip was aching badly, hobbling silently along beside her at her slow texting pace.

The turning point in the mood of the day came after they had got home, when Susie's mobile buzzed peremptorily as Valerie was getting out the cake tin for a little afternoon snack. When Susie saw the name of the sender her eyes lit up and by the time she had read the text message, her whole face had started to shine.

Valerie glanced at her. "From somebody nice?"

Susie had her head down already, thumb flying, her mouth curved up in a blissful smile. "Mm."

The text message she was sending seemed to go on forever. "So, are you going to go and look round for a new car?" she asked at last, sitting back with a happy sigh, though still keeping one eye on the mobile.

Did she understand how hard-pressed they were? Wasn't fair to ask her to help. She'd done enough. "I told you, love: we'll have to use the bus."

Susie didn't seem to have heard her anyway. "There seem to be plenty of used car places round here. You're okay, are you, staying in this house? Bit small, of course, but it seems quite nice."

Valerie looked around. Removing the dividing cupboard had opened up the kitchen, and the nice William Morris patterned grey-green and white wallpaper that they'd lashed out on for the sitting room and stairwell suited the little Victorian house. Mind you, it had really been too much for Andy; couldn't take the bending and stretching any more. With the smell of the freshly painted woodwork and the new grey-green carpet – cheap and off one of the warehouse rolls scorned by Camilla, but quite a pretty colour – at least the house didn't smell of cats. "Oh, yes," she said. "It's fine; we'll be all right here. We won't be troubling Ollie."

"How much do you think it's worth, as a matter of interest?"

She shook her head. "Ooh, I don't know. They do say prices are going up a lot round Bolton."

Susie's mobile buzzed demandingly again and her face brightened once more as she read the little screen. She laughed aloud, her thumb flickering over the mobile keys. "So how much did you say it might be worth?" she asked eventually.

Valerie pursed her lips thoughtfully. "Somewhere between eighty five and a hundred and five, I'd say..."

"That's not very much."

"I could be wrong."

Susie burst into laughter. Valerie was puzzled. "Eh?"

"Nothing, nothing." Susie's thumb flickered. "Go on."

"The Birkheads' house is worth more. It's made a huge difference having the two knocked through into one."

Eyes glued to her mobile screen, Susie smiled vaguely. "Mm. Mm!"

"They're ever so nice, the Birkheads. She used to be a teacher. They've got a house in France, too. Not sure what he did before he retired."

Susie nodded and smiled blithely. Valerie watched her thumb jabbing away thirty to the dozen.

She isn't listening properly to a word I say.

Chapter 20

Text messages zoomed backwards and forwards right through to suppertime. "I think I'll make an early start back tomorrow," Susie said casually, as she helped Andy with the drying up. No dishwasher here: no room. It was that or the washing machine, and there had been no contest.

He held up a glass to the light, and began to re-polish it. "Oh, will you, pet? Yes, I suppose that'd be wise. Got the M6 to contend with. Don't want to get stuck there at dinnertime. Though if I were you, I'd go M6, M5, M40 and down the A34." He was looking more comfortable already, Valerie thought, watching him affectionately; somehow he was making the little house fit.

"I'm going to London, Dad."

"Oh, so you are."

True to her word, she was up very early rounding up the kids. "Come on, have you got everything? I want to get away. Thomas, have you got all your things? Your Gameboy? The charger? Sleeping bag? Toothbrush? Poppy, have you got your phone?"

It was only ten to nine when Valerie and Andy presented themselves ready to wave them off down the road. "Come again soon, then," Valerie told Susie as she kissed her. "Or maybe we'll come down to you next time."

She glanced at her watch. "Yes, do."

Andy glanced forlornly at his old parking space before they walked back slowly along the Ginnel. "Bloody sod's law, isn't it? Sod's bloody law."

"What are we going to do then?"

"You'll never manage that hill. It's more important to have a car than to push on with doing things to the house."

She sighed. It would have been so nice to have the bathroom done and a new stair carpet, but needs must... She sighed again. "Yes, you're right."

Susie rang to say they had got back safely, but she sounded in a rush. It was quite difficult to get hold of her after that; she always seemed to be out. "No news is good news," Valerie said frequently, trying not to mind.

At last, she rang them, though. "Mum, I've got something to tell you. You know Joe?"

"Joe?"

"The man you met in London. The man you met at my flat."

"The nice man. Joe? The Kiwi?"

"Yes, that's right. Well, I told you he was going to be going back to New Zealand, didn't I?"

"I'm not sure..."

"Well..." There was another phone ringing somewhere. "Look, hang on a minute."

Andy had picked up the name 'Joe.' "He's still around, then?" He rolled his eyes. "Don't tell me: she's getting married again."

"Don't be silly." Valerie flapped him away. She heard Susie talking and laughing for a long while before she came back to the phone.

"Sorry, Mum."

"That's all right."

"Anyway, whether I did or I didn't: Joe's going back to New Zealand."

Valerie shook her head. "Oh dear, you are going to miss him. He's been company. Will he be coming back?"

"Yes. No, I mean, no. No. The thing is, Mum –" She drew in a deep breath. "He's going in six weeks' time and the thing is, Mum, the thing is, I'm going with him."

Valerie turned excitedly to Andy. "She's going for a holiday to New Zealand!"

He rolled his eyes. "All right for some!"

Susie interrupted, sounding a little strained. "Not for a holiday, Mum."

She was puzzled. "What do you mean, then, love?"

"He's got me a job out there."

"A job?"

"A friend of his is a really successful photographer and I'm going to help run his gallery and he's going to train me in black and white."

"What about the children?"

"Oh, we're all going. I'm going to live with Joe, Mum. We're together."

Andy nodded when she told him, though his expression was very strained. "I told you so! Even so, though, I must say, I'm very surprised."

"Why?"

His lips were tight. "I just am. I'm just very surprised."

"Why? That's she's going with this Joe?"

"No, that she's going at all."

So was Valerie, indeed she was, but she couldn't bear to say so; her instinct was to defend. "Oh, I don't know! If I were younger..."

"That's the whole point, Val; you're not. She couldn't get further away. What's she doing traipsing off to the other side of the world when you're going to need her more and more as you get older? Bad enough at the other end of the country."

"I've got you."

"You might not have much longer."

He did look very pale. She could feel panic rising. "Why, aren't you feeling very well again? Is it your heart?"

He shook his head. "I'm fine, I'm fine, I'm just saying: one day before too long one of us is going to be left on our own." He rose, staring at the phone, his fingers twitching. "I think I'll tell her."

She struggled hastily to her feet. "No, no, Andy, don't do that."

"Why not? She needs telling. You wouldn't have done it, not when your Mum got to your age. You'd have waited, at least."

"It's her life. It's different these days. They don't think the same way."

"But it's her *duty*, Val."

"I think as they see it now, their first duty is to be happy.
I *want* her to be happy. I'm glad she's got a nice new man."
"Hope she's picked the right one this time." He frowned.
"But what about the kiddies, then? You'll never see them.
I wonder what Oliver had to say about that. Is he still with
that woman?"

"I forgot to ask. He probably is, come to think of it, if he
hasn't raised any objections to Susie taking the children.
Camilla doesn't like children, and she's very clever. She'll
probably have got him to agree."

She had to sit down. Her head felt swollen and her heart
was fluttering. "We'll have to go down to London, Andy,
and see them before they go," she said, when it had calmed
down a little. "I'll have to take the camera, too. I haven't got
any recent snaps."

"I'll make you a cup of tea."

"It's all happening in a bit of a rush, isn't it?" he muttered,
as he carried her cup carefully in.

She took it from him with a shaking hand. "As I understand it, Joe wants them to travel with him and have a
holiday there before they settle down: take a few weeks,
explore both islands. It sounds lovely."

The tea was too hot, but she sipped it anyway. "Do you
think we'd be able to manage a trip out to New Zealand to
see them, pet? Perhaps maybe next year?"

"Well, it'd be that or a second-hand car, if we can afford
either. We certainly can't afford both."

"No. Hm." She swallowed another drop. It burned her
throat. "Should we try it out for a while, then, without a
car? See how we get by on the bus?"

It was a strange time: they were both really grieving inside.
It was very difficult to involve themselves with anything.
The idea of trying to move somewhere else just seemed too
big to think about. Another move would only add to their
expenses, anyway, and rule out any hope of a trip to New
Zealand or a car – and, after all, as long as they didn't try
to compare Number 3 with *The Bury* or with *Penny Cottage*,
and so long as there was no mention of their old family
house, it was adequate and certainly cheaper to run. Not
being in the mood for outings, not having a car didn't worry

Valerie too much. She had to park herself on walls from time to time in order to get back up the hill, but the bus service wasn't too bad. Andy, though, missed having a car quite a lot.

The prospect of a trip to New Zealand, though, drove her to ring Susie and tell her to go and have a look at the things that they had in storage and help herself to anything she wanted and to sell what she could of the rest, something she had kept putting off just in case they did move one day, and for old times' sake. She was very disappointed with the outcome. Of course, the only bits of furniture they still had that were really worth anything were the dresser and the sideboard, both genuine antiques, and you didn't get very much for second-hand furniture these days, but there had been a few nice pieces and, of course, the dining set as well.

The cheque that Susie sent her wouldn't go anywhere towards the trip.

Andy put his foot down about taking National Express all the way to London, so they went by train to see Susie and the children before they departed for their new life. It was still ever so expensive, even though this time they booked two weeks in advance.

It was a very sad few days. They both managed put a brave face on it when they were all around, but at night Valerie cried quite a lot into Andy's shoulder; his pyjama top got very soggy. Joe wasn't Ollie, and they were all three a little awkward round each other, but he seemed a nice young man and they were reasonably content he'd keep a careful eye on Susie. They'd hope so, anyway.

Thomas was very excited at the thought of New Zealand. It was going to be massive, which apparently meant sort of extra-cool. They were going to go rock-climbing, abseiling, canoeing, bungee jumping and parachuting, whale watching... He couldn't wait.

Poppy hadn't a great deal to say on the subject. In fact, she hadn't very much to say about anything; she was very withdrawn. "Are you worried about going, pet?" Valerie asked her, hoping to get her chatting.

Poppy just shrugged. "Not really."

"You're quite, um – cool, about it? You're going to miss your friends. And Daddy. Aren't you, I expect?"

Another shrug. "Don't worry. I'll be fine."

"Have you seen much of Daddy recently?"

"We stayed with him last weekend."

"Oh, good! And how was he?"

"He was fine."

"We're going to pop in to see him sometime before we go home."

"I'd give him a ring, first."

"Is *she* still around? Camilla?"

"Oh, yes."

"Really! How are you getting on with her?"

"I'm not. I hate her. Hate her!"

"Oh dear, don't say that!" She felt very guilty. It was peculiarly satisfying, in a wicked sort of way.

In view of the possibility that they might bump into Camilla, they gave Ollie a ring instead of calling round. He sounded very cheery, even though his children were going away. "So how are you getting on in the house, Valerie? Comfortable, I hope? How do you like living 'oop north'? Bit different from Hampshire, hah-hah!"

"Oh, yes, we're fine." She sounded like Poppy. "Fine. Fine."

"I've only seen it the once, of course – nice little surprise, that, finding I'd got a great-aunt, eh, Valerie? Bit of a surprise inheritance, ha ha! I gather that area's now on a bit of an up?"

"Oh, I think it is, yes."

"Mm. Oh, well, that's good. Limit to what we can do on mine, though…"

"Yes, I'm afraid so. Yes."

"Nice to talk to him," she said to Andy when he'd put the phone down after having his turn.

"Nice lad. Pity he doesn't ring us. Thought he would."

"Mm." She felt a bit tearful. "I do miss him."

Andy looked very sad.

She managed not to cry when the weekend came to an end and they had to say goodbye – at least, she did until they had turned the corner on their way back to the station. Andy had to hold her for a minute and lend her his hankie then.

"Susie kept asking if I was going to be all right," she told him, blowing her nose hard. "I think she's feeling guilty."

He was quite hard-eyed. "And so she should, Valerie. So she bloody well should."

There were repairs and hold-ups on the railway line, naturally, being a Sunday, but she barely noticed. She had to keep swallowing hard and her eyes threatened to spill over whenever she tried to stare through the window. When she wasn't thinking about them all being at the other side of the world and wondering when, if at all, she would see them again, an image of Thomas bungee-jumping and the elastic thing snapping filled her mind, followed by another of Poppy jumping out of a plane and her parachute failing to open, and that image in turn replaced by one of Susie falling off the sheer side of a mountain, and she pushed them away quickly because they were making her feel sick.

Andy didn't want to chat, either. He seemed to be dozing a lot.

They lashed out on a taxi when they got to Bolton. Shona Birkhead had offered to pick them up from the station, but they hadn't liked to take her up on it. "Doesn't seem fair, not on a Sunday especially," Andy had rightly said.

It was dark but still warm when the taxi dropped them off at The Ginnel. Somehow the sweet smell of dry summer grass as they walked up the short path made the lump in Valerie's throat even bigger. "I think I'll sit in the garden for a bit, pet," she told Andy.

He nodded. "I'm going to have a scotch." He hesitated before going inside with their suitcase. "Do you want anything? Shall I make you a cup of tea?"

She deliberated for a moment. "I think I'll have a drop, too, pet. Just a tiny one."

"Okay." He looked quite pleased.

There were quite a few moths and mossies about. Even in the dark she could make out the white flowers of the lavatera and the cosmos that Andy had planted for her. They were keeping going well, too. She'd done the pots herself, the geraniums and things, but he'd planted all the rest, the salvias and penstemmons and pinks and things they'd got when Shona took them to the Garden Centre, and mowed the small rectangular lawn, and did the regular weeding. She'd hardly heard him complain at all.

"I was just thinking, you've done a good job on this little garden," she told him when he came back out with their drinks.

"Bloody hate gardening."

She sniffed. He glanced at her defensively.

"Yes, I do!"

She sipped at the scotch. It was comforting.

Time passed, as it always does in old age, remarkably quickly. The year ticked by, and then the next, and gradually they got used to the idea that Susie and the children weren't even in the same country, and that there would be even fewer phone calls. Andy gave in and unpacked and set up the computer in the back bedroom now that they wouldn't be needing the room for Susie, so at least they could keep in touch with her by email, which saved on the expense of the phone. She seemed to be having a wonderful time. She loved Joe's houses – there were two, apparently, that he and the family spent time at – one on the Bay of Islands that belonged to his parents, which sounded beautiful, and one in Nelson, which Susie said was ever such a nice place and where Joe's house was, and the gallery that she was working in.

Thomas, it seemed, loved life in New Zealand, though, true to form, Poppy was not so keen. She was doing reasonably well in school. Susie said the educational system was very much more old fashioned and strict. There was a fight on at the moment, as she wanted to get her nose pierced. She'd already done her ears.

Susie emailed a lot of lovely photographs from time to time and Andy bought an H.P. photo printer and printed some of them up. They were really artistic; Valerie put them up all over the walls. He tried to get her more interested in the computer, but beyond emailing, which she did with two fingers once he'd set it up, she was afraid of it.

Not exactly the *living together as a family and sharing lives* thing that she'd imagined the future would be like. It felt very odd.

Number 3 didn't grow on them. Andy still mourned the loss of the car and fretted about Valerie struggling to get up the hill. "I don't know," he said, frowning, after they had been on the bus into Bolton for a nice Pensioners' lunch to celebrate Valerie's seventy-fifth birthday and were battling up the hill in what felt like a Force Nine gale. Took both of them a long time now; she had company perching on the wall. "I think we ought to ring Ollie after all."

The very same day, a 'For Sale' sign went up on Number 4.

"Oh, I wish we could buy it," Valerie murmured longingly as they watched the man from the estate agency erecting the sign. "If we only had the cash! It would be a lot different if we could knock through and make the two into one like the Birkheads have done. Think of all that extra room!"

"The hill would still be there, wouldn't it? That's what worries me."

"What are they asking for it, though, I wonder? If we knew that, we'd have a better idea what Oliver would get for this one." She was eager to find out. "The local paper's not due out until Friday; why don't you ring them and ask?"

He shook his head. "No hurry; no, we'll wait."

One hundred and nine thousand, it was going for. That was more than Valerie had expected. "So what does that make this one, then?"

"Possibly even a bit more. I mean, we have titivated this one up a bit and Number 4's been empty for ages. Might have a bit of damp."

"So, if we call it – oh, I don't know, a hundred and ten? Is it worth looking around again in that price bracket? We only looked at a couple before, after all."

He shrugged. "No harm in having a look, I suppose, though prices are bound to have gone up all round."

"Or should we ring Ollie first, see how he feels?"

"I'm loathe to do that unless we know we're likely to find somewhere he'd like."

"But there's no point in looking if we don't know he's going to agree."

"You like looking at houses."

"Yes, but you know what I mean."

They hummed and hah-ed and bickered about it for the next couple of days, but then, early one morning, the decision was taken out of their hands.

Valerie was still in bed when Andy saw the car. "That's

a bit flash!" he murmured, staring out of the bedroom window, still in his dressing gown and nursing a mug of tea. "By gum, who's got a Porsche?"

She was very comfy; she kept her eyes closed. "I've no idea."

"Has Keith Birkhead got a new car?"

"I don't think so, no."

"Bloody hell..."

"What?"

"Bloody hell, it is, too."

Startled, she emerged, blinking, from under the duvet. "Who is? What is? What?"

"It's Ollie."

"At this time? Don't be silly, it isn't."

"It is. It bloody well is."

"And he's go that that whatsit, too – whatsername..."

Valerie shot bolt upright. "Not Camilla?"

"They're coming in." He stepped away from the window quickly. "Hey, Val, you'd better get up!"

She scrambled hastily for the clothes she had left on the bedroom chair. "What time is it, anyway?"

He glanced at his watch. "It's a quarter past nine."

She was all fingers and thumbs. The tights she had had on yesterday had a great big hole. "Quarter past nine! Quarter past nine! What am I still doing in bed at a quarter past nine?"

"Don't panic. It's Sunday. You're entitled to a lie-in."

The doorknocker rapped smartly and she gestured wildly. "You'll have to go to the door. I'm still not dressed."

"I'm going to have a shave."

"Open the door first. I haven't done my hair or washed my face or anything. Go *on!*"

He stomped down the narrow stairs harrumphing. A woman's voice murmured something undecipherable in response to his greeting at the door and then Camilla's supercilious and precious tones carried up the stairs as she walked into the sitting room. "I'm afwaid we're a little early. Did we get you up? Oliver will be along in a minute. He's just popped in next door."

Andy was plainly mystified. "Oh, does he know the Birkheads?"

Camilla was on the prowl. Valerie could hear her voice travelling towards the back of the house. "What a simply sweet little house. And this is the kitchen?"

The cheek of the woman! What's she doing in my kitchen? Hastily Valerie pulled yesterday's cardigan on over yesterday's dress and made her way out of the bedroom. Andy was standing at the bottom of the stairs, staring into the kitchen and looking rather helpless, tying and untying his dressing gown cord. "Go and get dressed," she hissed as she squeezed past him, pasting a smile on her face. "Well, well, well, this is a surprise. Can I help you, Camilla?"

Camilla, wearing expensively-cut jeans and a cream blouse with a matching sweater slung about her neck, unwound herself gracefully from the examination she had been making of the under sink shelves. "Mrs Bwyce, good morning. You're looking vewy well?" Her iceberg blue eyes flickered over Valerie's unkempt hair and crumpled cardigan. "We have a meeting in Manchester today. Boring, boring, but unavoidable, so Oliver suggested we might as well stay the night somewhere and pay you a little call."

Valerie was struggling not to appear as flustered as she felt. "Oh, well, I see! Oh, I see, well!"

Camilla raised a finely drawn eyebrow as the door-knocker rapped again. "That'll be Oliver."

"Hello, Nana!" He greeted Valerie chummily as she opened the door. "Sorry: Valerie. Slip of the tongue there, hah-hah! I have to remember what to call you now, eh? How are you?" He kissed her on the cheek.

"It's lovely to see you, Ollie." It was lovely to see him; it made tears spring into her eyes. She gave him a little hug. "Come in." She peered into the garden expecting to see a large brown furry bulk. "No Henry with you today?"

He looked a little uncomfortable. "No. No, he, er – I'm afraid he had to go."

Camilla sashayed out of the kitchen. "I can't abide dogs."

"No, no, she can't."

Valerie nodded. "Ah, I see. Would you like a coffee?"

Ollie glanced at Camilla. "Do you want a coffee, darling?"

Darling!

There was no reply. Camilla had disappeared. He thrust his hands into his pockets, staring around the room. "I see somebody's been decorating since I last looked around: looks rather better than I remember. I wonder who that was, hah-hah?"

Valerie was too busy wondering where Camilla had got to, to do more than nod distractedly. "Yes, we've done quite a lot to it. Andy's been very busy." She heard the stairs creaking, but it was Andy who emerged at the bottom, looking very neat now in a clean blue shirt and with his face all pink and shiny after his shave. His face broke into a broad smile when he saw Ollie.

"Well, well, well, my son!"

"Good to see you, Andy," said Ollie, grinning broadly. They embraced awkwardly, but with real affection.

"How are you, Oliver?"

"I'm doing all right, Andy."

"Well, then. Well, that's good. That's good!"

They broke apart a little clumsily. "Haven't seen Camilla, have you?" Ollie asked Andy with a grin. "Don't know where she's gone."

Andy scratched his head. "Well, actually, yes. I think she must have been waiting to use the bathroom. She seems to be in our bedroom."

In our bedroom? Valerie started for the stairs but Ollie forestalled her. "I'll pop up, Valerie."

She hesitated then turned back to the kitchen. "All right, then. I'll put the kettle on." She clattered the crockery and cutlery quite a bit while making it. Cheek of the woman, *cheek* of it, wandering all over my house...

Camilla and Ollie were upstairs long enough for the coffee to have brewed by the time they came down again. Conversation whilst they were drinking it was a bit strained. The obvious topic was Susie and the children, but they didn't want to touch a nerve.

"So how's work going, Ollie?"

Ollie shook his head. "Ah, that's a long story, Andy, hah hah..."

"Oh?"

"Yes, um... Things have changed a bit. Not with the old company any more."

"You're not?"

"No. Been on a bit of a bumpy ride for a long time, actually. There was a takeover, don't know if you knew that?"

"No?"

"We've been – I should say *they've* been – an American company for some time now."

Andy shook his head gravely. "Redundancy, eh? I see. I didn't know."

Ollie looked a little bashful. "Well, not exactly..."

Camilla pushed her coffee cup away with a delicate fingertip. "The long and the short of it is, Oliver's in business with me, now," she purred. Both Andy and Valerie turned and stared at Ollie.

"Are you?"

"With *Camilla*? My goodness me!"

He had become a bit flushed. "Yes, well, you know, hah-hah, new start, new start..."

Andy shook his head. "And what is it, this business? What are you, um, doing, actually?"

Camilla rose gracefully to her feet, looking pointedly at her watch. "We weally ought to go, darling. We don't want to be late."

Ollie glanced at his watch, nodded and jumped up with alacrity. "You're right, you're right."

She smiled sweetly. "I usually am."

He laughed, grimacing at Andy. "Women, eh?"

"Women."

"We'll catch up sometime later then. Well, Andy, Valerie," Ollie made his way to the door. Valerie kissed him again on the cheek. "Goodbye, dear. Sorry it was so short but it was lovely to see you." She didn't say the same thing to Camilla. She just said, "Goodbye."

"Well, well, that was a turn-up for the books! What was that all about, then?" she murmured as she closed the door.

Still half smiling, Andy crossed to the window, watching as they moved off down the path. "Good to see him, anyway."

"Yes, it was, it was. Could have done without *her*. "

"He's a good lad." He frowned. "Pity about losing his job. He's had a bad few years hasn't he, one way and another?"

"What on earth is he doing going into business with Camilla? That woman, Andy! The *cheek* of her, poking about in my kitchen! Wandering off upstairs!"

He wasn't listening. "They're going next door."

"They're not."

"They are. They're going to the Birkheads."

She hurried to peer over his shoulder. "What for?"

"Well, I don't know, do I?"

It was a mystery.

Chapter 21

It was Susie who unravelled it. She rang from New Zealand in the middle of the night a few days later. The sound of the telephone ringing at half past two gave them a panicky shock; Valerie went through the whole bungee jumping, parachuting, rock-climbing scenario all over again in her mind before she had had managed to clamber into her slippers and dressing gown and stagger downstairs to pick up the receiver. As it turned out, Susie'd been so wound up she'd forgotten the time difference, but what she had to tell them still came as a nasty jolt.

"She's bought Number 4."

"Who has?" She struggled to clear her head; she was still half asleep.

"Oh, Mum! Camilla!"

"Camilla?" Valerie's heart sank into her slippers. "Don't tell me she's going to be living next door."

"Oh, no!" Susie gave a knowing laugh. "I know Ollie told you that they were going into business together, you said that in your last email, but did he say what kind of business it was?"

She tried to remember. "Um, no, no, he didn't actually. She said they were in a hurry to get off."

"Well it's property renovation, basically. You know, buy places and do them up. It all needs capital, and Ollie's already used his pay-off; it wasn't a huge amount. She won't let him sell his house; she likes living there. Did I tell you – did *he* tell you, they're getting married?"

That was another shock. "They're not!"

"They are! It's good that he's got somebody, but it's very odd; I never thought he'd go for anyone like her. This was all decided before he lost his job, of course, I don't know if it'll make any difference. She is a little gold-digger after all; she must have been really disappointed when she found out he'd lost his huge income." She gave another short laugh. "He wants his head reading, but anyway, that's by the by. The thing is, without selling the house in Primrose Hill, he's short of capital."

"Oh, dear, poor Ollie."

"And she's already raised money on her house and has bought property with it, including, I presume, the house next door. And now she wants him to get you to move out so that they can do what your neighbours, have done, and knock Number 3 and Number 4 through into one. If she goes up into the attics as well and has, maybe, a nice mansard roof or something, the agent's told her she'd get much more that way."

Valerie's lips felt stiff. She was a bit shell-shocked. "Ollie wants us to move out?"

"Oh, don't worry, he's said no. *BIG* trouble: there's a huge row going on. She's saying if he doesn't kick you out, she's going, and he's saying he can't do it and she's saying he doesn't owe you anything since we're divorced, you're not related any more, he's done enough and he's got to think of his future."

Valerie swallowed. "She is right, though, Susie."

"I've told you, don't worry."

But that, of course, was an impossibility. They were up for the rest of the night. Andy got paler and paler and more and more red-eyed, and Valerie worried and worried till her hair was practically standing on end.

"Maybe he'll stick to his guns. But it would still be a lot easier for him if we just went. Got out of his hair, you know."

"We ought to put up a fight, Valerie. I mean – this is our home. What do you reckon would happen if we just stayed put? I know Ollie has said he won't ask it of us, but you know she'll win eventually, won't she? Carbolic, or whatever her name is. You know her; you saw him with her. She's got him wrapped round her little finger. Oh, no question – she'll win. I think we ought to fight."

"Oh, Andy, I couldn't face it..."

"I don't know that I've got the energy for it myself."

"I should think not, not at your age. I mean, it won't be all that long before you're pushing eighty."

He was indignant. "Pushing eighty?"

"Well, I'm seventy-five."

"So that makes me seventy-seven." He rolled his eyes. 'Pushing eighty'...!"

"Well, you know what I mean; only a few more years, you're not far off. And it could turn out to be a court case. Can you imagine what that would be like? I'd never be able to sleep. Besides, this is Ollie. Can we really turn round and make things difficult for him? Can we? After all he's done?"

"You know, what, Val? I don't think we ought to tell Susie. It's our problem, not hers. We'll sort it out. Don't want her worrying over there, or falling out further still with Ollie. She's got her new life now. Don't want to rock her boat."

As the milk float rattled and whined down the hill, they both knew what they had to do.

"So we have to go, Andy."

"No question. He's done too much for us already, has Ollie. We can't stand in his way now."

"You're quite right." *Mind you,* she thought, *we spent enough ourselves, all those carpets and tins of paint and curtains and bits of furniture and things. Can't bear to remember how much it totalled.*

Andy seemed to be having the same thought. "It cost us a lot of money, too, you know, that house."

"I know it did,"

"It's not as if we'll ever be able to make that money up again."

"I know we won't." The thought of all that money spent was beginning to make her feel panicky and she wished he would stop talking about it. "But I am right, aren't I, Andy?" she added hurriedly. "We can't stand in his way. No two ways about it."

"No, no."

"We have to go"

"But where? Far too expensive to try to rent down south. And it's all right round here, but it doesn't feel like home."

She felt weak from exhaustion. She reached out a hand. "You can hold my hand if you want to."

"Thanks."

"That's okay." She smiled, heartened by the strength and familiarity of his warm hand as it enveloped hers.

"Where is our home, Val?"

"Home is where you are, Andy. But I don't want to stay around here."

They were silent for a while.

"Glynogol, then?"

It was going to have to be back to the Glyn.

The first sight of familiar places through the white clouds of steam flowing past the train window as it had slowed down coming into the station had seemed exhilarating to her when she was a child. "We're coming home – we're coming home," the chugging wheels had sung. It had been her town, hers. Now she felt like a stranger. She stirred, uncrossing her feet. She had a touch of pins-and-needles. "Well, here we are, then."

Andy cleared his throat, and folded up his newspaper. "Mm."

"Hope we don't have to wait too long for a bus. At least it's not raining. Wonder what it'll be like?"

"Dunno."

Don't let it be too bad!

She was dreading seeing it. Norma and Leon had been to look at the flat, of course, as soon as she told them about it on the phone. "Well, it's big enough, but it's over a café, Val! Are you sure about that?" Norma had been quite upset. "Oh, Val – after your lovely house!"

"Can't be helped, Norm. At least it's central. It'll do to start with. We'll look around when we're there."

That's what Andy had said once they'd realised how few private rentals were available; with all the studio-flats and bedsits now, not much left in town. "Somewhere to start with, Val – that's what we need. We can look round for something better once we're there." He had refused to take up Leon and Norma's offer of an indefinite stay with them.

"If we're going to go I want to go under our own steam, Val – make our own arrangements." His pride, of course. *Of course*. She understood that.

Many of the grubby windowpanes in the platform frontage of waiting rooms had been broken. The old newsagents' stall had been boarded up and the platform was littered with wind-blown fragments of cigarette ends and fast food detritus.

"Give me your suitcase."

"I can manage."

He brushed her aside. "No, give it to me."

They caught a bus from the station square: only ten minutes to wait. Nobody they knew walked by them. She knew he was relieved. It hurt too much to look at him so she stared out of the grubby window instead. "Still no Debenhams, then."

"Fat chance."

'Di's Diner' it was called, and it was clean, anyway, as far as Valerie could tell by pressing her nose against the glass door whilst they were waiting for the agent who had arranged to meet them there, and it looked nice and neat and tidy, too: it was obviously cared-for. Plastic chairs had been neatly stacked up on small tables, and the floor and the counter looked scrubbed and clear. The porch area to one side that led to the door to the flat was unpleasantly neglected, though. It was littered with cigarette butts, dead leaves and bits of old paper and the light blue paintwork of the door looked as if a big dog had spent a lot of time scratching and pawing at it.

The agent was a bit late. A short, dapper little man with a rather loud jacket, nice smile and startlingly yellow teeth, he was very apologetic. As he forced open the door, the bottom edge gouged out even more of a worn black crescent, scoring what looked in the half-light of the hall like peeling greyish-green linoleum. A narrow staircase ran up from the narrow hall into the gloom above. Andy made his way upstairs after him, eyeing in passing overlapping wallpaper seams and testing the wall surface suspiciously with the palm of his hand for damp, but Valerie lingered behind, sifting through the junk mail that had been left behind the door and on a small rickety hall table.

A flier for a Chinese takeaway, free home delivery over £15; no order they might make would be likely to get to that much. Another flier for a take-away service, pizzas this time. Several copies of a free local paper, most of them well out of date. An invitation to a Karate club opening. A child-minding service. A tattoo parlour. Car insurance, home insurance, life insurance, loose covers...

A postcard from somewhere in Greece for a Mr and Mrs T. Wilson, dated several months ago: 'Having a lovely time, Ray got the soles of his feet sunburnt, what a plonker!'

An appointment had been made for Mr Wilson to have a Complementary Home Visit and Fitting for an Invisible Hearing Aid. She set that on top for Andy.

"Val? You coming up?"

She peered up, doubtfully. It looked a long way. "Yes, hang on, I'm coming!" Another narrow staircase at the far end of the landing led up to a second floor. There were three doors, all open. She stood at the top of the stairs, hesitating. "Where are you?"

The agent called back. "This way, Mrs Bryce, *bach*, we're in the kitchen." The linoleum on the landing gave loosely beneath her feet against the hardboard, or whatever it was under it as she crossed.

She found herself in a small, empty room and stared around. Linoleum again on the floor, brown this time, a few chunks knocked out of it here and there; a small grate with beige and brown tiles set into the party wall; a high, uncurtained sash window at the back, which, though the glass was very grubby, made the room quite light. "Where?"

"Through here."

She made her way into what could only properly be described as a scullery, though it did have a few rickety-looking wall cabinets, an under-the-sink cupboard and a rusty-ringed upright electric stove.

"Ooh, dear..."

Mr Griffith affected not to hear her.

Andy was standing disconsolately in the middle with his hands in his pockets, gazing up at a water-stained ceiling. "Lucky that ceiling didn't come down."

"Tenants are responsible for interior decoration."

"Should have been an insurance job."

The wall cabinets, painted a harsh marine blue, were rather high up. She tried to pull open one of the sliding doors, but it jammed. "At least that one's got a door." He slapped the shelf of another one. "This hasn't."

"*Duw,* yes, they should have been done, though..." Sucking his teeth, Mr Griffith withdrew a notepad from his pocket and scribbled in it with a Bic. "Kitchen cupboards: they should have been fixed."

She looked around helplessly. "Where will we put the washing machine? And the fridge?"

Andy shrugged disconsolately. "Who knows?" He seemed rooted to the spot.

She patted his arm. "Come on, let's see the rest of it. Come on."

As they processed back through the room with the big rear window, she glanced out, paused, and gasped. "Goodness me, what's all that?"

"Good God!"

Whereas the yard behind Di's Diner was empty except for a large cluster of big cooking oil tins, a couple of mops and a bucket, and a tangle of overgrown weeds, the yard on the other side of the fence to their left was piled from one end to the other and to the top of the fence with old furniture, broken bits of table and shelving, television sets, old music speakers, rusty bicycles, rain-sodden boxes and oddments like mangles and plant pot holders and fire-places, all heaped higgledy-piggledy on top of one other. She could see a piano and a couple of sofas, one of which looked quite nice. Fancy leaving them out there to get wet in the rain!

"Whatever is all that?"

Andy peered out. "Must be where the lad next door keeps the stuff he collects."

She frowned. "What lad? What stuff?"

Mr Griffith joined them at the window, sucking his teeth again. "*Duw,* yes, bit of a mess, isn't it? Next door, you see, it's a reclaimed furniture shop."

"Junk shop, you mean." The deep lines about Andy's mouth were like ravines. "'Kevin's Bargain whatsit.' I noticed the sign. I'm surprised the Council allows him to keep that lot."

She moved a little closer to him. "Andy! Do you think there'd be rats?"

The room at the front looked out to the street through another sash window above a narrow flat roof below which was the big blue-and-white sign saying 'Di's Diner'. The room had a thin beige carpet, with a nasty stain on it near the hearth where somebody had obviously spilt red wine or such. A fairly new-looking imitation-log electric fire stood against a sealed-off chimneybreast. One of the upper windowpanes was cracked and the sash cord was dangling. There was a very unpleasant, stale cooking sort of smell. She nodded, trying to seem encouraging, but unable to think of anything to say. "Uhuh."

They followed him to the narrow stairs up to the second floor. Andy brushed past her. "Let me go first. Here, give me your hand..."

There were three bedrooms, two at the front and a tiny one at the back. The bathroom had a narrow bath and a mouldy, dripping shower. Wedged in between the bathroom and the back bedroom was a separate lavatory with a badly-stained bowl. She decided not to dwell on the toilet facilities. "Quite big, isn't it, for a flat?"

The agent showed them where the electricity meter was and then handed them the rent book, two sets of keys and said he must be off. Someone would be in to sort out the kitchen cupboards. He'd have a word about replastering the kitchen ceiling. He flashed his yellow teeth in an engaging smile. Last Thursdays in the month the rent was due.

They were quite glad he'd left. It was easier looking round without him there.

It didn't improve on second viewing.

Poor Andy looked wretched. "What are we doing here, Val?"

"I don't know, pet."

Embarrassment and loss were coiled within him like twin poisonous snakes. "How did we come to this?"

It was unbearable to see his mind so heavy. She turned away, rummaging in her handbag so that he wouldn't see her tears. "Now where did I put my...?

"Well, now, are you hungry, lovey?" she asked, when she had blown her nose and got herself under control. They'd feel better when they had eaten.

"What time's the furniture van due?"

"They said about half past four. We've got a couple of hours."

"Have you got any sausages?"

She snapped, a little bit tetchy. "Of course I haven't got any sausages! We didn't bring any food. I was thinking about maybe getting the bus back down and going to Morrisons."

"I don't know about that..." His face brightened. "I tell you what, why don't we nip downstairs? They do chips, don't they? We could try that All Day Breakfast that's advertised in the window. Quite fancy an All Day Breakfast: bacon and egg, black pudding, tomato, sausage, mushroom – few rounds of bread and butter, bottle of HP sauce. Hot mug of tea." He was practically salivating.

"I was thinking of buying some ham and some bread and a bit of lettuce. It would be better for you."

He was already making for the door. "Hang the expense, Val and hang being sensible. Let's give ourselves a bit of a treat."

She had a look at the opening hours for Di's Diner as Andy locked the flat door: Monday to Saturday, closed Sundays. Open at eight in the morning, but no problem with late night opening; they closed at half past six.

They introduced themselves to a short, squat woman with a dark, prickly-looking moustache and small, wary, blackcurrant eyes – presumably Di. Valerie decided she was probably Turkish. Mr Di was thin and wispy, with sad, liquid eyes and a balding head. When Di called to him to come and meet them, he appeared from behind a curtain, enveloped in a large apron and accompanied by a waft of chip fat, raised a hand and mumbled, 'Allo', and disappeared again. He was obviously the cook.

"I'll have the All Day breakfast, please," Andy told Di, hungrily.

"Youwanoneegggeortwo?

He frowned, puzzled. "Sorry?"

"Youwanoneegggeortwo?

Valerie raised her voice. "Do you want one egg or two, pet?"

"Oh. Um – two, please."

"Antips?"

"Sorry?"

"Youwanlargeshipsorsmaw?"

That almost floored her. "Chips! Oh, yes, please, he'll have some chips. And I'll have some, too, please, but just with an egg and some peas. Oh, and tea, please. Two teas." She looked around. "Well, this is very nice."

The food was a little on the greasy side, but hot and very welcome. Mrs Di didn't seem to be much of a conversationalist; she did have a few other customers to serve, to be fair, but she spent a lot of the time counting up money at the till. Mr Di popped his head out from behind the curtain from time to time and stared at them, but disappeared as soon as he caught their eyes. He was probably shy.

"I don't know about having a curtain there instead of a proper door. Bit of a fire risk." Andy eyed his empty side plate. "Do you fancy a bit more toast?" He was beginning to get some colour back.

Valerie set down her mug. "So what do you think? Are we sticking with it, then?"

He shrugged. "You won't be very good with those stairs."

"Won't be too bad if I don't get any worse."

"Hm."

"Horrible kitchen."

"Look a bit better when I've painted it."

"If we stay. Have to have the fridge in the dining room."

He nodded through the window. "Pub on the corner. Bit of a dive by the look of it, but at least it's handy."

She winced as a green double-decker came noisily to a halt outside the café window. "And it's also handy for the bus."

Once it had driven on, she delicately fingered the knife and fork, laid neatly on her plate. She couldn't quite bring herself to meet his eyes. "So...?"

He shrugged baldly. "Do for now, I suppose. Haven't got much choice."

Their furniture arrived more or less on time as estimated, and was carted upstairs and distributed without incident. The removers hadn't had any trouble with the M6. Andy expressed himself pleasantly surprised.

By the time they had been and gone Valerie and Andy were quite exhausted. She had secreted some biscuits, small plastic bags of tea and sugar, and a tin of milk powder in her suitcase, so they left their shopping till the next day.

It wasn't a quiet night.

It started off all right, with only occasional traffic passing and a bit of noise and laughter from passersby, but it got worse after midnight. Much, much worse. Having the pub so close seemed likely to be a handicap rather than a boon. Most of the raucous din that kept them awake until the early hours was caused by the infuriating bass thump, thump, thump of live rock music, and much of the remainder by the raucous shouts and laughter of the hoards of young people spilling in and out and gathering on the pavement.

Some of it was rather closer to home. At around half past twelve a strident male conversation began to waft up from below their bedroom window. She peered out through the net curtain. It was difficult to see down because of the flat roof.

"I think they're in our doorway," she whispered to Andy, who was poking his head up, blinking irritably, above the duvet. "That's why there's all that mess of cigarette ends and stuff in the doorway. They obviously think it's a great place to have a midnight chat."

Whoever they were, they hung around there for hours. Andy wanted to go and clear them off, but she wouldn't let him. "Let's leave it for a while, they may go somewhere else." It wasn't that they would be aggressive, necessarily, just drunk and loud, but you never knew. And it might not be just drink that was fuelling their excitement. It could be drugs as well.

The road might not have been heavy with grinding tractors and farm lorries at the crack of dawn, as it had been at *The Bury*, but from half past eight till half past six at night the traffic was pretty well nose to tail and the air above the pavements was thick with vehicle fumes. As the morning wore on, the source of the unpleasant smell in the front room became apparent. The thick odour of Di's All Day Breakfasts oozed through the floorboards, so that, especially between eight o'clock and twelve, it reeked sulphurously of eggs as well as of chip fat. The smell was horrible. Even Glade and Airwick, when she brought them back from Morrisons, wouldn't shift it.

They only saw one person they knew while they were doing the shopping. Fortunately he didn't ask what they were doing back.

Andy wasn't sure about a declaration from Leon and Norma that they were coming over.

"They're not, are they? This place is a pigsty. I wanted to get some of the decorating done first."

She shook her head. "You can't, lovey: you can't possibly. We can't put them off. They want to make sure we're all right."

Leon brought Andy a special bottle of scotch, Johnny Walker Black Label, as well as two bottles of wine, and when Norma saw the flat-roofed frontage, she went next door to the junkyard place and came back with four big garden pots. "You can put these on the bit of flat roof over the front of the café."

Valerie was dubious. "Do you think I ought to?"

Andy was, too. "Don't know how safe that flat roof is. Once they're full of soil, they're going to be very heavy."

Norma was determined, though. "She's going to be miserable without a bit of garden of some kind, Andy."

"How is she going to water them?"

"Through the window."

He looked extremely dubious. "Oh, I don't know about that..."

Norma nipped Valerie over to B&Q and stocked her up with geraniums, begonias, lobelia and lavender, got the pots out there and they planted them up anyway, whilst Andy and Leon were across at the pub.

"So are you going to be all right here, then?" Norma asked as she clambered awkwardly back in and dusted herself down. "What do you think, honestly, Val?"

Valerie sighed. "Oh, it'll do for the time being."

"You know what you ought to do, don't you? Apply for a Council flat."

She was shocked. "We couldn't lovey; it'd be the last straw. Andy'd hate that. Fancy a cup of tea?"

"You've still got your nice dresser, I see," Norma said as

they walked into the back room.

"I have." Val eyed it thoughtfully. It did look very big and cumbersome in the small sitting room; you had to wriggle past it to get to the kitchen door.

Norma shook her head as she stared out at the yard packed full of flotsam and jetsam. "That is a right old mess!"

Valerie shrugged. "There's a limit to how long our money's going to last, even for somewhere like this – and I do want Andy to have a car. I don't mind the bus, but he hates it. I think it'd make him feel a little bit better." She stroked the warm, dark wood of the old dresser. "Don't say anything to Andy, but I've been thinking, actually, of selling this dresser and putting it with the money we got for the other furniture, see if there'd be enough then for a decent car."

"But you always said you'd never sell that dresser."

"Well, I don't want to, I wanted to hand it down, but it's not going to be any use to Susie now, is it? She won't want it out in New Zealand."

"I suppose not, no."

Andy was actually in a much happier mood after their visitation. He even went for a ride with her on the bus along the coast as far as Conwy and back. They bought some nice fresh dabs (little flatfish, Andy's favourite) on the quay.

Chapter 22

While they were on their way back on the bus, she spotted a second-hand car showroom through the bus window and it reminded her. "If you were going to buy another car, Andy, what would you go for? What sort of figure would you be talking about?"

"We can't afford a car. If we had the money, I'd rather take you to New Zealand."

Wonderful to have gone to New Zealand. Nicer though, to see him happier. "I mean, just a second-hand one. Just suppose."

He didn't say much more about it, but was obviously thinking about it, because when they got back and while she was cooking their dabs, he got out the local paper and began studying the section on cars. She was pleased.

She opened the kitchen window. They could do with an air extractor in here. The small room was thick with blue, fishy smoke. "So what do you fancy, love?" she asked over her shoulder.

He looked up, puzzled. "Thought we were having fish."

She chuckled. "No, silly. I mean, what kind of car?"

It took her a bit of a time to work up to selling the dresser, though; her sentimental attachment to it was very strong. It was to be a secret, she resolved – and there was no great hurry. His birthday would be a nice time to give him any cheque.

When the time came, she went down to see Kevin in his cramped and overstuffed shop. He would have had the dresser like a shot. He offered her a ridiculous price, though. She knew he was just trying to pull the wool over her eyes, but she was very hurt. "But it's worth much more than that! I know it is; my mother had it valued. It's a genuine antique! It's been in my family for years! It was my grandmother's mother's dresser and her grandmother's before that."

He sniffed. "Gettin' a bit past it, then, isn't it?"

She could feel the hair on the back of her neck standing up. "Don't be ridiculous; it's a genuine antique!" He said he hadn't got room for it really, anyway, it would have to go out in the back and take its chance with the weather, and put the price he was offering up by £50.

"My mother's dresser out in the rain in the yard piled on that heap of garbage?" She wouldn't carry on, walked out and opened her door again in a bit of a huff.

It was a bad day. Mrs Di had been watching for her. She rang imperiously on the door just as Valerie reached the top of the stairs. It seemed the watering of the pots on the flat roof was causing water damage to the shop ceiling and they would have to be taken off there. She was not pleased; in fact, she was very rude. Valerie was very apologetic, but there was no need for that kind of language. Surprising that Mrs Di knew it, not having very good English, truth to tell.

In the heat of the moment, she took the opportunity to mention, none too delicately, the smell from the eggs. Perhaps a better extractor fan? Mrs Di flounced off in a huff.

Andy got in a huff, too, when he came back in from doing the shopping and had to heave the heavy flower pots back in. He nearly did his back in, struggling in with them over the windowsill.

The whole day put her off selling the dresser for a while.

Andy had been thinking of her, too, it seemed, and he beat her to it. He gave her the letter from the allotment society as she was drinking her mid-morning tea.

"Here you are, pet."

"What is it?"

"Read it."

She scanned the address at the top. 'The Secretary, Brackley Allotment Cooperative.' She stared at him over her glasses with raised eyebrows. "What have you been up to here?"

He had an odd smile on his face. "Read it."

Dear Mrs Bryce, I am pleased to welcome you as a new member...

She gasped. "Andy, pet, you didn't!"

He was as pleased as Punch. "I did!"

"You didn't!"

"I did."

"You got me an allotment."

He was so pleased with himself he was almost shining. "Yep."

How the dickens did he think she was going to take care of an allotment? With her hip? Not to speak of her knees?

"Oh, pet, that's wonderful! Thanks ever so much." She read the letter again. "Where is it, then, this allotment? Is it far?"

"Turn left down at the end by the Newsagents, cross over, up Rhosaber street, up the hill and round to the left."

"Sounds a bit of a way."

"Oh, it's not bad. Five minutes if we had a car, fifteen, maybe twenty minutes walking?"

"Your pace, or mine?"

"Well, mine. It's me that'll be going there most days, won't it?"

"Will it?"

"Well, I don't except you to dig the wretched thing, do I?"

"I was wondering about that."

He shook his head firmly. "No, no, you direct things, oversee me, tell me what to do. It'll be your operation, I'll be just the labourer. We've got a shed, by the way – a lock up. Should be safe enough to leave the tools. Where are they, by the way, the gardening things?"

"You said there was no point in hanging onto them when we weren't going to have a garden. I've got my trowel and secateurs, but that's all."

"Have to get some more, then. I'll need a spade and a rake and a riddle and a hoe."

"Maybe he'll have some odds and ends next door." She hugged him tightly and kissed him affectionately on the head. He was getting balder by the minute. "That's lovely, though, pet. It's really lovely. A lovely surprise."

He was quite pink. "'S all right. Glad you're pleased."

"You are my little hero."

"Don't be daft."

She woke up during the night. Andy was breathing softly by her side. Made a nice change: no snoring. As she lay quietly, he turned over and edged closer, linking his fingers with hers. "I love you," she said, the firmness and clarity of her voice in the darkness taking her by surprise.

He shifted a little closer still and squeezed her fingers, so she knew he had heard her. "Hm..."

"I love you more than anything in the world."

His voice was surprisingly strong, too. "So I do you."

There was silence for a moment and then he squeezed her fingers again and murmured sleepily, "You are a silly cow."

It made her giggle.

He was very good; he traipsed off up to the allotment almost every day. Having him up there made it possible to get people in to see the dresser. She found one who wasn't as insulting as Kevin, and who offered her a reasonable price, though not as much as she had hoped. To get anywhere near the sort of figure that Andy had been talking about for a decent second-hand car, the sideboard had to go too, and the old Royal Stafford dinner service that she had stored in it, and the treasured bone china plates that had been on the dresser, and her great-grandfather's silver pocket watch, and her mother's Clarice Cliff teapot. The flat looked very empty, and when the door closed after the removers, she did shed a bit of a tear.

Andy was very surprised when he got home and noticed the dresser was missing. "What did you get rid of it for?"

She blew her nose, hoping he wouldn't notice her pink eyes. "Well, you said it often enough; it was in the way."

"Yes, but you didn't have to get rid of the thing. How much did you get for it?" He hadn't noticed that the sideboard had gone too.

She took the cheque out of her pocket, then put it back again before he could see it. A nice card, that's what it needed – a nice card with a glossy picture of a car on it. At breakfast time, perhaps, propped up against the teapot. *FOR ANDY WITH LOTS OF LOVE. ONE CAR.*

"Oh, not much – tell you about it in a minute, I just need to pop downstairs for a – for a thingummybob."

He was already sinking into his chair and opening the newspaper that he had had tucked under his arm as she opened the door. With the paper to read, odds on he'd have forgotten all about the missing furniture by the time that she got back.

He was ever so pleased with the cheque. The enormous delight that he took in considering what he was going to buy made the loss of the dresser and other things sink into comparative insignificance. He settled eventually on a blue Ford Focus. She was glad it was blue: her favourite colour.

It was nice having a car again. They had lots of outings and it was very handy for the allotment. Valerie pottered about there quite a bit, but mostly she sat in a deckchair, watching and offering occasional and carefully diplomatic words of advice. "So what do you fancy growing, then love?" she had asked. "Cabbage? Carrots? Peas? Tomatoes? Sprouts? Potatoes?"

"*You* tell *me*. Anything except lettuce."

She had to smile to herself. She knew he didn't want to do it. He was doing it for her. There was no question but that it was his, though: it was very neat, very *Andy*. All his vegetables came up in neat straight rows with plenty of bare earth showing in between. She'd have sown a lot of annuals in it, poppies, larkspurs, things like that, but that would have made it messy.

They had already renewed the 6-month lease three times, but as the next renewal date drew near, in the evenings, when she had finished rubbing his back, they spent a great deal of time reading out rental offers from the local paper, and talked about the pros and cons of a move. As time went by, they had become inured to the traffic and the smell of eggs, but the noise from the pub was still problematic. Eventually, in desperation, they had moved their bed into the small back bedroom and climbed in every night from the foot. They had had to leave everything else in the front bedroom, but it was much quieter, though it also made it very difficult to make the bed.

"'Refurbished ground floor flat benefiting from UPVC double glazing...' he read out. "Bloody hell, not UVPC again. Lounge with bay window, kitchen, double bedroom and bathroom. Shared garden and drying area. £425."

"For one bedroom?"

"Too far from my allotment, anyway." She had to smile. *My* allotment, eh? He glanced up. "Do you need any peas, by the way? Got plenty of peas."

She nodded. "And a bit of parsley and maybe a few more carrots?"

"Okay." He returned to the paper. "Communal garden?' She wrinkled her nose. "Don't fancy communal."

"No." He shrugged, frowning as he stared down at the paper. "I don't know, maybe we should stay put, Val?"

She considered for a moment. The upheaval of moving again! If he was reasonably settled with it... "Yes, love. I think we should."

It was one morning the following September that they got the call from Susie. There was laughter and happiness bubbling in her voice. "Guess what we did yesterday?"

Her exuberance was catching. Valerie chuckled. "I don't know, what?"

"We got married!"

"You didn't!"

"We did!"

"Oh, my goodness!" She glanced across at Andy, wide-eyed. "They've got married, Susie and Joe."

"Why? Is she pregnant?"

"She didn't say so." She returned to the phone. "Are you – I mean, you're not, well –"

Susie giggled. "Expecting? No, no, bit of an impulse, really. Just seemed like a good idea."

Valerie found it difficult to analyse her feelings. "Well, well, well, darling, my goodness me! Was it – did you, I mean, where, I mean – was it a big wedding?"

"Just a Registry Office. Oh, don't worry, Joe's family weren't there – we didn't even have friends there – so you didn't miss out. We just decided to do it, so we booked it, and well, there you are, just the children and us! We dragged in some people as witnesses from the street."

Valerie was lost for words. "Well, goodness me."

Andy was raising his brows. "Does Ollie know?"

She shrugged. Not the moment to ask. "Well, well! Congratulations, lovey! So, well, you're Mrs... what?"

Susie sounded very airy. "Oh, I'm keeping my own name."

"She's keeping her own name," she told Andy afterwards, when he had poured them both a sherry as a toast.

"That Ollie's name or ours?"

She hadn't thought of that. "I didn't ask."

"What are we going to give them for a wedding present?"

"I don't know. I don't know what they've got. I'll have to ask." What they could afford out of what was left wasn't likely to mean very much to Joe or Susie. Still, it was the thought that counted, after all.

Andy was shaking his head. "Well, well, well...! Saved us a lot of work and expense, that's one way of looking at it." He studied her shrewdly. "You're hurt aren't you?" She shook her head fiercely. "Yes, you are, Val. I can tell."

She swallowed hard, but a tear trickled down her cheek. He rose quickly. "Come here, you silly old thing."

When she'd done having a sob on his sturdy shoulder and had blown her nose hard, she chuckled wetly. "Sorry, bit of a surprise, that's all."

"Shouldn't have got the car. We could have been there; I could have taken you."

"Didn't ask us if we wanted to, did they?" Annoyingly, a sob was rising in her throat again; the words came out in a sort of bubble. "It's all – it's just – it's just not turned out the way I expected, you know, how I thought it was going to be. When we started out. With the family. All in all."

Valerie had a very early appointment at the hospital to see an orthopaedic specialist at last about her hip. Andy drove her there, but she insisted that he left her to get the bus home. "No point in your hanging about, I've no idea how long I'll have to wait, it could take ages."

He didn't take too much persuading. "Well, if you're sure, I could use the time to get on with finishing the bathroom. Costs a bloody fortune in the car park, too." She was pleased. With Andy's eightieth birthday coming up, she had one or two secret purchases to make. It was a fine day, bit too windy, perhaps, but dry at least: perfect for taking her time traipsing around.

She was quite a while at the hospital – a couple of hours waiting to see the specialist, then a trek down to the X-Ray department, which was very busy, then another long wait to see what he made of the results. A morning gone; twenty past one when she came out.

It wasn't easy finding suitable presents in Glynogol. She browsed round most of the shops, but short of yet another cricket book or a volume of wartime memoirs from W.H. Smiths, and a quite nice but ordinary short-sleeved shirt and some socks from Peacocks, nothing had yet stood out. What menswear shops there were were geared to skinny lads who liked jeans and sweatshirts with big, bold, and often, very rude lettering all over them; she had had a look at one or two of them, but, really! It would have to be another bus ride, then, to the nearest Marks and Spencer. At least there wasn't any hurry; with Andy busy decorating, he'd be happily occupied all day.

She had a cup of coffee and a cheese roll in a café when she got off the bus and then hurried quickly into Marks. Half past three already! She deliberated for quite a long time over the shirts, but eventually picked a long-sleeved one in a rather nice blue-and-beige check, with a pair of beige cords to match. Instead of a packet of socks she bought him a bottle of wine; he'd like that much better.

Just a card, and a packet of watercress and a small carton of cream for a soup, now, and she was done. Andy's birthday cake – chocolate, because he liked that best – was ready baked and iced and hiding in the tin she'd stowed away under her dressing table. The Bolognese sauce for the pasta that he loved was ready in the fridge.

She was all set quite quickly. Time to get the bus.

The bus route back home took her by their old house. The *For Sale* sign that had been there last time she had passed it had gone. So it had changed hands again! The paintwork was blue, now, Oxford Blue. The garden wasn't looking too bad, though the shrubbery was rather overgrown. There was a swing on the side lawn and a great big children's slide. A grey estate car was parked on the drive. No sign of the lovely climbing Hydrangea she'd had creeping up the front wall.

The sight of it always made her sigh. Nice house. Very graceful. Big. She clutched her Marks & Spencer bag tightly to her as the double-decker swung away around the corner.

The traffic was very heavy today. There must have been an accident somewhere; the driver had to pull in to let an ambulance and two fire engines howl past them as they drove along the straight. Opening the M&S bag, she peeked inside at the shirt, fretting already. Nice cotton, but would he have been happier with the green check? Pulling the package out, she studied it closer through the cellophane. Hope he's still a 16. He might have preferred a stripy one to the check... Too late now. Putting it back at last, she closed her eyes and took a little half-doze. She judged the distance very satisfactorily. When she opened them again, they were nearly home.

For some reason, the driver pulled the bus up a long way away from the stop. The traffic seemed to have snarled up there nastily. Vehicles were backing up and reversing. "What's happening?" she asked the man next to her, who was getting ready to get out. He was taller than she was.

"Road's closed."

She frowned in irritation. Her hip was aching after all her wandering. "Oh, that's annoying: it usually stops right outside my door."

The driver was on his feet. "Sorry, ladies and gentlemen! If the next stop's yours, I'd get off now. I've got a choice, now: I can wait, or I can turn around and try another route. Just going to ring the Depot." He slid back into his seat.

There was a rustle and a murmuring amongst the passengers and several stood up and began to move along the aisle. Heaving herself awkwardly to her feet, Valerie joined them. Somebody down at the front of the bus started coughing heavily. The woman in front of her turned round, her nose wrinkling. "Can you smell burning?"

The air in the bus grew thicker, heavier, more murky. People peered out. "There's a fire engine."

"Two. I can see two."

"And an ambulance. That means somebody trapped."

"Oh, dear!"

"Ooh – what's on fire?"

"Can you see what's burning?"

Valerie could; she had reached the front of the line. As she clambered down the steps, the Marks & Spencer bag fell from her grasp and the wine bottle shattered on the pavement. Oblivious to the pain and stiffness in her hip, she began to run.

The shop and café signs had charred and crumbled. Blackened windowpanes were broken. Tongues of flame and thick black tarry smoke poured from what remained of the terraced roof, sinking down to roll across the street and billowing up to darken the sky above. The fire crew must have had had their hoses playing for ages; the street was awash with blackened, stinking water. Her heartbeat was so loud it shook her from head to toe and made her ears hurt. Her eyes and nostrils burned from the acrid smoke. A youthful policeman barred her way. "You can't come through, love."

She struggled to find a way past him. "I have to, I must! My husband's in there! Andy!"

He caught at her sleeve. "Where do you live, love? What's your name?"

"Val. Val." Her mind wouldn't work. She couldn't remember her surname or what the address and pointed her fingers again wildly. "There! There!"

He grasped her arm more firmly. "You Mrs Bryce?"

Yes, yes, of course I am, that's who I am... Nodding, she pulled frantically against him, scanning the flat front. There were firemen everywhere. They had one of those cradle things at the end of an extension up to it, and a ladder. She reared up on tiptoe. "Andy! Andy!"

The policeman shook his head. "He's not up there, love. He wasn't in the building."

"Yes, he was, he was, he is, I know he's in, he's decorating the bathroom, I know he's up there!"

"No, love, no, he isn't, they've searched. Anyway –" He was pale pink, with smooth, baby-soft skin and very blue eyes, the young man, and he had the faint hint of a fair moustache. There were beads of sweat caught on the fine hairs. "Anyway, love, we know he wasn't."

"Oh, thank goodness!" The relief was enormous. It was as if it had only been the air inside her that had been holding her up and when she let go of it in a huge sigh, her legs wobbled. She needed to sit down.

Mrs Di appeared at her elbow, her black-moustached upper lip quivering. "Ah, poor lady. You comealongame." She looked very woebegone. Of course she did, she'd lost her café. And we've lost our home, of course, but never mind that for now. Valerie brushed her aside. "No, no, it's all right, I must go and find Andy."

Mrs Di put a firm arm about her. "Itakeyou. I showyou. You comealongame." There were tears in her black, beady eyes and they seemed to be tears for Valerie. She was puzzled. "What's wrong? He wasn't in the fire."

The baby policeman was at her other side. "No, love, he wasn't."

She looked around eagerly as they led her through the crowd. "Is he looking for me? He'll need me; he'll have had a shock. He's got a weak heart, you know, bit of a weak heart."

"A history of heart attack, was there?"

"Well, he did have one."

"I'm very sorry, love."

Why were they leading her towards the ambulance?

The policeman was trying to explain something. "He went with a bang, Mrs Bryce. He really went with a bang, love. He wouldn't have felt anything. It'll have been the shock, you see. He was shouting, pushing, trying to get upstairs. They wouldn't let him, of course. He thought you were up there."

"I wasn't! I told him, I'm coming home on the bus, I'm going out shopping!"

"He must have thought you'd have been back by now. It is getting dark."

Mrs Di patted her arm. "Gonetoallotment, I think. A bagofpotatoesandveg and things. He drop them ona pavement. I have when you wanathemback, jus say."

Valerie was exasperated. "Silly man, what was he doing that for? We've got plenty, we don't need any more veg!"

She felt strangely calm, an onlooker, almost, when they

let her sit beside him in the ambulance and gently lifted back the sheet so she could see his face.

Of course, she found herself thinking: of course, this is how it all ends. This is what is going to happen.

His face seemed smaller than it had been when she had last seen him, very neat featured. She slid her finger down his nose. There was still a hint of warmth. She swallowed hard. "Oh, poor little thing..." The covering sheet had made his hair untidy. He wouldn't like it like that. She smoothed it back from his forehead gently. Her lips felt cold and numb. "Oh, Andy. Oh, my Andy."

Chapter 23

The Homeless Welfare Officer had stuck his glasses together with a well-fingered bit of sticking plaster. It bothered Valerie because it looked as if it was coming undone and she didn't want his specs to collapse on him. She twisted her fingers together, staring hard at it and willing it to stay on.

"Mrs Bryce? What do you think? Is that all right for you? Do you think you'll be all right there? It's a bit of out of town, but I think it's the best place I can offer you." He kept fiddling, squeezing the bit of sticking plaster on more tightly and adjusting his glasses more comfortably behind his ears. He obviously hadn't got the length of the two arms matching properly. Andy would fix that for him very nicely; he was ever so good at little things like that. "We're a bit hard-pressed at the moment. The alternative at present would be B&B accommodation, which wouldn't really be appropriate. Can't have you wandering round the streets!"

"Hm."

"So, is that all right, then? Shall I set that up?"

"I don't want to go into a Home."

He shook his head. "*Rosemount* isn't a Home, Mrs Bryce. As I said, it's a private hotel which has a contract with the Council to provide temporary accommodation for people like you, emergency accommodation for elderly people who've lost their homes and so on."

"I've lost my home."

"I know you have, I know you have. I'm very sorry."

She remembered suddenly. "I've lost my husband, too."

"Yes, yes, I know. I'm truly sorry." He took off his glasses and began to polish them with his handkerchief. He was going to snap the arm off again if he rubbed as hard as that.

Once they were back wobbling on his nose he reached for the telephone. "*Rosemount*, then, okay, dear? We'll get you there right away."

"We have got a car, but I don't drive. Always meant to learn, but I never got round to it." There was a rush of icy coldness round her middle. Her fingertips felt frozen. "Andy ran me everywhere. I always had my Andy."

"Oh, we'll get you there. We'll organise something. Don't worry about that, Mrs Bryce."

She had started to fret now, thinking about their little blue car standing there all alone waiting for Andy. "Will it be all right, do you think, parked there, I mean, just left on the main road? We had our other car stolen before; I don't want it to be stolen. There are gangs, you know, gangs of boys roaming around, especially in the evening. They don't half make a mess, tin cans and empty bottles and things, what-you-may-call-it, spraying up graffiti. I don't want anything to happen to it. I mean we will be insured, we've got proper insurance again this time, but still... We made a bad mistake taking out only Third Party before. Andy didn't want to do that again; he loves that car."

The Homeless Welfare Officer pushed aside the documents on his desk and moved his chair back. "Look Mrs Bryce, we won't worry about it for tonight, eh? You usually leave it out there, do you?"

"Oh, yes, we haven't got a garage." Her shoulders ached. There was a tearing pain deep down inside.

He stood up. "Well then. It's been all right till now, presumably, but I'll have a word about it and we'll sort it out. Is there anybody you want us to phone for you, Mrs Bryce? A son, a daughter?"

"My daughter's in New Zealand." She couldn't remember for the moment what Susie was doing there.

"We can get a message to her. She'll need to be told, won't she? Do you have her number? Her address, dear?"

Her mind was a blank. "Neptune Street, I think, something... Nelson. It'll be in my diary." She looked around, but couldn't see her handbag. Panic began to rise up in her throat. "I don't know what I've done with my handbag."

"It's all right, it's all right, hang on..." He opened his door and stuck his head out. "Have we got Mrs Bryce's handbag, Angela?"

Valerie wrung her hands anxiously. "The last time I remember having it I was on the bus..."

He was back, with her big brown handbag held triumphantly in the air. "Here we are, Mrs Bryce. I thought the police station would probably have it but Angela says you put it down while you were waiting out there. Shall I look in it for you? Find your diary?"

"No, no, I'll do it." She found her little grey diary and opened it, with trembling fingers, to the address page. "I keep forgetting to ask what name my daughter's using. She remarried, you see, quite recently, so I put her down under 'S'. Susie, her name is. Her name's Susie. Oh, and her husband's Joe."

He took the diary, nodding. "And is there anybody else in here who could come and see you?"

There was only one person. "You could ring Norma. Yes, please try Norma for me; she's under 'N. & L.'"

Norma and Leon came very quickly; in fact, Valerie was still sitting in the housing Department's outer office, waiting to be taken to *Rosemount*, when they burst in. Norma looked as if she had just come from the hairdressers without having her styling finished; she was red-faced and shiny and her hair was in little tight sausages. Valerie shook her head. "Oh, my goodness, Norma, you shouldn't have rushed!"

Norma threw her arms about her tearfully. "Oh, I am so sorry, Val. I can't believe it." She was shaking. Leon put his arms about them both. His cheek was pressed hard to Valerie's temple and he hadn't shaved. It was rather uncomfortable, but she didn't say.

Norma backed away at last, wiping her eyes. "And the flat's gone? Everything?"

"Everything."

Leon sat down beside her with his arm along the back of her chair, his head drooping and shaking disbelievingly.

"Bloody hell."

Norma took the chair on the other side and clutched Valerie's hand in both of hers. "Oh, you're cold, lovey. You're ever so cold." She began to rub Valerie's hand vigorously. Valerie wished she would leave it alone.

"She's in shock."

"So am I, Leon. I'm in shock, too. I can't believe it."

The woman called Angela put her head around the door. "We've managed to arrange transport to *Rosemount*, Mrs Bryce. Sorry to have kept you waiting such a long time."

Norma frowned. "*Rosemount*? What's that?"

Valerie couldn't remember what the Homeless Welfare Officer had said. She could only remember his broken glasses. "It's a – I don't know, some kind of hotel place. They've very kindly found me a room there." She managed to withdraw her hand from Norma's and looked at Angela. "Shall I come now?"

"If you're ready, dear. They'll find you some washing things and clothes and whatnot when you get there. Somebody'll call tomorrow to talk to you and, you know, arrange things."

"She's not going anywhere. She's coming with us." Norma squeezed Valerie's hand. "You're coming with us, pet. Isn't she, Leon?"

"Yes, yes, of course, of course she is." He jumped to his feet. "You're coming with us, Val. No question." They were very kind.

It was odd, seeing the world out there outside the car window, with people carrying on just as normal, hurrying, strolling, talking, laughing: schoolchildren wending their way home from school now, in twos and threes, squabbling and chatting: mothers with their babies and toddlers. How could that happen? It was very strange.

Norma and Leon were very wound up. "Now you don't need to worry about anything, Val," Leon told her resolutely. "We'll see to everything, the funeral and things. You just let us know what you want when you've had time to think."

Norma leant forward, clutching the back of her seat. "Has anybody let Susie know? I'll ring her myself, anyway. She'll have such a shock, won't she, poor girl? Will she come back, do you think?"

"Of course she'll come back for the funeral, Norma."

"Well, you don't know that, Leon, do you? It might not be possible. By the way, we'll both drive over tomorrow and then Leon can drive your car back and park it in our road, Val." Norma clapped her hand suddenly over her mouth. "Oh, lovey, I've just thought: how terrible. It's Andy's birthday today!"

Valerie's voice sounded strangely echoey. "I know. I've bought him a shirt. Don't know what's happened to it." She seemed to hear the shattering of breaking glass. "I've bought a bottle of wine for him, too, but I think that smashed."

It was what was going to happen. It was always going to be this way. She knew what it was now. How it happened. She felt very calm.

"Now why don't you have a lie down, Val?" Norma suggested when they got to the house. "Slip off your top things and get under the covers? Have a little rest."

"I think I will."

"Would you like a cup of tea?"

Leon was hovering in the hallway. "Would she like something stronger?"

"Would you like something stronger, Val? A drop of brandy, perhaps?"

"I don't think so."

Norma led her up to the back bedroom, the room her daughter Tricia and her husband used when they were home. Her other daughter, Karen, being single, used the small front bedroom. "Tricia's room will be best for you, pet: nice and quiet. Shall I sit with you, lovey?"

"That's kind of you, Norma, very kind, but I think I'd like to be on my own."

Norma seemed loath to go. "Sure you don't want a brandy, lovey?"

She shook her head firmly. "No, no."

Norma left the door a little ajar; she heard her chattering with Leon in what they probably thought were hushed tones in the hall. "Well, I'm going to have a brandy. What a shock!"

"I can't believe it. Andy!"

"Poor Val."

"I know, I know! And everything: everything gone. I suppose they might find some bits and pieces. I wonder if it was the café, where the fire started?"

"I don't know any more than you do. It might have been that junk yard place next door."

It didn't matter where it had started. It had started, and it had finished. Everything had finished. Nothing was the same now, not any more. She quietly closed the door.

Norma had it nice these days, Tricia's room, with a dark blue counterpane on the bed and matching curtains. She drew the curtains and then folded up the counterpane carefully and spread it out on a chair so that it wouldn't get creased. She didn't bother taking off her dress and cardigan, just her outdoor shoes.

Lying on her back listening to the muted voices and noises from downstairs and occasional traffic sounds and voices from outside felt very odd, really. It was like being in bed on a school day when she had had mumps or chickenpox and was feeling better. Norma or Leon dropped something downstairs. She heard the clatter and then the scratch of Norma's voice saying something crossly.

Turning slowly onto her side and drawing up her knees, she curled up into a ball, one hand between her thighs where Andy used to put his and the other tightly about her chest. The whole world was spinning. Well, she knew it did that, didn't she? Any child knew that. It was obvious now, though. She could hear it hum.

The funeral was delayed, so that Susie could fly home. With Susie holding her hand and Norma on the other, she got through it somehow. The service was a blur. She did remember about him wanting a cremation, but she didn't want the jar with his ashes in it. It didn't mean anything. It wasn't Andy.

Seeing Susie made the aching bubble of something that she was carrying round in her stomach press upward and upward so that she could hardly breathe, but strangely enough, though Susie was very tearful, Valerie was dry-eyed. It was lovely having her there, of course, and she was very glad that she had come, but she didn't know what to say to her really. She asked about the children, of course, and about Joe, about the plans for the new house and Susie's new job and what it was like living in Nelson, but she didn't really take in what Susie had to relate. Her words went in one ear and out the other. It was as if they were talking about other people.

Susie had just started her latest job, so she had to fly back the following Friday. Sitting on the arm of her chair on the last but one night, she reached over and stroked her hair. "What are we going to do with you, Mum?"

Valerie shrugged. "I know, I know, I must go to the hairdresser. It's gone ever so dry." She felt the ends of her hair. "Dry and rough like a little dog's with distemper. I've still got a cold nose, though, so that's a good sign!"

Susie shook her head. "No, no, I don't mean that. I mean, what are you going to *do*, Mum? Would you want to come out to New Zealand? I don't know where they stand on parents coming over, but I should think they'd have you as you haven't got anybody else."

What was she going to do? It didn't matter. "I'll think about it. I might."

"We'd love to have you, you know."

She stared at her hands. Can't think about it. "I'll think about it, love."

"But where are you going to live, otherwise, Mum? Have you considered sheltered accommodation?" She held up a hand as Valerie opened her mouth. "I know, I know, you've always said you didn't want to go into a home, and I don't mean that, but there are lots of places about, private sheltered accommodation places, you know, with a warden, where you can be fairly independent. I'm going to be a long way away, and to be fair, you are getting on, and there's your hip... I do think you need to be somewhere where they can keep an eye on you, you know. Perhaps somewhere with proper nursing staff?"

She was getting rattled. *Wish you'd leave me alone!* "And how do I pay for all this?"

"You must have some money, Mum. You sold your house!"

She really hadn't a clue, had she? "Yes, but we've spent most of it, Susie, over the years, with all the moves and things. Furnishing houses, removal costs, solicitors, doing places up, buying another car... It *was* a house up here, you know, we sold, not down south. We've only had our pensions."

Susie looked horrified. "So that's how you came to be living in that dreadful flat? I couldn't understand it when I saw the place. When you said you were going to let Ollie have the Colbury house and move back to North Wales, I thought it was just you being noble and you were probably doing the right thing with him having lost his job – or the Bitch Witch had browbeaten you. I didn't realise it'd put you in such a difficult position – and you didn't tell me you were living in such a grotty place! I suppose that's why you didn't want to buy a new car, too. I wish you'd told me! Why didn't you tell me? And he didn't have any life insurance, Dad?"

"No."

"Not buildings insurance, either, I suppose, but what about contents insurance? You must have had that."

Valerie was beginning to get a nasty headache. What did all this talk of where she was going to live and money matter? None of it mattered. She frowned, rubbing a hand over her eyes. "Well, yes, we did."

Susie shook her head. "So who was the insurance with?"

"I don't know. I put down what we spent on things and what we'd got left in my little notebook, and Dad would tell me how much he was paying for things on a monthly basis – like road fund licence or the insurance – and I would just jot them down. I had it down in my book: 'insurance'. I didn't put down who it was with."

"And the policy's gone? Bank statements?"

"Bank statements too, I imagine. Everything."

"Ask the bank; they'll know."

"Will they?"

"Of course they will; they'll know who they've been paying out to, or they should do. And you mustn't forget to apply for a Widow's Pension."

Susie was obviously worrying about it; she tried to talk about it again the next day, but Valerie couldn't be doing with it; she knew she ought to be thinking about it, but she couldn't somehow, so she kept fobbing her off. Susie said she'd forget the new job and stay on for a bit. Valerie told her not to be so daft. She tried again to persuade her to go out to them in New Zealand. Valerie just shook her head. Susie said that she'd talk to Joe and they'd find some way to help financially. Valerie said she had helped enough that way already and she wasn't taking any more. Susie got cross. In the end, she heard Leon whispering to Susie that she should leave it for a while; they'd have a word with her, he and Norma, sort something out, when she felt more like it, get in touch. It hadn't hit her properly yet. She was still sort of in shock; let it all sink in first, give her time.

Susie hugged her for a long time at the airport; and she cried, which made Valerie's blouse shoulder uncomfortably wet. Valerie patted her reassuringly. "Don't worry, lovey. I'll be fine."

There was a nasty cold wind blowing as they emerged from Departures. It must have been her wet blouse: even after they got in the car, she shivered for quite a long time.

Norma tried again a bit later. She shook her head over their evening nightcap. "I think you *should* go to Susie, you know, Val. Whenever are you going to see them again?"

She nodded, staring at the pattern on the carpet. "They'll come over."

Norma tossed her head sardonically. "Oh, yes, they'll come over. Next year, Susie said. Perhaps. Or the year after, or the year after that, when they've got their house built."

Leon tried to quieten her. "Sssh, Norm. The time's not right." She was very grateful. Norma hadn't given up, though. "What about seeing the children, Val? They grow up so fast. Poppy'll be leaving school before you know where you are. Is she staying on for A levels or whatever they have out there?"

"I think so, yes."

Norma leant forward excitedly. "Leon, could we get a web cam?"

He shrugged. "I suppose, so, yes. Have Susie and Joe got one? And an internet phone? They probably have. Well, they could get one anyway." He nodded enthusiastically. "That's a good idea, actually, Norm. You can talk to them and they can see you, you see, Val, and they're bound to have a digital video camera, too. They can send films of them over the internet."

She shrank a little. "I'm useless with computers, Leon."

He shook his head vigorously. "Doesn't matter, doesn't matter, it's very easy!"

Norma nodded, beaming. "You'll be able to see the children when you're talking to them."

"That'd be very nice."

They went up to bed soon after. It was good to be on her own. It was cold and lonely in the bed, though: her mattress went on for miles.

C ome to Morrisons with us today, Val. Have a walk around the shopping precinct."

"Oh, I don't know." Apart from the trip to the airport and for the funeral, Valerie hadn't left the house. From time to time Norma and Leon had tried to suggest a bit of fresh air, maybe a little outing in the car, but she hadn't fancied it. No point. "No, no. Just let me be."

Leon seemed more determined this time, though. He was very persuasive. "Oh, come on!"

At last she gave in with a sigh. "Oh, all right. Just let me get my bag."

She thought he was going an odd way round, a much longer way, up Station Road and around the back. "Have they got road works?"

He looked a bit sheepish. "Um, um – no."

She realised as they passed the entrance to the allotments: he was trying to avoid passing the flat.

Peering over the hedge she could see the tops of runner bean poles and the corrugated tin roofs of sheds and all of a sudden, without really thinking about it, she leant forward and tapped him on the shoulder. "Leon! Leon, could you stop here, please?"

He turned his head to glance at her. "Did you want to see your allotment, Val?

Norma frowned. "It's raining a bit, love."

What was a bit of rain? "It doesn't matter."

Leon stopped and put the car into reverse. "Well, if you're sure. Hang on." They roared backwards till they were level with the gate. She opened her door. Norma was fastening on a headscarf. "Wait a minute, love, I'm coming too."

Fresh air, damp with fine raindrops, was clinging to her skin. She shook her head. "If you don't mind, Norm, I'd rather be on my own." She thought for a moment. "In fact, if it's all the same to you, I'll pass on Morrisons. I've got my handbag. I'll get a bus home."

Leon looked anxious. "No, no, I'll wait for you, Val – or if you really want to stay here for a bit, we'll come back after we've done the shopping,"

Norma was worried, too. "But is there anywhere you can shelter? You're going to get awfully wet."

"If it gets worse, I can stand in the shed."

Leon frowned. "I thought it was a lock-up?"

She had forgotten that. "It has a padlock, yes."

Leon slumped back in his seat. "Well, that's no good, then." A thought appeared to strike him suddenly. "Unless –"

Climbing out of his seat, he hurried round to the boot and reappeared with rain-damped hair, triumphantly flourishing a large pair of pliers. "Here we are, here was are! I knew I had some. I was thinking the other day we ought to get old Andy's tools over. Might as well get them now as not. I'll pick them up on our way back. So which shed's yours?"

Their allotment was overgrown, of course. Take your eye off it for a minute and thistles and nettles had re-colonised it. Must be an irritation to the other allotment holders. Maybe they'd sent a cross letter to the flat. Suddenly, she itched to get at it. It wasn't supposed to be like that. He had it so nice. It should be all bare brown earth and neat, weed-free rows.

She stood outside the shed, though, for a long time after Leon had gone before entering it. The air felt thick inside when she did, very composty and mouldy. The small grimy window had a broken pane. The corrugated iron on the roof had rusted away in one corner and there was a dark damp patch on the hardboard flooring underneath. Good thing he hadn't put the bags of compost or the lime or bonemeal there: falling to bits, it was.

At least here, it was still very tidy. Bundles of canes graded by length and tied up tightly with string were propped up in one corner. Pots, similarly sorted according to size, were piled up beneath the narrow potting shelf. On the shelf itself were trays that had held seedlings. They'd keeled over, of course, poor things. All dry as dust. She scanned the handwritten labels. *Broadbeans. Lettuce.* He'd been trying to grow flowers, too; he'd said he would. The seed packets were tucked into the desiccated trays.

Larkspur. Stocks. Antirrhinums. Some of them had come up, too. They had shrivelled up now, withered away into a thin crust of brittle fur. There were notes pinned up with drawing pins into the wooden wall above. Notes to himself. Things he'd read up. Things she'd told him. Step-by-step instructions: 1)... 2)... 3)... The last one she looked at was in her handwriting: she remembered giving it to him: a reminder for on his way home. It just said, 'MILK!!'"

Turning around, she caught sight of Andy. She hadn't noticed him when she had walked in. he was standing in the corner behind the door. The rush of relief that filled her up was sweet and all-encompassing, making her forget to wonder why he'd left the seedlings to die for want of water. "Oh, there you are, pet!" she cried. "Oh, Andy, I had this terrible dream! I thought you were dead!" He didn't answer.

She blinked and it came to her. It was his old raincoat, that was all: his old brown raincoat with the torn pockets, hanging on the hook, with his muddy wellingtons neatly placed side by side beneath it. As she stared, a large black spider edged itself out from beneath the collar and made a skittery dash to the floor. The glorious relief had vanished. Instead, the ripping, tearing, bear-clawed thing in her stomach swelled up now, like a huge bubble. Sharp, almost sweet ripples of pain stabbed through her fingers and toes. It was hard to breathe. The pain could see daylight now. It surged relentlessly upward, pushing through her chest and up in to her throat, emerging at first voicelessly and then ringing around the walls of the shed in an unwavering animal wail.

When Leon came back to look for her, he found her still keening, but curled up amongst the compost bags and the fertilizers on the dusty floor. Her legs had given way and all the muscles of her body had tightened inexorably, drawing her up into herself until she was curled up tightly like an armadillo. It took him a while to unfold her.

"Come on, Val, love. Come on. Let's get you home."

Chapter 24

Norma tucked her up in bed when they got back. When she had left the room, Valerie pulled a pillow down beside her and hugged it very tight. If she'd had a jumper of Andy's or his pyjama top, or even if she'd brought his old mac from the shed, she could have wrapped it up in that, so she could at least smell him. But she hadn't; there wasn't any trace of him, except, of course, for the tools and bags of compost and things at the allotment. And his vegetables.

She wept a lot all night. She didn't sleep.

She did try to pull herself together and to help Norma about the house as time went on – after all, they were getting on, too; it was hard for them having an extra body – but she was more of a hindrance than help, she knew that, too, full of pain, too lost in her continuing grief. It felt continually as if a metal brace was fitted tight about her forehead. Her eyes felt sunken, dry and hot. Tears flowed without notice. She had no energy at all. Petals that fell from a vase being carried to the sink stayed on the floor until someone else noticed. Saucepans boiled dry. Leon sighed a little too heavily on occasion; Norma occasionally got a little sharp. Valerie didn't care. She was wrapped up in herself. Every tiny bit of her hurt. It hurt to touch things. It wasn't her arthritis; it was an Andy pain.

She saw him several times again, once on the bus, once in the library and twice in Morrisons.

At other times, it was the guilt that had her writhing: if I'd left things as they were, not dragged him down to Susie, none of this would ever have happened. We'd still have been in Andy's lovely house; there'd have been no stress, no dragging ourselves around, no worrying. Andy wouldn't have died. When the guilt forced itself up into her mouth and the tears were flowing down her cheeks she let it out loud sometimes. In the middle of the night or even once or twice on the bus, it came pouring out of her. "I'm sorry! Sorry!" Most of the time, though, she still couldn't shake off the feeling that it was just a long, bad dream.

She got angry with him, too and she shouted about that as well, sometimes, when the pain got too much. "How could you do this to me, Andy? How could you go and leave me? How could you do it? How?"

Time passed somehow. She had no idea how much, but all at once it was time to move on, she could sense it. She couldn't stay there forever, occupying the spare room and being a gooseberry every evening.

Besides, though nobody could have been kinder or more patient than Norma and Leon, she wanted to be alone now. Alone, so she could talk openly to Andy. It was time to go.

She went to see a Housing Association. There was a bit of a wait, but eventually they called to say a place had just come up, a one-bed roomed flat in an old hotel in the middle of town that had been converted. Norma ran her over to see it. The building had a press-button bank of entry buttons by the front door like Susie's London flat had had, but though they could hear loud voices arguing coming from behind one of the doors, and there were pushchairs and a bicycle in the hall and a couple of empty lager cans in the lift, they didn't meet a soul inside.

The flat turned out to be on the fifth floor and at the back, overlooking the dustbin area. It didn't consist of much: a claustrophobically narrow sitting room with a high square window: a tiny kitchen area off the sitting room: the bedroom, very small: bathroom, no bath, just a small, cracked shower behind a torn plastic curtain: grimy orange wallpaper throughout. It stank of stale smoke.

Norma eyed the garish pub opposite and then glanced at her carefully as they walked back into the busy street. "You didn't like that much, love, did you?"

"I thought it was bloody horrible."

Norma looked at her in astonishment, then chuckled. "Val! I've never heard you swear!"

She had to chuckle herself. "Must have caught it from Andy." It was probably him saying it. They say when somebody you love very much dies, they get inside of you somehow. She caught the echo of him a lot these days. *What do you think, then, pet?* she asked him silently. *Shall I take it? Do you fancy me living there?*

She heard him quite distinctly this time. *No, Val, I bloody well do not!*

She had been in their hair, though, for quite long enough. Besides, she ached for some things of her own: any things. She wanted to make her own food. To eat when she was hungry, not when Norma said. It was wonderful that they were so caring, so kind, but they were too much on top of her. It was making her crabby.

"I suppose I could go and live in a Travelodge, you know," she said to Norma when they were having a nightcap that evening. "Like those people Whatsit, can't remember their names. I read about them, did you? They lived there for years and years, you know. Andy and I used to say it would be quite cosy, living in a hotel; no cooking or cleaning, laundry service, even get your beds made!"

"Be very expensive, Val, and you wouldn't like it on your own."

"No, I wouldn't." Had to find somewhere, though. A thought struck her. "Where were we, Norma, when we saw those whatdoyoucallthem, mobile home things? Was I with you or Andy?"

"Caravans, you mean?"

"No, not caravans."

Norma frowned. "Campervans, then?"

"No, like, I don't know, like little prefabs. Little bungalows. Do you think they rent them?"

"Oh, I know where you are! Down on the Brynmor road." Norma shook her head. "Oh, you wouldn't want one of those, Val, they're horrible! And they get flooded, you know. You wouldn't like living there."

"I need to move out, Norm. I need to give you and Leon some space."

"You don't need to."

"Yes, I do."

Norma chuckled as she reached over to set her cup down on the mantelpiece. "You could always have our caravan, love."

"Your caravan? The one you used to have in Benllech?"

"My turn now. I *was* joking."

"But is that the one you mean?"

"Mm. It's not there any more of course."

"It isn't?"

Norma laughed. "No, silly, hasn't been for ages! You must have seen it."

"Where is it then?"

"At the bottom of our garden."

"Oh!" Valerie frowned, trying to picture it. "I've never noticed."

"You're blind, you are. Been there for ages now, I'm sure I told you."

"You probably did. My memory! And I've not been very observant recently."

"Of course, not. No." Norma shrugged. "It is plugged in, got proper electricity and such; Leon uses it as a workshop. It's bit on the small side and it's a bit dilapidated, but it's not damp or anything. At least I'd be able to keep an eye on you there!" She shook her head decisively. "But you're not up to living in a caravan, Val, not in your state of mind. Or health. You're very wonky!"

Valerie pretended outrage. "Don't call me wonky!"

Norma stuck her tongue out. "Well, you are."

The idea of the caravan began to grow on Valerie. She brought it up the next evening while they were watching television. "I'd be taking Leon's workshop if I had the caravan. What would he do for a workshop?"

"What's that? My caravan?" Leon rolled his eyes. "Oh, don't worry about me."

"We were joking about Val having our caravan," Norma waved a hand airily. "Oh, he hardly ever uses it; it was just one of his ideas. But you're not thinking of it seriously, are you Val?"

She was surprised to find she was. "I am, yes, if you're offering."

"Well, if you did, Leon would just have to find somewhere else to store his tools. He can put them in the cellar."

Leon shrugged plaintively. "Oh, thanks."

She was very tempted. "Shall I try it?"

"Well, I suppose it has some advantages. You'd have your own little space, be self-contained, but you'd be close enough for us keep an eye on you." Norma was a decisive woman. "We could try it. It's not a bad idea. Yes. Okay. It'll take a bit of time for him to get it liveable-in, though. How long d'you think, Leon?"

He rolled his eyes. "Oh, if I slog my guts out, do without any food or sleep and work all hours, maybe a couple of weeks."

Val felt an anxious flutter. "Oh, Leon, love, I wouldn't want you to..."

"He'll be glad to do it; take no notice." Satisfied, Norma settled back in her chair. "Oh, good. That's settled, then."

I t took much longer than two weeks to renovate, but they wouldn't let her go inside the caravan till it was all ready. Leon was down at the bottom of the garden at all hours and there were times when Norma, doing something mysterious with her sewing machine in the dining room, shouted to her, "Don't come in! Don't come in!"

She felt really quite excited as they eventually led her down the garden and told her to keep her eyes closed while they helped her up the step. She gazed around in amazement when they told her to open them. It was really quite sweet. "Oh, Norma, you've got it lovely."

Norma surveyed it proudly. "It's not bad, is it?"

"I recognise that carpet." Swirly browns and oranges; if you looked at it too long, it made you dizzy.

"It's the one we used to have in the lounge. I kept it in the garage for a rainy day. Leon's put this together for the caravan out of the best bits that we hung on to; knew it'd come in handy one day. It's well stuck down, don't think you'll trip."

The coverings on the seats were mostly orange, too: big squares of dark orange and cream. The curtains were off-white, with little green and brown saucepans and frying pans in some of the squares. She remembered them from years ago, too; they used to be in Norma's kitchen.

"And you've painted everything, Leon! It's a very nice shade of cream."

He was looking very proud. "And I've made you some shelves and cupboards. The only thing is, Val, the bed. There's a bit of a snag."

"What's that?"

"Well, you see, your bed folds up. It's here, see it? Against the wall. You have to let it down when you want to use it."

She stared at it daunted. That was tricky. "Oh, I see."

"Show her, Leon, Show her."

It came down heavily ready made-up. She shook her head in admiration. "That's very clever!"

"It might be awkward for you, it's a bit cumbersome, so Leon will come over and get it down for you each evening. "

She was guilt-ridden again. "Oh, I wouldn't want him to have to do that. I'll leave it down."

"You can't. Well, not if you want to have a table."

"Oh."

"And you'll need a table, won't you, in the day?"

Leon looked around, rubbing his hands together and beaming. "What d'you think, then, Val? Be all right in here, will you?"

She kissed his cheek. "Oh, Leon, it's lovely! Very cosy."

"We've had some good times in this. Used to be a complete breeze to tow, didn't it, Norm? We only had the Vauxhall Victor – d'you remember it, Val?" He patted the wall affectionately. "But old Maudie didn't sway at all, did she, Norm?" Norma chuckled. "Good old Maudie. She didn't jump around."

Valerie slid into one of the check-covered seats by the small formica table. It was all coming back. "We stayed in this with you when you had it in Benllech a few times, Leon."

He had forgotten, obviously. "So you did, so you did!"

She looked around, puzzled. "How did we do that? Where did we all sleep?"

Norma chuckled. "Don't you remember the hammock?"

It came slowly back to her. "Oh, yes, yes, the hammock! How could I have forgotten? There was a big hammock somewhere funny. Wasn't it hanging above the bed?"

Leon nodded. "It was, you're right, you're right."

"Hung right down over my nose. You fell down once."

"I didn't."

"You did, you rolled out and landed right on top of Andy, didn't he, Norma?"

She chuckled. "Had too much to drink, the pair of them, little demons!"

"I don't believe you."

Laughing Valerie appealed for confirmation. "Didn't he, Norma? Andy got a black eye. We did laugh! Mind you, serves us right for nicking your bed."

Leon assumed a pious expression. "Well, you were guests. We like to look after our guests."

"I'll say." She gazed up at where the hammock had been, reflecting. "You'd have a problem with it nowadays, eh? Even if you could get in it, how would you keep nipping in and out to spend a penny?"

"Speaking of spending a penny, Val," Leon beckoned to her, sliding open a narrow veneered door. "Come here, come here."

Norma helped her to slide out from behind the table. "He's very proud of this."

He stood aside so that she could see into the small space. "There was an old chemical lav but I've put in a proper marine one now for you, see?"

She gazed at the little lidded structure. "Oh, you shouldn't have!" Edging in closer, she examined it. "How do I flush it?"

"Here, if you just -" Leon pushed in beside her and placed his foot over a floor button. "You pump it, like this, with your foot."

"Ooh, that's clever!" She hesitated, frowning. "Where does it go to? I mean – all the-you-know-what?"

He shook his head. "Don't you worry about that. See? Little washbasin...."

"Oh, very neat!"

Norma stuck her head inside. "You'll have to come over to the house for a shower, I'm afraid."

Val nodded uneasily. "Oh, I am still going to be a pest..."

"Don't worry about it; that's fine."

Leading the way back into the body of the caravan, Leon rubbed his hands again. "Now then, you've got a sink, too,

Val, but it's not piped in, the water: there's a drum outside, you pump the sink like this." He demonstrated enthusiastically. She watched what he was doing carefully, anxious to get it right.

"Right! Lovely!" She glanced around the kitchen area. "Ah, look, a little gas stove!"

Norma moved up to demonstrate. "Calor Gas, of course; works nicely, though, Val. You've got two rings and a little oven and grill."

Leon jerked his head towards the back of the caravan. "There's a bottle outside, next to the water drum."

Bending down, Norma pulled out a flat tray of cream plastic from between the sink and a cupboard. "There's this plastic worktop here, you put it on top of the sink when you need a space to work on. You put your pans and everything underneath."

"I'll need to get some small pans." Valerie was trying to take it all in. "All very compact."

Leon was still busy demonstrating. "Little electric heater, see? Another one if you need it, we can bring it in. Windows swing out; this one's got a dodgy hinge, so leave that shut."

She tried to quell the quiver in her stomach. "Very nice, Leon. Very nice, Norma. Oh, yes." It all made her a bit nervous. So this was to be her new home... She smiled determinedly. "Oh, thank you both of you. Thank you. Very nice."

Norma made them a special dinner that night to celebrate, though Val had to pretend she had an appetite. She tried to hide some of her pork chop under a little mound of potato and gravy, hoping Norma wouldn't notice. Afterwards, they watched a bit of telly. "We must fix you up with a television, Val," Leon said, leaning forward towards the set with his elbows on his knees and steadily flicking over with the remote control from one channel to another.

Norma clicked her tongue impatiently. "For heaven's sake, Leon, will you stop doing that? Settle on one programme, don't keep flicking round and round."

Val nodded, remembering. "Andy used to do that. Used to give me a headache."

"It's a man thing. Look, Leon, there's a quiz show – go

back to that, go back to that. That'll do; let's see if our brains'll still work." Leon changed channels obediently and settled back in his chair. The quizmaster looked very grave.

"*What is the coldest city in the world? Is it a) Moscow; b) Vostok; c) Ulaanbaatar; or d) Winnipeg?*"

They looked at each other. "Moscow."

"No, I don't think so."

"Well, it must be Vostok, then."

"Why? Where's Vostok?"

"Don't know. Sounds cold. Russia? Where's Ulaanbaatar?

"Could the coldest place be in Canada?" Leon was decided. "I think it's in Canada. I'm going for Winnipeg."

They all got it wrong. It was Ulaanbaatar. Leon flicked over again – 'Hang on, just want to see the football results...'" – so they missed the bit where the quizmaster said where it was.

She wanted to be on her own all of a sudden; it happened like this. She had to be on her own. She levered herself up. "I think I'll go over now."

Norma looked at her in surprise. "You all right, Val?"

She smiled tightly. "Yes, just a bit tired." It was difficult to speak; she had to keep swallowing. "Think I'll go and try out my lovely new caravan."

Leon struggled out of his chair. "Right-ho, love. I'll come and walk you back."

"Oh, there's no need."

"I'll need to get the bed out for you anyway. Just get a torch. Should have left the bed down while we were over there."

Norma came with them to the back door. "Will you be all right then, Val? Have you got everything you need?"

She stared hard into the darkness of the garden, swallowed hard again and smiled, hoping that they couldn't see her chin quivering. "Oh, yes. I'm fine; I'm fine."

"All right, then, love." Norma kissed her cheek. "Have you got that torch, Leon? Sleep tight, then, Val; I'll pop over in the morning. If you do want anything, don't be afraid to wake us up."

She managed just a faint murmur. "...'kay."

It was strange in the caravan, very quiet after Leon had

gone. It smelled a little funny; the enclosed, still air was both stuffy and earthy, like being in the shed on the allot-ment. The electric heater had been left on while she was at the house – have to watch that, she reminded herself, could run very expensive – so it was nice and warm. The bed actually looked quite inviting, if a bit hard. There were little wall lights on either side, with pull cords, which was quite handy, and Norma had found some orangey lampshades for them so they spread a nice glow. She was tempted to crawl in just as she was and to pull the duvet up over her head, but she pulled herself together. It wouldn't do. Besides, she'd only have to get out again to spend a penny.

"Well, here we are, then, love," she told Andy. She patted the bed beside her before making herself stand up. "Bit of a firm mattress, but that'll be good for my back, I dare say. I'll just have a bit of a wash."

She undressed stiffly and slowly. Seemed to have got worse, somehow, the arthritis: going into her other joints now. Getting her jumper over her head was a painful task, and getting her tights off was a dickens of a job, but she managed it eventually as always. Cutting her toenails, though – that was getting quite impossible. "I keep forget-ting; remind me to ask at the surgery about a chiropodist."

Pulling on her nightie and a cardigan, she shuffled over to the little wash compartment. The door slid open easily. "Leon's done a good job on that. Now then, let's see how we get on with this..." She managed to lower herself down onto the little lavatory, but it was a beggar to stand up again. "Ooh, dear, oh dear!" She had to haul herself up pulling on the door handle. "Hope I'm not going to pull that door out of its track."

It took a fair few heavy prods with her foot on the floor before the flush worked, but she got the hang of it at last and it emptied quickly, sucking the water away with a woosh. The water in the washbasin was cold. "Shall I boil up a kettle? What do you think?" She shook her head, frowning. "Can't be bothered. Need to take my tablets, though. Now then, shall I make some cocoa?" That meant making the gas stove work. "No, you're right; don't think I'll bother."

She climbed at last into the bed; she'd been right, it was a bit hard. Propped up against the pillows she stared out into the small space. Where would she put a telly if she had one? "Leon says we'll find me a telly; that'll be nice, won't it? I can watch *Newsnight* in bed."

Shouldn't have thought about that: remembering watching *Newsnight* side by side with Andy. Talking to herself, how silly. A plump tear slid down her cheek. "Wish you were here, Andy."

The wind got up in the night and the little caravan shivered noisily. There were night noises: bumps and clatterings, thirsty gurgling sounds that made her jump. Tomcats fighting, a train in the distance, the occasional car, but she didn't mind those. She wasn't even exactly frightened. She just felt so alone.

Chapter 25

V al, Val, whatever are you doing? You naughty girl, you really shouldn't be doing that!" Norma emerged from the back door and waddled crossly over the lawn. "Put that spade down now, you silly thing! Whatever do you think you're doing?"

Valerie straightened painfully. Startled tears sprang into her eyes. "You've got Creeping Buttercup and Ground Elder in here, Norm, I'm trying to get it up."

"Well, don't. Give me that spade." Taking it from Valerie, she shook her head. "I don't know! Well, really!"

"It needed doing."

"Well, you can't do it. I don't want to be nursing you as well, you know."

"No, of course you don't, Norm." Placing a hand in the hollow above her buttocks, she massaged the achy bit with her knuckles, trying not to grimace. "I just thought: it's the least I can do. Trying to get myself going a bit. If I could sort out the garden a bit for you, it'd be something. All I need is for Leon to get me some bags of compost and some bone meal and all-purpose fertilizer – and maybe some bark or spent mushroom compost for a mulch to put on top."

Norma was very snappy. "Leon's much too busy at the moment, Val. He's got his annual report to do for the Players and the balance sheet for the Bowls Club and all sorts of things to do. I want him to finish the shelving in the back bedroom. Besides, there's his back; he's got aches and pains too, you know. You're not the only one."

Valerie was stung. "No, of course not, no."

307

Norma seemed to be regretting her sharp tone. "I suppose I could manage to get a small bag for you myself when I do the weekly shop," she offered grudgingly. "Do they sell it in Tesco's?"

"They definitely do in Asda."

Norma rolled up her eyes and tossed back her head. "What am I talking about? I'm not having you doing yourself in struggling with my garden. No, and that's that. Look at your hands! They look really sore."

"Then what can I do to help, Norma?"

Norma sighed. "Oh, Val, you don't need to help. You don't need to do anything, really you don't." A bell rang faintly in the distance. "Oops! That's the front door bell; I'll have to go. Now you do as you're told. Go on back to the caravan, put your feet up. Have a little snooze."

The caravan enclosed her again like an orange and brown cocoon. She was beginning to get on their nerves. Been here too long. How long? Eighteen months? Two years? One year? She had no conception of time.

What now? Ought to make the bed, really, get it put away but what was the point? She was only going to get it down again later. Besides it was getting to be too much of a struggle for her, really, and she didn't want to trouble Leon. She sat down on it instead, staring down at her hands. They were certainly very painful; always were, some times more so than others. Used to be so strong and useful. Not all that much use now..

She sighed. *Come on, do something; don't just sit there.* "What d'you think, pet, shall I have something to eat? Haven't had anything this morning, just a cup of tea." She frowned, trying to remember what she had had the evening before. Had it been an egg? Or was it yesterday she had had the tin of beans?

"A drop of soup, d'you think?" Maybe have a drop of soup. Not yet, though. "Think I'll leave it for a bit, pet. Not really hungry."

What then? She stared around, then remembered, pleased. "Oh, by the way, did I tell you I'd bought another cookery book? It's by that what's-he-called, that something Rhodes, you know, the one with the sticky-up hair. I found it in the Oxfam shop when I went for that bit of a walk whenever it was – a few weeks ago. *New British Classics,* it's called. Thought we'd see what he's got to offer."

Smiling, she took it down clumsily from the shelf. Planning what she might get Andy for his dinner always gave her a bit of a lift. "What do you fancy, then, eh?" she asked him, smoothing down the enticingly illustrated pages. "What about roast duck with crispy hash and local beer gravy? You'd like that, nice beer gravy. Or how about buttered leeks with Whitstable champagne oysters? And I thought, maybe, for pudding, we could try a nice big custard tart."

It occupied her till almost five o'clock, choosing his perfect menu, though she did doze off for a bit towards the end of the afternoon. When she woke up and peered out through the window she was surprised to find how late it was getting. Her heart gave a little jump and a flush of pleasure washed over her as she saw Andy making his way back down through the shadowy garden, whistling. Back already! I must put the kettle on... When she blinked, though, he had gone.

She had a few cream crackers with some slivers of Cheddar and a tomato for her tea.

Leon rapped on the door as she was rinsing out her crockery. "Are you ready? Are you coming over, love?" he asked as she opened the door.

"Um..." She stared at him blankly.

He shook his head, exasperated. "You've forgotten again, haven't you? It's Thursday. Val. Thursday: your weekly call from Susie." He grinned. "You're a dozy Nellie. Come on, get your skates on, she'll be ringing before very long."

She *had* forgotten again. "Oh, dear me! Hang on Leon, while I just get my coat."

He gave an exaggerated shiver. "You'll need it! You'll need it, Val. It's blooming freezing out here."

"You go back, love – I'll follow you."

It was amazing, really, seeing Susie and the children right in front of her, large as life on his computer screen and growing up more every time. It always took her aback. Thomas was there this evening – a big lad, now, a real Kiwi already. Tall for his age, by the look of it: a lovely smile. Still shy. His answers were a bit monosyllabic, but it was a bit difficult being asked to chat to a granny he probably couldn't remember all that well.

Poppy didn't appear again; she rarely did these days. Valerie couldn't remember the last time she had seen her. Susie moaned about her as usual. "She's impossible, Mum. I can't deal with her. She's got a thing about this awful boy, too, a real dropout: hair down to his shoulders, older than her, no job. A layabout. Thank God he's off soon, going over to the UK. Poppy wanted to go with him, but I've said she can't."

She didn't mention coming over herself for a visit again, but then, she did seem very happy with Joe.

Nice having these calls. It was odd, though, Valerie thought, as she followed the bobbling light of her torch back to the caravan – she knew who they were and she knew she loved them, but it was difficult to get involved. To worry about them all was too much trouble.

She put on her little television when she got back in, just to fill the silence as she got undressed ready for bed. Her loneness – she didn't think of it as loneliness, exactly, because she didn't really mind being on her own – her loneness, without Andy, came swooping round her when it was nearly time for bed. No one to hug. No one to whisper to. No one to laugh with. No Andy by her side. No Andy.

Recriminations had become a part of the night time ritual, too, once she was under the covers and the light had been put out.

If only...

My fault, all my fault. Should have left us where we were.

I should have watched your diet. Less butter, fewer cakes.

If she did eventually drift off, she woke up after a brief respite and carried on exactly where she had left off. *Come back, come back! Be here when I wake up.*

So sorry...

She had a dream that night, so she must have dropped off for a bit and it must have been just before waking, because she had the hazy tail end of it still in her mind as she opened her eyes. Lying still, she drew gently on the misty thread, trying to bring the dream back into her mind before it dissolved entirely away. She had been so happy in that dream; she had been whole again. What she was going to do next was obvious now. Another revelation.

Of course! She knew now. Of course. That's what happens.

She had been with Andy.

There were a number of Travel Agencies on the High street, a surprising number, really, when by all accounts most people were making their own travel arrangements via the Internet. Thomas Cook, Going Places, Thompson Travel... They all looked much of a muchness; it was hard to choose. She hovered round each one pretending to read the signs and lists of bargains in the windows, then picked one that was quite busy but had one seat left free in front of an assistant. Glancing around at the colourful brochures lining the walls in racks, she perched self-consciously in the chair, nervously clutching her bag.

"Good morning!" The girl was red-haired and young, quite plump, and had one of those silver stud-things in one nostril, which was rather a pity. The turquoise blue of her uniform suited her rather, and she'd have looked much nicer without the stud. She beamed, revealing another one, set in one of her front teeth. "How may I help you?"

"Um, yes." She dragged away her gaze from the young girl's teeth and cleared her throat, doing her best to pretend that they were on their own. "Could you tell me, please, how much would it cost me to get to Ulaanbaatar?"

The girl frowned. "To where?"

"Ulaanbaatar. I'm not sure where it is."

"How d'you spell that?"

"U-L-A-A-N-B-A-A-T-A-R; Well, I think so, anyway. Or is it an 'N' at the end? I know there are lots of 'A's."

The girl – Dawn, according to the name badge pinned to her uniform blouse – tippy-tapped rapidly at her keyboard, staring hard into her monitor screen. She raised her eyebrows. "Ah, there it is...Ulaanbaatar. It's an 'R'. Mongolia."

Valerie was taken aback. "Mongolia? Oh, goodness. Oh." Mongolia was a very long way. "And how much would it cost? A rough idea will do"

"When were you thinking of going?"

She glanced at her hands where her worn wedding ring

gleamed dully silvery-gold. "Oh, um, well, pretty well right away."

"Single? Return?"

"Single."

"Bear with me..." Dawn returned to her keyboard. "If you were to go on the 27th February a single to Ulaanbaatan would be... Well, depending on airline, between £800 and £1000."

She fingered her wedding ring. *I could afford it; I've got the contents insurance money – but do I want to go all that far? Sounds very onerous.* "How long is the flight?"

"Approximately fourteen hours including stopovers."

"Stopovers?"

"With Aeroflot it's via Moscow, or via Seoul with Korean airlines – or you could fly British Airways to Frankfurt and from Beijing with Air China."

"Oh, goodness me, Beijing?" *Stuck in a plane for all that distance; then not knowing what to do, where to go, when she got there? Would there be buses out to the countryside where there'd be nice deep snow? It was all a bit frightening. There had to be somewhere, some method, a bit closer to home.*

Dawn was waiting. Valerie nodded. "Right-ho, well..." Gathering up her handbag, she pushed herself out of the chair. *Five minutes in a chair and I get really stiff; how am I going to manage after fourteen hours?* "Well, thank you for that. I'll think about it."

She smiled back nicely at Dawn as she pushed the door open in case she was disappointed. "Thank you very much."

Andy was sitting a few seats in front of her on the bus. It made her catch her breath at first, but it wasn't him, of course, just somebody who looked like him. She was used to this disappointment. Inspiration came to her again, though, as she directed her gaze away from away from the back of the stranger's neat grey head and stared out through the window and she had to push her way back out again, apologising as she went. *Of course! So obvious!*

There were several other posters in the window of the travel agency next to the bus stop apart from the big one of the gleaming white liner sailing through azure blue seas that had caught her eye, and they all seemed to be about cruising. The shop was empty of customers, with only one man sitting behind the desk, a round-faced, middle-aged man in a suit wearing wire-framed glasses, who looked up eagerly as she walked in. "Good morning!"

"Good morning." Gripping her handbag on her knee firmly as she sat down in front of him, she summoned up her best voice. "I wanted to enquire about a cruise."

He nodded keenly. "Have you been cruising before?"

"Yes, yes, I have."

"What line?"

"Line?"

"Do you have a particular line in mind? I take it you're not a party animal?" He chuckled.

"No, not exactly."

"We'll rule out some of the lines, then, the non-stop-fun ships. A week? Two weeks?"

"The shorter the better."

"The Med, perhaps, then? That might be your best bet. When did you want to go? May? June? August?"

She shook her head. "Oh, no! Now, really."

He sucked air in through his teeth. "Have to be the Caribbean."

"Wouldn't the water then be, well, rather warm?"

He nodded reassuringly. "Warm? Oh, yes, it should be, oh, yes, you'd be all right."

The Caribbean didn't sound right, and it'd mean a flight. "Might you have anything going a bit more, well – north?"

"You mean the Fiords, perhaps? The Baltic?"

"Where's the coldest – I mean, the most northerly place the ships go to?"

He deliberated. "Reykjavik, I suppose. Fancy seeing the northern lights, do you? You might be better off with Trondheim. Or – how about Alaska! That's our most popular cruise."

Bound to be cold in Alaska. "That might be interesting, yes."

Scraping back his chair noisily, he opened up a filing cabinet. "As a matter of fact, there's this one, just come in – a lovely cruise; I've just printed it off. Mind you it is a fifteen nighter. 'Ultimate Alaska'. Millennium class ship. Inside cabin – would you be happy with an inside? Inside cabin starting from only £2,367. Mind you, single occupancy, could be quite a bit more."

How much? "Good heavens."

He shook his head, beaming. "I know, I know, astonishingly good value, quite fancy it myself. So let's see... 16th May, flying from London Heathrow –"

She shook her head vehemently. "No, no, no, too late, too late. I don't want to wait any longer than next week."

He puffed out his cheeks. "No chance. No chance. Not in that direction."

She was getting a little agitated. "In what direction might I go, then?"

He shook his head gloomily. "Might possibly find a last minute offer to the Canaries, a cancellation, perhaps." He returned to his monitor screen. "Bear with me while I have a look."

She leant forward, struggling to decipher what he had up on the screen. "What will the sea temperature be around the Canaries?"

"Thinking about swimming? Very popular again, of course, the Canaries during the winter. Winter sunshine, we all want it." He shook his head gloomily. "Nothing, I'm afraid, so far. Not having much luck."

"I suppose I could just take a ferry."

"Pardon?"

The idea was getting her quite excited. "The Channel's pretty cold, isn't it, at this time of the year? Could you organise a ferry ticket for me?"

He was disappointed, clearly, and losing patience with her. His face had lost its shine. "Where to? France? The Isle of Wight? Santander? Where from? Dover, Folkestone, Southampton, Portsmouth?"

Why hadn't she thought of it before? She was back in North Wales. Very little travelling, just a bus ride to the station, then fifty minutes, an hour or so, on the train. Very cold water in the Irish Sea, especially in February. She straightened, satisfied. She had it now. "I'd like a ferry ticket to Ireland, please. A single from Holyhead."

Leon and Norma were delighted to think she had managed to get herself together enough to decide on a little break.

"Dublin, eh? Very nice, very nice! Doing well these days, Ireland. I believe it's a very nice city. Expensive, though, these days, so I've heard."

"Don't go drinking too many pints of Guinness now! Bring me back a little bit of Shamrock!"

"I won't! I will!"

They were going away too, on the same date. She'd chosen that one carefully. If they'd been seeing her off, she'd have had to drag a big suitcase along. No point otherwise, just a handbag. Pity for them that the weather looked as if it was taking an even nastier turn: for her, perhaps a good thing. Not easy to spot a bobbing body if there were great high waves.

"I've booked a night crossing," she told Andy when she was having her bedtime chat. "You know, after what we said – less chance of somebody seeing me that way. The train for Holyhead leaves at 9.25." She had studied the timetable carefully. "The 8.15 bus should do it nicely."

There wasn't too much to do to get ready. Fortunately, her will was still with the solicitor, so it was all fairly straightforward, really, just a bit of a tidy-up, just a few letters to write.

It was hard, though, writing the letters. It made her cry a bit. And the sky was so overcast she had to have the lights on all day in order to see.

To Susie. Of course, to Susie: *Be happy, Susie, be happy. I love you.*

Don't be sad for me, Susie. I'm happy too.

To the children: *I am so proud of you; you have brought me great joy, hope you have wonderful lives,* that kind of thing.

A line or two for Ollie, for his past kindness and for old times' sake. She even managed to mention Camilla. Briefly.

For Norma and Leon, a special note: *You have been kindness and generosity itself. So sorry to do this to you.*

She was really sorry, indeed she was. They were in for a terrible shock.

By six o'clock the letters were finished, if a bit spotty and blotted. She set them out them on her pillow with a note about how to get hold of her solicitor. She was very tired – drained, really – and her hip ached badly from sitting too long and too still. Good thing it wasn't a very long journey. She stared at the kettle. "Cup of tea, next?"

Once the tea was finished, a dilemma raised its head. "What to wear, you see, pet? That's the thing. Ought I to be putting on heavy layers, clothes that will weight me down, or something very light, so that I'll get cold more quickly?" She surveyed the few items in her tiny wardrobe. A thick tweed skirt and blouse and jumper and woolly tights, or the pale blue summer dress he liked that she'd bought at Peacocks? "Bit chilly on the train, don't you think, pet?" She considered for a moment. He did like that dress. "No, you're right. I can put my big thick beige cardi and my winter coat on top and take them off before I jump. Or not. I'll think about that one on the way, decide which would be best."

The dress seemed a bit big on her now, but it didn't matter, especially with the chunky cardigan on top. Bit of time to kill...

She had made herself chuckle.

Collecting the photographs emailed over from New Zealand that Leon had printed up for her, she sat down heavily with them on the bed. Smoothing the glossy paper with her hand, she studied each one carefully before putting it in her handbag. All looked as if they were having fun. They'd be shocked, upset – well, Susie would, anyway – but they *would* be all right. "They have a full life out there, Andy: a *good* life. I'm sure they do. Susie and Joe. Thomas. All of them. Even Poppy, though perhaps she doesn't always believe it." She chuckled, holding a photograph up to the light. "Looks like you in one of your moods. Have you seen that scowl?"

She closed her handbag when she had finished and looked around the little caravan again. "Well, there we are." She felt like saying 'thank you', so she did. It had looked after her, after all.

It was a wild night. It was pitch dark as she locked up the caravan and there was rain in the icy, gusty wind as she picked her way up the garden path. She popped the keys onto Norma's kitchen table, and then locked the back door up again. Poor things. What a shock it was going to be. At least, though, she wasn't leaving them a body.

It was difficult to open the side gate; she couldn't see the bolt at first, but she found it eventually and closed the gate again carefully behind her, though only on the latch. Cross fingers. Shouldn't be any intruders. Should be all right. Next step: Norma's back door key: put it through the letter-box. The icy wind took her breath away as she rounded the corner to the front of the house. My goodness, it was cold! Maybe all this travelling was unnecessary; maybe the garden would have done it after all.

When she made out the large dark shape on the step and saw it move, she ground to a startled halt, emitting an involuntary squeak of alarm. Throwing a hand to her chest, she could feel her heart thumping. "Who is it? Who's there?"

Chapter 26

The shape unfolded itself and spoke. It was a female: a young woman by the sound of it. "Sorry! Sorry! Did I frighten you? I didn't mean to. Sorry!"

Valerie clutched her handbag tightly, gazing suspiciously around at the front gate. Was it a trick? Were there others, burglars, hooligans, ruffians, lurking out there in the road behind the hedge, hoping she'd open the door?

Whoever it was bent down and picked up a big dark bundle and then moved down off the step towards Valerie. "I'm waiting for my gran? There's nobody in. Have I got the right house?" She sounded very young and rather nervous herself. A little bit like a whatsit – like Joe did – like an Australian or a New Zealander.

Valerie couldn't make out her features. She eyed the shadowy face warily. "I don't know. What's your gran's name?"

She didn't sound too sure. "Erm – her name? Oh, um, Valerie. I think it's Valerie. Valerie Bryce?"

Valerie blinked. Raindrops were trickling into her eyes. The girl pushed back the hood of her drenched cagoule and took a step towards her, peering closely at her in turn. Her voice was shaking a little bit. "You're my gran, aren't you? It's me, Nana. It's Poppy."

Valerie's tongue was stuck to the roof of her mouth with surprise. She could only stutter. Tears were stinging the backs of her eyes. "No! No... Well, well! My goodness me! I never did!"

"Don't you recognise me, Nana?"

"Is it you, Poppy?" She took a step closer. If it was Poppy, my, she'd grown.

"It is, Nana."

It couldn't be. It wasn't. It was! "Poppy, lovey! What are you doing here, pet?"

Poppy gave an exhausted chuckle. "It's a long story."

The step was nothing but a puddle. "And you've been sitting there! How long have you been sitting there on that wet step?"

"A couple of hours. Thought you must be away. I was just wondering what to do next."

"Well, I don't know! What a surprise! Well, let's get you into the dry for a start. You'll need a hot bath, catch your death, sitting there. Norma won't mind. I've only got a back door key; we'll have to go round." She headed back towards the side gate. "Come on in, lovey, this way. Come on in."

Poppy's huge wet backpack took up a lot of floor space in the kitchen. However did they go around carting heavy loads like that! It made her tired to think about it. Valerie made her take off her cagoule and trainers and fetched her a nice dry towel, then took off her own coat and sat down in a kitchen chair to struggle with her boots. She wasn't sure how she felt. "Well, well, well, just fancy! There's a turn-up for the books!"

There was a big empty space inside her somewhere; her stomach hurt: must have got herself very pent up.

At last the boots were off. Rising stiffly, she held out her arms. "Come here, then, lovey, and let me give you a hug." Poppy felt sturdy and warm, like a young pony. Funny to see her so tall: tall, like her Dad, still looked like him, too, same pale skin, same blue eyes and fairish eyebrows, although she had dyed her hair; looked as if she was growing it out, though; there were a good couple of inches of fair hair showing at the roots. Good job, too. Black hair really didn't suit her.

She smiled as Valerie hugged her, but held back some-what, rather stiffly. "Nice to see you, Nana."

"Lovely to see you, too." Valerie was all in a spin: difficult to think clearly. "Now, then, I'll show you where the bath-room is and run you a bath. Would you like a hot drink first?"

"Just hot water."

She blinked. "You don't drink tea?"

"No tea or coffee."

"Oh." She saw Poppy's eyes flickering towards the biscuit tin. "Are you hungry?"

"I am a bit hungry, yes."

Would Norma mind if she pinched something from her fridge? Her own little larder cupboard was empty: no plans for eating in the caravan any more. She peered into Norma's fridge. Not a great deal there, either. "Would you like some bacon and eggs?"

"Don't mind."

"Hm. Don't you? Oh. Fried eggs or scrambled? Or I could make you an omelette?"

Poppy shrugged again. "Don't mind."

Valerie pulled out the egg carton. "Omelette, then. Her hands were trembling quite a bit, she noticed. "Plain one, or cheese?"

"Don't mind."

"Plain, then."

She studied Poppy surreptitiously as she boiled up the kettle. Looked as if she'd slept in that dusty grey, baggy sweatshirt and raggedy jeans for days. Poppy caught her eye and smiled awkwardly and Valerie smiled back, feeling suddenly rather shy. "Well, well, well! So what are you doing over here, lovey? I didn't know you were coming over to see me. Your Mum didn't say."

"Mum doesn't know."

Valerie almost dropped Poppy's mug. "She what?"

"She doesn't know."

"That can't be right, lovey; she must know, she'd be worried stiff." Poppy shrugged. She had a little silver ring piercing one eyebrow, and a stud in her nose like the girl in the Travel Agent's: silver, this one of Poppy's, with a tiny turquoise stone. Quite pretty, really, if you liked that kind of thing.

"Oh, it's all right, she knows I'm over in Europe. I'm in Greece at the moment, back-packing with a friend."

Valerie was relieved, and not a little touched. "Oh! Oh, I see! And you just thought you'd pop over to the UK and see me? That's very nice."

"Well, yes." Poppy dodged her eyes sheepishly. "Well, not exactly, no." It didn't look as if she was going to explain any more. She was eyeing the mug of scalding hot water hopefully: probably too thirsty.

"Here you are, then, lovey." Valerie handed it over. Cupping her cold hands gratefully about the mug, Poppy fell on it with closed eyes and apparent relish. Valerie put an extra large spoonful of sugar in with her own teabag to compensate: no accounting for taste! Even she, though, had to have it without milk; there was none in the fridge. "Well, I don't know!" she said again. She felt very bemused.

Poppy had big dark circles under her eyes. Mustn't push her. Very tired, no doubt. "Well, you can tell me all about it later, perhaps when you've had your bath."

Whilst Poppy was upstairs, she whipped up the eggs, then opened the bread bin. It was empty. She found some tomatoes, though, and some Jacobs Cream Puffs, and a nice Penguin for after. She took one for herself, too. Needed the sugar. Good for a bit of a shock.

When she came down, wearing Leon's navy towelling dressing gown, Poppy golloped the lot. She must have been starving – it was all gone in minutes. Her eyelids were drooping, though, as she pushed away her plate. "I'm shattered."

"Are you, lovey?" Explanations had better wait till morning. Have to put her in Tricia's room: nowhere in the caravan for her to sleep. She picked up the key to it from the table and slipped it into her pocket ready. "I'll show you where you can sleep, pet, and then I'll see you in the morning. I'll nip off home."

Poppy looked bewildered. "Home, Nana? I thought this was your home."

"Oh, no, love! This is Norma's house – Norma and Leon's. I live in a caravan out at the back."

"A caravan!" Poppy widened her eyes. "That's neat! That's really cool! Can I see it? Can I come with you?"

Valerie frowned. "Are you sure you want to go outside again in this weather? You've just got nice and dry."

"Oh, I don't mind!"

Valerie shrugged. "Well, if you want to, I suppose so. That mac thing of yours is soaking, though."

Poppy had already pulled it on and was tugging on her equally soaked trainers. "Oh, it's fine, it's fine!"

Fastening on her own coat, Valerie opened the back door. The wind whipped it out of her hand, gusting into the kitchen laden with icy droplets of rain. "Oh, my goodness, what a night!" She turned up her coat collar. "Bring that torch there, that's right, that's Leon's torch. I'll lock the back door while we go over, so you'd better have the key – and lock it again, after, won't you, when you come back in?"

It was very difficult to pick their way. They had to bend almost double against the force of the wind. Would have been lucky if there had been a crossing tonight. Not meant to be, perhaps? She was relieved and touched when Poppy slipped an arm through hers and gripped her tightly. "Don't want you falling over, do we, Nan?"

Poppy was really taken with the caravan. "Ah, it's so cool! Can't I sleep in here, too?"

"There's only one bed, lovey."

"But it's nearly a double."

Spotting the envelopes lying on the pillow, Valerie removed them quickly, slipping them into her coat pocket. "We did both sleep in it, your granddad and I, when we were younger."

"Well, there you are, then!" Poppy bounced on the edge. "Ah, come on, Nana? It'd be amazing! Go on! Can I?"

It felt very strange at first, lying beside another warm, softly breathing body once again. Couldn't stretch out very much. Bit afraid to move. Poppy was a lot thinner and lighter than Andy, but even so... Couldn't see a blooming thing once the lights were off: like thick black velvet. She stared up into the blackness.

Been a funny day, pet. Have to watch it, though, only do it in my head tonight. I'll wake her up, otherwise, if I start talking aloud – she'll think I'm going potty! She heard him chuckle. *You're right, you're right, I probably am.* She frowned into the darkness. *You must have been wondering where I'd got to. Couldn't get the ferry, you see. But you probably know that.*

She pictured him rolling his eyes. Bit of a turn up for the books.

I said that, I know, I know! What a surprise, wasn't it! Fancy! Poppy!

As if she had heard her, Poppy rolled heavily over with a sigh and Valerie turned her head blindly in her direction. *She looks like her dad, you know – like Ollie; can't see Susie in her at all.*

The caravan shook noisily as a doubly strong gust of wind caught it. Something heavy started clattering around outside. Caravan roofs came off sometimes in the wind. It could blow them over. Poppy murmured something softly in her sleep and threw an arm around Valerie's waist. She let it stay there. It was rather nice.

Listen to that wind! Funny, you know, love, normally, on a night like this, without you with me, I'd have been a bit scared. All right, though, with Poppy here. 'Course, it's not the same, not the same at all! Can't relax the same; can't hug her, can't snuggle up properly, can I? Not like having you next to me, Andy: not like that at all.

Poppy started to snore very gently. It made her smile. *I say, though, she is your granddaughter all right.*

She drifted off surprisingly quickly and was barely aware of the gusting winds that continued to rock the little caravan that night, but a particularly savage squall that even had the curtains at the windows flapping brought her to consciousness as it grew light. She peered in the dim grey morning light at the fair strands of hair and the dim features of her sleeping granddaughter. *Here's somebody I hadn't expected to see! A day I hadn't expected to see, either.*

Not sure how I feel about that.

Poppy must have sensed her staring at her. She opened sleepy eyes and stared back. "Oh, hello."

Valerie felt a little awkward, almost shy. "Hello, lovey. Did you sleep all right?"

Poppy struggled up onto one elbow. "I was out like a light."

Valerie pushed back the duvet and sat up stiffly, feeling for her slippers. "Want a cup of tea? I mean, of hot water?"

Poppy licked her lips. "Wouldn't mind some juice."

Valerie pulled her dressing gown round her shoulders and shuffled over to her little fridge. "I've got a drop of grapefruit here. That do?"

Poppy wrinkled her nose, but she nodded. "That's fine."

Valerie sat down on the bed beside Poppy and watched her whilst she gulped the drink down with her eyes closed. Pretty girl, underneath the hair. No teenage spots, I see; her skin's flawless. "Well, this is very nice!" She took the glass back. "So how old are you now, lovey?"

"Nineteen. Well, I'll be nineteen this year."

"Nineteen! My goodness gracious, how time flies! I'm looking forward to hearing all about New Zealand. How's Thomas?"

Poppy grimaced. "A pain."

Valerie chuckled. "Brothers, eh? Well, hopefully, I've got plenty of time to hear all about him – and about everybody else. How long are you able to stay here, pet?"

Poppy shrugged her shoulders. "A day or two maybe."

Valerie was taken aback. "Is that all? A long way to come for a day or two, pet! And then what, then? Back to Greece?"

Poppy glanced away. "Not straight away. While I'm here, I might have a, like, a wander round some other places."

"You mean, like London?"

She nodded casually. "London, maybe..."

"Hm. Are you hungry?"

"Mm. A bit."

Valerie pictured her empty fridge and half-empty cupboard. "I haven't got very much in." Better not raid Norma's kitchen again; they'd be back later expecting to have something edible there. She peered out of the little window; didn't seem to be raining. Too tired for it, really, but must make a bit of an effort..."Would you fancy going out for breakfast? We could go to a café."

Another shrug accompanied by a faintly hopeful look. "Don't mind."

Valerie nodded. "All right, then, I'll get dressed."

Feeling self-conscious, she collected her clothes and went into the small shower area to change. It wasn't easy. When she was trying to get her arms into her sleeves, she bumped her elbow on the wall, and when she bent down to pull up her tights, she bumped her head on the washbasin. In the end, she sat down on the loo to do it. When she emerged, Poppy was sitting waiting on the bed, dressed in her still damp cagoule and crumpled jeans. Valerie rolled her eyes. "Ooh, goodness, we'll have to get those dried properly for you; haven't you got anything else to wear?"

Poppy stood up. "They're fine. They'll do for now."

"Want to borrow a coat of mine?"

"No thanks." Her expression was priceless. Valerie smiled to herself. Wear her grandmother's clothes? Of course not.

"Well, we'll get them over to the house and wash and dry them after." *Ought to put the bed away this morning: no room otherwise for the two of us. Leave it, though, till we get back.* She struggled to button up her coat with morning-stiffened fingers, found her walking stick and assumed a bright smile. "Right, then, are you ready?"

The wind was still blowing stiffly outside and it was an icy wind, too. One or two bins had gone over during the night; there were fragments of rubbish and old bits of newspapers tossing all over the place. She clutched her coat tightly about her with her free hand. "Oh, my goodness! Should have put on a hat."

"Here," Poppy unravelled a multi-coloured scarf from her pocket. "Use my scarf." The wind kept tossing the ends away as Valerie tried to fasten it over her head and Poppy had to step in to tackle it, tying it firmly at the back. "That all right?"

"Much better; keeps my ears warm. Can I hang on to you?" clutching tightly to Poppy's arm, she directed her down to the promenade, to the Seagull, the little café at the top of the shingle where she sometimes went to have a cup of tea. The Seagull was very ordinary, with plastic chairs and wipe-down tablecloths and such, and it smelled quite strongly of yesterday's chips, but it was quite clean: nice and warm inside, too, after the cold wind outside. Poppy unfastened the scarf for her again. "You don't need this in here."

"No, I don't. It's lovely and warm." It was nice to be fussed over.

They took a table near a sea-facing, salt-stained window and Poppy stared through it with astonished eyes. "Is that the beach?"

"Yes." Valerie stared out with her. "Why? What's wrong with it?"

Poppy rolled her eyes scornfully. "Well, I mean, look at it! It's pathetic, isn't it? Now in New Zealand we have *beaches*. We have *sea*."

"Do you, indeed!" Poppy's remark reminded her now of her last, dispiriting view of it as she and Andy had been leaving North Wales. The beach did still look very dull and ordinary, not very appealing at all: muddy brown sand and a strip of oily pebbles littered with bits of rubbish, scummy grey waves. There were nicer places; she'd have liked Poppy to have seen them if she got the chance. A lot of Wales was very beautiful. It wasn't all like this. She felt a bit ashamed.

"Just a bit of toast for me," she said, having studied the plastic-coated menu. "And a cup of tea; that'll do me fine."

"Really?" Poppy's face fell.

"I don't eat much."

"Oh." Poppy pushed away her menu. "Same for me, then."

Valerie pushed it back towards her. "Oh, no, no! You must have a proper breakfast, pet – don't do without just because I'm not having any. Bacon and egg? Sausage? Have something else. Have a poached egg."

"Oh, I don't know..."

You could tell she was starving. Trying to be polite, poor kiddie. Picking up her own menu again, Valerie studied it carefully. "Actually, I think I am a bit hungry!"

In the end, they both ordered fried eggs and bacon, tomatoes, mushrooms, hash browns and toast and butter, with a glass of orange juice for Poppy and a pot of tea for Val, and tucked in heartily. It was a good thing they had so much on their plates, because it wasn't easy to make conversation. Valerie was still somewhat shell-shocked and Poppy was clearly having a bit of struggle knowing what to say. The shade of Andy hung between them like a spectre at a feast.

"So how are you these days, Nana?" Poppy asked at last politely, with her mouth full of toast. "Mum says you've got a bad hip."

How odd; she hadn't thought about her hip this morning. Hadn't felt a twinge. She reached greedily for the butter. Not had a breakfast like this for ages, not since Andy... She smiled. "Yes, yes, I have, I'm on the waiting list now, but

I'm all right really, you know. Up and down, Poppy. Off and on." Draining her cup, she poured more hot water into the metal teapot and gave the teabags at the bottom a vigorous stir. "So... You said you didn't tell your Mum that you might come over?"

Poppy's eyes were fixed steadfastly on her plate. There was silence for a moment and then she squirmed. "Well, I did *sort* of tell her. I asked her where you lived."

Valerie studied her carefully. "And she thinks you're still in Greece."

Poppy buried her nose in her mug of tea. "Back-packing with a friend."

"I see."

Poppy glanced up at Val with a wicked glint in her eye. "We've just moved from Mykonos to Paros, at least, my friend Heather has. Santorini next. I wrote all my postcards when we got to Athens, and she's posting them."

"Well, well!" Valerie shook her head. "But why don't you want her to know?"

"No reason." Poppy's lips tightened. "I'm not a child, Nana, I don't have to keep reporting my every move to Mum!"

"No, no." *Leave it alone for now.* She drained the last dregs from her cup. "Well, she probably ought to know. Just have a think."

On the way back to the caravan, they had to stop in one of the dilapidated shelters on the prom so that Valerie could have a rest. Poppy wrinkled her nose. "Peeuw! Nana, it's not very nice!"

"Sorry. Won't stay more than a minute. Just rest my hip. At least it's got a roof on and a bit of glass; most haven't."

The seat was broken at one end so they had to share the other. Poppy, her shoulders hunched, hood of her cagoule pulled down over her brows and her hands thrust deeply into its pockets, stared out at the grey and windswept sea. "I don't remember any of it round here, Nana. Did I come here at all, when I was here before?"

"You did when you were little, lovey, when you were staying with your Grandad and me. Probably too young for it to have made a mark, and it has changed. But there are some lovely places in Wales, you know pet. If I could drive,

I could take you a few places."

"Like where?"

"Oh, goodness me, the Lleyn Peninsula, Snowdonia of course. Pembrokeshire..." The perfect place came to her suddenly. "I tell you one place I'd like to take you to see, just a little place. It's called Porthlas. Tiny place, really. Haven't been there for years." It wasn't so much the little harbour nestling at the edge of a lovely inlet of crystal clear water from the estuary that she remembered, but the small upstairs room with the soft feather mattress and crisp white sheets at the little B&B, *Swn-y-Mor*, where they had stayed for the their first night. She peered out once again in her mind's eye over the wonderful view from the small window across the estuary to the headland and the misty Blue Mountains beyond. "Mind you, we were on our honeymoon when we went there, so I was probably looking at it through rose-coloured whatsits, spectacles, and it was a very long time ago. We were always talking about going back to it one day, but somehow we never did."

Poppy was on a different track. "Where's Builth Wells? Is it somewhere round here?"

Valerie's mind still in Porthlas. She was taken by surprise. "Builth Wells? Oh, not sure, pet. It's quite a way down south."

She looked disappointed. "Oh. A long way, then."

"Why? Is it somewhere you were hoping to go?"

"Maybe."

She could see Poppy shivering and gathered herself together. "Come on, pet, I'm all right now, shall we move on? So these friends of yours, pet, that you're island-hopping with; are they nice girls? Old school friends?" she enquired as they set off slowly again along the prom.

"Heather is, Nat isn't, she's Heather's cousin. Yes, they're good."

Maybe this was the moment to explore a bit further the mystery of Poppy's reluctance to tell Susie where she was. "And am I right in thinking, pet, that you've got another friend, someone who's over here, too, somewhere in this country?"

"Um, I don't know!" Poppy widened her eyes in innocent fashion. She coloured slightly. "Oh! Iolo, you mean?"

Valerie frowned. "Yellow? Is that his name, pet? Yellow?"

"No, Nana – Iolo!" She wrinkled her nose "Well, it's Iorwith really, but he's always called Iolo. That's a Welsh name, isn't it?"

"Iorwerth, perhaps? That's an old Welsh name."

"Yeah, that's it. His family came from Wales. That's partly why he's here."

Valerie peeped at her from under her eyelashes. And what's the other part, I wonder? "And is that where this Iolo was heading for – Builth Wells?"

Poppy looked a bit shifty. "Well, he said he might. Maybe not till May, though. There's a motorbike rally or festival there, he said."

Valerie felt a twinge of anxiety. "Rides a motorbike, does he?"

"Oh, yes. He's hired –" She corrected herself quickly. "Said he was going to hire one."

Oh, dear, oh dear. "I see."

Chapter 27

I t's this boyfriend of hers, you see, Andy," she told him as she was making up the bed again after Poppy had excused herself and had gone back outside. Through the small window she could see her texting away on her mobile. Who was she talking to? Iolo?

"She's chasing after him, isn't she? Planning to meet him. Well, you heard. The thing is, the thing is, pet: do I ring her mother? I mean, Susie needs to know, doesn't she, where she is? Poppy doesn't want to her to know, though. She doesn't want her to know she's on the track of this who'd-you-call-it, this Iolo. Susie doesn't approve of him, as you know."

She made herself another cup of tea and sat down heavily with it once the bed was safely away. It had taken a bit of a struggle; should have got Poppy to help her. Her limbs felt like lead now after the long walk and her head felt muzzy. Taken it out of her. Quite a traumatic day yesterday, one way and another.

Poppy clomped back in up the caravan steps, bringing in with her a penetrating draught of cold, fresh air and slamming the door so hard that the frail structure shook. Valerie peered at her, concerned. "You all right, pet? Why don't you go and have a look round the shops? Not a lot there, but still! Do you need a bit of money?"

Poppy shook her head fervently. "No, Nana, really; I have got a bit; I don't want your money."

"Didn't you take any money with you to Greece?"

"Yes, but I spent a lot of it on the flight to Manchester.

It's all right; I'm going to get a job."

"Where? Here?"

"No. Somewhere. When I meet up with –" She bit her tongue.

"When you meet up with Iolo?" She was reddening again. "He knows that you're here, then? I see."

Poppy sighed heavily. "Oh, well, you might as well know – you've pretty much guessed, anyway. When Mum went ballistic and said I couldn't see him any more, wouldn't let me come over with him, it was too much hassle to go on arguing with her, so we set it all up. I'd tag onto Heather and Nat – Mum would be happy with that – and then I'd slip off and join him here. I love him, Nana."

Her tone and her expression touched Valerie; she seemed so earnest and innocent. "Do you, lovey?"

"I really do. But I have got a problem. He's got my number but he hasn't rung for ages, and he's not answering his mobile. I've left loads of messages, but he doesn't call or answer my texts."

That didn't augur that well. "Maybe he's lost it."

Poppy shrugged moodily. "Could have. I don't know."

Norma and Leon arrived back at lunchtime, and finding Poppy there gave them a real surprise. Norma gave her a big hug. "Ooh, I say, Val, doesn't she look like her dad!"

"So how long is she staying, love?" she asked Val, when Poppy had gone over to the caravan. "She can stay in the house if you want, you know; Tricia won't be wanting her room for a bit. And you must come over this evening; have a bit of a meal."

"Oh, she won't be staying very long; she's determined to go off after this lad." Valerie told her the story behind Poppy's visit.

"What does he do, then, this Iolo? Does he have a job?"

"According to Susie he's a bit of a layabout. Rides a motorbike."

"Oh, no."

"Bit of a drifter. A carpenter by trade, I believe."

"Carpenters can make quite good money."

"Her mum says she's too young for a serious relationship and she could do better."

"Hm." Norma raised her eyebrows. "It is serious, then?"

"She thinks it is. Like I say, now she can't get in touch with him."

"And she's set on going hunting for him? On her own?"

"Talk about a needle in a haystack..."

They shook their heads slowly in unison, united in misgiving. "It is worrying."

"It is."

Poppy refused Norma's offer of the bed in Tricia's room. "If Nana doesn't mind, I'm quite happy sharing in the caravan. Do you mind, Nana?"

"Not at all, pet, if you're comfortable." It had been quite nice, last night, having her in her bed.

Poppy, her tongue loosened by Leon's wine at supper, was in talkative and curious mood when they got there at last. "Do you miss Grampie?"

"I do, pet."

"How long were you married to him?"

"Almost fifty-six years."

Poppy pulled herself up onto one elbow and peered at her disbelievingly, then threw herself back onto her pillow. "Fifty-six years? Wow! That's like – wow! That's so cool. That's so sweet! No wonder you miss him, then."

Valerie smiled wistfully. "It is a long time, isn't it? Mm."

"Wish my mum and dad had stayed together. Why didn't they, Nana?"

She sighed. "I don't know, Poppy love. Mum wanted something else. Maybe your dad did too. Maybe they'd just picked the wrong people. Who knows?"

"I don't know any of my friends' parents who aren't divorced. How do you manage to stay with one person for all that time, though? Didn't you ever want something else? Didn't you get fed up with each other, Nana? Weren't you ever – well, you know, tempted?"

She had to chuckle. "Oh I suppose so, yes, we were only human."

"But you stayed together, though! You didn't break things up."

"No, we didn't. It gets easier, actually, as time goes on, Poppy, if you've picked the right one. You – I don't know..." She frowned trying to pick the right word. "I suppose, *cleave* to your husband."

"What does 'cleave' mean?"

"Stick together, grow together, belong together, sort of become parts of a whole."

Poppy shook her head wonderingly. "It must be terrible, then, when one of you dies."

The pain of it still made every inch of her ache. 'Cleave' also meant to violently divide a whole something, as you might with an axe.

Poppy was frowning. "So if the cleaving's set with the two of you, and your husband dies, or your wife..." She turned her head to face Valerie, and there were quick tears in her blue eyes. "Oh, Nana, that's awful. You must feel as if you're only half a person, somehow. Half of you's disappeared. However do you cope?"

Her empathy made Valerie catch her breath. "It's very hard. Everybody's been so good, but it's not what I want, pet. Well, I do, but it's not the crux of the matter, it won't make me feel right again. The only thing that'll d-do that is to –"

"Have your other half back again." Poppy sat up and held out her arms. "Ah, Nana, don't cry!"

She was ashamed. "Oh, I'm sorry, Poppy, I'm sorry, lovey, this isn't fair, it's all that wine."

"It's all right, it's all right!"

It was so nice to be held again: to be touched.

Poppy's voice took on a solemn tone. "Could I ask you something, Nana? Do you believe in God? Do you think we go on to somewhere when we die?"

Valerie tried to chuckle. "I don't know, love. I'll have to wait and see."

Poppy was very serious, though. "I do. I truly think that Grampy is somewhere waiting for you. In heaven, or wherever it is."

"Well..." Valerie was a bit lost for words, but very touched. "Well. Well. That'd be very nice."

Poppy was frying herself an egg when Valerie woke up next morning, and the smell made her feel quite queasy. Poppy seemed bright enough, though, as she glanced at Valerie over her shoulder. "Good morning! Fancy an egg?"

"Ooh, no thank you, love. You're early."

"Thinking about getting off."

See, now: there! All that maudlin nonsense; you've frightened her off. "Today? Hang on, hang on..."

She had to sit up. Sudden anxiety was setting her heart racing. "Is it wise? How do you think you are going to find him, lovey?"

"I dunno." Poppy glanced at her mobile, lying beside her on the sink. "Still can't get a reply. Don't worry, Nan, I'll track him down." She searched about, frowning. "Have you seen my other jeans and my black tee shirt?"

"They're in the wash. And I mean, where are you going to start looking? Where are you going to stay?"

"Dunno. I'll find it." Poppy shrugged. "Hitchhike."

Valerie quailed. "Ooh, pet, I don't like the sound of that: hitchhiking. We used to do it a lot, but these days... What about National Express? Or couldn't you go on the train?"

She could see that Poppy was getting a bit annoyed. "Don't worry, Nan. I'll be all right."

She tried to calm down. "Wait till tomorrow, anyway, pet, I would, till your clothes are dry and we can have a proper think about it. Don't go off in a rush!"

"I want to go now!"

Suddenly Valerie felt like crying. "Don't go yet, pet, please. It's so nice having you. Give me another day."

"Oh, Nan!" She glanced at Valerie, frowning, then paused. "You're crying again."

"No, I'm not."

"You are! Oh, no, Nan, don't!" Dropping the pile of undies she was holding, she fell onto her knees at Valerie's side. "Don't be so daft!"

Valerie smiled feebly, sniffing. "You sound just like your Grandfather."

Poppy put her arms about her and hugged her tight. "Of course I'll stay till tomorrow, Nan," she promised. "And I'll come back to see you, I will. I'll bring Iolo." She chuckled. "You can come with me, if you like!"

Valerie had to smile, telling Andy about what she had said when she was talking to him about it in the garden: "The very idea! Me, backpacking! But I am worried, pet. When I ask her where's she's going to stay if she hasn't any money, she just says, 'Oh, I'll doss down somewhere!' I can't bear the idea, a young girl like that, in a doorway somewhere or on a park bench. And I shall miss her."

When he put the suggestion into her head, she had to chuckle. "Me? At this time of my life? Don't be so daft!"

She thought about it all day and all night, though, and when the next morning came, she went over to see Leon.

"Leon, will your caravan go on the road?"

He lowered his newspaper, looked puzzled. "Why? Does Norma want it moving from the garden?"

"No, I mean, would it go on the road? Could you tow it? Would it be safe?"

He grimaced doubtfully. "Oh, I don't know about that..."

"If it would, would you sell it to me, Leon?"

"Sell it to you?"

"Yes, if you don't want it; just tell me how much."

"I don't want to sell it to you."

That was a bit disappointing. "Would you lend it to me, then? Could I hire it?"

He sat back in his chair, examining her quizzically. "What do you want it for, Val?"

She shrugged. "Just fancy it."

"You mean – the open road?"

"Sort of. Would Andy's car be strong enough to tow it?" She hadn't been able to bear parting with this last piece of her beloved Andy, so there it had stood.

He pulled a face. "Good God, been stuck in my front drive for over eighteen months, don't know if it still goes."

"Yes, but if I got it serviced?"

"A Ford Focus? Oh, I don't know, maybe: caravan's fairly light." He shrugged. "Well, I mean, if you want it, love, you can have it. It isn't any use to me now I've got my workshop in the garage. I know what you're thinking of, though; you're thinking of going off hunting for this lad with your Poppy. I presume she'd drive. But you're not serious?"

She thought for a long minute. "Do you know, Leon, pet, I think I am?"

Poppy was equally, if not more surprised.

"Well, you said I should come with you."

"Yes, but I was only joking." She looked quite horrified. "You don't really want to, do you? Even if I took the caravan, Nan, you wouldn't have to come. In fact, I could just take the car, if you were offering, if that was all right. I could sleep in the back."

"Just a suggestion." She was amazed to find how disappointed she was with Poppy's reaction. Of course she didn't want her gran with her; it was a daft idea. "Of course, you take the car, then, love, if you'd rather that I didn't."

Poppy flushed. "No, no, no, it's not that."

"I'd keep out of your way, I mean, if I did come, if –" She corrected herself. "*When* you find Iolo. We could come back then and you could go off on your own. I wouldn't be a what-you-may-call-it, a gooseberry. I'd just be a bit of a – oh, I don't know, an anchor, maybe, till then? Somebody to keep an eye out, in case of emergencies. Someone to have an idea where you were exactly. Your mum would be pleased."

Poppy rolled her eyes. "My mum would think you had gone stark staring mad, careering round the country in a caravan. She thinks you should be in a home."

Valerie's insides wobbled. "I know she does."

Poppy stared down at her hands. "I'll think about it."

She was very quiet for the rest of the day, but towards evening she dragged out her rucksack from the underseat storage area and started quietly stuffing things in it. So that was a 'no thank you', then.

"Those songs are quite right, you know," Valerie told Andy, whilst she was washing her face ready for bed. "You know, about not having anybody to need and not having somebody who needs you. Not being needed any more – it's very hard."

When she came out of the little washroom, Poppy was perched on the bed with her voluminous tee shirt tugged down over her knees, studying her very gravely. "*I* need you, Nan."

Valerie flushed. "Was I talking aloud? I'm sorry, pet, I forgot I wasn't on my own."

Poppy unravelled herself casually and leant back on her hands. "I've been thinking, you know; it might not be such a bad idea. It might do you good, you know: a bit of an adventure, a change of scenery. We could go to that place of yours…"

"Porthlas, you mean?"

"If you like. And I would feel better if I had you around."

Valerie could feel her cheeks getting a bit pink. "Would you, really?"

Poppy shrugged. "Yeah! Well, what I'm saying is, well, if you really want to do it, Nan, it's fine by me."

Valerie sank onto the bed beside her. "Well, if you're sure, lovey…"

"If *you're* sure! I mean, of course, if it's going to be too much…"

"No, no… Oh, it won't be. Ooh, I say! Where would we start?" Excited, she looked round for something with which to celebrate. "Do you fancy a cup of cocoa?"

Poppy grinned. "I wouldn't mind. Have we got any bics?"

"Digestives, that's all; but they are McVitie's."

Poppy slid off the bed. "I'll have a bit of jam on mine."

She didn't take after her mum and dad when it came to eating: took after Andy. She told him so, later, when, too wound up to sleep, she went for a moonlit wander in the garden. "Reminds me of you! Don't know how she stays so thin." She could smell the delicate scent of daffodils on the night breeze. "I'm glad to think I won't be losing her just yet, you know, lovey. Be nice to see something of Wales, too, again, before I go." She paused, frowning, staring up at the blank back windows of the house. "I'm still going to do it, mind, just waiting now till I'm back on my own." The cold, daffodil-scented breeze blew through her hair, down the back of her dressing gown and icily up its skirt, and she shivered, remembering the absolute emptiness before. "Don't get fed up waiting, lovey. Won't be too long."

In the morning, she made Poppy stay at the table after they had had their breakfast. "We've a lot to do, but before we go off on a wild goose chase, though, pet, you are sure about this, love. I mean, about this Iolo? He's not, you don't think he's – I mean he hasn't been trying to –" She tried to find the words to put it delicately.

"Dump me you mean?" Poppy shook her head vehemently. "No. There's definitely something wrong. I know it."

"All right then, love, we'll go. If it does me in, I'll save on another ferry fare."

"A ferry fare?"

"Oh, nothing." She chuckled. "You know who you remind me of, love? Alice. You must have Alice's genes"

"Who was Alice?"

"She was – hang on, my grandmother, so your great, great grandmother – that's right. She ran off after your great, great grandfather, Tom, to Canada, when she was only just eighteen."

Poppy widened her eyes. "Cool! Younger than me. When was that then? Before the war?"

"Before the *First* World War. He'd gone off to find work, and she went off on a ship across the Atlantic to New York, and then up to Ontario to look for him all by herself. Very daring; very brave."

Poppy was all agog. "Amazing! And did she? Find him, I mean?"

Valerie chuckled. "Of course she did, you silly thing, or you wouldn't be here!" She patted Poppy's hand. "What I'm saying is, you must take after her; history is repeating itself. She found him and you'll find Iolo, if he's the right one and if it's meant to be. Compared to Canada, Wales will be a snip! Only one thing, though, pet."

"What's that?"

"Promise me you will ring and tell your Mum."

It was a real palaver getting the little caravan out of the back garden. Leon said he hadn't had the back gate open for years. "We'll take her round the block just to try her and then, if she seems all right, I'll have her checked over," he told Val when he had it parked at the side of the road. "Bodywork's all right, but I'll need to make sure the tyres are okay, and the handbrake and the battery and the connectors. In fact, I'd better book it in for a full service."

"I'll pay for it, of course. And could they do the car?"

"Sure she's up to towing a caravan, young Poppy?"

"She seems very confident. Perhaps you could sit with her, give her a bit of practice?"

He gave her a very straight look. "Are you up to this, Val?"

She paused for a long moment. "I don't know; Leon, but I'm going to try."

Once the Service people had pronounced the car and the caravan fit for duty, Leon took Poppy and Valerie down to the big car park behind the shopping centre after the store had closed and began the lessons. There was lot to remember.

"Start with your hands at the bottom of the steering wheel and lift the hand in whichever direction the van should go, see what I mean? If the rear of van needs to go left, lift your left hand. Do it a bit, then straighten your wheel again. Straighten – straighten – that's it, slow and steady! Keep it slow and steady."

They spent hours practising on the car park, backwards and forwards, and pretending to manoeuvre into spaces, then he let Poppy take it out on the road. She was remarkably good. "I think you're going to be in good hands, here, Val – she's pretty cool, your Poppy, isn't she? Pretty cool!"

Susie, when Valerie took over the microphone from Poppy after her confession, didn't seem surprised at all. "I might have known! I thought it was too good to be true. Doesn't often take any notice of me. Well, she is over age, I suppose, so what can you do?"

She was intensely surprised that Valerie was going with her, judging by the expression on her face, and not a little worried. "You will look after yourself, won't you? You ought to be taking it easy. Make her go back to Norma's if you've had enough and don't try to do too much."

Valerie eyed Poppy, hovering near the desk. "Hang on a minute, pet," she told Susie. "Poppy, lovey, I'm ever so thirsty; would you do me a favour? Nip into the kitchen and ask Norma if you can make me a cup of tea."

When she'd gone, she turned back to the microphone and lowered her voice, just in case. "Susie, I don't think we will for a minute, seems clear to me he's done a whatsit, a runner, but what do you want me to do if we find this Iolo? I mean, am I to let her – well, you know – go off with him or what?"

"What can you do, Mum? She's got a will of her own; never did listen to me. So long as she gets you home first. Look, if she wants to sleep with him, she will. She already has, actually, so it wouldn't be anything new."

She was a bit taken aback. "Oh. I see."

Susie seemed to be fairly easy with it. "If it happens, it happens."

"Perhaps it's meant to be."

"Who knows?"

Chapter 28

Norma had been fussing around Valerie ever since she'd heard about the plan. "Are you quite sure, Val? You're quite mad, you know! I wouldn't do it. It's not going to be too much? These girls, really! What if we get a thing from the hospital to say they've set a date to do your hip?"

"I've got my mobile, Norm, and Poppy's got hers. I'll leave you her number too. In any case, I'll ring every couple of days."

"Have you got everything you need? All your medicine? Your repeat prescription? It's a bit early in the year for touring, you know. I don't know if many sites will be open and it might be very cold; take plenty of warm clothes. What will you do for washing?"

"We'll have to use a laundrette."

There was still a deathly silence from Iolo. Poppy was clearly struggling to keep her spirits up and to put on a brave face. She looked up the Motorcycle Festival on the Internet. "It's not till May the seventh. If I still haven't heard from him by then, that's my best bet." She spread out Leon's road map. "If we go to this place whatitsname, Porth-whatsit, wherever is it, first, and anywhere else you want to go…"

"I just want you to see some nice places, lovey, while you're here. Harlech, maybe? Aberdovey?"

"Wherever you want." She stabbed at the map. "Oh, yes, there it is! Porthlas. Well, it's not direct, but it's sort of on the way."

"Let's have a look!" Leon couldn't resist putting on his reading spectacles and poring over the road map with them. He was shiny and pink, almost completely bald now, Valerie noticed with a secret smile. Just a little white tuft on top. Andy was lucky: kept most of his hair. "Well, you could take the coastal route to Caernarfon and then down through Snowdonia, but what I'd do is take the A470 down through Llanrwst and Dolwyddelan to Blaenau Ffestiniog, I think that's your best bet. Then you can take the A487." He tapped authoritatively at the map with an enthusiastic finger. "See it? To Porthmadog; that'd get you to Porthlas. Easy!" Valerie had to smile; loved a road map. Just like Andy.

It was exciting, though: getting ready, planning. "Talk about an outing, Andy! This is something else." The money from the insurance was taking a bit of a beating, but never mind; what else was it of use for? All in a good cause. Leon showed them how to plug in on-site to mains electricity but gave them a back-up battery just in case, and showed Poppy how to use it. "Don't overload the mains, though; you don't want to blow the park's fuse!"

They both had their hair done, too, in honour of the expedition. Poppy wanted to get rid of the black dye before seeing Iolo, and thought that Valerie should have hers cut really short. "You know, like that old film star."

"Katherine Hepburn?"

"Who? No, I mean the old one, she was in *Notes on a Scandal*, and that thing about Queen Victoria..." She grimaced. "Oh, you know!"

"Judy Dench!" Valerie shook her head. "Oh, but she's very pretty, lovely bone structure, she can carry it. I couldn't, not in a month of Sundays."

Poppy shrugged. "Well, come with me anyway, see what the hairdresser has to suggest. Come on! It'll be fun!"

Hang the expense, Valerie thought, just as she was about to dial the number for His 'n Hers. "Which is the best hairdressers in town?" She asked Norma.

"Ooh, well, there's only one now, isn't there? It's got to be Peppe's. None of them is that much cop, but if you want the best we've got, it'll have to be Peppe's."

"We'll go there, then."

She looked dubious. "Doubt if you'll get an appointment."

But they did: only a trainee, though, and Poppy had to wait while Valerie's hair was being done, but still, the girl did a decent job. Not a Judy Dench, of course, just a nice bit of shaping. Poppy had to have a lot of hers cut off because of all the dye, so it ended up very short, but with a few fine streaks of silver blonde put in after to lighten it up, she looked really very pretty.

Afterwards, they wandered round the shops. When Valerie's hip started to ache, Poppy gave her her arm. While Poppy was busy at the lipstick display, Valerie bought a little bottle of scent for her, by some celebrity she'd never heard of, just as a special 'Finding Iolo' present. Very expensive, the perfume was, though, so she just got the eau de toilette. She was really tired and achy when she got home. Frivolous, really, and another packet of money gone today, but most enjoyable.

Then, suddenly, everything was ready and it was time for the off. The weather wasn't good, unfortunately; it was still very cold, with a steady drizzle. Norma and Leon came out to wave them off. "Have you checked the lights?" Leon made for the back of the car. "Hang on – let me just check the coupling again. Got your jockey wheel up?"

"We have."

"Caravan's handbrake off? Everything inside secured and tightly fastened?"

Poppy sighed. Valerie shook her head. "He's like your Grandfather."

"Iolo's the same when it comes to his bike."

They shook their heads in sisterly solemnity. "Men!"

"Okay!" Poppy turned on the engine and the windscreen wipers, which set up a rhythmic squeak, squeak, squeak. She grimaced. "That's going to drive me bananas. Does it always rain here, Nana?"

"Wait till we get to Blaenau Ffestiniog."

"Why, will it dry up by then?"

"In Blaenau Ffestiniog?" Valerie chuckled. "Not a chance."

"Right then!" Norma came fluttering round to Valerie's window. "Now take it easy. Have you got your tablets? Both got your mobiles? Poppy, don't let her do too much; don't let her get tired. Ring us if there's any problem." She peered in anxiously. "Give us a kiss, then! Good luck!"

The traffic though the town was heavy, so progress was rather slow at first, but at last they were on the open road. Valerie's stiff neck made it very difficult to look back to check, as she was driven by nerves to do, that they were still all connected and that the caravan was following neatly in line. At first, she was very agitated. "Look out, pet, there a heavy whatsit coming up from behind! He's trying to pass!"

She put her foot down hard on an imaginary brake every time they started to go down a hill, and cowered each time a heavy goods vehicle accelerated past making the little caravan sway. "Are you all right, Poppy? My goodness, he was close!"

Nearer Llanrwst, the traffic built up again and Valerie's panic started to increase with it. "You know, you've got a long line of cars and things behind you – why don't you pull in a minute and let them pass?"

Poppy got quite exasperated with her. "Oh, Nana, chill! Chill! It's quite all right."

As they drove on towards Dolwyddelan Valerie, sucking a Polo mint and feeling a little calmer, was struck once more by how beautiful it all was. She'd forgotten; it was so long since she'd been down this way. Most of the time what she and Andy had seen on a daily basis had been the steady deterioration of a town. The years between, spent away in Hampshire, too, had made her forget that, beyond the reaches of the town itself, it was all so lovely.

Poppy glanced at her as they began to climb up the Crimea Pass. "Are you all right, Nana? Do you want to stop?"

"No, no, I'm fine. Carry on, unless you want to."

"Got anything in the car to eat, Nana?"

She strained to see the carrier bag that she had placed behind her seat. "Are you hungry, pet? I made some sandwiches, some tuna and some egg-mayonnaise. Don't know if we can stop here – shall we stop in Porthmadoc for a bite, or would you prefer to go straight on to the site?"

"I think we'll get the van parked up, Nana, then we can decouple the car and do any exploring in that. Okay with you?"

"Of course!" Secretly, she was very relieved. She was feeling very tired and living in a caravan was one thing; having it gliding and bumping along behind you was another. "Got a KitKat."

"Mmm! Yummy!"

Smiling, Valerie unwrapped the multipack of two-finger blocks she had put in the glove compartment with the Polo mints just in case. They had melted a little. "Hm. Didn't put them in the most sensible place."

"Doesn't matter." Poppy slowed the car. "Might just stop here for a minute and stretch my legs."

Valerie looked around them anxiously. "Are you sure it's all right to park here, pet? It's very narrow."

"There's nothing coming. It'll be fine." Pelicanning a chunk of sticky KitKat, she opened her door. "You coming?"

Valerie opened her door. "Ooh, I say, it's ever so cold!"

"It is a bit. You wait in the car, then. I'm going for a run."

She left her door open and watched as Poppy pulled up her cagoule hood and set off at a trot, leaping over low-growing clumps of heather. It was good to feel the draught of fresh, gorse-scented air in her lungs, despite the rain and the cold wind.

She's enjoying herself! Ought I to be warning her about adders?

Too early in the year and too cold. Too wet. Not too much fear.

Poppy paused a little distance away and fumbled in her pocket, and then Valerie saw her thumbing at her mobile phone again and shook her head. "She's still trying, bless her. I do hope she finds him, Andy. Just imagine if I'd been trying to find you."

As she had anticipated, Blaenau Ffestiniog, with its towering slopes of blue-grey rejected pieces of slate, was thick with cloud and drenched in rain, but as they neared the coast she pointed towards the sky above the distant horizon with delight. "Look, told you so! There's enough blue sky up there to make a sailor a pair of trousers!"

Poppy glanced at her in mystification. "You what?"

"Old wives' tale. Means it's going to clear up." Everything looked better when the sun shone. She smiled to herself, anticipating, with an almost proprietorial pleasure, showing her little harbour off to its very best.

Hope it hasn't changed too much. Wonder if *Swn-y-Mor* is still a guesthouse? It might be.

Not the same, without you, though, Andy. Not the same.

S he stared in consternation at the sign above the gate to the caravan site she had selected from a book from the library. 'OPEN MAY TO OCTOBER.' *Botheration.*

"Oh, fiddlesticks! I should have rung."

It would have been perfect, too, in a proper field backed by woodlands, with views down towards the Mawddach estuary, up to the Lleyn Peninsula, back towards Snowdon, and across the sea towards the setting sun. Supposed to have proper washing up and washing and drying facilities, too. "Would have been ideal!"

Poppy sighed and glanced over her shoulder, ready to reverse again down the rather narrow lane. "Okay, then, so where now?"

"I'm sure there are more caravan parks round towards Penglelli."

"So where's that, then? Which way?"

"Keep going, then down. We can walk into Porthlas from there – at least, I used to walk it, there and back, but of course I was fitter then."

The site they chose because it was closest to the beach was a bit crowded with caravans, but mostly they looked empty and there were a few spaces dotted around the ground. Poppy went up to check with Reception, and then came back grinning. "No worries, and they don't need us out in a hurry. I wasn't sure how long you wanted to stay." She pointed. "We're down there on the left."

"We've still got a couple of weeks till your motorbike thing. We could stay here and go off exploring for while in the car, or move on with the caravan. It's up to you."

"I think you'd probably be better staying put, Nan. If you're not up to it any time, I could go off on my own."

Perhaps she wanted to do that. "Stay here, then. That's fine."

They drove down the field slowly and Poppy reversed carefully into the pitch with their back to the sea next to a wind-blown hedge. "Are we level? Looks okay, doesn't it?"

"Hang on, I'll get out and see." Valerie climbed out and trudged round the caravan, trying to judge with her eye. It was very muddy. "Seems all right."

"Right. *Wheel chocks. Lower the jockey wheel and tighten. Safety breakaway cable...*"

Valerie rolled her eyes. "What a palaver!"

Poppy got it all done, though, and before too long she had the caravan decoupled and the electricity hook-up and water and waste pipes and containers sorted. Valerie looked on admiringly. "What a practical girl!"

"Get the kettle on, then – but don't count your chickens; I might have got it all wrong."

Valerie saw her fiddling with her mobile again whilst she was making the tea. She threw it aside after a few moments dispiritedly.

Poor child.

Even though the sun was trying to shine, it was too cold outside for a picnic, at least for Valerie, so they sat inside at the little table. "Do you want to go round to the Porth place, then, after, Nana?" Poppy asked with her mouth full, scooping up crumbs from her egg mayonnaise roll. "Hey, these are yummy."

Valerie was pleased. "Grampie always liked them." She considered for a moment. Seeing Porthlas – and especially *Swn-y-Mor* if it was still there – might make her tearful when she was tired, and she didn't want to inflict that on poor Poppy again. "Let's see a bit later, pet. I am a bit tired."

When they had had their refreshments they waded through the mud and walked slowly arm in arm down to the sea. The beach was empty and the water was rough and dotted with white horses. Valerie was sorry that it didn't look more inviting. "Pity it's not calmer."

Poppy shivered. "Not thinking of swimming, were you? It'll be freezing."

She raised her eyebrows carelessly. "Who, me?"

Poppy chuckled. "It'll be the Atlantic, I suppose."

"No, the Irish Sea. Or is it Cardigan Bay?"

"Do you think there are seals?"

"You do see them on the Lleyn. Oh, no doubt they'll be around."

Poppy kicked at the rain soaked sand. "Iolo's a good swimmer."

"Is he, pet?"

"Sometimes works as a life guard."

The heavy, steady sound of the breaking waves drew Valerie's eyes back to the sea. "Oh? That's useful."

"That's where I met him – on the beach."

It was chilly, standing still. Shivering, Valerie urged Poppy on a little so that they were keeping their circulation going, meandering parallel to the sea. "Tell me about him, pet. You haven't said very much. You say his family came from Wales? Do you know whereabouts?"

Poppy frowned. "I can't remember what place he said, that's half my problem. That's where his house is, anyway."

"You mean he's got family living here still?"

Poppy shook his head. "No, no, it's his house, only he's never seen it. That's partly why he's over here; it was in the will."

Valerie was surprised. "Whose will?"

Thinking of Iolo had prompted Poppy, though. "Hang on, I'm just going to try again." Pulling away, she strolled away a little, drawing out her mobile. When yet another fruitless attempt was over and she had stuffed it back disconsolately into her pocket, she glanced up the beach, frowning. She looked so unhappy, it made Valerie's heart sore. "Think I'm going to go for a run, Nana. Can you make your own way back? Will you be all right?"

"I'll be fine, love. You carry on."

She took a last long look at the sea before heading slowly back up to the caravan park. *Could I, after, if she finds Iolo? Maybe. Maybe not. We'll see.*

Poppy was a long time coming back, and she was in a depressed and silent frame of mind when she did so. Valerie had prepared them some salad and ham, but she didn't eat much of it, and none of the half-melted KitKats or the fruitcake for afters, either.

"Do you mind if we don't go to your place this evening?" she asked, slouching dejectedly at the little table. "I'll drive you over in the morning. Promise."

Valerie shook her head. "No, that's all right, pet. No

hurry, and I am a bit tired. The forecast's better for the morning anyway. Sunnier and possibly a bit warmer, it said so on the news."

She so much wanted Poppy to like Porthlas; no point in dragging her then when she wasn't in the mood.

There were some cows in the field next to them; there was quite a bit of impatient lowing and mooing before the farmer collected them for milking the next morning, so they were both awake quite early. To Valerie's delight the sky was clear and blue. It was cold outside, though, as she found when she put her nose out. The smell was lovely, a mingling of salt air and damp long grass and vegetation, with a strong hint of manure. She felt a ripple of pleasure. A lovely day for seeing Porthlas. "Shall we have breakfast outside?"

Poppy was still monosyllabic. With the duvet tented up over her bent knees, and with her hands behind her head, she lay staring glumly up at the low ceiling. "Don't mind."

Valerie was already having second thoughts. "Might be a bit cold. What do you fancy? I brought a bit of bacon. I wonder if the little shop at reception does fresh farm eggs?"

"Dunno."

"No, I know you don't. I might just pop over."

It took her a bit of a while to get there over the rutted, muddy and uneven grass, and it was even colder than she had thought, but the dewdrops on the grass glittered in the early morning sunshine. The sea beyond and below the hedge was calm today and as blue as the sky, and the trip was worth it, because they did have eggs, nice big brown ones, too, and they sold fresh bread and Bara Brith and scones and homemade marmalade as well.

A huge whoop of mingled joy and admonishment from Poppy still lounging on the bed almost made her drop the eggs when she came back in, laden. "Iolo! Where have you been? Bloody hell, I've been ringing your mobile for days!"

She threw herself out of bed, tossing the mobile onto the table when the call was over, and scrambled into her clothes. "You'll never guess: he's been in hospital!"

"He isn't! No! Oh dearie me! What hospital? Where?"

Poppy's eyes were shining. "Somewhere with a funny name. Uzbuzzy-somewhere or something."

"Ysbyty Gwynedd?"

"Where's that?"

"Well, if it is that, it's in Bangor, north of where we are, an hour at least or so. Well, goodness me!" Valerie unburdened herself of her treasures and slipped off her coat and scarf. "So how is he? What's been happening? What's been the matter with him, pet?"

"He had a crash on his motorbike, had a bit of concussion, cracked a few ribs and broke his leg in two places, silly bugger. I thought he'd dumped me! Can I take the car? I'm going to pick him up." Jigging around the tiny space, she flung her arms around Valerie. "I found him, Nana! I found him!"

Valerie chuckled. "I know, pet, I know, darling! You'll have me over – steady on!"

Poppy was ready to set off for Bangor, so delirious with excitement that her hands were shaking. "Do you want me to drop you off at that place first?"

"Forget about me, pet. You just go. Will you be coming straight back?"

"Yes. No. We might go off somewhere first. Don't know. "

"Well, I'll be all right. Have you got the map? Have you got your mobile? Have you got my number? Have I got *your* number?" Poppy had. She had. They were all set.

It was very silent after her departure. Valerie stared round the cramped space. So, what now? I could go out for a bit of a walk, but I am feeling ever so tired. I wonder if there's a bus to Porthlas? What if they come back straight away, though? What about the key?

Where are we going to put him? That's a bit of a problem. More than a bit of a problem, actually: there's definitely no room for three, especially with one with a broken leg. Wonder if he's on crutches? That'll be difficult.

Two's company; three's a crowd.

She stared out though the small window. "You're right. Poppy's happy now. She's not going to need me. I'm going to be a bit of a whatsit, Andy, aren't I, now? A bit of a gooseberry. Oh dear me."

She dozed most of the morning, and they were back just after midday. Poppy was over the moon, he hopping along with a crutch and she clinging happily to his free arm as she introduced him. "Isn't he lovely? Told you Nana, told you he hadn't dumped me!"

He grinned hugely. "Would I?"

She was relieved. He looked much better than Susie's tirade had led her to expect. With dark hair tied back in a scruffy ponytail, smooth toffee brown skin and bright blue eyes, he was unusual looking, certainly. About, what? Twenty-three, twenty-four? It occurred to Valerie that he could be partly Maori: difficult to say, especially as she had never been face to face with one. He was a bit scruffy, maybe, for her taste – jeans with big holes in the knees – but then, it could well be fashionable and he had been travelling – and he had a silver earring, silly man; he had intelligent eyes, though, a pleasing voice, nice hands and a lovely sleepy smile, too; it was quite endearing. He seemed shy. Well, not shy exactly, but unexacting. Easy to be with. Valerie liked him immediately.

It was still worrying her, though. She asked Poppy. "Where are we all going to sleep?"

"Iolo says he'll get his sleeping bag out and sleep on the beach. We left his backpack and his motorbike leathers in the car."

Valerie was horrified. "He can't do that! It's much too cold at night, and much too hard for a man with a broken leg and cracked ribs."

"Well, he'll be sleeping in a tent at the festival." Poppy wasn't all that sympathetic. "Let him try it. He likes to do things his way."

He grinned. "Thanks, mate."

"And he wants to see if he can get another decent motor-bike on the way."

"How is he going to ride a motorbike with one leg in plaster?"

"I'll drive it. I've got a licence. He can hang on behind." She ruffled his hair, and slung her arm around his neck, resting her head against his and beaming broadly. "Isn't he cute? Don't you think he's cute, Nana?"

Valerie chuckled. "Yes, lovely."

"We want to get off soon, anyway, to Builth Wells. Need to run you home and then got to go and look at his house on the way – it's in Mach – Mach – What is it, Iolo?"

He grinned shyly. "Machynlleth. Near Machynlleth." He pronounced it very well. Valerie was impressed.

"Do you speak Welsh, Iolo?"

He shook his head. "Oh, no. My mum does, though, and my gran. They're all Welsh way back on that side, though my dad's a New Zealander."

She felt ashamed. "I ought to speak Welsh. I've lived in Wales long enough, but I don't, just the odd phrases and words. And somebody's left you a house?"

He grinned again. "I suppose I'm like – the heir."

"That's very nice." Valerie looked about, smiling. "Well, now, let me get you something to eat."

"Can't we go out to eat, Nana? Can't we find a pub somewhere and have a drink? Iolo's got plenty of money."

Valerie frowned. "I'm not going to take your money – you're going to need it."

He shook his head. "Ah, there's no problem."

Poppy was already rummaging through her bag. "He's got oodles of it. He's rich! Come on, Nana – let's celebrate! I'm just going to tidy up."

Whilst he was up at the car fishing out his pack, Valerie double-checked with Poppy. "Are you sure about this, pet? I mean, I can pay, you know. I got the impression from your mum that he – well, that he was a bit of a – well, that he hadn't got much money."

"Yes, but that was before."

"Before what?"

"Before he inherited the house."

"There really is money, then?"

"Well, not that much, but some: plenty for now. And he's going to work, and so am I. I'm going to do an upholstery course. He's made some fantastic chairs and things; you ought to see them!"

Perhaps Susie had got him wrong. "Well, that is good news!"

"I tell you what," Poppy suggested, when he came back in. "Why don't we drive round to your special place, Nan. Is there likely to be a pub or a restaurant there?"

She tried to think back. "Well, there used to be a nice little pub, and a tea shop." A cramped little tea shop, as she remembered it, with white tablecloths and blue and white willow-pattern china – and delicious sponge cakes. Andy had loved those sponge cakes. Of course, it wouldn't still be there. "There's bound to be something."

"Okay then. Everybody ready?" Poppy threw open the door. "Come on, then, Nan – let's go and see!"

Chapter 29

"Oh, this is cute! Look, isn't it sweet, Iolo?" Poppy jumped up onto the low grey-stoned harbour wall and turned, gazing around in a slow circle. "Ah, what a pretty place, Nana. No wonder you like it."

"It is nice, isn't it?" It hadn't changed, not that much. She had been worried by the number of new houses that seemed to have been built along the narrow road leading down to Porthlas, but down by the harbour itself all was much as she had remembered it. A double row of old grey-stoned, slate-roofed houses and tiny cottages, some colour-washed pink or cream, nestled cosily together around the apex of the small, horse-shoe shaped bay. The water itself was not the clear translucent blue she remembered, still a bit cloudy after yesterday's weather, but she could have sworn that those were still the same small fishing boats bobbing gently alongside the sun-bleached and splintery old wooden jetty. The familiar hazy blue mountains were distantly visible across the estuary, and to each side of the hamlet, sea holly and furze bushes glowing like jewels on sandhills reached out softly towards the two rocky purple and golden headlands standing guard on either side of the bay.

"So where did you stay?"

"It used to be called *Swn-y-Mor*. Let me see..." Looking for a squat, grey stone house, with ivy growing thickly up the walls and two thickly buttressed chimneys, in the front row, somewhere to the right of the quay... Her stomach gave a jolt as she spotted it. "That's it there!" It looked as if it was still a guest house, too.

Goodness me. Fancy that.

"There's a hanging sign by the gate, can you see? It's got light blue paint."

Poppy shaded her eyes. "Oh, yes, I see." Iolo moved to her side and put an arm about her, and she put her arms about his waist and kissed his cheek. "Nana and Grampie stayed there for their honeymoon, Iolo, in that little house there."

"That was our room, the front one, above the front door." Valerie narrowed her eyes to make out the sign. Still the same name, then! Well I never. "Sound of the sea, it means, *Swn-y-Mor*. Sound of the sea."

She wanted to go and have a closer look, but she could see that Poppy and Iolo were hungry. "Shall we find somewhere to eat?"

"Ooh, yes!"

The pub that they had made a note of was on the road into the village. They walked up slowly, with Poppy and Iolo linking Valerie's arms with theirs. She made them stop once or twice, pretending to look at the view, so that she could gather her breath and take a bit of a rest. Too much excitement, perhaps. Goodness me, she was tired!

The Ship promised a comprehensive bar menu, freshly-caught fish and live music on Fridays, but it was closed until six o'clock. Fortunately, the little tea shop on the quay that Valerie remembered was still a café, although it had been extended into the shop next door and it looked very different, all bamboo, white wipe-down tables, wickerwork and ferns. The menu had altered, too, with not just cakes, tea-cakes, sausage rolls or scones on offer, but also sandwiches, toasties, chicken curry, pasta bake, baked potatoes, and various things with chips.

She was exhausted by the time they had walked back down and had settled at a table. "Open till nine p.m.," she read out from the front of the menu card as they were waiting for their order of fish and chips for Poppy and Iolo and a pasta bake for her. "If we stay on for a while, that might be handy."

Poppy and Iolo exchanged a fleeting glance. "Actually, Nan," Poppy murmured a little awkwardly, "we were thinking of getting you back tomorrow. Would that be all right?"

Of course they were. They had things to do. They wanted to be on their own. She felt an even deeper wave of exhaustion, but smiled as brightly as she could to hide her flush of disappointment. "Oh, yes! Yes, of course, That's fine."

Poppy looked relieved. She tugged at Iolo's sleeve. "Where's that photo, Iolo? Show Nana the photograph. You must see the photograph, Nana, of Iolo's house!"

"Oh, yes, I'd like to see that." An idea was coming slowly to her and she wanted to articulate it, though she waited whilst he found it in his wallet and handed it over to her with a shy grin. "It's called *Hafod.* My gran says that means something like 'Home'."

The small, dog-eared photograph showed a graceful, slate-roofed and grey-stoned Victorian house standing foursquare beneath a gently-sloping hill. At one side there seemed to be a long–neglected apple orchard and some kind of outbuildings, and the corner of a large greenhouse or conservatory could just be made out behind. She shook her head admiringly. "Oh, my word, very nice! But it's not that 'little', is it?"

Very nice. Andy would have liked this. Bound to have nice straight walls.

"It's perfect, isn't it?" Poppy took back the photograph, looking very excited. "With all those outbuildings, we can have a lovely workshop."

She rubbed her tired eyes, puzzled. "So what are you doing, then? Are you thinking of staying over here, then and not going back to New Zealand?"

Poppy nodded. "If it all works out."

Surely it wouldn't be as simple as all that. "Will you be able to get a work permit, Iolo?"

"I've still got a British passport." Poppy giggled, throwing an arm about him. "He won't need one if he marries me!"

"You're thinking of getting married!"

They exchanged shy grins. "Maybe not yet, but soon."

She had lost her breath. What was Susie going to say about that? "Well, well, well, well!"

"You'll have to come and live with us, Mrs –" Iolo looked embarrassed. "Sorry, I don't even know your name. Can I call you Nan?"

It sounded rather catchy with his accent. She was touched. "Of course you can. Or Valerie; I'm Valerie Bryce. I don't mind which."

Poppy was frowning. "Do you know, Nan, that's not a bad idea? Of course! There'll be bags of room. You can come and live with us!"

She could feel herself shrinking away. "Oh, no, I couldn't!"

Iolo was frowning deeply, too. "I could make you a nice granny flat; I'm quite handy."

Poppy rolled her eyes. "He's *very* handy! He'll even make your furniture, if you ask him nicely."

He shrugged and threw Valerie a lovely slow smile. "Anyway, like Pops says, Nan, there's plenty of room. If we stay, we'd be happy to have you. It's, like, a genuine invitation."

Poppy giggled. "You'll be very useful, Nana, when we have fourteen kids!"

She felt very muddly and a bit shell-shocked. No, no, it was ridiculous. It was extremely kind of them, but obviously they hadn't thought it through properly. They probably didn't even mean it, not seriously. They probably expected her to say no.

And would she really want to?

Would I really want to, Andy? You know – in view of you-know-what?

Their food arrived then, and saved her from answering. They were starving, too, poor things – they fell on their fish and chips like hungry wolves. Her pasta bake smelled good, too, though she had no appetite. It was bubbling and nicely browned. With a sigh, she picked up her fork to make an attempt on it, pushing further consideration aside. For the moment, what concerned her more than the future was where they were all going to sleep tonight.

"Do you know what I think?" she asked them as they all gathered afterwards on the quay. "I think I should see if they've got a room for me at *Swn-y-Mor*. If they have, you two go back to the caravan; I'll stay here. In fact," she added, gazing over at the first floor window above the door of the pretty, grey-stoned house, "I'd actually like to stay on here for a bit, rather than going straight back. Would you mind that, Poppy?"

Poppy shook her head vehemently. "Oh, no, Nan – it's your caravan. We could stay here, if you'd rather that."

She felt a momentary panic. "Oh, but I want to. I'd like to! For old times' sake, you know. Just for a few days. I'd really like to stay here on my own."

Poppy glanced at Iolo. "Well, if you're sure."

"Oh, I am, I am!"

"Did you mean we could take the caravan?"

She hadn't, actually, but – why not?

Poppy was getting excited. "Because if you did, that'd be amazing. We could take it to your rally, Iolo. It'd give us somewhere to stay."

He nodded slowly. "Yep. Yep, that'd be cool. Are you sure, though, Nan? Would you be all right down here on your own? We could nip your stuff over to you in an hour or two and then pick you up again on our way back."

All she wanted for now was to lie down. She couldn't think beyond that. *Please have a room, whoever you are who's now running* Swn-y-Mor.

"Oh, yes, I am. Quite sure."

The original proprietress, a scrawny little woman with a bun, Mrs Llewelyn Evans – she had never forgotten her name – had been ageing then, all those years ago, and she had gone, of course. The woman who opened the door and showed her up to her room today was a Mrs Williams, middle-aged, comfortable-looking, big and well-cushioned, with greying dark hair and an open, pleasant face. She said she had been baking. A voluminous floral apron was tied tightly over an emerald green skirt and a pale blue polyester blouse. The door she flung open on the landing led to a single room at the back of the house, but when Valerie, disappointed, told her about the honeymoon and asked if the same room was by any chance vacant, she was touched.

"Well, well, fancy that! And you've come back! Ah, that's nice. Yes, yes, number 1 is vacant. It's a double of course, but in view of your reason for wanting it, you can have it for the same price. I might have to ask you to move, mind you, if I need it. You're lucky at the moment, the season isn't yet properly underway. Will you be taking an evening meal, Mrs Bryce? £6.99 for two courses, £8.25 for three."

"We have just eaten. I'm not very hungry tonight." Tomorrow – well, tomorrow was another day. "I probably will after that. Could I let you know?"

In the old days, the room at the front had been mainly brown, like the rest of the house – brown and beige, with touches of white and orange. Beige walls, brown linoleum and beige, brown, orange and white rag rugs on the floor and an orange candlewick bedspread and plain white curtains at the window. Now it was rather pink. In fact, it was very pink, Valerie decided, when Mrs Williams had left her alone to make herself at home. Pink walls, a pale lavender carpet, darker pink curtains at the window. There was even a tiny en-suite, now, also in pink.

The bed had been moved. She sat down on it wearily. It wasn't the same bed, of course. The one they'd had had been a high dull metal bedstead. This one was much lower, and its headboard was all white curlicues and things, and it had sheer pink nylon curtaining draped over a ceiling ring and tied back above the headboard, like some little girl's Barbie's four-poster. When they had stayed in the room last, the bed had been under the window. Now it was against an inner wall. She told Andy. "It isn't quite the same."

There was a tray with a kettle and tea-making equipment on top of a low shelf in the corner, underneath one bearing a small telly. "All mod cons, now, pet! Shall we have a drop?" It was almost too much trouble to get up and cross over to it, but she was glad that she did so, because when she passed the window and looked out, it was all exactly the same. Blue sea, blue sky, blue distant hills... She sighed heavily.

"Well, look at that, love. Do you remember?" The two of them kneeling side-by-side on the bed at the window staring out at that view, not a stitch on and who was there to care! *Forgot to go to breakfast twice – shows how wrapped up in each other we were, especially you, Andy. Not like you, eh, to miss a meal!*

She filled the little white half-sized kettle and plugged it in, and then brought over the chair from the dressing table and put it beneath the window and sat on it, and forgot the kettle. It was a good thing it had a cut-off switch.

It was almost dark by the time she moved again, and then she only did so because Poppy and Iolo arrived with a bag with her clothes and wash things in it. They were both flushed and happy, but a little bit anxious. "You are sure? Quite sure? You're looking very tired, Nana; you have a good rest. We're going to set off first thing in the morning – go down to, where is it, Iolo? Harlech Castle? We'll maybe stay there a night and then over to Machiwachi."

Iolo grinned. "Machynlleth. We can't move into Hafod yet, the paperwork's not finished, but we're going to have a look round it. Someone's going to meet us with a key."

"We'll tell you all about it." Poppy flung her arms about Valerie. "'Bye, then, Nana. We'll take good care of the caravan and the car. We'll bring them back in one piece."

Valerie held her tight. "I'm sure you will, lovey. I'm glad to see you so happy, Poppy. If you speak to your mum..."

"Yeah, I'll ring her tonight."

"Well –" She had thought about it carefully. "Give her all my love. Tell her where I am, tell her I'm in a nice place. Tell her I'm satisfied that you're safe and happy. Tell her I like Iolo, I trust him to look after you. Tell her *I'm* happy. Tell her that whatever happens, it's quite all right."

She went down to breakfast the next morning, but only to stop Mrs Williams worrying if she didn't turn up, and she only had a drop of coffee and a bit of toast. Then she went back and sat in her chair by the window. She had sat there all night.

When a nice young girl came to make up her bed around midday, she put on her coat and went out to the quay. It was a beautiful day: fresh, though, very fresh. There were a few people about and one fisherman was out in his boat, but the tiny crescent beach was deserted. *Too early in the year for most people, April, especially with Easter having been in March this year and the school holidays over. Summer, when we were here. We went swimming.*

She wandered along the quay slowly and went up the road as far as the pub. Pity about the new houses, but people did need homes: very hard for young people, especially, with the housing market as it was. At least it looked as if Poppy would be off to a good start, assuming that her relationship with Iolo flourished.

I think it will, pet, don't you? She's very young, of course, but they seem serious about it. They make a nice couple.

She was tired again, then, so she sat on a wooden seat near the edge of the sea wall. She felt very happy. Andy felt very close. Strange, how she had come almost full circle. This was where she was meant to be, then. Here.

"It all works out, doesn't it, pet? You do one thing and you don't know why, but you realise eventually. Right time and the right place... It makes sense, doesn't it, somehow, Porthlas? Kind of – of, I know it sounds daft and you'll laugh at me – but *romantic.*"

It wasn't time yet. She went back to the house. At least it wasn't like the old days, when landladies weren't too keen on letting you in during the day. "Any time," Mrs Williams had said, as she had handed her a key. "Come in and out as you like, love; I shan't mind."

The room looked nice and fresh after the little girl had been round and cleaned it. She must have sprayed something, too, or she'd had some nice polish; it smelled of lavender.

Bet she wondered why I hadn't slept in the bed. Maybe she thought I'd made it for her. Tonight, even if I don't want to go to sleep – no time for sleep, too much remembering to get through: only up to when our Susie was being born – I'll lie in it for a while. Make it look crumpled.

For now, though, she sat back down in the chair. The girl had left it by the window. Kind.

Mrs Williams came knocking mid-afternoon, and caught her dozing. The last thing she remembered thinking about was the day that Susie had discovered the big doll with the long golden curls and the blue Alice-in-Wonderland dress that they'd hidden behind the sofa for her seventh birthday. She'd said it was lovely, but had not been as pleased with it as they had hoped she would be.

"Mind you, love, you know Susie." She remembered saying that to Andy. "She had been hoping for a horse."

"Will you be having an evening meal today, Mrs Bryce?" Mrs Williams asked, popping her head around the door when Valerie called to her to come in. "You didn't say."

She thought for a moment. There might be other people

in the dining room. Even if there weren't, Mrs Williams was bound to try to talk. She shook her head. "No, no, don't worry about me, Mrs Williams. Unless –"

Mrs Williams proved to be a bit of a mind-reader. "You'd like to be on your own, wouldn't you? Thinking about old times. I know. I tell you what I could do as we're not very busy – I could put you a drop of soup and a little light supper on a tray, would that be better?"

It would. Just a bite of something, just a little bite to keep her going, just for a while longer. Just for a little while. "If it's not too much trouble?"

Mrs Williams nodded, satisfied. "Then we'll do that, shall we? It'll be at half past six. Mushroom soup today, dear and either a nice shepherd's pie or braised beef for after – unless you're a vegetarian, in which case I've got some macaroni cheese?"

She shook her head. "No, no – a small portion of the shepherd's pie will do nicely."

"Right-ho, dear. And a bowl of jelly trifle for after? Will that be all right?"

She smiled gratefully. "That would be very nice."

She ate the soup and the jelly trifle, but only picked at the shepherd's pie.

When darkness had fallen and the same little girl who had cleaned her room that morning had taken away her tray, she moved around the room a little for the sake of her stiffening hip, and then switched on the small flickery television, crept under the duvet and propped herself up against the pillows, vaguely watching a gardening programme in Welsh. It was quite interesting, despite the language difficulty, but her mind kept drifting again, so when the programme finished she got up again and switched it off and went back to her chair. She took the duvet with her this time. Last night, it had been draughty round her knees.

Chapter 30

When the girl came in to do her room again next morning, she went out as she had the day before, but this time only as far as the sea wall, where she waited on a seat until she thought it might be done, and then went back in. Lovely blue sky again today, but still chilly.

Almost there, now. Having their Mediterranean cruise. Wandering round Venice.

When she got to the dreadful bit, in late afternoon, and had wept till no tears were left inside her, she got ready. She felt quite tranquil, quite calm as she dressed. She left her bag on the dressing table, with her key. The pink front room seemed almost like home now. She said goodbye to it with affection.

This time she took the narrow path leading through the dunes to her right and over the small headland. From the foot, it looked daunting, winding up and up through the prickly overgrowth, but it was only the first bit that was really steep, and with her stick to help her and by taking her time and stopping for regular sits at the side and little breathers, she managed it. Someone had built a large and rather expensive-looking white-painted bungalow near the top, its steep, green-fenced garden backing onto the gorse and bramble thicket fringing the path. Lovely views. They had planted a palm tree in the garden, or somebody had. It must have been growing for some time. It looked a bit incongruous, but in a way, against the cloudless blue of the sky, quite charming.

At the top, it was breezier and quite chilly and she turned up her coat collar. The waters below the headland on either side, clear today now that the wind had dropped, shone turquoise below her as the sun filtered through to the sand underneath. When she was ready, she took her time and clambered slowly down. At the bottom, she walked a short way along the beach and then sank, tired and breathless, on a rock, peering back up towards the bungalow. The few windows she could see looked blank. Nobody at all in view. Silence surrounded her, apart from a few sea birds and a thrush somewhere high up in the greenery behind her and the soft, sibilant swoosh, swoosh, swoosh of the water dragging at the pebbles. She gazed out at the sea again. "It's lovely here, Andy."

It didn't take him too long to answer. "Feel like a swim?"

"Don't be daft! Water's too cold."

"A paddle then? Bit of a paddle, maybe?"

It was tempting. "I wouldn't mind."

It was difficult to make her way across the rocks and pebbles – a good thing nobody was watching; she must have looked like a drunken old fool, lurching from sandy patch to large stone and trying, occasionally unsuccessfully, to dodge small rock pools. The water, when she reached it and laid down her stick and took off her shoes, was as clear as crystal and as cold as splinters of ice. She sucked in her breath. The hazy blue mountains on the other side of the estuary weren't visible from here and the aloneness of the empty beach behind her and the huge expanse of water in front of her startled her. It was disconcerting, making her feel very small.

When she began to move out again, it was very slowly. The bottom felt soft and squidgy: not pebbly here at least, which was a relief. There was some sort of trough, though; it got deeper quite quickly, throwing her momentarily off her balance. She stabilised herself quickly, but the hem of her long coat and skirt were already sodden, clinging to her calves. She was cross with him. "Why didn't you tell me to take my coat off?"

"Didn't want you catching cold."

A myriad butterflies of light seemed to be skimming and dancing over the water's surface. Cold, cold it was;

she couldn't feel her feet or her calves. Twisted her ankle, suddenly: slipped on a hidden rock.

"It's all right, Val, I've got you."

Pushed slowly onward against the incoming water, feeling its slow, rhythmical power. Couldn't feel her legs, at all now. Coat, sodden, clinging to her legs, dragging at her hips, fighting against any forward motion. Made it difficult.

Frightened. Hesitated. Pushed on.

Water washing suddenly on her stomach. Freezing. Made her suck in her breath. "Andy..."

Might be easier to swim.

It was even harder getting back up across the pebbled stretch when she finally turned back and slowly waded out, progress not helped by the fact that she couldn't find her shoes or the walking stick that she had laid down. Either she had come out at a different place or the tide must have come in a bit and washed over it, or washed it away. Breathless, staggering, shivering, the exposed soles of her feet painful and tender against sharp pebbles, twisting her ankles and jarring her hip again, with wet skirts heavily and scratchily clinging to her, she scolded herself all the way up the beach. Foolish! Foolish. What a silly old woman. Her hip hurt now, so much.

She turned back for a moment to rest at the head of the beach and stared back out to sea. What a waste. What a shame. Why hadn't she had the courage? Whatever had made her think she could jump off a ferry? For two pins, if she had the energy, she would have gone back in.

She was exhausted by the time she got back to *Swn-y-Mor* and could barely stay on her feet as she hovered in the porch.

I'm dripping all over poor Mrs Williams' porch floor. Can't go in like this, I'll ruin her carpet.

She was trying to pluck up the courage to ring when the door opened and Mrs Williams' appeared anxiously in the doorway. "I saw you coming up the path – what's happened, Mrs Bryce, dear? Have you had an accident?"

It was impossible to speak. She was shaking all over with cold and her teeth were chattering. She tried to take a step towards Mrs Williams but her legs failed her. Mrs Williams caught her, calling over her shoulder, "Nev! Can you give me a hand?"

Mr Williams was a big, burly man, and together they got her inside. Mrs Williams darted into her sitting room and brought out a warm tartan rug, which she wrapped around her tightly. "You're soaking! Soaking! You've got nothing on your feet, dear! Where are your shoes?" She glanced at her husband. "Can you help me to carry her up to her room, Nev, and then ring for the doctor?"

It was all a blur. Somehow Mrs Williams got her wet clothes off and a thick nightdress and cardigan on and helped her into the bed. Leaving the room for a moment, she came back bearing another duvet and a pair of fluffy pink bedsocks. "Here, dear, let's get these on."

Her lips would move enough to speak now. "I don't need a doctor."

Mrs Williams surveyed her dubiously. "I think we ought to get him to look at you. Your lips are quite blue, love. You've been thoroughly chilled."

She shook her head vehemently – or as vehemently as she could. She felt terribly weak. "Please. No. I'll be quite all right. Really."

Mrs Williams looked unconvinced. "Well, let's get a nice hot drink inside you, then we'll see. Go and make a nice hot cup of cocoa, Nev, and put in plenty of sugar. Fill a couple of hot water bottles, too." She shook her head as she tucked the second duvet over the top of the first. "My goodness, dear, what happened?"

There was no way of explaining. The warmth of the night-clothes and of the feather duvet was beginning to thaw out her body, though her fingers were still painfully frozen and she couldn't feel her feet. "Was just having a paddle. Nice day. Must have slipped."

"Paddle! At this time of the year! Good gracious me!" Mrs Williams tucked in the two hot water bottles that Mr Williams brought her, wrapping each one first in a towel, and placed them carefully, one alongside Valerie and one down at the bottom of the bed well away from her feet. "Don't want to have you touching these, dear: just to give you a bit more warmth."

After she had helped Valerie to take a few sips of the hot cocoa – all she wanted – she tucked her in again and drew the curtains. "I've put a little bell by your side, dear, here, see? Ring it if you need me and I'll be back in any case to look at you in a little while."

"Thank you." Valerie was getting warmer. She tried to smile. "I'll be fine. So sorry to be such a trouble to you. You're very, very kind."

She was so tired that she couldn't be bothered to try moving a muscle. The warm bed was very comfortable; luxurious, really, despite the numbness in her hands and feet. The scent of lavender was in her nostrils. Her eyelids were already closing as Mrs Williams quietly left the room.

Sorry I couldn't do it, pet. She barely had the energy to say goodnight to Andy.

She woke once during the night, hearing some clock downstairs somewhere striking three, and an owl hooting, then drifted off again. She was swimming somewhere in a deep, dark sea: no, not swimming: sinking. Above her head, she could see patches of turquoise blue near the top where the sunlight struck through the water, but the depths she was falling slowly through were a very dark green and cold. Translucent though, very clear. She could see lots of fishes around and below her, all the colours of the rainbow, darting in and out of a forest of great, towering, gently swaying fronds of seaweed. Didn't know there were such pretty fish around the North Wales coast. Somehow expected to see a heart-shaped little face peeping out from between the tall tree weeds, flowing golden tendrils drifting with the current, and disappearing again with the flick and swish of a gleaming silvery tail, a mermaid child. Just like Disney.

There was a buzzing noise in her head. She was getting very tired. How long have I been in the water? Should try to get up there somehow. Somebody up there... Somebody I ought to be getting back to... Can't remember who.

Falling faster now and feeling a little frightened. Sinking down steadily through the deep green water: impossible to slow her downward drift. Tight, round her chest. Couldn't lift her arms. Colour around her now – all around her, forming the shimmering walls of a cylinder. Luminous bubbles, streaming upwards; she stared at them with delight. Like a child's bubble mix, they were, crimson and golden-yellow, lavender-purple and rose, soft blue, greeny-blue, pearly pink, silvery and orange; tiny balls of light, glowing with light and colour and rising and bouncing like bubbles in a glass of fizzy water – millions of them, no, billions – shimmering, luminescent, changing colour, some of them silvery white like Christmas baubles, some minute, like tiny diamonds, others whole tennis balls of light. She was enthralled with watching them. They were fascinating. The little spheres seemed to be making music: or was it the buzzing in her head?

Peering down past her feet, she saw down at the bottom of the bubble cylinder on the ocean floor a silvery, lumi-nescent starfish. She tried to see it more clearly. Was it a starfish? Could it be a sea anemone? A hand? The glow of it increased steadily, its silvery whiteness reaching a degree of intensity and radiance that should have, but didn't, hurt her eyes.

Falling faster now. Panicking a little, she looked up again towards the surface. The patches of turquoise sunlight were receding further and further away. Darkness was encroaching overhead. The water felt as if it was growing heavier.

She began to struggle. "I don't like this, Andy! I don't know if I like this..."

Suddenly, part of the glowing, luminous light from below was shimmering all around her. "You'll be all right pet. Come on, give me your hand."

At his touch she sighed. She was home again. "Oh, you're there! Where are we going, Andy?"

"It doesn't really matter, does it?"

"No. Not if you're here." She felt his sturdy arms closing gently about her.

"Moving on. Just moving on again, pet, that's all we're doing."

"It's all right, isn't it, Andy?"

"Doesn't hurt at all."

She was at total ease in his arms now as they sank together towards the light. "Hmm..."

She pressed her nose into the warm saltcellar at the base of his neck and breathed in the familiar scent of his skin. "Not sure if I'd have moved in with Poppy and Iolo."

He chuckled. "No, pet. Probably wiser not."

THE   END

ABOUT THE AUTHOR

Jenny Piper lives with her husband in rural Hampshire and has been variously an actress, an artist, a teacher, a lecturer and a psychologist. She has had a lifelong love of books and nowadays spends much of her time writing.

Moving On is her second book. Her third, a sequel to ***Someday, Maybe,*** is currently underway.

Visit Jenny Piper at jennypiper.moonfruit.com, or at author-jennypiper.blogspot.co.uk, or join her on Twitter @ jennypiper6, or on Facebook.

THE MOUNTAINS BETWEEN
Julie McGowan
THE MOUNTAINS BETWEEN
A searing and powerful novel from one of Wales' best-loved authors
Julie McGowan

Part One

1929 ~

Jennie

J ennie heard Tom's voice calling her, but she ignored him and scrambled over the gate into the ten-acre field. She ran head down, forcing her legs to go faster and faster, her breath coming in great racking sobs, until she reached the corner of the field where the land sloped down towards the railway line, and she would be hidden from the house. As she flung herself face down onto the grass and the sobs became bitter, painful tears, Mother's words echoed in her head, refusing to be quelled.

You were never wanted! You were a mistake!... A mistake... a mistake!... Never wanted...!

The day had started so well. The Girls were coming home and Jennie had been helping Mother in the house – as she always did, but more willingly this time, excitement tightening her chest because her sisters would soon be here and the summer holidays would then have begun in earnest. Mother, too, seemed happy; less forbidding, and the crease between her brows that gave her such a disapproving air had been less pronounced.

Never wanted!... A mistake... Your Father's doing!

Eventually there were no more tears left to cry, but the sobs remained; long drawn out arpeggios every time she inhaled. And the more she tried to stop them the more it felt as if they were taking over her body.

She sat up and wrapped her arms around her knees in an effort to steady herself. A small girl dressed in a starched

I

white pinafore over a blue print summer frock, with two mud-brown plaits framing a face whose eyes looked too large for it. She stared at the mountains – her mountains, her friends, keepers of her secrets. But today she wasn't seeing them, could draw no comfort from the gentle slopes of the Sugar Loaf which stretched out like arms to encompass the valley. Today the mountains were majestic and aloof, wanting no share of her misery. In her head the scene in Mother's bedroom replayed itself endlessly before her.

She'd been returning a reel of thread to Mother's workbox – a sturdy wooden casket kept in a corner of the bedroom. Inside were neat trays containing all Mother's sewing things, and one tray full of embroidery silks, the colours rich and flamboyant as they nestled together. Jennie had lifted the silks up and let them run through her fingers, enjoying their smooth feel and the rainbows they made.

Then, for the first time, she'd noticed that what she thought was the bottom of the workbox was, in fact, too high up.

She lifted the rest of the trays out and pulled at the wooden base, which moved easily to reveal another section underneath. There was only one item in it; a rectangular tin box with a hinged lid on which was a slightly raised embossed pattern in shiny red and gold. She traced the pattern with her fingers. It was an intriguing box. A box that begged to be opened.

Jennie had lifted the tin clear of the workbox when suddenly Mother appeared in the doorway, her face bulging with anger.

"What do you think you're doing? Put that down at once!"

Taken unawares by her mother's arrival and the harshness of her tone – excessive even for her – Jennie turned suddenly and the box had fallen out of her hands, the hinged lid flying open and the contents scattering over the floor. Had she not been so frightened by Mother's anger, Jennie would have registered disappointment, for the box, after all, held only a few old papers.

To Mother, though, they seemed as valuable as the Crown Jewels. With an anguished cry she'd pushed Jennie aside and scrabbled on the floor to retrieve the documents.

"I'm s-s-sorry," Jennie stammered, "I didn't mean ..."

But Mother wasn't listening. She was too busy shouting.

"Why don't you ever leave things alone? This is mine! You had no business! You're always where you're not meant to be – always causing me more work! Either under my feet or doing something you shouldn't!"

Her voice had grown more shrill as she spoke, with a dangerous quiver in it, so that Jennie didn't dare offer to help – or to point out that the things her mother was accusing her of were grossly unfair. She'd given up doing that a long time ago. "... It's not right – I didn't want... Three babies were enough!"

Mother had been looking down, thrusting the papers back in the box, continuing to exclaim about the unfairness of her lot as she did so, almost as if she were no longer addressing Jennie. But then she'd snapped the box shut and swung round to face her daughter.

"You were never wanted, you know! It was all a mistake! All your Father's doing!" She turned back to the workbox, her shoulders heaving with emotion.

There was a moment's silence.

"What did Father do?" a crushed Jennie had whispered.

Mother's hand had swung round and slapped Jennie across the ankles. "Don't be so disgusting!" she'd hissed. "Get out of here!"

Jennie knew, as she sat on the grass, that Mother had meant it. She was used to her mother's tempers, her insistence that the house, the family, and at times the farm, were run exactly as she wished, but this was different. The expression on her face as she'd spoken the dreadful words was one that Jennie had never seen before. It had been full of a strange passion – and something else which Jennie, with her limited experience, couldn't identify. But it had frightened her.

Never wanted! A mistake!

It changed everything. Nothing in her world would ever be the same again. Her eight years thus far had been secure ones; lonely at times, being the youngest by so many years, and hard when Mother's standards were so exacting. But happy, too. Happy in the knowledge that she was well-fed, clothed and housed; well-cared for (didn't that mean loved and wanted? It appeared not). Happy on the farm, surrounded by her mountains, and in the company of her beloved father.

Father! Jennie's heart beat faster in alarm. Did this mean that he didn't want her either? That he too saw her as some sort of mistake? Her relationship with her mother always held uncertainty, but Father's affection never seemed to waver.

A kaleidoscope of images of herself with her father rushed through her mind. Making her a wheelbarrow all of her own, so that she could 'help' him on the farm, when she was only four. Holding her in his arms when she cried because a fox had got in and wreaked havoc in the hen-house; comforting her because she'd been the one to discover the terrible decapitated remains. Letting her help to make new chicken sheds, safely off the ground – not minding when she'd splashed creosote on the grass. Urging the cows to milking, his voice kind and gentle, calling each cow by name and helping her to do the same until she could recognise each one.

Surely he loved her! He had to love her!

Panic was rising inside her and she wanted to run to her father and beg him to tell her that it wasn't true; that she wasn't simply a mistake. But fear stayed her. There was the awful possibility that he might tell her even more dreadful things that she didn't want to hear. It would be the same if she asked The Girls, and as for Tom, well! – he had never disguised the fact that a sister six years younger than himself was fit only for endless teasing.

The words were still playing in her head when suddenly the panic eased. What else had Mother said? ... *All your Father's doing!* She didn't know what her father had done, but surely if he'd done it then he must have wanted her?

She lay back on the grass and closed her eyes. Perhaps if she went to sleep she would wake up and everything would be just as it was. She could go back to the house and carry on as usual and the lead weight in her chest that was making breathing so difficult would be gone.

The hot July sun soothed her. Mother would be cross if her skin burned, but Mother being cross about such a thing didn't seem quite so important at the moment. Convincing herself that her Father loved her and wanted her was, she instinctively knew, the only thing that would help her to push her mother's awful words to the back of her mind.

Katharine Davies sat on the edge of her bed, her shoulders sagging uncharacteristically, her breathing rapid and shallow. The papers were safely stowed away again but the episode had unnerved her too much for her to return downstairs just yet. Jennie was too young to have understood the implications of what the papers contained, but what if she told the older children of their whereabouts? A hot flush spread over her anew as she considered what they would think of her. She tried hopelessly to calm herself, but memories of nearly seventeen years ago refused to go away.

"Edward! Oh Edward!"

The voice was her own, urgent, pleading as his hands caressed her, explored her; and she wasn't urging him to stop. Oh no! To her everlasting shame she wanted him to go on, to satisfy the craving that had taken over her whole body. And he had: gone on and on until she felt she was drowning; until she had screamed her ecstasy.

I love you Katie. I'll always love you! Edward had held her afterwards, murmuring into her hair, promising to take care of her. And he had. But it hadn't been enough.

The memories sent prickles of shame up her spine until her neck was on fire. Yet, unbidden, the feeling was there again; that same burning physical wanting that had gnawed away at her in those early years, trapping her with its demands, its insatiability.

She stood up abruptly, angry that her body should be betraying her after all these years when she'd thought she had it firmly under control. She clenched her hands tightly in front of her. She must, she would, maintain that control.

She forced herself to think of what must still be done, which chores in the dairy or in the garden would best exercise her treacherously unreliable body.

She thought fleetingly of Jennie as she moved swiftly out of the bedroom. She shouldn't have spoken to her as she did, but doubtless the child would get over it – would probably look at her with those sheep's eyes for a day or two and then it would pass.

But you meant it, nagged the mean voice of Conscience.

She clutched the crucifix hanging round her neck, as if gathering strength to push the voice away. *I'll pray about it tonight,* she vowed, making for the stairs.

"Bessie! You'd better see about scalding the milk or it will turn in this heat! Then come and help me clean the dairy."

The girl, plump and homely, turned from the large stone sink where she was peeling potatoes, ready to make a cheery remark until she saw the expression on her employer's face. Best not look in the churn, madam, she thought, or the milk will turn never mind the heat.

Jennie saw her mother in the dairy as she entered the back of the house and tiptoed up the back stairs. She didn't want Mother to see the grass stains on her apron.

She'd thought long and hard once she'd finally stopped crying, and had decided that if she tried, really tried, not to let Mother see her doing anything wrong, and not to argue with her ever again, then perhaps Mother would forget that she was 'a mistake' and decide that she was the best-loved and most wanted of all her children.

She sighed as she reached her room. It would be hard work. There seemed to be so many things that Mother had definite and immovable views on. Take her apron, for example. Aprons weren't meant to get dirty. Mother's aprons always stayed spotless – except for the apron she wore over her apron to do 'the rough'.

Not that Mother ever did the really dirty jobs. They were done by Bessie, the latest in a long line of girls who stayed until they could take Mother's demands for perfection and her sharp tongue no longer.

She put on a clean apron and went to the recently-installed bathroom to wash her hands and face, careful to wipe the basin clean afterwards and replace the towel just so. The bathroom was a sufficiently new addition to be treated with exceptional respect. Then she returned to the kitchen by the front stairs so that Mother would think she had been in the house all along.

"May I go now, please – to meet The Girls?"

Jennie didn't want to look Mother in the face; instead

she fastened her gaze on the shiny gold crucifix.

The crease between Mother's brows deepened as she surveyed her daughter. She opened her mouth as if to speak, but closed it again. Then her shoulders dropped a little as she appeared to relent from whatever it was she had been going to say.

"Very well. But wear your sunbonnet – and keep your apron clean!"

Jennie went meekly to the little room behind the kitchen and fetched her sun hat before letting herself out through the back door, forcing herself to walk sedately in case Mother was watching her as she crossed the farmyard – immaculate as ever because the cows weren't allowed to cross it lest they make it dirty.

Once round the corner of the barn she ran again to the gate of the ten-acre field. But she didn't climb over it this time. Instead she divested herself of her apron and sunhat and hung them on the gatepost before turning to a smaller, iron gate which led to the lane running parallel to the field.

She began to skip along the lane, sending up little clouds of dust as she went. It was impossible, somehow, to walk once you were out-of-doors and alone, even when you were feeling pretty miserable. Had she been feeling happier she would have tucked her skirts up into the legs of her knickers and tried a few cartwheels. But as she thought this, the awful words bounced up at her in time to her skipping... *Not wan-ted... not wan-ted... not wan-ted...*

The engine hooted as it pulled out of Nantyderry Halt, diverting Jennie. No need to think about anything else now The Girls were home! She broke into a run as they appeared at the end of the lane. They were each wearing their school uniform and carrying a small case; Tom would take the van down later for their trunks. Their uniforms bore the badge of the convent school at Monmouth, which they attended not because they were Catholic but because it was the best school in the area, and they boarded, not because it was far away but because that was what the best families did.

Jennie threw herself into the arms of her eldest sister, sure of a rapturous response.

"Steady on!" laughed Emily, swinging her round. "You nearly knocked me over! Let me look at you! You've grown again while we've been away! Laura! Don't you think she's grown?"

Laura, a year younger than sixteen-year-old Emily, but inches shorter and already more buxom, hugged Jennie more steadily.

"At least an inch taller," she agreed.

"Does that mean I can use your tennis racket this summer?" Jennie asked excitedly, turning back to Emily. "I've been practising like mad against the barn wall with the old one, and you promised me yours when I was big enough."

"We'll see," came the reply. "You'll have to show me how good you are."

But Emily's eyes held a merry promise and suddenly she caught hold of Jennie and danced round with her again.

"Isn't it wonderful? I've finished school for good! My very last day! I can hardly believe it!"

"It won't be so wonderful if we're late for dinner," Laura reminded her, picking up her bag and beginning to walk up the lane. "Jennie, your dress is terribly dusty – Mother will have a fit!"

"It's alright," said Jennie, "I can cover it up with my apron – I've left it on the gate."

But as they reached the gate, there was Tom, Jennie's sunhat perched ridiculously on his head, and the apron held aloft.

"Give it back, I mustn't get it dirty!" Jennie cried, hers arms flailing wildly as Tom held her easily at bay with one gangly arm.

"Please, Tom!" Laura sounded as urgent as Jennie, as the gong for lunch sounded from the house. "You know she'll get into trouble."

Emily sauntered through the gate behind her sisters. "Give her the apron and the hat, Tom, and carry these bags in for us." Her voice sounded almost lazy, but Tom was aware of the authority behind it. He was taller than both his sisters, but Emily always managed to make him feel small.

He relinquished the garments to a relieved Jennie, tweaked each of the long brown plaits hanging over her shoulders, and then grinned. "Better not spoil the homecoming, I suppose."

But he didn't move to embrace his sisters. Instead they all hurried in for dinner.

C ome along! Come along!" said Mother as Father stopped to kiss and hug his two elder children. "This dinner will be getting cold."

Jennie contrived to sit between Father and Emily and at once felt happier, although tears threatened again when Father asked her in his gentle voice what she'd been doing all morning. Fortunately Mother began speaking to Emily, and as it was unwise to talk at the same time as Mother she didn't have to answer.

Edward Davies surveyed his family with a degree of pride as they sat round the large, scrubbed kitchen table. All four children well-grown and healthy – no mean achievement when you compared them to the malnourished rickety children over in the valleys, many of whom would be lucky to survive infancy. He would have liked another boy, for the farm, but he loved his daughters nevertheless.

Not that Katharine would have been happy with another boy – there'd been enough fuss as it was when Jennie came along, so he'd thanked God that He had seen fit to bless them with another girl. For some reason Katharine saw girls as a blessing and boys as a kind of blight. *Poor thing,* she would say whenever she heard of a mother being delivered of a son, no matter how longed-for. She treated Tom well enough for all that, Edward allowed, although he never saw the look of pride in her eyes that he had seen other mothers bestowing on their sons. But then, he reflected, Katharine was not like other mothers in a good many ways.

He watched her now, talking to Emily. She was still a handsome woman, despite her nearly forty years, with no hint of grey in the coils of rich brown hair which she wore piled high like Queen Mary. She'd kept her figure too, which was petite, with delicate wrists and ankles, but her body had always curved in and out in the right places.

Beautiful she'd been, when he first met her; beautiful with no idea of her beauty, which was what he'd found so appealing. Large grey-green eyes, more green when stirred to anger or passion, had beguiled him, and a relentless determination to set the world to rights according to her own view of things had been particularly attractive in one who looked as if she should languish and be pampered all day.

They first met when she was only eighteen, and had returned home from being a children's nanny to care for her younger brothers and sisters following the death of both their parents – her father having discreetly drunk himself to death after losing his wife from septicaemia.

Edward had watched her over the next few years as she struggled valiantly to prepare her siblings for adult life, while he himself was struggling to make a go of his first smallholding. But it had been some time before he'd plucked up courage to court her formally; there had always been an elusive quality about her that held him back, whilst at the same time tantalising him. She was twenty-three before the demands of her family had ceased and she had begun to take Edward seriously and allow him any degree of familiarity – and then, to his joy, what sensuality had been unleashed! And he had loved her! Oh, how he had loved her!

And I still love her now, he mused sadly. But it had been many years since the passion which had simultaneously driven and mortified her had been given rein. The determination which had enabled her to take over successfully from her parents had been channelled into 'getting on' in the world – or at least in the important bits of the society in which they moved, while the passion had been supplanted by a strange mixture of worldliness and godliness.

And, he thought with a sigh, *if cleanliness really is next to godliness, then she'll have a special place reserved for her when she gets to the other side.*

END OF SAMPLE CHAPTER
"The Mountains Between" by Julie McGowan
can be purchased from all good online stores,
or better still, ask for it from your local independent
or chain book store.

About

THE MOUNTAINS BETWEEN

by Julie McGowan

Despite its physical comforts, Jennie's life under the critical eye of her tyrannical mother is hard, and she grows up desperate for a love she has been denied. As she blossoms into a young woman World War II breaks out. Life is turned upside down by the vagaries of war, and the charming, urbane Charles comes into her life – and he loves her ... doesn't he? ...

On the other side of the scarred mountain, in the wake of a disaster that tears through his family and their tight-knit mining community, Harry finds the burden of manhood abruptly thrust upon his young shoulders. He bears it through the turmoil of the Depression years, sustained only by his love for Megan. But his life too takes many unexpected turns, and the onset of war brings unimaginable changes. ... Nothing is as it was, or as it seems ...

Blaenavon and Abergavenny surge to life in this vibrant, haunting, joyful masterpiece – a celebration of the Welsh people from the 1920s to the 1940s. It's the saga of two families and their communities, and the story of two young people who should have found each other much sooner. It's the story of the people of the mountains and the valleys who formed the beating heart of Wales.

__The Mountains Between__ became a regional best-seller almost immediately. Now in its 3rd edition, it was author Julie McGowan's first book, and is based in her much-loved homeland of Wales. Her second book, __Just One More Summer,__ is a wonderfully intricate read based in Cornwall, while her newly-released third book, __Don't Pass Me By,__ is also a Welsh spectacular.

ROSE & CROWN, BLUE JEANS, BOATHOOKS, SUNBERRY, CHRISTLIGHT, and EPTA Books

MORE BOOKS FROM the SUNPENNY GROUP
www.sunpenny.com

A Little Book of Pleasures, by William Wood
Blackbirds Baked in a Pie, by Eugene Barter
Breaking the Circle, by Althea Barr
Dance of Eagles, by JS Holloway
Don't Pass Me By, by Julie McGowan
Far Out, by Corinna Weyreter
Going Astray, by Christine Moore
If Horses Were Wishes, by Elizabeth Sellers
Just One More Summer, by Julie McGowan
Loyalty & Disloyalty, by Dag Heward-Mills
My Sea is Wide (Illustrated), by Rowland Evans
Sudoku for Christmas (full colour illustrated gift book)
The Mountains Between, by Julie McGowan
The Perfect Will of God, by Dag Heward-Mills
The Skipper's Child, by Valerie Poore
Those Who Accuse You, by Dag Heward-Mills
Trouble Rides a Fast Horse, by Elizabeth Sellers
Watery Ways, by Valerie Poore

FROM OUR ROMANCE IMPRINTS:

Uncharted Waters, by Sara DuBose
Bridge to Nowhere, by Stephanie Parker McKean
Embracing Change, by Debbie Roome
Blue Freedom, by Sandra Peut
A Flight Delayed, by KC Lemmer

Sᴜɴᴘᴇɴɴʏ
Pᴜʙʟɪsʜɪɴɢ
Gʀᴏᴜᴘ

ROSE & CROWN, BLUE JEANS, BOATHOOKS, SUNBERRY, CHRISTLIGHT, and EPTA Books

COMING SOON:

30 Days to Take-Off, by KC Lemmer
A Devil's Ransom, by Adele Jones
A Whisper On The Mediterranean, by Tonia Parronchi
Brandy Butter on Christmas Canal, by Shae O'Brien
Broken Shells, by Debbie Roome
Fish Soup, by Michelle Heatley
Heart of the Hobo, by Shae O'Brien
Raglands, by JS Holloway
Redemption on Red River, by Cheryl R. Cain
The Stangreen Experiment, by Christine Moore
Sudoku for Bird Lovers (full colour illustrated gift book)
Sudoku for Horse Lovers (full colour illustrated gift book)
Sudoku for Sailors (full colour illustrated gift book)
Sudoku for Stitchers (full colour illustrated gift book)

Lightning Source UK Ltd.
Milton Keynes UK
UKOW03f0124270814

237623UK00002B/16/P